M000073668

Dear John,

I'm sorry. I will never forget you...

Love, Anne.

"I'm Sorry....

Love Anne."

A novel by

Andrea Peters

ISBN: 0-9758933-7-8

1/05

"Every life has a story."

- A&E Biography

"You are the same today that you are going to be five years from now except for two things; the people with whom you associate and the books you read."

– Charles Jones

Chapter 1

"We're OVER!"

The words resounded in her head like a rung bell. He had meant them. He hadn't meant them. She would have said them. She SHOULD have said them. He was no good for her. She was too good for him.

"We're OVER!"

It was as if her MP3 earphones were attached to her head, which they weren't. In fact, she mused, they were probably in HIS car, right next to the rotting banana peel from last Friday, behind the passenger seat. The notion made her smile.

A cloud of exhaust enveloped her from a passing Metro bus and Anne looked around and realized she had no idea where she was. The new Hotel 71 stood in front of her, the self-proclaimed 'smart and stylish' place to stay in downtown Chicago, right by the river walk.

She stopped for a moment to adjust her right shoe, in which her sock had ignominiously bunched up. With her left hand she reached out for the nearest newspaper machine.

"Yech!"

It was an instantaneous reaction to the translucent liquid that her once clean hand now bore. She looked around, frantic for something to wipe it off with, and chose the least dirty of three paper napkins that someone had discarded in the nearby trash. The liquid was resistant to her attempts to wipe it off and left a disgusting grayish residue. Anne extended her hand and kept it open like a leprous member as her eyes moved down the street to see if there was any place she could wash up.

The nearest store was an old bookshop a half a block away and she hurried to the front door.

The musty smell of millions of pages of old paper and bindings invaded her nose and her face wrinkled up as she tried to withhold a sneeze.

"Do you have a restroom?" she asked.

The young woman dismembering a stack of books looked up at her and her still outstretched hand and nodded to Anne's right.

"Over there," she said.

There was only cold water in the sink but, more important to the immediate situation, there was soap and Anne excitedly lathered up several times before finishing and drying off with a towel. She used the damp paper to open the door, then ceremoniously tried to throw the waste into the basket on the far side of the small bathroom. She missed by a mile and grimaced as if Tony, her ex, had watched her. She allowed the door to close.

Anne felt the gaze of the sales girl as she exited the door and felt obliged to at least peruse the stacks of half-price books on the table in front of her. *Twenty Thousand Leagues Under The Sea*. She remembered Captain Nemo; he reminded her of Tony. If only a large Sea Creature would come and eat him. Mark Twain's, *Tom Sawyer…* Now there was a boy destined to be a macho, narcissistic pig! Patricia Cornwall's, *The Body Farm*. Hey, that sounded pretty good right now.

The Woman in White by Wilkie Collins… She had heard about this book but couldn't remember where. The book was in rather good condition and she picked it up and thumbed through it. It was quite obvious that it was old, but it did not fall open like worn books do. The pages were not creased and the binding was stiff, as if new. She turned to the front to find the publishing date and stopped when she saw the cryptic inscription on the first page.

"Dear John. I'm sorry. I will never forget you." It was signed. *"Love, Anne."* It was her name, written in pencil, signed with a sad flourish. Just like she signed her letters, and the name was the way she spelled it—with an 'e' at the end. A 'good English name,' to match her porcelain complexion, as her grandmother used to tell her.

There was an old address label, barely readable, on the front cover. It was from Kent, England. She wondered how this old book had made the long journey to this dingy bookstore in Chicago.

"Two-Fifty," the salesperson said, without even looking up from her now half decimated pile.

Anne handed her the exact amount and left. She really had no intention of reading it but it was a curiosity and it felt good in her hand as she continued her walk.

"We're OVER." Yes, we are, she thought as she turned toward the river.

Good riddance.

Chapter 2

It was another fitful summer night in Chicago—way too hot. Her old apartment didn't have air conditioning and the fan just re-circulated warm, stale air. Anne sat up and looked at the old analog clock on her dresser. She had put it specifically where the streetlight shone so she could read the dial anytime of night. 3:30 a.m. Well at least that was better than last night when she had woken up at 3:17 a.m. At this rate she could expect a good night's sleep in about two weeks.

She got up and walked to the kitchen, a scene that had become her sleepless night ritual. The fridge was her only source of cool air, and she stood close in front of the open door, as if melding with the shelving. The cool moist air was refreshing and she tugged at her T-shirt to get some circulation around her chest.

At least there was no more beer in the fridge. She always hated the smell of beer. It reminded her of her not so well spent teenage years. A lot of regretful things were done under the influence of that particularly rabid high school liquid. Anne reached for the pitcher of water and delighted in the coolness of the glass, then walked over to the cabinets and poured herself a cup. She sat at the square oak kitchen table and her feet hunted for their favorite worn spot in the wood floor.

The book she had purchased almost a week ago still lay on the tabletop unopened. For some reason she just had left it there, as if it had told her to please not put it back with the other books, to let it revel in its solitary comfort. As she had done the previous three nights, she flipped open the cover and read the inscription again.

"Dear John. I'm sorry. I will never forget you. Love, Anne." She ran her fingers slowly over the faded pencil writing and stopped when she had traced the complete message. There was something so sad about the note—a yearning. A love lost. She wondered what story it held.

She finished the water, turned off the kitchen light and made her way back to the bedroom by feel. The clock said 3:52 a.m. She lay down in the bed, and covered herself with only half of a sheet, willing herself to sleep. But she just lay there, her body rigid and her fingers intertwined and fidgeting. Her mind was just too much in turmoil, which was not all together unusual except this time she thought it wasn't about Tony. Thank God. Perhaps she had finally put him out of her mind.

Anne found herself wondering what had happened to the Anne in the book. Who was John, and why was she sorry? Why couldn't they have been together? So many questions!

Anne finally gave up and turned on her light. She took out a piece of stationary, then a well-chewed black ballpoint pen from her nightstand.

Dear sir or madam, or whomever lives at this address:

I have no idea why I'm writing this. I don't know you and you certainly do not know me. And you probably are not even the correct party. But I just purchased an old book called 'The Woman in White' from a bookstore here and it had your address in it. There is an inscription written on the first page from someone named Anne to a fellow called John.

For some reason I can't get this note out of my head – as you see – my name is also 'Anne' and, in fact, that is why I purchased the book, which is probably ludicrous, but – well – that's the truth. So... I was wondering if you knew anything about these two people and what happened? I have no idea why this has piqued my interest so but, if you have the time, I would very much appreciate a response."

She signed the letter *'Anne'* with a sad flourish, and added her address to the bottom of the page.

There, she thought. Maybe now I can get some sleep.

She curled up in a ball with a pillow between her legs and arms, her auburn hair now a tangled mess, and finally drifted off.

The next day Anne mailed the letter to Kent, England. She licked three stamps and put them on the envelope, because she had no idea how much a letter to England cost, and then she put it in the nearest Post box on her way to work. She really didn't expect an answer.

Almost a month later Anne returned home from work after a terrible day and opened her little mail slot while Mr. Morris watched her. He always watched her.

"Hi, Mr. Morris," she said, "Do you like my new dress? You know, if you stare at it any harder, you're going to start seeing dinosaurs or something."

He looked at her, puzzled.

"You know, like those 3-D pictures..." she said. It was obvious he didn't get it.

Without looking at them, she took her few pieces of mail and walked up the stairs. She could feel his eyes watch her walk up the steps.

"Goodbye, Mr. Morris," she said.

He just grunted.

As she took each step up, she was acutely aware of her calves, as without a doubt Mr. Morris was. She was used to men looking at her but it still gave her the creeps. And she found herself very self-conscious as she tried not to sway too much until she turned the corner to the next flight.

She wondered if his wife knew about his little postal habit. Then again, she couldn't remember seeing his wife in at least a couple of weeks and wondered if she was still alive. Maybe he had killed her and she was rotting in their apartment. She slowed down just a bit in front of their door and took a tentative sniff.

Gross! What was she thinking? That was too sick even for her inquisitive mind.

The top step creaked on the landing, which meant she was home, and she unlocked all four locks and went inside. She re-locked every one of them and then placed the mail and her purse on the coffee table before taking a seat on the couch where she gazed out the window. She pulled her dress up over her knees to cool down.

It wasn't a bad view of the city.

She leaned over and picked up the envelopes, half paying attention as she flipped through them until something caught her eye. A foreign letter.

Kent, England.

The excitement in her throat was palpable.

Chapter 3

The envelope was thick and yellowed. It felt almost handmade, and the writing was in black. The ink was deep and pronounced, like it was written with an old inkwell stylus. She took a key and fit it under the flap. With great care she cut it open and withdrew a matching single piece of paper. She immediately noticed the large watermark, a kind of crest or logo. The paper was heavy vellum, with the alternating thick and thin ribs running horizontally along its entire length. The letter smelled of mold, not unlike the old bookshop.

There was a single sentence in an overly large printed script.

"Who is this?"

She turned the paper over but there was nothing else on it. She checked in the envelope… nothing. She read it again.

"Who is this?" At first she thought it to be just a question. Perhaps someone had received her note and had no idea what Anne had referred to. But then the words started taking on an ominous meaning. Anne wondered if somehow she had opened a box that was best left alone.

What if the letter she had written had opened an old wound, or worse yet, hope?

What if this person was a lunatic? Anne had given this stranger her address! Her NAME!

Anne stuffed the letter back in the envelope and placed it in the book that started the whole thing. She sat for a moment and stared at it.

The Woman in White. The book almost seemed to speak to her and she felt compelled to open it and start reading.

> *"THIS is the story of what a Woman's patience can endure, and what a Man's resolution can achieve…It was the last day of July. The long hot summer was drawing to a close; and we, the weary pilgrims of the London pavement, were beginning to think of the cloud-shadows on the cornfields, and the autumn breezes on the sea-shore."*

Anne sat engrossed in the story of Walter Hartright and his mysterious midnight encounter with The Woman in White, an encounter that drew him into a maelstrom of crime, poison and kidnapping.

By one in the morning Anne was convinced more than ever that she should never have written the letter. What if the story of the Woman in White was actually true? And she was Anne! Then Walter was John and this whole thing was very, very bad.

Anne's heart nearly jumped off the sofa of its own accord when the telephone rang. She started laughing, half-hysterical and half-amused. She smiled as she reached for the handset.

"Hello?" she asked.

No reply.

"Hello?" again. "Hel..lo? Hell-ooo?"

"Who is this?" A male's voice replied.

Anne dropped the phone, jumped up and stared at it. Then she bent over, grabbed it like a dead mouse and threw it on the cradle. She stood and gawked at it. She looked down at the book where it had fallen from off her lap. The illustration of The Woman in White gazed up at her with her blank eyes. Anne took a pillow and threw it over the book and ran into the kitchen where she reflexively opened the fridge and looked inside—at nothing.

After a few seconds, she closed the door and walked to her bedroom where she saw her own shaking hand as it reached for the knob.

This was ridiculous! She was a twenty-four year-old independent woman who had just dumped her unappreciative boyfriend and she was scared brainless over a book? She had a good notion to just toss the thing, and she walked back out to the living room, removed the pillow, and stood above it contemplating what to do.

She screamed when the phone broke the silence.

"Dammit!" She surprised herself at the volume of her voice and looked at the telephone like it was Beelzebub himself.

"Hello?" She held the handset between her thumb and forefinger.

"Honey?" It was her mom's voice.

Anne fell onto the sofa and started laughing.

"Honey? I know it's late… What's so funny?"

Chapter 4

"Mom! It's one a.m.! Where are you?" Anne said.

"I'm sorry, dear. I thought it was just Eleven. Your father surprised me with a trip to Hawaii. I'm watching the most beautiful sunset on a beach on Kauai… just thought I'd let you know where we were if you tried to call us."

"Hi, Anne!" She heard her father's muffled voice above the crashing waves in the background.

"Hi, dad." Her mom relayed the message.

"So, honey, what are you doing up so late?"

"Oh… I'm…. umm… just reading. Got engrossed and didn't realize what time it was. I'm headed off to bed right now," Anne replied.

"What book?" her mom asked.

"The Woman in White. Some 19th Century novel of intrigue…"

"I read that when I was pregnant with you! Isn't that crazy?" her mom said.

Anne started shivering uncontrollably. She pulled her knees up and wrapped her arms around them. Her mom continued.

"When I first picked it up I remember it started really slow. But when Walter is walking down the street in the middle of the night and sees the Woman in White just standing there out of the shadows, I was hooked. I remember that I stayed up all night to finish it. It was really long!"

"Uh huh…," Anne said. She was numb and didn't know what to think about this weird turn of events. But she knew what was coming next. She had already read that part of the book.

"In fact, dear… I named you because of that book! My heart always went out for that Anne Cather… something. You know, the missing girl."

Anne was shivering so intensely she had to remind herself to take deep breaths to try and calm down. Her voice was shaking.

"Mom. I really have to go now, can we talk tomorrow?"

"Sure, honey. I just didn't want you to loose sleep over me. Goodnight."

The next morning Anne got up, took a shower and spent extra time in front of the mirror trying to hide the obnoxious bags under her eyes. She picked out a knee-length white dress and put it on the bed, then, just as quickly replaced it with a blue skirt, tan blouse, a matching pair of flat sandals and a simple scarf to tie back her hair. Finished, she appraised herself in the mirror, gave her approval, and went out into the living room. She picked up the book and the pillow in one motion and placed it on the bookshelf with her dozen or so unfinished novels before walking out the door.

She had work to do today and, for God's sake, it was just a book she just happened to pick up in an old bookstore!

Entering the sidewalk from her apartment building was like trying to merge into traffic during rush hour. She paused for a second, timed the tempo of the pedestrian crowd, and took her place in the fracas. She found the tap of the hard concrete was somehow reassuring. It felt good to be going somewhere.

Three blocks later, a stop at Starbucks for a rare but much deserved frappuccino and a low fat muffin prompted her to smile. Within ten more minutes she entered Argyle and Associates, a suite of offices on the fourteenth floor. A placard greeted all visitors as soon as the elevator opened: "LAW OFFICES."

"Hi, Anne!" Susie, the receptionist, greeted her.

"Hi, Suz." Anne smiled and walked on by.

Her desk was sparse, with not too many personal effects. There was an empty picture frame on her desk that used to be of her and Tony at last year's Jazz festival. She hadn't found a suitable replacement yet. None of her coworkers even commented on the empty frame. On her desk were a paperclip bowl, a stapler, desk calendar, a single pen and the ubiquitous flat screen computer monitor that showed the login screen. It was just the way she liked things, organized and uncomplicated. The sign on the wall to her right said *'Anne Compton –Paralegal.'* She needed to work on that. A couple of more years of night school and she could take the bar exam.

Chapter 5

The call came three months later at 4:00 p.m. on a Friday afternoon. "Anne?" It was her boss Harold Lawton the III. He wasn't nearly as stuffy as the name sounded.

"Yes, Harry." Anne was tired and had cradled the phone on her neck as she pulled her purse out from under the desk and put it in her lap. She had every intention of leaving early.

"Ever been to England?" Harry said.

"What?" The memories flooded back into Anne's consciousness.

"England? You know, the little island north of France? The United Kingdom and all that?" Harold put on his best English accent, which really wasn't that bad.

"I… I know where England is, Harry," Anne said.

"Well, ever been there?" he asked.

"No… why? You plan to take the wife to the land of Buckingham Palace and Big Ben? Or do you just want to know what bangers and mash are?" Harry often proposed incomprehensible questions that he rarely volunteered reason for.

"Actually, my dear.." Harry said, "I was going to request your presence to accompany me on a trip there. Seems an honorable client is having a bit of a problem with some quite dishonorable practices of a certain gentleman in their London office, and they have prompted some…rather judicious review by law enforcement over there. I may need a bit of a hand with your counterparts in the Old Country." Harry's accent was turning more into a Celtic Brogue.

"When, Harry? Can't we discuss this Monday?"

"Well, actually, the matter is of rather an urgent nature and we must leave in, well…about three hours."

"Three hours! Are you crazy, Harry? I have things that I planned on doing this weekend." Anne knew that Harry knew she likely had no such plans.

"Come on, Anne. I realize your social calendar is well booked, however, could you consider this a favor? A first class favor." At least he had given her some dignity.

"England, huh?" Anne said.

"England. Tally Ho and all that!" Harry said.

"As long as you quit with the terrible accent, Harry."

"Remember your passport," Harry said, as she hung up the phone.

:

Anne had never flown first class. That was as good a reason as any for a trip to England. She went home and packed a light suitcase, just enough for a couple of days, and headed out the door, only pausing for a second at the bookcase to grab something to read. She reached out and grabbed a Grisham novel that she had started a couple of years ago, pulled it half way out, then pushed it back in and stood and stared at the books. She unconsciously straightened her back, tossed her hair with her head and firmly grabbed *The Woman in White*, stuffed it into her bag and walked out the door.

The taxi took her to O'Hare, where Harry waited anxiously at the Security Check point.

"You really shouldn't look so worried, Harry," Anne said. "They'll think you have something to hide." She smiled and nodded to the mass of guards up ahead. Harry started sweating even more.

They made it through without incident.

Chapter 6

"Would you like some Champagne or a Mimosa before we take off, ma'am?" The flight attendant was a bit too smiley for Anne's taste. But the cool leather seat felt good.

Harry chirped in. "How about a scotch, no rocks." Harry tried to grin when he said it, but Anne could see that something was wrong.

"I'll take a Mimosa, please," Anne said, then turned to Harry after making sure the attendant was out of earshot.

"You alright?" Anne asked.

Harry shook a small bottle of pills, which he held in his hand. "Hate flying," he said, as he popped two of them and swallowed dry.

"Now you tell me?! Anything else I should be aware of?"

"We-ell, I left my will in my desk drawer if something happens," Harry said.

"Harry, I'm flying with you," Anne said.

"Oh," Harry said as he closed his eyes and leaned back in the seat.

Anne took the opportunity to look at him and thought he really wasn't all that bad looking. He was even kind of funny at times, successful and respected. She wondered why he never talked about his wife—assuming they were still married.

The Mimosa did the job and Anne felt more relaxed though wide-awake as the plane leveled out at 42,000 feet. The little map on the front wall of the cabin showed a little less than 4,000 miles to go—about eight hours.

She was unsure if Harry was asleep or just feigning it as the late supper was served. The flight attendant laid out real silverware, except for the plastic knife, and Noritake china plates. Anne enjoyed the Asian Red Snapper, 1994 Napa Valley Cabernet, Camembert cheese and some wonderful crackers. She finished the meal with a fruit plate topped with just a tad of whipping cream.

Quite satiated, she flipped channels on her private video screen, finally choosing a documentary on Charles Dickens. With her blanket pulled up to her chin and the seat in full recline it was only a matter of time till she fell asleep. She missed the part at the end of the show that spoke about the relationship between Wilkie Collins, author of *The Woman in White*, and his mentor and friend, Charles Dickens.

They arrived a little after 9:00 a.m. at Heathrow and took the train into the city. It was a gray London day, laced with fog. The moist air felt like a cobweb draped over her face. She followed Harry, who seemed delighted to finally be on the ground. The cobblestones made it difficult for her to walk in her short heels, and she found herself trotting every minute or so to catch up. She noted, with wry amusement, the LOOK RIGHT, LOOK LEFT signs printed in very large letters on each corner. She thought, they must have lost a lot of tourists to put all those up.

Harry acted like he knew where he was going, and hadn't asked for directions, so she assumed they were going in the correct direction. Then Harry slowed his frantic pace and had a bewildered look on his face at a corner that looked like the last ten or so they had already passed…. Another antique shop and book store, another Starbucks. At least America is exporting something important, she thought, and hoped Harry would stop long enough for a latte.

"Hey, Harry, mind if I get a coffee?" she asked.

"Uh… no. Go right ahead. Ask where Russell street is while you're in there."

The shop had the wonderful smell she experienced everyday in Chicago. She liked the familiarity of it all. She began to understand why Americans eat at McDonalds when visiting Moscow.

"Double tall latte, please," she said, reading it off the board.

"Is that for take-away, Miss?" the black haired, pierced, Gothic looking girl asked her.

"Take… a what?" Anne said.

"Take–away. You want that for here or are you leaving our wonderful establishment?" the servant, or whatever they call them in England, spoke again.

"OH! To-go. Yes. Take-away," Anne said.

"Whatever," the girl turned around and muttered something about the Yankee to her colleague, who looked up at her from under his red hair, then turned back toward the machine. Anne wondered if Mr. Schultz, the President of Starbucks, knew about London's seeming predilection toward punk rock servers.

"That'll be two quid," the girl said.

Anne froze. She hadn't thought about the money. She didn't have any British currency. She looked down at her wallet and noticed a little box that looked like a debit card machine and fumbled through her purse till she located her ATM card. She swiped it and held her breath until the little box indicated 'approved.' Anne took her latte and turned around to leave, then remembered what Harry had asked. She turned back around toward the girl.

"Can you tell me where Russell Street is?"

"Sure, straight ahead, about a hundred meters, er...yards, love. You can't miss it."

The girl pointed up the street with her black fingernail.

"Thanks." Anne left the counter and exited the café.

"About 100 yards that way," Anne said to Harry as the door closed behind her and a red double-deck bus rumbled by. She sipped on her hot latte as she pointed with her other hand toward the bus. Harry looked at the latte and then up at Anne.

"Oh, did you want one?" Anne said with a smile. She had just a tad of cream on her upper lip. She licked it off.

"Uh. No. That's OK. Later." Harry looked at her wistfully for a second and then took off at his old pace. Anne tried to keep up while carefully holding her cherished cup.

Chapter 7

Turnberry & Sons was a small import-export company specializing in Eastern European antiquities. They had only two offices, one at 15 Russell Street, London, and one in Chicago. A Mr. Edward Turnberry, no relation, ran the London office for the owners. Anne followed Harry into the small suite of offices on the second floor of the old brownstone building. The stones, however, were more exhaust soot black in appearance than brown.

The offices were just as she expected them, adorned with lots of wood, old brass fittings and a woman, about 50, with spectacles. She sat there like the Sphinx and peered over at them when Anne and Harry walked up.

"Hello. We are here for Mr. Turnberry. He is expecting us," Harry said.

"Ay! Edward, the Yanks are 'ere." The Sphinx broke a small smile as she yelled into a small intercom box on her desk. Anne had only seen those in movies… *old* movies.

In a few moments a short, balding man in a brown three-piece suit appeared.

"Mr. Lawton, we've been expecting you. Please follow me." He didn't even acknowledge Anne, which was fine by her. Harry signaled for her to follow them and the Sphinx watched as they walked by. Anne hoped she wasn't staring at anything amiss about her appearance. She hated to think she had walked all over London with something in her teeth, or worse yet, really bad hair.

They passed by a wastebasket and Anne threw the empty latte cup into it as she tried to surreptitiously steal a glance in a pane of glass. She was relieved that she didn't see anything wrong with the way she looked.

They entered what had to be Mr. Turnberry's office, and he gestured for them to sit. Anne sat on the couch, while Harry took the only chair facing the desk. She had no idea what this emergency trip was about but she had a feeling she would soon find out.

"Sorry, Harry, about the reception. It's been really bad here this week," Mr. Turnberry said.

"No problem, Edward. Why don't you fill us in on what's going on, and perhaps we can head over to the attorney's... er, barrister's office after this and get started on our end of things."

Edward let out a sigh. "About four days ago, Stephen returned from Georgia, one of the former Soviet Union countries." He looked up at Harry and Anne to make sure they were following. Harry nodded. "No big deal there. He has been going back and forth for several months to this little town outside of Kutaisi, a large city. He was working on this connection for some icons that a particular priest had. Seems he needed some hard currency to fund a little social dissent. Anyway, Stephen had been buying him lots of vodka and staying at his house trying to work him through his *remorse* over selling God's possessions." Edward stopped to frame 'remorse' with finger quotes. It really is a common ploy to elicit a higher figure, but we are used to that."

"This was the sixth or seventh trip that Stephen made, including a trip to the border crossing town into Azerbaijan from which we have connections to import to the West. Unknown to us, it seems the priest had a pretty young daughter." Edward stopped to take a drink of water. Anne watched Harry look at the glass, much like he had looked at her when she bought the latte. Poor Harry.

"No big deal. The girl was eighteen, so... young love and all that. Stephen bought the icon and took the item and the girl to Azerbaijan. Then he worked his way back to England." Edward pointed with his left index finger to a spot against the wall where Anne sat. There was a small wooden icon of Madonna with child. It was only about a foot and a half square, and the wood was splintered.

"We were very happy with the acquisition, but the priest was furious. He's here, now, in London." Edward took a moment to loosen up his bow tie and unbutton his top shirt button.

"He claims we *stole* something from him," Edward said.

"The icon or the daughter?" asked Harry. Anne had no idea why this involved the Chicago office.

"Neither, actually, a gold and silver cross. Something supposedly from the first Century, from some Church in Turkey..." Edward said.

"But, I thought..." Harry looked confused.

"Yes. A moment...." Edward took another gulp of water. "Evidently, the girl took it with her. Her father has hardly mentioned her at all, but this cross is supposedly worth a fortune, and Stephen and the girl have it—or so says the priest. He's in London as we speak, raising a big stink and thereby jeopardizing our delicate import business... as well as causing political grief about thieving Westerners. That would be *us.*" Edward gestured with his hand and slumped in his overstuffed chair.

"Here is where you come in," he continued, "Stephen knew he was in trouble with us, and may have known about the cross, so he and his girlfriend are now in New York. Seems they had this planned all along! The priest is demanding that we return the cross to him immediately. We need to find out how to get it back. The US has laws on antiquities, like we do, and we need to find out how to get that cross back to this Orthodox clergyman with his tall black hat, and get him back to Georgia, and out of our hair!"

Anne finally understood the reason she was here.

"OK. Let's start with the names, places, and dates, and go on from there. Anne, would you take some notes as well, please? You'll be coordinating the research on extradition and the legal aspects of the antiquities." Harry spoke directly to Anne.

"Stephen Butler, twenty three, English passport..." Edward continued with the particulars.

Chapter 8

The barristers were named Henry & Sons. It seemed like almost every professional service company was an '& Sons'. Anne looked at the sign and guessed you had a lot of sons when your nation had been around for a millennium.

Anne's counterpart at Henry & Sons was a tall, stalwart English man, with a boyish face named Jarred Mulberry.

"Yes, as in the tree. Also known as Morus Nigra or on your continent Morus Rubra." Jarred rambled on with what was obviously a well-rehearsed explanation.

Anne smiled. "Ah, yes. I've partaken of the fruit of the mulberry tree before." She immediately blushed. "I mean, I really have tasted mulberry before, I believe it was a syrup on pancakes, or it could have been ice cream, I can't remember..."

Jarred smiled and raised his hand in the international sign of 'Stop.' "Got it!"

Anne felt the blush as it ran up her neck onto her alabaster cheeks. She didn't look back at him and sat down with her raincoat still on.

"So, you have that desk over there. I'm over here." Jarred pointed out a desk about ten feet from his own, kitty corner to his.

"If you promise to behave yourself, I'll promise to not tell anyone of our little conversation," Jarred said.

Anne put her hands over her face, and tried to hide her red cheeks by peering over her fingers at him.

Jarred laughed. "I'm going to enjoy working with you." Then he took his grin and coat, and left the room.

Anne sat in the seat, mortified and flushed, but oddly pleased. Yes, she thought. It was going to be fun.

There was a note on the computer with a guest password, which she typed in. There were links to the Westlaw library, a legal database of case law, in the States, as well as an Internet browser—everything she needed for her search. For the next couple of hours she sat alone in the room researching case law on antiquities and extradition of foreign objects unlawfully brought into the United States. The good news was that there were laws providing a basis for taking such an action. The bad news was that it sounded like it would be at least partially political. But that was not her concern. Her job was to research the options.

"Is it safe to come in?" Jarred had walked back into the room with a large smile.

"Very funny," Anne said, as she stood up and stretched. She was wearing a pair of casual black slacks and a simple peach blouse. She rotated her head around to work out some of the kinks.

"May I help you with that?" Jarred took a step forward and Anne had no idea what he had in mind so she backed up into the wall and bumped her head.

"Ouch!" she said.

Jarred was half holding back a laugh and had half a look of concern on his face.

"I'm OK. I make such pleasant first impressions. But really…I grow on people!" Anne said.

"Yes," Jarred said, "like a mulberry tree!" He chuckled at his own pun.

Anne pretended to not be amused, so Jarred quickly added. "I have lunch!" He lifted up a brown paper bag. This was a good thing, because Anne was famished.

"What have you brought me?" Anne held her head with a slight tilt, her auburn hair brushing against her blouse. "It smells delicious."

"Bangers and Mash, our London pub specialty. Thought that would be an appropriate first meal for you in London. This is your first time, is it not?" Jarred smiled.

"First times are always special," Anne said.

This time Jarred blushed. She liked it.

"And of course we have a pint to make sure the experience is complete." Jarred pulled out two bottles of London Pride.

"At work?" Anne said.

"Good for any occasion," Jarred said, and handed her a bottle with a smile.

Anne didn't comment that she hated beer. It was a nice gesture anyway.

They sat at his desk. He served her a portion of what looked like bratwurst and mash potatoes, and she took a small taste. Her suspicions were confirmed.

"So, what brings you to London?" Jarred asked just as Anne had put a bite of food in her mouth. She looked at him with wide eyes, and he burst out laughing.

Chapter 9

After lunch she worked alone researching case law on extradition of foreign antiquities and found herself reading the same line over and over again. Still unable to comprehend the sentence, she went to make a note of the information on her pad, but no matter how much she wrote she never seemed to finish.

"Morning!" A voice came from somewhere in the darkness.

"Hellooooo?" This time she felt someone's hand on her shoulder.

"Anne?" It was Jarred's voice. Anne woke up with her face resting on her arm. She could feel a bit of drool on her lips and wondered how she was going to lift up her head without him seeing it. She pulled her hands over her face and rubbed as she sat up.

"They let you sleep at work back home?" Jarred had a very large smile.

"Uhhh." Anne tried in vain to think of something witty to say.

"That's what I like about American women. They are never at a loss for words!" His grin never left, and Anne wanted to grab his nose and twist it until he squealed.

"Oh, I wasn't taking a nap. I was concentrating on an important case." Anne smiled back.

"Ahhh. I see. Then those wet marks on your sleeve must be from your exertions," Jarred said.

Anne wanted to die.

"I'm joshing you, Anne. You must be exhausted. Shall I take you back to your hotel? Harry left about an hour ago. I said I would look after you."

"Yes. Please. I have no idea what time it is. I'm not even sure what day it is." Anne tried to smooth out her blouse and pants but soon gave up and just put on her raincoat.

She was happy to take the arm Jarred offered her as they walked out onto the street.

They passed by an old bookstore and Anne found herself looking in the window briefly.

"Do you want to get a book to read?" Jarred asked.

"Oh, no. I have one... Say—how far is Kent from here?" The words came from Anne's lips but she didn't remember saying them.

"Actually, Kent is an area, do you know what town?" Jarred said.

"Uh, Canterbury?"

"Sure. About 65 kilos, 40 miles or so by train. Do you want to go there for some reason?" Jarred said.

"No. Oh. I don't think so... Just heard about it somewhere. Is that my hotel?" Anne pointed out in front of her to the Jury's Great Russell Street Hotel.

"I believe it is." Jarred looked at her and raised his eyebrows slightly. He walked her to the front desk and asked for the booking, which was under his company name, and handed Anne the key.

"Would you like me to come by and fetch you in the morning?" Jarred asked.

"That's really not necessary. I can find my way back just fine." Anne smiled and turned toward the elevator. She was thinking about Canterbury.

Jarred watched the elevator doors shut and left the hotel.

:

The next morning Jarred was already at work when Anne arrived late, at 9:00 a.m.

"Good morning, Jarred," Anne said.

"Hi, Anne. I trust you had a reasonable night's sleep," Jarred said.

"Yes, I feel much better today." Anne took off her raincoat. She was wearing a flattering pair of cream flat front slacks and a brown blouse, with a single strand of pearls.

"Nice shirt," Jarred said.

"Blouse actually," she smiled.

"Ah. I stand corrected. Nice blouse!" he said. "Here are the notes from Harry. He had some specific questions regarding international law on religious artifacts." Jarred handed her a single half sheet of yellow paper and grazed her hand with his.

"Thank you. I'll get right to work on it." She sat down in the old wooden office chair. It was cool to the touch and it made her shiver slightly.

"I don't suppose there's any coffee nearby? I was in a bit of a rush this morning," Anne said.

"I think that can be arranged… latte even better?"

Anne smiled and Jarred disappeared around the corner. About ten minutes later Anne smelled the comforting scent of coffee wafting through the hallway and in through the door. She stopped what she was doing, and looked up just in time to see Jarred come into view with two cups. The steam from the frothy liquid was swirling up to the ceiling through the little sip hole, and Anne inhaled a full breath as he handed it to her. Anne was so fixated on it she didn't notice that Jarred looked at her the way that she looked at the cup. She gingerly took the cup from his hands and held it for a moment before taking the first sip.

"Yum," the word escaped her lips.

"So, what do you want to do today?" Jarred asked.

"Uhh, what do you mean? I need to do this research, and I suppose I should ask Harry if there is something else…" Anne's voice trailed off.

"Well, I was thinking you might have a little time for some sightseeing." Jarred said.

Anne looked down at her cup as if concentrating on the vapors circling toward the ceiling.

"I…" Anne's heart was beating loud enough that she thought he could hear it.

"That's OK. Just thought I'd ask." Jarred smiled, then turned around and walked out the door.

Anne closed her eyes and let out a long breath. She put the coffee cup down and looked at it. Somehow it just wasn't as appealing anymore.

Anne spent the next couple of hours doing the research for Harry. Jarred came in and out several times, but she feigned concentration on her computer screen. She felt his gaze, but just couldn't get herself to look up. Thank you, Tony, she thought. Thanks for absolutely nothing.

Around 1:00 p.m. Jarred appeared with a small box, which he placed on her desk next to the still full, but now cold, latte. He stood there just long enough to get her to look up at him. He didn't say a word, just grinned a little and left the room.

Anne opened the box to find a sandwich, a piece of chocolate and a small orange juice. She looked up to where he had been and sighed.

During lunch she looked up CNN to get the news stateside. A little pop up window came up asking her which edition she wanted and she selected Europe just for the heck of it. There was nothing but the unfinished war in Iraq, soccer, which she knew nothing about, and something about a meeting on the proposed EU constitution, a typical day in the life of the world.

She did notice an advertising link for a phonebook reverse directory though, and she paused for a moment, her fingers poised on the left button of the mouse. Why not? She clicked on the link and a web page came up with the prompt in query box. "Address?"

She reached down and pulled out the book and opened it to the front cover. She had kept it with her, just in case she had time to read a little, but Jarred had been distracting her so much that she was no closer to finishing the voluminous thing. She typed in the address in Canterbury and, in an instant, a name appeared. "Cornwall Est.." Now more curious than ever she Googled *"Cornwall Estate Canterbury Kent England."* Amazingly no search results were found.

She redid the search and put in "Cornwall Canterbury Kent England."

Google came up with over two dozen results, the first several of which referred to a shipment of thirty million pounds sterling of gold that was shipped from England to Canada in 1939. King George VI and Queen Elizabeth had sent the gold to protect it from a possible invasion by Germany. Another ten million pounds were sent on October 16, 1939, ten days after Hitler authorized war on England. A Duke Ellias Cornwall of Canterbury supervised both shipments.

Anne clicked on another link about Duke Ellias Cornwall. 1884-1956.

> *"After World War II both shipments of gold were returned to England by the Canadian Royal Navy. When the gold was repatriated and counted, it was found that over half a million pounds had disappeared. The Duke of Cornwall publicly denounced the theft and promised a full investigation but the bullion was never recovered. The Duke and his infamous son Michael Ellias….."*

"Anne!" Anne nearly jumped out of her seat and looked up to discover Harry beside her.

"Harry! For God's sake, are you trying to give me a heart attack?"

"Ah... but I come bearing good news," Harry said beaming. "We're leaving!"

"What do you mean? We're leaving? Here? Now? England? Turnberry & Sons?"

"We're going home!" Harry said, then paused and rubbed his chin. "Well, actually that is not quite true. *I'm* going home."

Anne looked at him, her eyes squinted. "What do you mean, Harry?"

"Harry?" Anne repeated.

Harry stood there a moment, squirming in his patent leather shoes.

"Well.... Actually, we'd like for you to make a stop on the way home..." Harry said. He wasn't looking at her anymore.

"Exactly where, Harry?" Anne asked. She felt like she was extracting teeth.

"New York." Harry had decided to look at her, and smiled. "But! I've got some tickets to Lion King!"

"What in heaven's name for?" Anne said.

"Well, I thought you would prefer that over Puffy Combs new play," Harry said as he looked back at his shoes.

"No, Harry," Anne said and put her hand on his. "What in heaven's name would I want to go to *New York* for?"

"Oh!" Harry looked at her again. "Well, it seems Stephen, and his new girlfriend Natasha are there trying to find buyers for the Cross."

"And...?" Anne signaled with her hand for him to continue.

"And... Turnberry & Sons would like you to try and negotiate the return, or purchase if necessary. Seems that their insurance company is willing to forward a bit of dough to make this thing go away," Harry said.

"Harry, why me? I'm a paralegal, for God's sake. Why don't *you* go?"

"Good question. Well – seems that the powers that be here," Harry jerked his head toward the side wall indicating Edwards office, "think that Stephen would react much better to a woman."

Anne just waited.

"And..." Harry's eyes rolled up a bit in thought, "We'll put you up in The Four Seasons, you get the concert tickets, and I remembered your sister lives in New York and my kid has a baseball game tomorrow… Please, Anne! I promise, I'll make it up to you."

Anne still had her eyes squinted. "And all the room service and limo rides I want, PLUS I get a week paid vacation when I get home." It was a statement not a question.

"Uh. Sure. I mean yes." Harry said. That was going to cost him with the boss.

"When do I leave?" Anne asked.

"In the morning. You can take the rest of the day off."

"Perfect!" The voice came from the door, and both of them turned around. There stood Jarred.

"Then you have no excuse not to go with me. We shall do afternoon tea at the Dorchester, St. Paul's Cathedral and the Chiswick House Gardens. Then, if you are especially nice to me, I shall take you to Balti food for supper," Jarred said. He stepped toward Anne, grabbed her bag and offered his arm. She paused for a moment as Harry looked at her with wide eyes, then she took his arm, grabbed her book and walked to the door with him.

"Harry—be a doll and leave the itinerary for me at the front desk," Anne said without looking back. They both laughed, and vanished down the hallway.

When they reached the stairs, Anne tenderly removed her arm and followed Jarred down the stairs. She carried the book in her sweat soaked palm.

Chapter 10

Anne stood in the lobby of her hotel with Jarred facing her. It had been a wonderful night and a fantastic Balti supper, which she had discovered, was East Indian or more correctly Pakistani food.

Jarred's face had lost his smile.

"So. Can I email you?" he asked.

Anne paused just a little bit too long.

"Look, I don't want to push anything here but I thought you enjoyed my company. You are six thousand kilometers away and I'm really not a great danger. No outstanding warrants. I brush my teeth and my mom likes me." Jarred smiled slightly.

"I'm sorry, Jarred. It was a nice day. I thoroughly enjoyed the time, the conversation. You are an intelligent, witty man..." Anne said.

"But?"

"But... I don't know if this is something I am ready for," Anne said.

"Boyfriend? Husband? I promise not to tell!"

"No. Well, not at least anymore. Can I...well...can I have some time or something...?" Anne drifted off.

"Sure. It's not a problem. I'm sure we'll be in contact about this cross mess," Jarred said. His smile was gone but the kindness in his eyes remained.

They stood, awkwardly looking at the floor. Then Anne extended her hand and Jarred took it gently, turned it over to expose the back of her hand to his thumb, and brought it up to his lips. She could feel his warm breath on her skin as she looked down at his head.

Jarred smiled one last time and left. The back of her hand was on fire as she watched him disappear through the turning doors.

:

The first class lounge at Heathrow was quiet and gave her time to ponder the previous day. Her mind was confused with colliding thoughts and emotions. She watched an older couple across the room sit down and drink some tea together and wondered how long they had been together.

Anne thought about Jarred. She wondered if the connection she felt was strong enough to last a lifetime. Her only serious experience with a man had been with Tony, so the thought of entering another relationship did not sit easily with her. Perhaps she was confusing attraction to connection. Still, the well being she felt around Jarred was different. It had never been there with Tony. In that relationship she had always tried to become what Tony wanted. With Jarred she didn't feel the need to hide her needs and thoughts. In fact, she wanted to reveal too many things, and had to stop herself from doing so in order to keep her distance. At times she felt like he already knew what she was thinking and it scared her. It meant that the longer she was around him the greater the potential that she would lose control of her feelings.

As she watched the old couple drink their tea, Anne found herself wondering what kind of tea Jarred liked, or if he liked it at all. What were his dreams and desires? She didn't need them to be the same as hers because, no matter the answer, she knew it really wouldn't matter to either of them. The lack of logic to that made the whole thing very confusing.

Anne took out *The Woman in White* and started reading where she had stopped three days before.

Chapter 11

The Newark airport was crazy. It took her thirty minutes to make her way through the maze of security doors and exits. Finally, she found herself at the Ground Transportation and waited in line for a taxi. She certainly wasn't taking the bus on Harry's dime.

"Hello, Jen?" Anne said. She had her cell phone up to her ear.

"Anne?" Jen, her sister, replied. "Where are you? It's like really noisy. I can barely hear you."

Anne put a finger in her other ear and pressed the phone to her head as she huddled in the back of the taxi.

"I'm in New York!" Anne smiled when she heard the reaction.

"New York!? Where? When? Where are you staying?" Jen asked.

"Where? Just came in from Newark. When. Now. Where am I staying? The Four Seasons. Want to join me for the day?" Anne asked.

She could hear Jen's muffled voice talking to her husband.

"YES!" Now? Oh. What time is it anyway?" Jen paused.

"Actually, I just came in from London—so I have no idea… seems like lunch time to me," Anne said.

"OK. Robert is just heading off to work anyway. I'll meet you in a couple of hours or so."

"See you then, love," Anne said, and hit the end button.

Anne dialed in a number on the itinerary that Harry had given her.

"Hello? Is this Mr. Johnson?" Anne asked.

"Yes. Who is this?" Mr. Johnson returned. The phrase made Anne hesitate for a second.

"This is Anne Compton. I believe you are expecting me."

"Oh. Yes. Ms. Compton." Anne hated it when they presumed that. She liked the unambiguous 'Miss'.

"Are you in New York?" Mr. Johnson asked.

"Yes. However, if possible, can we meet tomorrow? The trip was rather long," Anne said.

"Sure. Ten am - OK? Can you get to my office?"

"I'll be there," Anne said, as she hit the end button and took out the Lion King Tickets for that night's show. Harry was right. She was going to enjoy her visit to New York on their company's money.

Anne slumped into the back seat of the yellow taxi and watched the massive gray Manhattan skyline come into view. It had been almost five years since she had come here as a teenager. She remembered getting lost in Chinatown, where she had almost freaked out at the dead animals in the windows, and the permeating smells of the countless restaurants that lined the streets. Of course, she didn't show that she was scared. She had held her head high, gripped her newly purchased fake Gucci bag, and walked straight down Canal Street until she found Jen, who was haggling with a street vendor. She never even told Jen she had been lost.

The Four Seasons hotel was located near Central Park and she was greeted by a uniformed valet who opened the door for her, then took her single bag and followed her into the beautiful foyer.

There was a huge bouquet of flowers that adorned the marble table in the middle of the room and she thought, for a moment, that it was artificial until she saw the single brown petal of a daisy, which drooped toward the table. Her shoes clicked on the marble, and the smell of Jasmine filled the air as she approached the front desk. She declined the offer from the valet to take her bag to her room and waited behind a woman wearing a short red and black business suit, and carrying a Chihuahua.

"Hello, ma'am," the young man said. Only in the Four Seasons did the uniforms actually fit.

"Hi," Anne said. "I have a reservation under Compton, Anne."

His fingers typed much longer than it seemed they should have.

"Ah. Yes. Two nights. Queen bed. City view," he said. Anne thought that two nights was not going to be nearly enough to do everything she had planned.

"Actually, I believe it was supposed to be a King bed, park view." Anne looked straight at him.

"Oh?" His fingers tapped furiously again. "We do have a park view, king room available, but the rate is slightly higher." He looked up at her.

"No problem. I'll take it," Anne said, and handed him a company credit card.

After another couple of minutes and some signatures, Anne found her way to the elevators where the woman in the red suit and dog was just disappearing into a car. Anne waited for it to close before pressing the up button.

Anne was on the 23rd floor—Park view. She opened the drapes while she feasted on a free chocolate from the box they had so thoughtfully left. Anne looked out over the huge man-made park and saw a couple climb into the back of a black, horse drawn carriage, and trot off. She turned away and plopped on the bed, where she pulled a pillow out from the cover and laid on her back. The residue of chocolate melted in her mouth, and she savored the taste. She closed her eyes for a moment and wondered where Jarred was. The thought made her reopen her eyes and she looked at the neo classic painting on the wall. Even in a nice hotel like this the art looked a bit forced. The frame was just a little too big.

She got up and went to the bathroom, where she unpacked a few things while she ran the bath. She opened the free amenities and smelled the shampoo and conditioner then realized they had provided a package of bath crystals so she added them to the water and the room filled with the smell of ginger. Anne removed her outfit, briefly looked through the vapor at her ghostly image in the mirror, and stepped into the tub for a long, leisurely bath. She wished she had a candle, and turned off the light.

:

Jen's knock on the door came almost three hours after she had called her, but Anne had anticipated the tardiness, and was just finishing getting dressed.

"Ta da!" Anne opened the door as if presenting a reward on a game show. She was dressed in a black knee length spaghetti strapped tea dress, with matching pumps, a fake pearl choker and a cream white sweater. She had pulled her hair back with a single barrette placed at the crown of her head. Her shoulder length auburn hair laid loosely around her neck. It nicely framed her exposed collarbone.

"Oh. Annie!" Only Jen would dare use the childhood nickname. Jen gave her a big hug, then pulled back while still holding on to her.

"Wow! Why so dressed up?" Jen said.

Anne splayed the two theatre tickets and presented them to her now very attentive sister.

"Fantastic! Why didn't you tell me? I would have gotten dressed up!" Jen said.

Anne knew this, of course, but with Jen's beautiful face, slender figure and blonde hair, Anne was quite certain she would draw enough attention.

"You always look great Jen," Anne said. "And I'll take you to an early dinner anywhere you want. On me." Or rather on my company, Anne thought.

"Chinatown?" Jen asked with a smile. She remembered, quite well, Anne's last visit.

"I was thinking something just a little... less exotic." Anne squeezed her sister's arm.

"OW! OK. I'm just joking. Let's go to 21." Jen said.

"Fine with me," Anne said, and let go of her sister's arm. Jen rubbed it a little with her hand.

21 had recently opened an upstairs restaurant. It was elegant and intimate, adorned with salon type seating and early American rich fabrics. A pretty young redhead in a short yellow dress seated them at a private salon.

As soon as they sat down, Jen put her hands on the table and moved forward to look at Anne.

"So? What happened to Tony?" she asked.

"Ouch, Jen. How about a little chit chat first? You know: how's the job going, been anywhere exciting lately?"

"Come on, Anne—you have neatly disposed of all my questions about your love life for the last several months. I assume Tony is history?" Jen said.

"You presume correctly." Anne took a sip of the water that had just been served. The glass was sweating with so much moisture that it slipped a little and Anne reached up with her other hand to support it, happy for the distraction.

"That's it?" Jen said. "What happened?"

Anne sighed. "Nothing really too exciting, Jen. It just didn't work out." Anne fidgeted with her silverware.

"Didn't work out? Like he cheated on you?"

"No... well, I don't think so. He just didn't treat me well. You know, like I deserve to be treated," Anne said.

Jen widened her eyes, waiting.

Anne sighed again and started with a little hesitancy. "I... I think I deserve to be treated like a lady." Anne took her napkin and laid it on her lap, then leaned back straight in her chair and looked at Jen.

"I think you do as well," Jen said.

"Can we move on to another subject now?" Anne said.

"OK. Meet anyone new?" Jen was relentless, and Anne couldn't help but blush a little.

"OH! You *have* met someone!" Jen said.

"No. Not really. I was in London for a couple of days…"

"London? What were you doing in London?"

"For business." Anne shrugged.

"Oh. So. Who is he?" Jen leaned forward to listen.

"Just some guy. Nothing serious. I just had kind of a connection with him. We hit it off. But I'm not ready to do anything, and I don't really know anything about him. Maybe he's even married," Anne said.

"You didn't even ask him?"

"No. It didn't seem really appropriate. What am I supposed to say: 'Hi, good to meet you, are you married?" Anne said.

"So, are you going to write him?" Jen asked.

"Maybe," Anne played with her fork on the table. "If he writes… Maybe."

"So, ladies, my name is Stephen, may I tell you about my specials?" A handsome twenty-something waiter with a conspicuous grin interrupted them. His name flooded Anne with a reminder of why she was in New York.

Thankfully Jen didn't bring up the subject of men again until after the play. By then it was too late for much of a discussion, and Anne truthfully told her she was just too tired to deal with it.

Jen left her at the hotel and Anne got undressed, brushed her teeth with the mint flavored hotel toothpaste and tucked herself into the cool white percale sheets on the oversize king bed snuggling three pillows around her like a feather fortress. She fell asleep hearing 'The Circle of Life' playing in her head amidst the blaring horns of the streets of New York.

:

At 8:00 a.m. the alarm sounded and Anne sat up, looking out the window through the sheer drapery to a beautiful fall day. The sun was streaming in, and it looked like a scene from a cruise ship commercial. Anne smiled, got out of bed in her white tank top and favorite boxer shorts, and walked to the shower where she brushed her teeth and examined the jet lag toll on her face. All things considered, it could have been worse.

After a much needed shower and a brief, cool blow dry, Anne ironed a pink shirt and her cream slacks, put on a brown belt to match her brown flat shoes and picked up her cream sweater from the day before. She stopped to grab up the complimentary newspaper on her way out. It still smelled of fresh printer's ink.

In the lobby a good-looking forty year-old man in a three-piece business suit smiled and looked at her. Anne smiled as she kept walking, searching for a sign to the restaurant. She wondered if he had caught a whiff of the Chanel Chance that she had dabbed on her neck and pulse points.

After a breakfast of coffee, fresh fruit and yogurt along with two scrambled eggs ordered a la carte, she caught a taxi to Mr. Johnson's office on 33rd and Broadway.

Chapter 12

It was a dingy four storied building with a well-tarnished brass front door.

"Come in!" A booming voice came from the other side of the door, which was inlaid with obscured privacy glass with the words: "Harold Johnson, Private Investigator." The gold print was crescent shaped across on the top of the pane. Anne used the cuff of her sweater to open the door so she didn't have to touch the knob. Mr. Johnson sat behind a desk piled high with files. He was overweight, disheveled, and exactly how she would have pictured him. The only thing missing was the cigar, and she was relieved at not having to breathe the smoke. He proffered the plastic seat in front of his desk and Anne sat in it gingerly.

"Ms. Compton, I presume?" Mr. Johnson smiled. He had a single gold-covered bicuspid, and a large gap between his two front teeth. There was something stuck in the hole. Anne averted her gaze to the file he had open on this desk.

"Is that Stephen and Natasha?" she asked, pointing to the grainy photo of a young man and woman coming out of a store.

"Yes, ma'am," Mr. Johnson said. At least he had stopped calling her Ms.

"I talked with them right after this was taken," Mr. Johnson said. "They were a bit skittish to say the least. Seems her father was none too happy with dear boyfriend, Stephen. Something about bodily harm…"

Mr. Johnson grinned with his left over breakfast and his thousand-dollar smile. Anne felt a gag coming on, and again looked at the picture.

"Were you able to persuade them to meet?" Anne asked.

"Sure. I told them that I had heard on the street that there was money being offered for a near death experience." Mr. Johnson laughed, and the rolls of fat continued their jaunt long after he stopped. He wiped away a tear from his eye. "I told him that it would probably be best to give up the little trinket and call it a lesson in life. Ya know, instead of costing 'em his life." Mr. Johnson laughed again and the rolls that were not yet moving were now undulating back and forth. Anne could feel another gag coming on, and spoke quickly.

"Where and when, Mr. Johnson?" she asked.

"Tonight. Eight p.m. this address." Mr. Johnson offered her a piece of paper and she reluctantly took it with two fingers. "Stephen insisted that you sit in the lobby with this." He held up a bright pink umbrella. "And that he would contact you once he confirmed that you were alone. Me thinks the boy has watched one too many a detective show." Before he could start up his chuckling again, Anne interrupted.

"Did he say anything about the object?" she didn't know how much Mr. Johnson had been told.

"Oh. Yeah - almost forgot. He said it had been misplaced, but that he thought he knew who had it."

"It was *what*?" Anne said as she stood up.

"Stolen, absconded, picked, taken—you know..." Mr. Johnson said. "Hey, look Ms. Chapton, Chamton? No biggie here. I didn't really hear of anyone looking to kick the crap out of him, and he probably just didn't want to tell me he still had it. I'm sure it's fine. This guys way too scared to be a pro."

"That's what I'm afraid of," Anne said as she got up and left through the open door. She didn't bother to close it.

On the way back to the hotel, Anne thought about calling the police, but what would she say to them? Besides, Mr. Harold Johnson was probably right. They were just scared of Natasha's dad and this would all be over at 8:00 p.m. Still, she called her sister and asked her to meet her for dinner at six. That would mean she would arrive at seven and they could walk to the hotel, pick up the cross and then go to dinner. No need to burden Jen with the details.

As she walked back to her room, she noticed an Internet café and went inside. She needed to check in with her office email, let Harry know what was going on, and remind him how much he owed her.

She paid the guy with the almost twenty piercings, and in the almost white T shirt, three dollars for twenty minutes, and logged on to her company webmail.

She scanned the short list of messages and her heart skipped a beat to see one from Jarred. She would read that last.

Harry just wanted an update, and Anne made it sound much worse than it was. She hated New York, her sister was busy, the traffic was terrible, Mr. Johnson was a slob, but she did admit she liked the play. She ended the note that she would know more later that night, and would write again.

I'm Sorry… Love, Anne

The next email was from some other legal assistant asking about some expense report she had turned in. She told them to ask Harry.

The final email was from Jarred.

"Dear Anne,
Hope your visit to NY is going well. Such a crazy city! It's almost as bad as London. Really enjoyed our last day, and hope that I will hear from you. Oh. And it seems as if the priest is no longer in town. Maybe he's in New York! Just joshing.
- Jarred"

She wondered why he just signed it 'Jarred'. Not 'your friend Jarred', not "Jarred Mulberry," just Jarred. She wondered what that meant, exactly. Anne started to write a reply. She got about two sentences down and realized she didn't know what to say, so she just deleted what she had written and logged off. She would have to deal with that later.

With ten minutes to go, she decided to try and find out a little more about Lord Ellias Cornwall, the owner of the estate in Canterbury. She Googled him again and found a lot more information. One link, in particular, caught her attention.

> *"Lord Ellias Cornwall was a proud family man known for his patriotism. King George VI appointed him as secretary of finance and the sole caretaker of a very large sum of bullion in 1939. By some estimates, over forty million pounds sterling. At the end of the war, when the bullion was to be returned to the throne, it was discovered that a half million pounds was missing. Lord Ellias Cornwall allegedly investigated the missing gold, but it was never recovered. Because of the incident, the family was seen to be as out of favor with the Monarchy, and most of them left England to the territories in the early 1960's. Lord Ellias Cornwall II, his only male heir, sold off most of the family estates after his father's death, and moved to Hong Kong where he is said to be somewhat of an antiquities dealer and collector. Lord Ellias Cornwall's trusted aide, Sir Percy Harrision, assumed Lord Cornwall's duties, serving as an undersecretary of finance until early 1973."*

There were several links about Lord Ellias Cornwall II and Anne read one.

"Lord Ellias Cornwall's sole male heir assumed his title upon his death in 1956. The family had extensive estates in Kent, which the son sold off piece by piece until the early 1960's, at which point he moved to Hong Kong to take up his self -professed love of antiquities. Lord Cornwall was also survived by two daughters, Elizabeth and Anne."

The mention of 'Anne' riveted her attention and she read it several more times. The article continued.

"The mysterious disappearance of the gold bullion after the War was not the only incident in the family's history. In the early 1930's the Cornwall's were entangled in the murder of a young girl at the family estate in Canterbury. Scotland Yard never solved the murder, and given the low social status of the girl nothing much was ever revealed about her. Speculation suggests that the family arranged for the incident to be covered up, however, when the gold went missing a few years later, the Monarchy had had enough, and the family fell out of favor."

The flag on the computer screen warned her that there was less than sixty seconds left and it broke Anne out of her stupor. She couldn't believe the story she was reading. 'Anne' must have been the daughter of this no good Lord. But who was John?

"Hey Lady? You done?" A kid no more than fifteen stood beside her.

"What?" Anne said.

"You done? The computer…" he pointed to it.

"Oh. Sure. Yes," Anne said and grabbed her purse.

It was enough information for the day.

Chapter 13

The Woman in White, VIII, page 295

June 19th – I had only got as far as the top of the stairs when the locking of Laura's door suggested to me the precaution of also locking my own door, and keeping the key safely about me while I was out of the room. My journal was already secured, with other papers, in the table-drawer, but my writing materials were left out... Distorted by the suspicion which had now become a part of myself, even such trifles as these looked too dangerous to be trusted without a guard – even the locked table-drawer seemed to be not sufficiently protected...

Anne lay prone on the still made up bed engrossed in the book. Her stocking feet hung over the end of the mattress, with the book in front of her and a pillow under her chest. It was only a loud horn from the streets below that brought her back to the present. She looked up at the window, and then at the bedside clock.

"Shoot!" Anne said. It was 7:10 p.m. Where was Jen? She rolled over to the edge of the bed sat up at the same moment as the loud knock on the door. Anne ran over to it in her stocking feet, and yanked it open.

"Where have you been? We're late!" Anne was trying to get her feet in her shoes and, at the same time, exit the room while pulling Jen along. At the last moment she grabbed her purse and sweater from the floor by the door where she had left them in a pile, and rushed to the elevators with her sister in tow.

"Wh-at are you doing?" Jen asked, "I know I'm late, but.."

"But? We have an appointment across town in forty five minutes," Anne said.

"I'm sure they'll hold the reservation Annie, just call them."

The small bell signaled the elevator had arrived and Anne spoke as they boarded.

"Actually, we need to make a bit of a stop before dinner." Anne faced the doors with Jen beside her, but didn't look at her sister. The polished brass of the doors presented them a contorted view of themselves.

"What for?" Jen asked, as she faced Anne. Anne maintained her gaze at the doors. Her posture was stiff and her hands were wrapped around the strap of her purse, which she held in front of her.

"Annie? Fess up," Jen said.

Anne took a deep breath and looked at her sister and smiled. The elevator stopped for a passenger, and Anne nudged her sister as they both looked at the elegantly dressed handsome man that joined them. He looked directly at Jen, then at Anne, and took a place behind them. Jen leaned over to Anne's left ear.

"What is up Annie? This better be good." Anne just smiled and grabbed her sister's arm and held on.

The doors opened in the lobby and Jen and Anne exited first. They both felt a bit self-conscious as the gentleman walked behind them out to the reception area. They could hear the click of his leather soles on the slick marble.

"OK, Annie, talk." They had exited the hotel's main doors and Jen pulled Anne's arm from her and looked at her. They were about the same height and Anne wished she had Jen's brilliant blue eyes, instead of her hazel ones.

"Nothing that big, Jen. I just have a brief meeting with a client. Well sort of a client, actually the ex employee of a client. I'm just supposed to pick up this little religious artifact, and then we can go to dinner. I just didn't want to go alone. You know how I get in New York." Anne lowered her head so she could look up at Jen's face with wide eyes.

"Oh right, Anne. Like you're really a helpless teenager in a big bad city. You live in *Chicago*... by yourself! You're not telling me something."

"No. Really. That's the truth. This guy stole a cross. Well, we think he did, or his girlfriend did, and her father wants it back. He's been raising a ruckus over in England. That's why I was sent there. They needed some research on extradition laws and antiquities, but if he just gave it back, it would save a lot of trouble. It shouldn't take more than a few minutes," Anne said.

Jen squinted at her, but Anne smiled with closed lips and Jen gave up. They started walking. The streets were not nearly as noisy as that afternoon and, other than getting yelled at by an obnoxious cab driver as they crossed 50th street, the walk was uneventful.

The 'J' Hotel had experienced better days, about twenty years ago. The doors opened to worn red carpet and a lounge with high-back chairs in various shades of greens, lavenders and gold's along with the occasional wood table. The entrance to the combination restaurant and bar was over on the far side, beyond the lounge area, and a pretty good male voice rose above a jazz quartet. He was singing some old Cole Porter song that Anne recognized from her childhood. The reception desk was on the opposite side of the room, and two men were helping a couple of patrons. Anne noted wryly that the clerk's uniforms did not fit well. There were two staircases coming down into the lobby. On one of them a man flirted with a woman wearing a low-cut red dress. He smoked a cigarette and stood a step above her, looking down. He was obviously enjoying the scenery. An older woman passed them, and wrinkled her nose. Anne wondered if it was at the smoke or the public exhibition.

"Now what?" Jen had leaned over and was whispering in her ear.

Anne nodded toward a couple of chairs that faced the lobby, and walked over to them. She pulled the compact pink umbrella from her purse, and laid it on the table in front of them.

"What the heck is that for?" Jen asked. "There isn't a cloud in the dang sky?!"

Anne shrugged. "I'm just following directions."

"Let me guess. This guy is a clairvoyant, and expecting rain?" Jen crossed her legs and started swinging the top one. Anne noticed that it showed quite a lot of skin. The pose and the leg meant Jen was getting irritated.

"Look, Jen. I'm supposed to put out this pink umbrella and he, or someone, is supposed to contact us. He's just a little bit paranoid because someone told him there is a price on his head." Anne had leaned forward, and Jen was forced to do so likewise to hear her.

"Price on his head?" Jen said it a little too loud and put her hand over her mouth. "Is this dangerous, Anne?" Jen's face was starting to flush. She loved excitement.

"No, Jen. Calm down. Some P.I. told him that to encourage him to return the object. There is nothing to be afraid of."

"Oh." Jen looked disappointed. She leaned back in her chair, and commenced with the swinging leg again.

Anne surveilled the room, but she didn't know what Stephen and Natasha even looked like. She could guess from Mr. Johnson's photo, but there were at least six people that could have met the same description. Anne heard a telephone ring, and one of the front desk clerks picked it up and started to scan the room. He said something into the receiver and wrote a note, disappearing through a side door. Moments later, he walked out from a side hallway, walked up to Anne, and handed her the note.

"Nice umbrella," he said as he left.

Jen held up her hands in the international gesture of 'what the heck was that about' but Anne was reading the note. Anne stood up, smoothed out the front of her pants, and slung her purse over her shoulder.

"We're supposed to go to room 1416," she said.

Jen stood up, and narrowed her eyes.

"Are you sure this is a good idea?" she said. "This guy could be some perv or something."

"And that is why you are here, dear sister, to gouge out his eyes!" Anne smiled, half to pacify her sister, but also to calm her own nerves. No. She wasn't sure this was a good idea, but she knew she was going to find out very shortly.

"Want to walk it or take the elevator?" Anne asked.

"Right," Jen said, and walked over to the 'up' button and pushed it.

The fourteenth floor was actually the thirteenth, as Anne noted there was no thirteenth. She thought that if you were superstitious, you wouldn't want to stay on the fourteenth floor because it was really the thirteenth. So Stephen and Natasha must not be superstitious. She giggled at the thought and Jen looked at her, puzzled, but Anne just smiled and looked up at the lighted floor numbers above the door.

The doors opened, and the floor was eerily empty. The only sound they heard was the slam of the elevator doors behind them. It made both of them jump. Anne looked around to see where the stair well was, and saw it at the end of the hallway. She half wanted to go to it to verify that it was open, and actually went down, but she thought that would only freak out Jen, so she didn't. On the other hand, Jen was probably enjoying the adrenaline rush.

They walked down the hallway, side by side, just a little too close, and followed the increasing room numbers. The carpet was an old yellow and gold, with some floral pattern in it, and the wallpaper had a cream tapestry look to it. All in all, Anne thought, not as bad as she would have expected. Each door was varnished in a dark stain and had brass numerals designating the room. On each door there was a single universal hotel access card lock and a peephole. She noticed that the peepholes changed colors as they walked down the hall. It felt as if someone was watching them.

Chapter 14

Room 1416 was at the very end of the hallway, around a small corner. It was just out of sight of the rest of the doors, and Anne felt her hands moisten as they approached it. There was a 'Do Not Disturb' sign, which hung on the door handle. She looked at Jen, and they both looked at the door. Anne knocked as if she really didn't want anyone to hear her but, in the silence, they could hear someone start to move inside. A moment later they saw telltale signs of a shadow blocking the light of the peephole. They both looked down at the handle as they heard the deadbolt open. Jen and Anne stood about a foot away, transfixed by the scene unfolding in front of them.

"OH!" Jen exclaimed and stepped backwards as the outline of an unexpected person came into view.

"Ahhh… are you Natasha?" Anne said, as she also took a step back and tried to peek around the door to see what was in the darkened room.

"Yes," Natasha said. She was a short girl, just a little over five feet tall. Her hair was dyed red, and she wore a torn black jacket. Her black mascara was half worn off, and her eyes were puffy. There was a bright bruise on her right cheek that looked like it hurt. Natasha signaled for them to come into the room, and she looked nervously down the short hallway. Anne and Jen just stood there.

"There's no one here. Stephen is gone. You MUST come in. It is not safe," Natasha said. Anne's first inclination was to turn and run away, but perhaps it was morbid curiosity as something impelled her forward, and she entered the room. Jen remained standing outside the threshold until Anne grabbed her and yanked her in, which resulted in a small yelp from Jen. Natasha closed and locked the door as they all stood in the small entry. The smell of cheap coffee and cigarette smoke emanated from the recesses of the washroom. The sleeping area was a total mess. Obviously, the maids had been given the day off.

Natasha started to pace. She put a cigarette in her mouth and tried to light it with a match and book, but her hands shook too much. Neither Anne nor Jen offered to help. Natasha looked at the unlit member and threw it on the unmade bed. Good way to start a fire Anne thought.

"Where is Stephen?" Anne broke the thick silence.

Natasha plopped herself on the bed, crushing the cigarette, and threw her hands on her lap.

"I don't know. He's gone." Her enunciation was almost perfect, no hint of an English accent. Anne thought she must have attended school in the States. Natasha looked up at the half-closed curtains.

"I came back here around noon today, and he wasn't here. Someone did leave that, though." She pointed to a legal-size brown envelope on the light green upholstered chair. Jen went over to look at it.

"Don't touch it, Jen!" Anne said. It made Jen jump a little, but she looked back at Anne with a smirk, and picked it up. The action prompted Anne to rush to her side.

"How do you know Stephen didn't leave this for you?" Anne said, the letter now in her hand. It was sealed, at least eighty-pound paper, and thick to the touch. Something was inside it. Whatever it was, it had a concave feel to it. Anne shook it around a little and it moved.

"That's not his handwriting," Natasha said. The envelope had her name written on it.

"So why didn't you open it?" Jen asked.

"Because I didn't want to." Natasha was back to staring at the single stream of light coming in from the curtains.

"So, do you know who it is from?" Jen asked.

"Yes," Natasha said, still staring at nothing. Jen looked at Anne, and shrugged.

"Who... is it from Natasha?" Jen said. The note of impatience was noticeable to Anne, but she doubted Natasha heard it. She was in her own little convoluted world at the moment.

"My brother," Natasha said.

"Your brother is in New York?" Anne asked. Something was not right here.

"I guess. That letter is from him." Natasha looked at them, and pointed to the letter.

"Are you afraid of this letter for some reason?" Anne asked.

Natasha grabbed her left forearm with her right hand and stared at the floor. Off to nether land, Anne thought.

"Natasha," Anne said, but received no reaction. "Natasha!" The girl looked up and Anne continued. "Should we open this? Do you think this has something to do with the cross, and Stephen?"

The last comment got Jen's attention and she said, "What cross?"

Anne gestured with her right hand for Jen to be quiet. Jen's left hand went unconsciously up to her neck where a sliver cross, hung. She started to rub it and stared at the envelope in Anne's hand.

"It might. Probably. Poppa has not been too happy with me..." Natasha started to drift off again.

"Natasha! What do you mean? Could this be something really bad? Should we call the police?" The statement finally elicited some emotion from her.

"NO! NO police! I'm in enough trouble as it is. Just open the envelope and see what my brother wants," Natasha said.

Anne shook the envelope so that the contents settled to the bottom, and then slipped her nicely manicured pinky nail under the flap and sliced it open. There was a single sheet of paper in it.

Anne and Jen were both hunched over the envelope, but Natasha sat a few feet away on the bed wringing her hands. They were all fixated on the envelope.

"Here. It's written to you." Anne handed the envelope to Natasha, who took it with reluctance.

Natasha pulled the letter by one end from its envelope, which allowed whatever object was wrapped in it to fall to the bottom of the envelope. She obviously did not want to see what the item was. With the letter out of the envelope, she placed it delicately on the bed and unfolded the sheet of paper. Anne and Jen could see it was handwritten with large black lettering.

Natasha read the letter with no visible emotion, then fell back onto the bed, the letter still in her left hand.

Anne and Jen both went over to her, and Jen grabbed the letter. It was not in English. She handed it to her sister. Anne had a pretty good idea that this was Armenian.

"Natasha, what does this say?" Anne waved the letter in her hand and put it in front of her face. Natasha grabbed it while on her back.

"It says: My Dear Nattia, You have taken something that does not belong to you. God will ...what is the word...Smite?" Natasha looked up at Anne, and Anne nodded at her. "OK... God will smite thieves. You must return it to your brother immediately."

"My father wrote that," Natasha said, then looked up at them and pointed to some writing on the bottom. "This part is from my brother, Peter. He is not a very nice person."

She continued reading: "My baby sister. Stephen has joined me until you give me Poppa's cross. I left you a little memento of his in the envelope. I will call on you later today." Natasha shivered as she read the last part.

Anne reached for the envelope on the bed and shook the item out of it onto the white rumpled sheets. She screamed and Jen grabbed her mouth. Natasha didn't even look.

"It is a fingernail, no?" Natasha said. It was the first time they had heard even a hint that English was not her mother tongue. Anne and Jen looked at her in disbelief, and then looked at the bloody nail on the bed. Anne had no idea fingernails were actually that long. They must go below the cuticle a half inch or so. The nail was fresh enough to start to stain the white sheet but no one attempted to move it. Natasha broke the silence from the bed.

"This is my brother's favorite persuasion method. But not his only." She sat up and placed her spayed hands beside her for support on the bed. Both sisters noticed that she did not look at the dismembered nail.

Anne and Jen were morbidly drawn to look at Natasha's hands and she noticed them do so. She lifted up her left one and extended her pinky. There was something wrong with the nail.

"This one," is all she said.

Chapter 15

Anne had drawn back the curtains to let in some light, and opened the little side window for some fresh air. The two sisters stood facing the outside world while the shower ran in the background.

"Annie, we should really call the police," Jen said.

"Yeah. I know. But what about Natasha? She is going to go ballistic if we do that without telling her. You saw how she reacted when I mentioned it a few minutes ago." They could hear Natasha singing some song in the shower. It wasn't in a language they understood.

"She seems in shock," Jen said.

"Wouldn't you be?" Anne said. "Her boyfriend has been kidnapped, his finger dismembered and sent to you, her brother is a sadist and is looking for her, her father is some ego maniac zealot who is probably into all kinds of kinky stuff..."

They both stood there, side by side, for a few minutes staring at the building across the street. Some man was flirting with a pretty blonde. Anne was surprised at how close the building was to theirs.

"OK. So let's just return the cross and get this over with," Jen said.

"That would be my choice," Anne said. They could hear the water turned off and the bathroom door open. They turned to meet a still damp Natasha who was wrapped in a towel. Anne thought she was quite attractive without the entire body armor she wore. The piercings were mostly gone from her face. Natasha didn't look at them, grabbed some clothes, and went back to the bathroom.

Jen lowered her voice. "How come you didn't tell me this was about a cross? You know how I feel about these things." Jen pointed to her own icon around her neck.

"Jen, look, that thing is just a piece of metal. It can't *do* anything. I didn't think it was a big deal. This thing was probably melted down from a sword by some monk, put in a church in Turkey or Russia, and worshiped for the last dozen or so centuries. But it is definitely not a deity. I don't know how you can get into that bunk," Anne said.

"Actually, it was supposedly made by St. Jude, Jesus' half brother and patron saint of those in need, or lost causes." Natasha reappeared and spoke matter of factly. "How appropriate that I stole it, huh? Talk about someone who is a lost cause." Natasha stood next to them as she dried her hair with a towel.

"It is said that the cross has healed at least a dozen people and granted hundreds of prayers. I just thought that maybe it could answer one of mine…" Natasha drifted off.

"That's my point," Anne said. "It can't answer *any* prayers or do any miracles. It is just a stupid piece of gold or silver, or whatever." Jen looked at her, then turned to face Natasha.

"My sister is an unbeliever," Jen said.

"No, not an unbeliever. I do believe in God, just not all this other religious mumbo jumbo. What a waste of time," Anne said. "Do you realize how much pain religion has caused? I mean look at *this* situation!"

"Speaking of which," Anne said, "why not just give him the cross and get on with your lives?"

"I can't," Natasha said. Anne waited for her to continue, which she didn't.

"Why can't you Natasha?" Anne asked.

"I don't have it."

"Where is it, Natasha?" Jen was a little irritated at these snippets of information.

"I don't know. It was here when I left. Over there." Natasha pointed to the TV armoire. "Stephen put it on top, but when I came back it was gone." That explained the out of place chair by the armoire, Anne thought. She climbed up and reached over the crown to verify that there was nothing there.

"Do you think Peter took it?" Anne asked.

"No, then he wouldn't have taken Stephen, he would have just beat him up or killed him, then…" Natasha drifted again. "Stephen must have done something with it, but he'll never tell Peter. They hate each other. Steven is an Anglican."

Jen looked at Anne and questioned her with her hands.

"The Orthodox Catholics of some countries, especially the Greeks, Russians, and I'm gathering the Georgians, feel very strongly about any other religions. One would imagine that Natasha's relationship with Stephen was frowned upon by her father and brother," Anne said.

"Yes." Natasha said, as she combed her hair in the mirror. "Those two would barely even talk to each other back home and, when they did, it was always an argument. Peter was always trying to pick a fight with Stephen. He said that I was too good for Stephen, that the Archbishop of Canterbury was a pretend priest, that England was God's toilet."

"I know Stephen put up with it for the icon that he wanted from Poppa, but he used to tell me, when it was all over and we were leaving for good, that he was going to teach Peter a lesson. So, when we finally left that night, we took the cross. It was to be my brother's inheritance from my father and we all knew that. Peter hates Stephen, but what he really wants is the cross."

"I think I have heard enough, Natasha. I'm going to call the police," Jen said as she walked toward the phone.

"NO!" It was the reaction that they all anticipated.

"Look Natasha, by your admission Peter is a loose cannon. I mean, look what he has already done. You know, kidnapping is illegal in this country." Jen paused. " We are not qualified to do this, nor is it smart to do this, nor am I getting paid to endanger my life." She looked at Anne for support.

"But Peter won't hurt *us*. He only hates Stephen. If we just get him the cross, he'll go home and Anne will be off the hook with her boss, and I can go off somewhere and be a waitress or something." Natasha plopped back on the bed.

"Actually, Jen...." Anne started.

BEEP. BEEP. BEEP. BEEP.

The phone rang and they all stared at it. It was a black office type telephone with a gray mismatched handset cord. Natasha looked at them both and walked over to it.

"Hello?" Natasha said.

"Peter! You Son-of-a-Bitch! Are you crazy? This isn't Georgia..." Anne and Jen could hear a rising voice on the other end of the line and Natasha went silent. After a minute or so, Natasha said, "OK, OK. OK." She hung up the handset and sat on the bed.

"He's coming up. He said all he wants to do is talk."

"Are you nuts? We are calling the police. NOW!" Jen ran over to the phone and picked up the phone only to have it wrung with such force from her hands by Natasha that they all screamed when it hit the wall and shattered. '"I'm sorry!" Natasha pleaded. "Please don't! He said he has hidden Stephen, and if I call the police, and he is arrested, no one will ever find him!"

Anne and Jen just looked at her. They both thought about the cell phones in their purses. But neither made a motion to use them.

"I'm leaving." Jen said, and got up and walked to the door. "Are you coming, Anne?" Anne felt as if she were watching a plane crash in slow motion, but couldn't turn away from seeing the inevitable inferno.

"Annie! Are you coming?" Jen's hand was on the doorknob, but Anne had not moved.

"Whatever. I'll be waiting in the lobby. If I don't see you in ten minutes I'm calling the police, and I don't care what either of you think." Jen opened the door and walked out. Anne wondered if she was going to take the stairs. If so, she would undoubtedly see Peter. He didn't seem like one to trust elevators.

Chapter 16

Natasha and Anne paced around the room, saying nothing. Anne paused for a moment in front of the open window and held out her arms to allow the breeze to dry the perspiration from her torso. It was less than three minutes after Jen had left that a knock came on the door.

All of a sudden Anne changed her mind and didn't want to be there. She thought about hiding in the closet, or in the tub or under the bed, but couldn't get herself to move. Natasha was taking small steps toward the door, and Anne wanted to stop her, but she wasn't sure she could actually speak. By the time she opened her mouth and tried to form a word, Natasha had opened the lock and the door went flying open. It threw Natasha back, and she stumbled before regaining her balance.

Peter was at least six foot four, two hundred thirty pounds from the look of him. He had a long, black scraggly beard, and intense black eyes framed by a large uni-brow, with deep furrows in his forehead. He had to be at least forty. For some reason, Anne had in mind someone much younger. He wore a black, priestly smock and hat. Anne hated him immediately, but she didn't show it.

He was saying something very intense to Natasha that made her back all the way up to the bed and sit down, where she cowered. Anne regretted not calling the police.

"But I don't have it, Peter!" Natasha said as the tears poured down her face. Her hands trembled as she tried to wipe them away.

Peter picked up the torn fingernail from the bed and smiled at her. His teeth were black and rotten. Anne could only imagine the stench they put out.

"Ah. He screamed like a pig when I took this!" Peter said.

Natasha grabbed his hands, and held on.

"Peter, I don't have it. I would give it to you, but I don't have it. I think someone took it from the room today. I think maybe the maid?" Natasha looked up at her brother, pleading.

"Really, she doesn't have it." Anne was horrified to hear her own voice, and even more appalled when the humongous man turned and walked over to her. He stood much too close, and his mouth was open. Anne wanted to offer him some of the free minty fresh breath wash from the bathroom but thought better of it. She almost gagged when he spoke. He smelled of fish and rotten meat.

He pointed a finger at her and looked sideways at Natasha.

"Who is this?" he asked.

The familiar phrase confused Anne and her mind regressed to several days before, but the voice did not sound the same. The other voice had no accent, Peter's did. Anne looked up at him and refused to breathe.

"She is from Turnberry & Sons. She came, like you, to get the cross. But it is NOT here!" Anne was surprised to hear so much conviction in the young girl's voice. Peter narrowed his eyes and looked at Anne, then took his hand right and moved it toward her face as if he was going to caress her face. Anne tensed up and she tried to hold his gaze and not pay attention to the filthy fingernails and callused palm, which were inches away from her.

"PETER!" It was said with such force that they both looked back at Natasha. She was standing, still shivering, but standing. Yet it was obviously not her speaking.

They turned toward the movement in the doorway and saw a badly beaten up man with a bandaged right hand.

"I thought I told you to say put," Peter growled.

"I have a bad habit of not listening to directions, or hadn't you noticed?" the man said, as he cocked a worn baseball bat, and moved quickly forward, the bat poised as if to lay into a fastball. Peter reacted by grabbing the only thing nearby, Anne, who screamed and reflexively stomped on Peter's foot, then wrested out of his grasp. Anne saw the briefest glint of pale wood in the corner of her eye, and yelped as she catapulted herself in the opposite direction. Peter had his free left hand up trying to block the blow, but still held Anne, now on the floor, with his right. The blow had a sickening sound to it, a deep, resonating, painful thud, and Peter relinquished his grasp on Anne in order to strike back at Stephen with what ended up being a missing blow. Anne rolled out of the way to the wall.

Peter was bent over at the waist from the first blow and Stephen was walking around him, the bat upright as he waited for a vulnerable spot. Peter lunged at him with his body, catching Stephen around his chest and propelling him into the armoire. Anne couldn't tell where the splintering came from, but used the distraction to grab her purse and the frozen Natasha, pulling her toward the open door.

Stephen was being held off his feet by the much larger Peter, but the bat was raining down blows until finally Peter dropped him and staggered back, still menacing, but his forehead bleeding and his left arm dangling like a wet sock. Stephen was gasping for breath, holding on to his rib cage with his left hand but wielding the bat with his right. They watched each other out of their swollen eyes, and Stephen stepped backwards to where the girls were. Peter took one step forward, as if to test the other man's resolve and Stephen managed to raise the bat with both hands. Neither one said a word until, finally, Peter dismissed them with a wave of the back of his hand. Stephen backed out the door with Anne and Natasha.

"Get the elevator," Stephen said to Natasha. He continued to look in the room at Peter who had sat on the floor to watch him.

They heard the elevator bell ring and Natasha's voice.

"It's here!"

Stephen was barely able to stand, and Anne looked at him for a moment, then got under his free arm and they half ran, half dragged themselves to the elevator.

Once inside Stephen turned to Anne.

"And you must be Anne? I'm Stephen," he said, with a broken smile.

"I gathered," Anne replied.

When they arrived at the lobby, there was an instantaneous hush that spread over the room. Jen came running up.

"What happened!?" she asked.

"Later, Jen," Anne said, "Let's concentrate on getting out of here first. The four of them rushed out onto the street. Anne could hear someone on the phone with 911.

Stephen turned to Anne and said, "You two can do whatever you want, but we are out of here." He grabbed Natasha's arm and they limped down the street to the alley. Anne had the sudden urge to ask him about the cross, but decided better of it.

"Well, want to wait for the police now?" Anne said to Jen.

"Not really," Jen replied.

They both headed in the opposite direction of Stephen and Natasha.

"You really know how to show a lady a good time," Jen smirked at Anne.

"And you missed all the real fun," Anne said, smiling back. Jen didn't see her trembling hands, which hung at her sides.

"You hungry?" Anne asked.

Chapter 17

"No. I didn't get it," Anne said into the mobile phone. "Let's just say it was really bad timing, Harry… OK. Fine. You still owe me the whole deal. Yes, even the paid week of vacation, which I will be taking shortly. Later Harry." Anne pulled the handset away from her mouth and spoke into just the mouthpiece as she pressed the 'end' button.

They were sitting at Aldolpo's restaurant, which was comfortably far away from the 'J' hotel. 'J' for jinxed, thought Anne.

"So, let's see if I have this right. Witnessed torture, a beating… two beatings, actually, a small strange red-headed pixie girl, a kidnapping, large, huge, bad smelling priest and yet no cross." Jen was on her seventh finger as she finished the list.

Anne had just taken a bite of the chicken with vermicelli and red sauce. And she gazed up at her sister before chewing. Jen had just taken a breath.

"Which, by the way, means that the priest, the boyfriend, the priest's father, your boss and I have not gotten anything that you promised us." Jen finished.

Anne had an index finger in the air as she sipped a glass of the house Chianti. She swished for a second then swallowed.

"Actually, that's not quite true. You are having dinner with me. AND, you are alive, and you have a great story for your grandkids!" Anne said.

"But I don't even have children!" Jen said.

"We'll, that sounds like some latent Freudian hostility toward your husband, or something," Anne said.

"Annie. I'm serious. This is a mess. What are you going to do?" Jen said.

"First. I'm, no, *we're* going to finish this wonderful meal." Anne pointed to Jen's untouched Caesar salad. "Then we are going to go to the hotel and make love to the mini bar, but only in a non-prophylactic, kind of way. And after getting good and tipsy we are going to watch a good comedy. Because my life is not nearly funny enough right now."

"Then, in the morning, I'm going to fly back to Chicago, talk to Harry and explain how he almost got me killed. Then I'll get behind my boring desk and return all my boring phone calls and emails and wish I was on another adventure somewhere. I'll go home to my empty apartment, put on Dana Glover, and take a nice long soak in my tub. Maybe I'll light a vanilla candle or something, and fall asleep in my own bed. That about sums up my plans for the next couple of days. What about you, my dear Jen?" Anne said.

Jen ignored her and started picking at her salad.

Neither of them noticed the news report on the TV in the bar about a fight in the 'J' Hotel. Three women and one man were seen fleeing the scene. A beat up Georgian priest was found in a room on the fourteenth floor, unconscious. Police had no leads as to what it was all about. The TV channel put up several artist renderings of the suspects. They could have been half the people in the restaurant.

:

Across town, Stephen and Natasha were counting how much money they had between them. It was not nearly enough for where they needed to go. Natasha pulled a wrinkled pamphlet from the XiXi auction house out of her purse. There was a number written on the back and Stephen called it collect.

Chapter 18

Anne arrived back in Chicago just late enough to avoid work for the afternoon. It was another gray fall day in the windy city. They were expecting rain. Anne arrived at her apartment and unlocked all four locks, dropping her bag inside. As always, she re-locked all of them and dragged herself to the bedroom. There were three messages waiting for her, and she pressed the button and lay on the bed staring at the ceiling.

"Hi, honey! Just seeing if you are home. I had a fabulous trip. Call me…" Her mom.

"Anne. This is Harry, your um, boss. Um, you knew that of course. Well, um. Guess I'll see you tomorrow." She missed Harry. He had a way of making her feel so competent.

"Anne. Jarred here. Just checking in. Had a little bit of stuff happen with the priest over here. Thought you might like to hear about it. Call or email me."

Anne contemplated if she should call him. She did like him, felt some kind of connection, but she didn't think it was a good idea. There were too many reasons why it wouldn't work, and she couldn't be just a friend. Those kinds of relationships always seemed to end up going bad. On the other hand, when she was around him she saw so many open doors. She liked that feeling… options, opportunities. She felt almost too happy around him. That probably was the thing bothering her most.

She flipped over to her side and picked up *The Woman in White,* which she had tossed onto the bed, and opened it to page 309.

> *"June 19th – Once safely shut into my own room, I opened these pages, and prepared to go on with that part of the day's record which was still left to write.*
>
> *For ten minutes or more I sat idle, with the pen in my hand, thinking over the events of the last twelve hours. When I at last addressed myself to the task, I found a difficulty in proceeding with it, which I had never experienced before. In spite of my efforts to fix my thoughts on the matter in hand, they wandered away, with the strangest persistency…"*

Anne couldn't concentrate either. She flipped the book to the front cover and traced her finger along the handwritten message, *"John. I'm sorry. I will never forget you. Love, Anne."* She wondered what kind of person was it that you could never forget. What is your story, Anne?

She picked up the phone and dialed a number.

"Hi, Mom. Just got home," Anne said.

Maybe she would email Jarred later.

:

The next morning Harry waited for her in her cubicle. He didn't look very happy.

"Hi, Anne," he said.

"Hi, Harry. Sorry I didn't come in yesterday. The plane arrived after three, and with traffic and everything…" Anne said.

"We have a problem." Harry sat in her seat and looked sad.

"What's wrong, Harry?" Anne asked. Her arms were folded.

"Turnberry & Sons has just been served by Her Majesty's government for dealing in stolen antiquities. Seems the priest has some political connections, and they are not too happy with us. We'll, specifically, me."

"Harry, I tried my best, but there was no way I was getting that cross. Seems like everyone from Eastern Europe is after that thing," Anne said.

"I know," Harry said, "but what has made it worse is that there are rumors that it is being put up for auction. Turnberry & Sons are having an old fashioned conniption, because if that thing ends up in some private parties' hands, they will never find it again, and they are looking at a huge lawsuit. Seems their insurance carrier has declined coverage based on unlawful activity. So they are blaming *us*. More specifically, me."

"I don't get it, Harry, why do they think you are responsible for their gaff?" Anne said.

"It doesn't matter… well, actually they say I shouldn't have sent you to retrieve it, that you were not qualified, and that because of that it is now missing. It's just an excuse." Harry waived his hand flippantly.

"Did you realize that thing supposedly was made by St. Jude, Jesus' brother? I mean, if that were true, I can almost understand the significance," Harry said.

Anne had no desire to go back into that discussion.

"Harry, look, we have a special insurance rider for officer malfeasance and unknown unlawful activities, why not find out where this thing is coming up for auction and try to get our insurance company to bid on it? The insurance company will only need to parlay the funds to tie the thing up so it doesn't disappear. Then we can work on providing the provenance and do the extradition. The insurance company will be refunded the money, and everything will go back to the way it was. I can work on that today if you want. That would seem to solve everyone's problems," Anne said. Harry looked at her, and smiled.

"Why, Anne, that is a brilliant idea. Let's review our insurance coverage." By 'let's' Anne knew that meant her. "Sure, Harry, it's not a problem."

"I'll have Sonja get you the policies right away," Harry said.

"Actually, Harry, I'll talk to Sonja – don't worry about it." That made Harry smile even bigger.

"I'm glad you're back, Anne."

"You still owe me," Anne replied.

"Get me out of this and you can have anything you want," Harry said as he walked away.

By the time Harry came back, around at 2:00 p.m., Anne had talked their insurance carrier into coverage under a Reservation of Rights, which was good enough for Anne. It was a step in the correct direction at least. Anne showed him the fax, and the stress lines in his face relaxed. He broke out into another smile. Anne noticed he had eaten something with lettuce for lunch, and she indicated so by pointing to her front teeth.

Harry quickly covered up his mouth. She could see his tongue moving under his upper lip. He paused long enough to say, "Anne, what would I do without you?"

"Oh, you probably would be working many more hours and doing a lot more of your own research, your wife would complain a lot more, and your kids wouldn't know your name," Anne said. "Oh, and you would be happy to provide me two tickets to Cirque du

Soleil when they come here next month." She looked up at him and pushed over the newspaper ad. "Good tickets," she added.

"Consider it done." Harry took the ad and walked away in his drab, brown two-piece suit.

Anne loved this part of her job.

Her email indicated an incoming message, and she paused before clicking on it.

> *"Hey. Just thought I'd see if you were in. It's late over here but I did have some information I'd like to discuss with you about the priest. Let me know when you have a chance. J."*

She started to write an apology, but got worried that would send the wrong message. After the third attempt she thought the tenor was correct.

> *"Jarred,*
> *I just got back into the office from New York, things didn't go particularly well there. I did receive your message and was wondering if I could talk to you tomorrow about this. Jet lag and all. "*

She spent the next minute trying to figure out how to sign the stupid note and finally gave up and just signed it. "Anne."

She waited for a reply for about fifteen minutes, received none, then shut off her computer and went home. She needed to figure out a better way of handling this. One minute she felt mean, the next like she was leading him on, the next too business like. She had no idea where to put this relationship in her 'boxes'. He just refused to fit in one.

She stopped on the way home to pick up some groceries, but ended up wandering around the store not knowing what she felt like. She finally just purchased some peanut butter and bagels, an apple, and a Shape magazine, and then went to her apartment.

She picked up her mail at the bottom of the stairs and was greeted by the lascivious stares of Mr. Morris. She was wearing a beige fitted knee length dress with a brown suede belt and matching two-inch pumps, as well as a light fall coat. She knew her figure showed through the clothing but, for some reason, she just didn't care about his attentions today and she gave him a smile as she walked by him, toting her single bag of groceries and her mail, which she sorted through on the way up to the landing.

There was another letter from England. It was the same thickness and same color as the last one! With some hesitancy, she pulled it out to the front of the stack and looked at it.

It was addressed exactly the same as the last one.

Anne found herself on her landing and went inside. She entered the kitchen where she laid the envelope on top of the others. She found herself wanting to read the letter but also needing time to prepare for the unknown. Her mind was filled with possibilities and questions, so she distracted herself by making a peanut butter sandwich while staring at the unopened envelope.

Finally ready, she sat down, took a bite of the bagel, the warm stickiness of the peanut butter adhering to the roof of her mouth, and lifted up the letter to the light. She couldn't see anything.

The butter knife had remnants of peanuts on it, but she wiped them off with a corner of the paper towel, then slowly inserted the knife under the flap of the envelope and gently cut it open. Inside there was another single sheet of paper folded in thirds just like the first one she had received some months before. Anne took another bite of the bagel, wiped off her hands, pressed the top left corner of the letter to the table and unfolded it, one section at a time, till it was fully opened and flat on the varnished wood.

> *"Dear Anne,*
> *I suppose I could have provided more information as to who I was when I wrote you that last note. You're probably not who I suspected – are you? Sometimes my old mind gets the best of me! It's just that I hadn't thought of 'Anne' in a very long time. I live in a house in Canterbury, but you know that. I am a widow here, and have been so for some time. Many years ago I found a diary in an upstairs bedroom. It was written by someone who was called Anne… A very sad girl I gathered. I still have the diary if you ever want to look at it. It is like a porthole to someone's heart of a bygone era. If you are ever in England please stop by and I will show it to you. -* ***Betty Theison****"*

Anne was at once relieved and intrigued. She should have gone by there! What a blast that would have been.

Anne folded up the letter and put it back in the envelope. She walked to the nightstand in her bedroom and placed the letter in *The Woman in White.* It seemed the most appropriate place to put it. She sat there for awhile, lost in thought, then got up and went to the living room and dimmed the light. In the corner was a soft fabric case, which was home to a cello. She unzipped it and, with a tender grasp, wrapped her hand around the smooth neck and removed the instrument, then the bow with her other hand. She sat down on the edge of the wooden slat back chair and spun the cello around on it's endpin so that it was facing the other way. She ran her fingers lightly across the strings while holding the neck with her palm. They hummed in her hand. Then she took the bow and lightly grazed the strands. Her head lay gently against the scroll, and Anne played Bach's *Suite No. 1 In G Major.* It was a piece where she could lose herself, a piece in which the day could be washed away like fine dust. It was much like the inscription - of a time long ago – but not quite forgotten.

Chapter 19

Anne woke up after the best night of sleep she had had in months. She was already late, but she took the time to try on several outfits. She finally picked a simple sleeveless pink spring top, which exposed her arms, an orange, above the knee skirt, and a fun multicolored beaded belt. She left her auburn curls falling down on her shoulders and put on a simple gold chain with a treble clef around her neck, a cream sweater, and a flirty wide-brimmed hat. She thought better of the hat after checking the mirror, and took it off. It was sunny out, and she was going to make the best of it.

On the way, Anne stopped at Starbucks and picked up her requisite latte, along with a muffin, and took her time strolling along the waterfront to her office. She arrived almost forty-five minutes late, and Susie looked up at her with wide eyes.

"Something wrong, Anne?" Susie said.

"No. Why?" Anne knew perfectly well why she asked.

"You're never late!" Susie said.

"I know! Isn't it great?" Anne replied with a smile. She picked up the little stack of messages that Susie had placed on the counter, and walked slowly back toward her cubicle. Steve, another paralegal, walked by and smiled at her. As he passed, Anne looked back and caught him looking again. She was in a strange mood, she thought.

Her cubicle was just as she had left it the night before. Except today, Anne took out a picture of her dad and put it on the desk where Tony's picture used to be. She didn't care what her co-workers would think.

"Hello, Anne." Anne didn't need to turn around to know the voice.

"Hello, Harry. Did you have a good night?" Anne asked.

"I guess so. Actually, yes. A very good night!" Harry said. It made Anne turn around and look at him.

"How good, Harry?...No. Never mind," Anne smiled. "So, any word from our compatriots in England on my idea?"

"Oh, yes. They love the idea and are willing to help out in anyway possible. You are supposed to call Jarred as soon as you get in. He'll be finishing up his day soon." Harry pointed to the time.

"Thank you, Harry. I will do so this minute." She sat down at her desk and took one last sip from her coffee, then put it aside, took out a pad and pencil and picked up the telephone. Jarred's number was on the card he had given her, and she dialed it, waiting for the ring.

"Hello?" Jarred said.

"Hi, Jarred." Anne waited just a moment to see if he would recognize the voice.

"Anne!" he said, and she smiled.

"I'm sorry I've been so tardy getting back to you. Things have been a bit unconventional the last week or so," Anne said.

"Not a problem." Jarred paused. "It's good to hear your voice... So. Did you hear about the priest?"

"No. I did meet his very earnest son though... In New York, and not under the best of circumstances, I'm afraid. He may not have gotten the best impression," Anne said.

"You weren't there when that whole thing came down...where are you?" Anne wasn't sure if Jarred knew everything.

"Um... what do you mean?" Anne asked.

"According to the priest, his son was mugged in New York by some gang of thugs." Jarred paused.

"Hmm... well, I guess you could say that," Anne said.

"You WERE there!" Jarred said. "What happened? All we know is that the son is in some hospital in Brooklyn and the father, excuse the pun, is on his way back to Georgia. Of course, he did make it perfectly clear that he still expected us to deliver the cross."

"I would have guessed so," Anne said. "What actually happened is that I had a meeting set up with Stephen and his girlfriend Natasha, but Peter, the priest's son, kidnapped Stephen. He sent his dear sister Stephen's ripped off fingernail, and a warning. Then the son, who, by the way, is *also* a priest, comes barging into the room making threats, and Stephen appears, all banged up, but with a large baseball bat." Anne paused for a second to catch her breath.

"Oh, God," Jarred said, softly.

"So, Stephen and Peter go at it in the room and I grab Natasha and leave. Stephen manages to get away and he runs off with Natasha. I went back to my hotel. All in all, quite an exciting day." Anne's steady voice belied her shaking hands, but she was amazed at how calm she was.

"Wow. I'm impressed," Jarred said. "I can't believe you even agreed to continue to work on this case..."

"Actually, it made me think about my life a little, and I came to some conclusions." Anne wasn't sure whether she wanted to share those at that moment.

"Oh, like what?" Jarred asked.

"Like... doing something fun with my life. Something I want to do," Anne said.

"And you have something in mind?" Jarred asked.

"Yes. I do," Anne replied.

"Any chance you'll be coming to London to do that?" Jarred asked.

"Umm..." Anne was again unsure of what she should say. "I think that I will need to come to London for at least a couple of days to finish the work on the extradition paperwork for the cross. In the end, it is Her Majesty's government that will have to make the request to get it back, so better to get it all lined up there."

"And that's what you had in mind for *living?*" Jarred waited on the line.

"Well, no—there is something more. It has to do with a personal quest of mine." Anne thought about how that could be taken and added, "a personal book I'm researching."

"Oh," Jarred said. She could hear the disappointment in his voice. "So, when are you coming back over the pond?"

"I'll ask Harry and get back to you," Anne said.

Anne emailed Jarred a few minutes later to say she was coming in two days. She found herself very excited about tracking down Betty Theison and the diary, but she had to admit she also was looking forward to seeing Jarred.

:

This time, Jarred met her at Heathrow airport. He was in a blue sportsman's jacket, with a cobalt shirt, tan khaki's and brown shoes and belt. Anne walked through customs pulling her single carry-on baggage, and Jarred stood waiting with a sign that said: "Anne, our Savior." The play on words was not lost on Anne, who smiled, and took the sign away from him. The gesture also alleviated the decision as to whether to shake hands, hug, or just look awkwardly at each other.

"Can I give you a hand with that?" Jarred pointed to her case and reached for it.

"It's really not necessary," Anne said, but allowed him to take it.

"Chivalry is not dead on this side of the pond, love."

Jarred smiled.

Anne liked his smile.

"So, how was the flight?" Jarred asked.

"A funny thing happened on the flight." They had stopped to wait for the train, so Anne looked up at Jarred.

"The Air Traffic Controller told our pilot that we had traffic at six o'clock. But our pilot looked at his watch and asked the Controller for help…." Anne paused.

"OK. I'll bite…why?"

"Well, the pilot was wearing a digital watch," Anne giggled. Jarred was more amused at Anne than the joke.

"So, that is airport humor, eh?" Jarred asked as the train pulled up.

"No. Actually, that is plain, 'plane', humor," Anne said, which made her laugh more and she covered her mouth.

"OK. It was a long flight. Let's leave it at that," Anne said, still giggling as they boarded the train.

Jarred looked at his watch. "Analogically, speaking of time, it is now near 4:00 p.m. local. Do you really want to start work, or….?"

Anne smiled, a bit mischievously. "Or… what?" she asked.

"Or dinner? Dancing?" Jarred did a quick two step, much to Anne's amusement.

"Well, we could do that, or…" Anne knelt in front of her bag for a second and removed *The Woman in White,* handing it to Jarred. The train bounced around a little, and Anne steadied herself by grabbing Jarred's arm for a second. He looked down at her fingers, and she quickly removed them to grab the handrail.

"Or… you want to read this book?!" Jarred looked a bit confused as he turned it over in his hand. It was just an early 19th Century book in a red binding. It was in fairly good condition, but nothing he hadn't seen a couple of million times. He read the title: *The Woman in White.* He knew this story. It had been made into a movie in the Fifties or so.

"Want to rent the video? I think I know a place that has it," Jarred asked.

Anne sat down and gestured for him to do likewise. Then she opened the book and showed him the inscription.

"You wrote this?" Jarred asked, "May I ask who John is?"

Anne smiled. "No. I didn't write this, but someone named Anne did, many years ago. You see this?" Anne pointed to the address label. "I wrote to this address several months ago and recently received this letter. She pulled out the envelope and handed it to Jarred. He opened it unceremoniously and read it. Then looked up at Anne.

"You want to go meet this woman? This..." he looked at the letter again, "Betty Theison"?

Anne nodded along with the biggest grin she could muster.

"Sure. Why not," Jarred said, as he pulled out his PDA cell phone.

"So, this was why you asked about Canterbury on your first visit?" Jarred asked. Anne was surprised that he remembered.

"Do you think it would be good to call her first?" he asked.

Anne nodded in agreement, and he typed in something to the screen and waited a moment. He tapped on the screen twice and handed the phone to her.

"Here you go..."

Anne held the phone up to her ear, unsure of whether this was a good idea but her thought was interrupted.

"Hello?" An older woman's voice.

"Umm..." Anne's mouth was a bit dry, and she swallowed. Jarred urged her to talk. "Hello. Is this Betty, er, Mrs. Theison?" Anne said.

"Yes, it is. Who is this?" There were those words again, Anne thought.

"Mrs. Theison, this is Anne Compton from Chicago, USA," Anne said.

"Who? You're from the United States?" Betty asked.

"Yes. I wrote you a letter a while ago about an inscription in a book, *The Woman in White*," Anne said.

Anne was about to repeat the sentence but she heard something, and stopped.

"Oh..." Betty said as the line went silent.

"Hello? Hello? Can you hear me?" No one was paying attention, and Jarred took the phone from her.

"Sorry—happens all the time." He pressed SEND again and handed her back the phone.

Anne could barely hear the ring on the other side due to the incessant clacking of the tracks. She was about to hang up and try again later, in a quieter place, when Betty answered again.

"Hello?" Same sweet old voice.

"Hello, Mrs. Theison, it's Anne again. I'm on the train, sorry. I was wondering if I could stop by and talk to you about the book?" The words all rushed out in a torrent.

"Hello? Anne? I'm sorry, I'm a bit hard of hearing. I'm home all the time. If you want, you can come by." Anne didn't know whether Betty had hung up or the line had gone dead. She handed the phone back to Jarred.

"Well. That went sailingly," Jarred said. Anne smiled. She didn't know what else to do. She rubbed her temple a bit as she could feel the vague indications of a headache coming on.

"How far is Canterbury?" Anne asked when the train had stopped and they had gotten out.

"I'll tell you what. Let's get you checked into the hotel and then we can pick up my car. Should be about sixty to seventy minutes from here at this time of day. You know, we could do a little research on her first. I know this clerk at Scotland Yard. She loves to snoop!"

Anne noticed the 'she' in the sentence but let it go. "I really don't think that is necessary, Jarred. It's just some elderly lady."

"Well, OK. We can always do that later if you want."

Anne appreciated that he was trying to be so helpful. "Could we stop and get a bite to eat. I'm afraid I'm a bit run down from the journey." Anne rubbed her stomach, which growled back at her, and she opened her eyes wide, as did Jarred. They both laughed.

"Sure. We have McDonald's, Burger King, Super Mack's.." Jarred kept naming them.

"Super Mack's?" Anne said.

"Yeah. Don't they have those in the States?" Jarred asked.

"No," Anne said.

"Well. It'll be Super Mack's then."

They arrived at Jury's Great Russell Street Hotel, and Anne unpacked and freshened up while Jarred waited in the lobby. She appeared ten minutes later wearing a red sweater over a white shirt, slim fitting blue jeans and comfortable flat shoes. She could have been any of the thousands of University students that lived and played in London.

The sun had just peeked out from behind the clouds as they walked out the front door onto Russell Street. They walked a couple of blocks till Jarred found a Super Mack's, where they each ordered a cheeseburger. Anne had a strawberry milkshake and Jarred ordered chocolate. They walked out of the restaurant, and Anne opened the bag, inhaling the aromas as Jarred hailed a famous London cabby and gave him an address in the Docklands, by Canary Wharf. The driver did his best to show Anne why 'London's best' are amongst the most feared in the world.

Anne was quite pleased that they did, however, arrive in one piece.

Jarred drove an older Merkur, a black four-door sedan. He kept it clean, in good condition, and in a private garage under what Anne presumed was his flat. The alarm chirped and Jarred opened the door for her. Anne got in, allowing him to close it. It had been a long time since someone had done that for her.

The drive to Kent was uneventful, and Jarred crisscrossed several streets until he found Fleming Road. The rural estates made for a serene drive, and Anne rolled down the window and leaned her head against the soft leather headrest to enjoy the breeze flowing over her face and hair. The two-lane road turned to the East, and Jarred slowed down in front of an old gate. Jarred looked at the address, and the names that were engraved in the stone, for quite a while. Anne knew that it was the correct address, and was about to say something when Jarred got out of the car and pulled one side of the entry open, propping it open with a frayed piece of lumber. The wrought iron had long ago became an amalgamation of black paint, paint chips and rusted metal, and squealed as it moved. After he had driven through, Jarred removed the prop and the gate swung to what would be considered a closed position, though it left plenty of room for any size of creature to slip through. Jarred drove in silence up the gravel driveway, another hundred yards or so, to a larger estate. It seemed too decrepit to be lived in, and they continued around the back until they found a smaller cottage with a thatched and rounded roof. The chimney heralded that someone was home, but Jarred parked a reasonable pace away, and didn't seem inclined to get out.

He watched Anne as she opened the car door. She stretched her arms above her head and arched her back along with a spontaneous yawn and smoothed out the front of her sweater. They were parked just far enough away so as to not be in direct view of the cottage door. Anne opened the rear passenger door and removed the book, which she cradled in her hand as she walked up the cobblestone path. There were more weeds than cobblestones however, she could see that once upon a time the path held an intricate design. Jarred waited in the car and watched as Anne approached the front door, knocking on the splintered trim.

A few moments later an old woman, perhaps seventy-five, opened the door. She wore a shawl around her shoulders and an old beat up apron.

"Hello, dear. You must be Anne." The old woman smiled and gestured for her to follow her inside. There was a small fire in the hearth and a set of tea waiting.

Anne took a deep breath and spoke. "You must be Mrs. Theison?"

"Betty, dear. Betty is just fine. But yes… one and the same," Betty said.

"Thank you so much for seeing me! I'm so excited to meet you," Anne said.

Betty looked at Anne's face, and then her hair and clothing, much like one might regard a grandchild to see how much they have changed.

"You are a pretty thing," Betty said, and Anne blushed.

"Thank you, Betty." Anne looked around the small room. It was decorated with mementos and pictures of a long time ago. There was a particular picture of two young girls together, riding on a horse. It had to have been from the forties.

"Is that you, Betty?" Anne pointed to the small gold frame on the mantle.

"Yes, dear, my sister and I, when we were children. I think the horse was named Odd Fellow. I'm the only one left now. Would you like some tea?" Betty started to pour into the two cups. She added a lump of sugar in each and handed the saucer and cup to Anne. It rattled a little in her hands. Betty looked at Anne as they sipped. The fire popped periodically in the background. The room seemed uncomfortably warm to Anne.

"I brought the book." Anne broke the silence by showing Betty *The Woman in White*. Betty put down her tea and tenderly took the volume. She ran her fingers over the fabric cover, then opened it up.

"Ahh... there it is." Betty traced her finger under the inscription. She closed it and held the book to her chest with both hands.

"What a story you are about to learn, Anne," she said.

"You know, I moved into the cottage when I was already old. After my husband died I was offered this small place and, well, here I am. One day, about twenty years ago, I was up in one of the rooms of the main house. I have no idea doing what—perhaps setting traps for mice. Well, I stumbled upon a diary written by a girl named Anne, just like you. Only this Anne did not have a very good life. She was obviously a Cornwall, since that's who owned this estate. Have you heard of them?" Betty asked.

"I, um, I think I've heard of them." Anne didn't lie.

Betty looked at her as if she was waiting for her to say more, but Anne remained silent.

"Anyway, the diary mentions some things that I think the family would not appreciate, even after such a long time has passed. That is why I wrote you that cryptic first letter. I thought perhaps you were on a little hunting expedition." Anne was intrigued, but couldn't imagine that anyone would be concerned about this eccentric little old woman.

"No. I don't know anything about the diary. I only picked up that book on a fluke one day in Chicago. And since we have the same name, and share the name with one of the characters of the book, I was just a little curious as to who this Anne was."

"May I ask you exactly where you obtained the book?"

Anne rolled her eyes up toward the ceiling and saw the cracks in the plaster. "I can't remember the name of the store, but it was a used book store by the river front. It was just in a stack of books."

"Hmmm. It must have been there a long time," Betty wondered out loud. "Have you read it?" she asked.

"Actually, I am reading it now. It was strange that the book was basically brand new. Some of the pages are still stuck together," Anne said. Betty slowly flipped through the pages and she nodded in agreement.

"You know, Anne. You look a lot like my sister did when she was your age." Anne was surprised at the change of subject but accepted the picture that Betty showed her.

Anne held a black and white picture of a woman about twenty-five. By the looks of the automobiles around her, the picture must have been taken in the '40s or early '50s. Anne didn't really know her automobilia that well, but the long straight skirt and simple blouse confirmed the time period. Betty's sister was pretty, slender, and looked sad.

Betty took the picture back. "She died about ten years ago…" She placed the picture back on the mantle. "Oh. And that's my husband, Rupert, God bless his soul. He died twenty or so years ago…" Anne didn't know what to say.

Betty shook herself and laughed. "I'm sorry, dear. I just don't get many visitors. I know what you want to see." Betty leaned over and grabbed a small book from under her chair. It was about ten inches long and six inches wide. The cover was pasted with dried flowers and the scribbling of a child. It was stuffed with clippings and papers, but looked to be about an inch thick sans the extra paperwork. Betty handed it to her and Anne took it and placed it on her lap. She was dying to read it but didn't know what the protocol was, so the diary lay in her lap while her book lay in Betty's.

"Tell you what, dear. If you'll let me keep this book I'll let you borrow that one. When you are finished with it you can return it and we'll trade back." Betty took *The Woman in White* and pushed it under her chair, then got up. Anne followed her as she shuffled to the front door. It was obviously the end of the visit, Anne thought.

Betty opened the door and Anne could see Jarred in the car. The visor was pulled down to block the sun but she could see the bottom of his face.

"Thank you, Betty. Thank you very much. I'll get this back to you in a couple of days."

"You're welcome, dear. I know you will enjoy it. I think you will find it very exciting!" Betty closed the door behind her and Anne wondered if she really needed any more excitement given the way that her life had been going this week.

When Jarred saw her coming, he jumped out of the car and opened the door for her, then quickly ran around and hopped back in the driver's seat. Anne still felt funny sitting on the left side.

"Well, how did it go?" Jarred asked after he had opened the main gate and was on Fleming Road.

As they took a corner, Jarred's cell phone slid across the dashboard. Anne caught it and gave it to him. "Sweet old lady. She just wanted company," Anne said.

"So, what did she give you?" Jarred nodded to the book in Anne's lap.

"Wouldn't you like to know?" Anne asked playfully.

"Let me guess. You went in with your book you came out with this one… the sequel?" Jarred shrugged his shoulders. Just then his telephone rang and he picked it up. Anne held the diary in her lap with both hands.

"Hello?" Jarred said. "Uh…yeah, that's correct. Can I get back to you about that? Sure…." Jarred hung up. "So where were we?" he asked.

"About to miss our turn, I believe." Anne pointed to the London exit as it passed by.

"Whoops. Sorry about that." Jarred made no attempt to follow the turn. "Since we are out here, I happen to know something you must see." In a few minutes Anne found herself walking among the crooked streets of Canterbury, looking at the timber framed homes, with Jarred walking beside her. They meandered through the streets until they came upon a most beautiful cathedral. Anne followed Jarred up the stairs while he explained.

"Canterbury Cathedral contains one of the most prominent collections of 12th century stained glass in the world. It was paid for by the money received from pilgrims to the tomb of Thomas à Becket."

"You do know who Thomas Becket was, don't you?"

Anne shrugged.

"Thomas Becket was the Archbishop of Canterbury, who was murdered in December, 1170. It is said that Becket quarreled with King Henry II over the legal privileges of the clergy, and the king got sick of his meddling. The king is said to have asked 'Who will rid me of this meddlesome priest?' and four knights went to the Cathedral and murdered Becket in front of the altar."

Anne wrinkled her nose.

"However, Becket is said to have had the last laugh as he was made a saint in 1173." Jarred stepped into the church and they watched the rays of the sun pour through the stained glass. Anne thought it really was an impressive display.

"You know—the Cornwall's have been around almost as long as the Becket's," Jarred whispered in her ear.

"What?" Anne asked.

"The Cornwall's… the estate we were at today. They have quite a colorful history as well," Jarred said. "Under this Church there are said to be thousands of volumes of books detailing nearly every family from around here back to the twelfth century or so. The Cornwall's, the Becket's, the Harrison's…" He gestured to a historical row of names of prominent members of the church.

Anne didn't say anything and Jarred tried another subject.

"You hungry?" he asked.

"Sure. I suppose that you just happen to know a quaint little place near here?" Anne smiled and grabbed his arm as they left the church. As she passed by the stones with the names of the families engraved on them, she couldn't help but wonder about the muddied history of these lineages and how many secrets the vaults held. It felt like listening in to hushed voices echoing off the stone walls, voices which had spoken here over the past millennium.

She couldn't wait to read her own diary.

Chapter 20

That evening Jarred dropped her off at her hotel room and Anne undressed, brushed her teeth, washed her face then turned on a bed light, propped up three pillows on the mattress and laid on the cool fresh sheets. She opened the diary, which had waited so patiently all day and began to read.

"April 22, 1933.
My name is Anne Cornwall. Actually, it is Anne Marie Cornwall. I am thirteen years old today and my mother gave me this diary. She said I could write my thoughts down in it so I could read it when I was old. But I really don't know what to write about. Today I played Fur Elise on the Piano.

April 26, 1933.
Poppa is leaving today for London. The king wants to speak with him. Poppa is very important but I wish he would stay home more. I think Mums would like that to. Lizzy was acting up and she got a spanking. My Piano teacher says that I must practice more, but I wish he would let me play something I like.

June 20, 1933
We have been at the Yorkshire house for three days. I want to go home. Something bad happened last night and I don't like it here anymore.

Anne wondered what happened but nothing else was mentioned about it, so she skipped through the next few years until she noticed a tenor change around 1937, when the winds of war started to be felt across Europe.

November 10, 1937
There are many men at the house tonight. They are talking about Germany and some lunatic named Hitler. Momma has sent Lizzy and I up to our rooms but we can hear them talking downstairs. Lizzy is scared. She thinks that Poppa will have to go fight in a

war. I'm not sure what will happen. There are talks of submarines and ships and airplanes. I have never been on an airplane, but Poppa has. He said it makes you feel like a bird. I overheard Poppa talking about meeting with the King tomorrow. He says that George VI and Queen Elizabeth are good for England but that he is worried they are not doing enough to prepare England. I think he and Sir Percy Harrison are doing something for the Queen and that is what all these meetings are about.

November 13, 1938
Poppa caught Michael shooting squirrels again with his favorite shotgun. I think he also poisoned Margaret, Lizzy's cat last month. But I didn't say anything. Michael is acting so strange. He thinks there is going to be a war and he is always pretending to kill people. That is so disgusting. I heard Momma tell Poppa that she didn't think he was ready for the hunt this weekend. It is to be his Eighteenth birthday present. I saw the gun that Poppa has for him. It is hidden behind his armoire. I am not allowed to practice the Piano now. There are too many people and the teacher is not allowed in the house. I don't know how I am to be ready for the family dinner. Momma expects me to play.

November 16, 1938
I was able to practice a little while everyone was gone today. I have decided to play Chopin's Waltz in C sharp Minor. It is a beautiful piece and has much life. I love it when my fingers fly over the keys. There is such freedom. Well, Michael got his hunt. Killed a pheasant and also said he missed and hit one of the dogs by accident. Stupid boy! The doctor said Cody would be all right, but still… I don't think anyone should kill for sport. It seems wrong, and Michael likes it too much. Poppa is to be gone until Tuesday. Lizzy and I are going to ride horses today. I think the gray mare would be better for her but she likes the Chestnut stallion. Perhaps we will just go riding together.

November 24, 1938
It is our family dinner and Momma is frantic downstairs preparing the roast beef. She does this every year. My favorite is the Yorkshire pudding. It is grandmother's recipe. We made it this afternoon. My hands are still soft from mixing the eggs and flour.

There is supposed to be a special guest tonight but they haven't told me who it is. The table is set for sixteen people. That means there will be at least eleven guests. Michael is supposed to be here as well. I could really do without seeing him. I hate the way he looks at me and, before he left, I caught him in my room looking through my clothing. I confronted him but he said if I told anyone he would make sure I would pay for it. He scares both Lizzy and I.

Nov 24, p.m. entry.
What a glorious dinner. I hope I can host as good as Momma when I have my own family. Sir Percy came tonight. He was the secret guest, I think. He brought his son with him, John. He has turned into such a handsome boy! … Square face, fresh skin and dark blonde hair. He is taller than I, but I think about the same age. He was charming, clever and funny. Lizzy was laughing hysterically at his jokes. I didn't think they were that funny but I didn't mind his company. I wonder if we shall see him again. He sat nearest to me when I played the piano. For some odd reason I was not nervous to play. It was as if my fingers knew their own way and I was just there to observe. Momma was pleased as well, I'm not sure at what, but I saw her smiling at me after I finished. John complimented me and said he wished I had played longer! Perhaps it is a bit forward of me to send him a letter!

December 1, 1938
We are going to Yorkshire for Christmas. I don't like Yorkshire and I wish we would stay here. I will especially miss my piano. We do have one up there but it is not in very good tune and I prefer the touch of this one. Perhaps it is because I am used to it. I don't really understand why we have to move just for a few days. I would be just content to stay in one home. I like this one. Lizzy is next door and I can see the river from my room. Momma let me light a candle when I took my bath yesterday night. What decadence! Snow fell for the first time today. There is barely a dusting of it but the texture it adds to the landscape looks like powdered sugar on donuts. I like it on the frame of the window as I look out. Poppa mentioned war again today. I think England will soon have a new Prime Minister. I do not know him, some man named Churchhill. Michael is to join us in Yorkshire. He is

on 'assignment,' or so he says. Probably just visiting the floozies in London. He drinks too much.

December 22, 1938
When we were driving through the countryside today we saw our first military vehicles. They are painted like the forest. Poppa calls it Camouflage (?) or something. Michael joined us last night. I forgot to lock my door and he came into my room after everyone had gone to bed. He tried to touch me and I pushed him away. He said I should just let him do what he wants and that I would like it. He laughed. There is something wrong with him! I don't know whether I should tell Momma. She is under so much stress, because Poppa is gone so much already. I heard them discussing something. I don't know what is wrong, but Momma started crying. She didn't see me but I think something is wrong. I wish we would have some company. We have had no visitors in a week. There is a foot of snow on the ground and Lizzy and I are tired of playing games. Perhaps I shall write a book of poetry or start working on my new piece by Schumman. I am unsure if I like it, as it is both difficult and long.

December 25, 1938
Christmas. Poppa couldn't be here with us but Lizzy and Michael are here. I hate it when Michael is here without Poppa, he acts like he is in charge and bosses the servants around. Momma doesn't say anything. I think she is depressed. I read about depression in a book she has in the library. It is something about the mind being trapped in a dark place. I've taken to locking my door every night. Michael has tried to come in several times. I don't want to wake up Lizzy, so I try to make him go away, but he keeps trying. If Poppa was around I would talk to him, but I do not know when he will return. The days are much shorter now. I did receive a book for Christmas. It is called ***The Woman in White*** *by Wilkie Collins. It is a mystery novel. I think I will read it tomorrow.*

December 28, 1938
We are returning to the Kent home for New Years. Momma says we are to have a big Party. That means visitors! Hurrah! We shall

all have new dresses and we will have ham and sweet potatoes and strawberry rhubarb pie. Momma wants me to play again for our company. I think I will play Bach's two and three part inventions. They are always good for the listening ear. Momma is very happy today. She says that Poppa will return in two days, along with Sir Percy. I wonder if John will be with them. I would very much like to see him again. Michael has taken to following the servants around. I see him at night stalking them outside. I think they are terrified of him. The second maid, a girl about my age named Theresa, seems especially afraid of him. I've seen the way she cowers when he is around. I am happy he is leaving me alone, but I feel sorry for Theresa. Perhaps I will have a chance to speak to Poppa about it. We will decorate the house with a fresh tree tomorrow and mistletoe above the foyer! Momma says it is acceptable to do that for New Years eve. I should note that.

Jan 1, 1939
What a fabulous evening! Mum allowed us to stay up until midnight and I had my first glass of champagne. It was like drinking tiny crystals. They tickled. Michael drank too much and made a fool out of himself. Poppa finally made him leave the house. I think he slept in the barn. How appropriate for the beast that he is. Sir Percy and his son did come. John asked me to dance. He is very good at it. Not that I have a lot of experience, just with dad and Lizzy, but I think he was good. I think he likes me. There were several other girls there but he spent almost the whole evening with me. Momma bought me the most perfect dress! It was pink and white and had lots of lace. The petticoats were full and light and mum said it showed off my 'stately neck'. John was wearing a black jacket with coattails and white shirt and gloves. He looked so dashing! I do not know what he does for his father, but he is always traveling. He again sat near me while I played. I think he likes to watch my hands, but I don't mind it. It's not like when Michael looks at me. It made me want to make the music come to life when he was watching. What an interesting feeling that is! When he left, he kissed my hand. I think I shan't wash it for a day or two. Lizzy says I'm in love. But I don't think so. I've never felt anything like this before.

January 14, 1939
There is constant talk of war by the men. Poppa is here now, but men are coming from London almost every day. They speak of ships and gold and Hitler. I can only hear bits and pieces as the sound travels through the house by the air vents and servant calls. I'm not sure if I should be listening. But it is so difficult not to. I suppose if I were a man they would tell me more. Still, it is the women that support the men, so I think we should be told as well. Michael is back. He is doing things for Poppa and hasn't bothered me much. Theresa is nowhere to be seen if he is around. I wonder what he has done to make her so afraid. Mother has taken to spending most days by herself in the sewing room, but she is not sewing. She no longer takes care of her hair or clothing. Poppa is so busy that I do not think he has noticed. I have to be strong to take care of Lizzy. Most of the time she is happy because we play games and go for walks. I read her Aesop's Fables for bedtime stories. The snow has not melted in over 2 weeks. I must think of what to do tomorrow.

February 3, 1939
Mother is inconsolable now. There is something wrong with her. Doctors have come every day for the last week. Lizzy is scared. So am I, but I must be strong. Poppa and Michael are constantly in meetings in the drawing room, and there are men in army uniforms walking around the house every day. No one laughs anymore, we are not allowed to play music or take walks in the woods. There is an air raid siren somewhere in the countryside and almost every day there are drills. Lizzy and I are confined to the two topmost rooms during the day, but I sneak down to the kitchen to get us food. I have asked father if I can help, and he told me 'perhaps in a day or so.' I do not know what I can do, but at least I wouldn't be stuck this room all day. I am not allowed to practice piano unless no one is in the house. When they do leave, I play Schumann's Piano Concerto in A minor, or Chopin, the piece that John so likes. I look outside at the meadows covered in snow and everything looks so pretty and peaceful. I do not understand how there could be so much trouble in the world when things are so simple here.

March 8, 1939
Father has allowed me to serve the men food. Sir Percy and John are here almost every day. There are times when John and I can talk privately. He has told me that there are plans for a special navy party to depart England to Canada. These are the preparations that they are making. Poppa and Sir Percy are always on the telephone, and often they leave during the day, only to come home exhausted. I feed them what meat we have, but the butcher has not been coming as regularly. Mother is now bedridden and we are forbidden in her room. Only Sarah, momma's nurse, can visit her. Michael came to see me today. He was agitated and in a fit to be tied. We know that he stays out in one of the cottages, and everyone leaves him alone, but tonight I saw him, and he looked very angry. I asked him what was wrong and he pushed me away and called me names I cannot even repeat. I do not know how he has become such an abusive man, but father seems to need him. I have heard him tell Sir Percy that he will need men like him during the war. I believe that is why they leave him alone. I will be eighteen in just a few months, but I am afraid for the world I live in. John is very kind to me but I don't know what will happen...

{No date}
There is something going on tonight. It is around 2:00 a.m., and I am writing this by candlelight. I heard the cars and trucks come about an hour ago, and more than a dozen officers came into the house. I heard them downstairs, speaking about a shipment of Gold… 30 million pounds sterling! Everyone left in a rush and I crept downstairs to see if could see anything. The drawing room door was left open and I heard Michael's voice talking to someone. They were arguing about the gold. Michael said something about a commission, and laughed, and the other man told him to shut up. I think that Michael is involved in something very bad…

Chapter 21

"History will be kind to me, for I intend to write it."
-Winston Churchill

April 22, 1939 – Kent England – the Estate of Ellias Cornwall, finance minister for George VI and her Majesty - Queen Elizabeth I.

"Sir Percy, have you made the arrangements for the final shipment?" Lord Ellias Cornwall said.

"Yes," Sir Percy Harrison replied to the Finance Minister, his supervisor.

"The men that are arriving right now will accompany the final two million pounds by truck to the Port, where it will be stored for loading onto the ship in a fortnight." Both men refrained from mentioning the ship's name.

"Are all the controls in place?" Lord Cornwall asked.

"We have over a hundred men at the storage facility, along with several armored vehicles and MI5 personnel. Each individual shipment will be counted as it is unloaded and loaded. Every fifth container will be physically opened and verified. The Queen's gold is in good hands," Sir Percy said.

"Just in case—do we have our agents in place?" Lord Cornwall asked.

"Yes father, I mean, Sir." Michael Ellias Cornwall II walked into the room. He was dressed in casual clothes with a turtleneck sweater and black leather coat and boots. His father looked at him disapprovingly.

"Michael, are you and John prepared for the trip? Do you understand your job?" Lord Cornwall asked his only son.

"Yes, father. It's not astronomy. John and I will tail the convoy to make sure that no one hijacks it. We are the last line of defense." Michael used his fingers to draw quotation marks in the air. "Once the bullion is delivered to the Port, we are to confirm that it has all arrived safely and report back to you. Simple as pie. We'll be back before sunrise." Michael picked up a date and ate it. John, Sir Percy's son, watched him with narrowed eyes and did not say a word. The two men were the same age, but could not have been more different.

Michael walked over to where John was seated. "Any questions, old boy? Or are you too terrified to speak?" He shoved John's knee a little.

"Shut your mouth, Michael. This is serious business." John waived him on.

Michael continued his sojourn around the room.

"Good then. Shall we go?" he said, and the two younger men left the room.

Lord Cornwall and Sir Percy stayed a while longer discussing some other plans. Neither of them noticed Lord Cornwall's daughter, Anne, sitting on the staircase. They both left shortly after 2:30 a.m. and closed the drawing room doors. Anne went back to bed.

The night was cold and still. There was enough snow on the roads to make the driving a challenge, and John sat in the car planning the route in his mind. He looked up to the room where Anne would be, and saw a flicker of a light. She must be reading by candlelight, he thought. Michael was nowhere to be seen. In a few minutes, the back door opened and a young girl was shoved in. John recognized her as Theresa, a maid from the Cornwall estate.

"What the hell are you doing, Michael? This is no place for a woman." Upon hearing that, Theresa reached for the door but Michael held it closed.

"Mind yer own business, John. I mean to have me a fun time tonight." Michael liked to put on a common accent when in one of his moods. "And this here little girl has been most cooperative." He had moved into the front seat but was leaning over to the back where the girl cowered.

"Dammit, Michael. The convoy is leaving. We don't have time for this!"

"Well then, ye better get moving yer arse then!" Michael laughed at his bad cockney accent.

"Get her out of the car, Michael!"

"I don't think so, Johnny. You just better do your job. The convoy is nearly out of sight." John turned around and saw taillights in the distance.

"Dammit, Michael!" John started the engine and accelerated out of the driveway. He caught up a minute later and remained well behind the line of trucks moving south. In about a mile he would split off on a parallel road, where he could observe the convoy without being seen. The moon had broken through the clouds and it cast an eerie pale light over the countryside. John turned at the designated road and shut off his headlights. He could see the row of trucks, moving along at a good clip. Michael had climbed into the back seat to be with Theresa, which was fine with John, except for the noise he was making.

"Michael! Stop it! Now is not the time! We have a job to do," John said.

Michael sat up and pulled the girl to him with his left arm, lighting a cigarette.

"And exactly what is our job, Johnny boy?" Michael's voice was serious, and John looked at him in the rear view mirror.

"You know what our job is. To follow the shipment and confirm it's arrival. We've been doing this for weeks now," John said.

Michael laughed. "That is *your* job, John. I have something else to take care of. I'm just babysitting you. Your pop didn't want you assigned to do anything too dangerous, so you got this cushy job. Makes you feel all important, doesn't it Johnny?" He laughed again.

John just stared at him for a moment, then continued monitoring the trucks. They had been doing this for two weeks, and nothing had happened. He had no idea what he would do if something did happen, but he was following his orders. He didn't need to know.

Michael returned to harassing Theresa, who was half disrobed in the back seat. John tried to hit some large potholes to disturb Michael, but he only got laughter.

At the port, John rolled down his window and could smell the salt air. He watched as the shipment was unloaded from the trucks and was counted by the assigned MI5 personnel. It was then moved on carts to the rear of the storage facility, where John presumed it was added to the twelve other shipments that they had overseen.

Michael and John were parked about fifty feet away, watching the process, and several guards came over to see who was in the car.

Michael stopped messing around with Theresa and got out.

"Hey Michael, or should I say, Lord Cornwall!" One of the guards obviously knew him.

"How's it going, Rad?" Michael said to the man as they shook hands. A second guard joined him.

"You doing your super secret thing here?" Rad said, as he looked into the car at John and Theresa, then back at Michael.

"You know... government business and all. Some bloody serious preparations going on." Michael acted like he knew what he was talking about. He threw his butt on the ground and stepped on it.

"So, who's the skirt?" Rad asked.

"That's just some girlfriend of my partner there, Mr. Harrision. Can't make it an hour without his baby." They all laughed. John tried to ignore him.

Rad leaned into the car and looked at Theresa. The other guard also ducked down so that he could see her. Michael stood behind them. He made sure Theresa could see his face.

"Pretty thing," Rad said. "So this is your boyfriend?" He cocked his head toward John. Michael drew a finger across his throat and pointed to John. The message was clear enough and Theresa replied.

"Yes," she turned away and looked out the opposite window.

John had missed the signal and looked back, puzzled at Theresa. Her bare shoulders were covered with the blue wool scarf. John thought to himself, I might have a girlfriend but it sure isn't this one.

The two guards and Michael walked off and John turned back toward the front of the car. The girl was obviously in no mood to talk so he just watched the shipment being unloaded.

His thoughts were interrupted by a loud voice.

"Do you know who I am?" John knew who it was. Michael was somewhere out of sight, but within earshot. John got out of the car and ran toward the back of the facility where the gold had been taken.

There were two guards with rifles outside the entrance door, and Michael was in their face.

"I'm sorry, sir, we have no authorization to allow you through."

"Michael, leave them alone. What do you want anyway?" John said he was really tired of dealing with him.

"Shut up, John. This is between me and these brainless peons." Michael blew smoke into the guard's faces, then took a breath.

"I am Lord Elias Cornwall II. My father is the Finance Minister for Her Majesty's government, and I have specific instructions to verify that this shipment is fully secured." Michael took out a letter from his pocket and waived it in front of them. John had never seen the paper before.

"This letter authorizes me go wherever I want and to see whatever I choose." Michael stopped long enough to get a response.

"We know who you are, Lord Cornwall, it's just that we have been told to let no one through here..." the guard drifted off as Michael started in again.

"Then who is that?!" Michael pointed to a man that he could see inside the room. The guards looked at the man then at each other.

"Yes, sir." One of them said, and they moved away from the door to let Michael pass.

"Come on John, let's do our job." Michael went into the room. When he was beyond the guard's gaze he grinned at John, and waived him in. It was all a game to him. John didn't feel any need to go, but he didn't want to leave Michael alone either, so he went on in.

"Good evening Mr. Harrision." The older guard acknowledged John as we walked by.

Once inside the room they could see there were about twenty rows of carts, each with a dozen wooden boxes on it. Each box was labeled with a number and had a seal over the lock.

"What can I do for you, sir?" The man who they had seen inside the room had approached them. He was dressed in black slacks, with a dark shirt and black belt. His boots were well polished and his hair trim and in place. A single handgun adorned his left hip. The overhead lights made his skin look almost gray. John wondered how long he had been in this room.

"It is what I can do for you. I am Lord Cornwall, and this is Mr. Harrision. The Finance Minister has asked us to verify that all here is being handled correctly and according to my direction." John was embarrassed, but really didn't want to draw more attention to the situation. The armed guard looked at John and nodded then back to Michael.

"Yes, sir. As you can see, all is in place and ready for shipment. This room is guarded twenty-four hours a day and there is only one way in or out of the storage facility. I am Commander Julian Orson of MI5." Julian nodded his head in a brief sort of salute.

"Well done, Julian. I'll make sure my father is aware of your presence. Carry on." Michael turned away and rolled his eyes at John.

"Come on, John, we mustn't be late for our appointment." Michael beckoned John with his hand and walked out of the room.

"Sorry about that, Julian," John said when Michael was out of earshot. "I think the boy is really daft."

"Not a problem, sir. The blue bloods have a way of making you aware of their presence," He smirked. "But when the fighting starts, how quickly they vanish." Julian walked away and John followed Michael out the door.

Back in the car John turned to Michael and said: "What the bloody hell was that about?"

Michael was seated in the back seat with Theresa. He blew smoke circles up toward the roof.

"Just wanted to see if I could get away with it," he shrugged.

That's what I was afraid of, thought John.

As the car approached the Cornwall estate, Michael spoke: "We'll get out here. Stop the car."

John looked in the back seat and could see the girl was not pleased with the decision.

"Miss, is that OK with you?" John asked.

"Uhh, actually I'm really tired..." the girl started, then Michael whispered something to her and she took a deep breath.

"Sure. This is fine," she said, resigned.

John stopped the car and Michael got out, and half drug Theresa into the woods. John could see Michael turn on a flashlight about thirty feet from the edge of the road. He shook his head and returned to the estate. It was nearly 5:00 a.m. and Anne was asleep. At least the candle was no longer burning in her room. John went into the drawing room, laid down on a lounge and promptly fell asleep.

Five years prior - June 20, 1933

"Welcome to Yorkshire, Sir Percy," Lord Cornwall greeted his aide with a firm handshake.

"And who is this?" he asked.

"This is my son, John. He's thirteen. John, this is Lord Cornwall," Sir Percy said.

"Good to meet you sir," John replied.

"Come on in. We have some refreshments prepared. There are about fifty guests today. Several have brought their boys with them." Lord Cornwall walked up the stone steps to his country estate with Sir Percy and John following him. The doors opened into a vaulted foyer with a spiral staircase climbing along both sides. John was happy that a servant took their coats, as it was stuffy inside the house. He looked around at the grand paintings and sculptures as they followed Lord Cornwall into a spacious room. There was a tray of tea pastries and John immediately walked over to them looking at his father, but Sir Percy was discussing something with Lord Cornwall and a group of men.

"Go ahead," John turned around to see a boy slightly taller than himself.

"I'm Michael Cornwall, the Second."

John took his hand and shook it as he had been taught. "I'm John Harrison," he replied.

"I know," Michael said as he took a sandwich and stuffed it in his mouth.

"Want to see around my estate?" Michael asked.

"Uh. Sure, I guess," John turned toward his father, but he was still busy talking so he grabbed some more sandwiches and followed Michael out of the room. His father had said they were staying the night anyway, so he figured he could catch up with him later.

Michael had disappeared around a corner and John jogged to catch up. His leather soles tapped on the marble floor and he started to skid around the turn, which put him on an already occupied path with a pretty girl.

"Oh!" she exclaimed and jumped back toward the wall.

"Sorry! I'm sorry! I was just trying to find Michael," he said. The girl lost her smile and looked at him.

"Are you a friend of his?" she asked.

"Uh. Not really, we just met. I'm John." He extended his hand before he realized what he had done. She looked down at it but made no move to grab it.

"I'm Anne, Michael's sister," she said.

"Nice to meet you Anne." John had no idea what to say next. "I guess I better find Michael." He took off in the direction he had last seen him and twirled around to look at Anne again. She was still watching him, and he felt his cheeks blushing as he turned down a hallway and disappeared from view.

He found Michael a few seconds later standing with his hands on the shoulders of a servant girl. He was saying something to her and she looked uncomfortable. Upon John's arrival she wrested away from him and hurriedly walked off.

"I met your sister," John said, out of breath.

"And?" Michael said. He looked irritated.

"Nothing. She's kind of pretty," John said. Michael stared at him long enough to make John uncomfortable then he broke into a smile.

"You like games?" he asked.

"Sure. Like what?" John asked.

"Stuff. I've got all kinds of things we can play with outside. There's too many people in here."

"OK," John said.

Michael took him out to a shed in the back and shut the door. It was dark inside and only lit by a window, high up on one wall. Michael opened a box and took out some tobacco and paper.

"What are you doing?" John asked.

"What does it look like? Aren't you a man?"

"But my dad won't let me smoke," John said.

"And do you see your dad around?"

"No. But –" Michael cut him off.

"Look. If you can't handle it just go back inside with the women," Michael licked the paper and lit the end. The smoke filled the room and made John's eyes water. He wanted to leave but didn't.

"Good. It's our secret," Michael said, "You do keep secrets don't you?"

"Uh. Yes. I mean of course," John said.

"Ever shoot a gun?" Michael asked. John's eyes lit up.

"No? Have you?"

"All the time. Want to do it?" Michael asked.

"My father –" John was interrupted again by Michael as he threw down his cigarette and rubbed it out.

"Your father," he mimicked. "Your father isn't here. He'll never know. You want to or not?"

"I… I guess so," John said.

"Let's go," Michael dug out a long burlap sack and put something in his pocket. They walked for almost an hour until they had traversed a small mountain and entered a gully. Michael had obviously been there before, as there was a make shift shooting range. He took out the shotgun and loaded it, then handed it to John.

"Go ahead," Michael pointed to a torn up log about fifty paces away. John took the rifle and put it up to his shoulder like he had seen his father do and pulled the trigger. Nothing happened and Michael laughed.

"You have to cock the trigger, you idiot!" Michael said as he walked over and did it for him.

"Now try it," he said.

John repeated the motion and pulled the trigger. The force of the blast threw him on his rear end and sent Michael into laughing convulsions. He felt embarrassed at his lack of skill.

"Here. Let me show you how," Michael cocked the other hammer and pulled the trigger. He had his right foot behind him to stabilize his body and the shot came off cleanly.

"You want to try again?" Michael asked.

"Yes," John was determined to do it correctly, and this time he managed to stay on his feet.

"Good job, Johnny. You'll become a man yet," Michael said.

For the next several hours John followed Michael around the estate playing barbarous games. It seemed that every game ended up in someone getting hit or slapped or tackled. It didn't really hurt and, once in awhile, John would get the best of Michael and he liked the adulation he got when he did.

They headed back to the house for supper as the sun was going down.

"So, you want to do something really fun tonight?" Michael asked. John was tired but he was almost afraid to say no.

"Uh. I don't know. Maybe tomorrow," he said.

"What tomorrow? You've got to live for today. I promise you'll never forget it," Michael said, but John still hesitated. "I'll get a couple of beers, ever had one?"

"No-o. I don't know," John said.

"What a chicken. I can't believe you are so gutless," Michael started to walk off.

"OK. Fine, when?" John asked. Michael smiled, but wiped it off when he turned around.

"9:00 pm. Meet me here," Michael said.

Sir Percy and John ate supper that evening with the Cornwall family and the twenty or so guests that had stayed. Anne sat across from John and he glanced at her every chance he got. After the dishes had been cleared they were invited into the piano room, and Anne sat down and played *Fur Elise* for the group. John thought it was the most beautiful thing he had ever heard.

At a few minutes to 9:00, John snuck downstairs and met Michael outside the back of the house. He had brought a lantern and two beers.

"Come on," he said and headed to the shed where they had been earlier.

The room was pitch black and Michael put the lantern down, then sat on the boxes. He opened the beers with a wrench and handed one to John, who watched him.

"Good, huh?" Michael asked. John found it actually a bit hard to swallow.

"Yeah. It's good," John took another swig. They sat there saying nothing until the beers were gone. John felt a little woozy but Michael hopped up on his feet and started rummaging through a box. He pulled out some baggy pants, shirts and a canister, laying them on the wood.

"Let's have some fun," he said. John looked at the pants, then at Michael.

"What are we going to do?"

"We are going to play a war game. I'm going to be the commander and you are going to be the guard. We're going on a secret mission," Michael said.

John didn't know what to say, so he followed his lead and put on the pants and shirt. Michael had opened the canister, and it smelled like shoe polish. He started smeering it over his face.

"What are you doing?" John asked.

"I'm putting on camoflauge. Come on, don't you know anything about war?"

John looked at the canister and then at him. Michael took a glob of the black paste and, to John's horror, wiped it on his face, then laughed.

"Just do it. I promise you it'll be fun."

John put his hand up to his face and felt the cool, slick paste. It was already all over his cheeks, and he wiped it around his forehead and chin. Michael looked at him, his face completely hidden in black. All John could see was the whites of his eyes. Michael wiped off his hands on a cloth and opened the door to the shed.

"Let's go," Michael said. He led him to the back of the house and enetered the wet room.

"But I thought we were playing a game?" John said.

"That's what I said. We are on a secret mission and I'm going to be a spy. You'll be the guard. Come on," Michael walked in the house and held the lantern in front of him. Within a few turns John was lost.

"This is it," Michael had stopped in front of a door and was whispering.

"What is it?" John asked.

"It's a secret, remember?" Michael said. He put his finger up to his lips.

"You stand guard. Don't come in, no matter what. Do you understand your orders?" Michael asked.

"Yes," John said. He reasoned that this was Michael's house and he could do whatever he wanted.

Michael opened the door and crept in, then shut it behind him. John strained to hear any sounds and noticed a dim light appear under the crack in the door. For a second he thought he had heard something, but then it stopped, and he stood there in the darkness trying to keep calm. A few minutes later there seemed to be heavy breathing and then a second person's muted voice, like someone was trying to say something with their mouth covered. John wasn't sure what to do and the sounds seemed to go away, so again he waited. The next noise was a high pitched muffled scream. It sounded like a tea pot at boil, only with a cover on the spout, and John's heart started thumping madly. Then came an unmistakeable sound, it was a slap and John had heard enough. He grabbed the door knob and opened it. The room was lighted by the lantern, which Michael had placed on the floor. It cast an eerie shadow up to a bed where Michael was staring at him. In his right hand were two pale wrists with clenched fists. John looked below him and was horrified to see the profile of a girl, with tosseled hair, and tears streaming down her face. Michael's left hand was over her mouth, and John could see her eyes trying to look toward him. He wanted to both cower and run to her aide at the same time. For that moment he felt detached from his body and found himself backing up to the shadows as he watched, as if in slow motion. Michael bent down and whispered something in the girl's ear. Her body went limp, and Michael got up from on top of her. John was relieved to see that she was still covered by the blankets. It was then that she began to turn and look toward the door, and he panicked, stepping back out of sight. In the brief second, John immediately recognized the profile. It was Anne.

Michael joined him outside the door as he shut it. John could hear Anne crying from inside and it made his heart hurt.

"Now we both have a secret," he said, and then bent in closer to him. "If you dare tell anyone what happened, I'll tell Anne you helped me. For now, she doesn't know anything." He turned around and walked off, leaving John in the dark. In that second of time John hated him more than he had ever thought possible.

It was years later that John fully understood what he had seen, and by then it was too late to try and explain anything to Anne. It was a secret he swore he would carry to his grave.

Chapter 22

London, 2004

Anne awoke with a start with her head on the bed, her pillow tucked between her arms. She was conscious that it was daylight but not much else. She had been dreaming about some war or something... and she cautiously opened her eyes and found herself looking sideways at the diary, which lay open beside her. The sound that had awoken her finally registered. It was the telephone. She reached over the diary and picked up the handset, simultaneously looking at the time. *9:00 a.m.*

"Oh God..." she mumbled. "Hello?" It was the best attempt at an awake voice she could muster.

"Anne? Just checking with you. It's a bit after nine and I was wondering when we could expect you?" Jarred said.

"I'm sorry, Jarred..." She tried to think of a good excuse, but couldn't. "I just awoke. I forgot to set the alarm. Can I meet you in about forty-five minutes?"

"Sure, not a problem. I'll have the coffee," Jarred said. The thought started her mouth salivating and she rushed out of bed, yawning and stretching, to brush her teeth.

It was another unusually sunny fall day in London, and Anne enjoyed being out in the sunshine, taking in the rays. She wore a simple floral print tea dress with waist darts and a portrait neckline with a white sweater. Since she was in London, she might as well look English.

As promised, Jarred had the latte ready for her when she entered.

"Wow!" said Jarred when she walked into the office. When he realized he had spoken it out loud he turned a slight shade of pink.

"Uh, sorry. You look nice, Anne." He sat down at his desk. Anne smiled.

"Thank you for the coffee." She stood briefly by his desk to tip her cup, then turned back toward her accustomed place by the wall, where she sat down in her familiar wooden seat.

"So, did you finish your diary?" Jarred asked, as he looked up at her, his coffee in hand.

"Actually, no. I think I ended up around 1939."

"Do you know anything about a shipment of gold that was sent from England before the war?" Anne asked.

The question stopped Jarred in mid sip. He looked up at her.

"Yes. I have heard of it." He hesitated, then continued. "The Queen was worried about Hitler invading and wanted to have funds available overseas in case the fight needed to be continued from foreign soil. I believe two shipments were eventually sent. Somewhere around forty million pounds sterling."

"Hmm. Interesting," Anne said.

"Why do you ask? Is it in the diary?" Jarred asked.

"Perhaps...." Anne smiled, and looked down at some papers at her desk. Just then the phone rang, and Jarred picked it up.

"Yes. She is here. I'll put her on." Jarred put the call on hold.

"Line three, Anne. It's your boss," he said.

"Hello, Harry!" Anne answered the phone. She doodled on a pad of paper as she listened.

"I don't have it yet, but I'll ask..." She mouthed the word FAX to Jarred and he disappeared from the room.

"Well, that's good news, hang on a sec..." Anne took the fax from Jarred and mouthed *thank you* to him. "I have it here... Yes, I'll fill it out and get it back to them this morning. Bye." Anne hung up the phone.

Jarred had brought over a file and some loose printouts.

"These are our current thoughts on extradition and such. The printouts are of two case laws that took place recently in the EU. I think you will find them favorable," Jarred said.

"Thank you, Jarred." She took the file. "I appreciate the help. I have to fill out this form for the insurance company, then I'll start drafting an extradition request. This is assuming, of course, we find the stupid cross." She said it a little too vehemently and looked up. "Sorry. I'm not much into religious malarkey. I suppose you're Catholi... I mean Anglican?"

"Yes. My family actually. At least for the last three hundred years or so. But I understand what you mean. Seems a bit much for an icon, even if it did belong to Jude."

"You know, that is what bothers me so much. It *couldn't* have belonged to Jude. Christians didn't use the cross until well after the death of Christ. But you know, it's not even that. It's the fact that these men use religion as an excuse to do anything they want..."

Jarred sensed something more to the outburst. "OK. So I know what NOT to get you for a present."

Anne smiled at him. "Sorry. I don't mean to push my personal doctrine of religion… speaking of which…. this questionnaire asks me to describe the item. I wonder if they would prefer the priest's viewpoint, or mine?" She gave Jarred her best innocent look.

"Best go with the priest. I think you'll have a better chance to get money if they think it actually has some monetary value." Jarred smiled, and went back to his desk. Anne committed herself to filling out the insurance form and then asked where the fax machine was. Jarred directed her down the hall.

When she returned she overheard Jarred speaking on the phone and didn't want to disturb him, so she paused for a moment outside the door.

"I'm not sure how much she knows… I really don't think it's a big deal at this point, but you may want to check it out." Jarred was silent for a moment.

"No. I haven't mentioned it to mom… I will. Bye." Jarred hung up the phone and Anne walked into the room. He looked at the phone in his hand and then at Anne.

"Hi there. I take it you had no difficulty in finding Sarah?" Jarred put the cell phone in his coat pocket.

"None at all," Anne said, as she walked back to her desk. She found it strange that they named their fax machine.

They both worked until around 1:00 p.m. Anne was conscious of the sounds of the street below her, and the ticking of the office clock above the door. It wasn't a completely comfortable silence, but more of a mutually understood one. Still, it did enable her to get a lot of work done.

"You want to eat in or out today?" Jarred interrupted her thoughts.

"Hmmm. Any place I can get a salad?" Anne asked.

"I think I know a place. It's right around the corner. Shall we…" Anne noticed that he didn't ask her if she wanted to go, which was OK with her.

"After lunch, I'd like to stop by the…" Anne looked down and picked up a piece of paper, "Department for Culture, Media & Sport, 2-4 Cockspur Street." She looked up at Jarred.

"Sure. We can catch a cab to Trafalgar square," Jarred said. Anne stuffed the paper in her purse and followed him out the door.

The restaurant was an English version of Zuppa's, basically a Sizzler with a buffet salad and soup bar. Anne and Jarred purchased their own lunches and sat at a booth.

"So, you were telling me about your diary," Jarred said.

"Actually, you assumed I was telling you about the diary," Anne said. She looked at him and smiled. "Anne Cornwall. That was her name. The diary starts when she is thirteen years old in 1933. I guess her father was a government official back then. She had a difficult time growing up." Anne paused to look at Jarred and took a bite.

"Lord Cornwall was Finance Minister for Her Majesty's government prior to World War II. You realize that was part of the family estate we were at?" Jarred said.

"Yes. Figured that out. This girl's mother was sick or something and there was a sister, Lizzy. You ever hear anything about Lord Cornwall's children?" Anne asked

Jarred looked up for a second. "Yes. I seem to recall he had a son."

"Michael," Anne said.

"I thought it was Ellias, but it could have been a hyphenated name or something. You're probably correct." Jarred said.

"How about the girls? Anne and Lizzy?" Anne asked.

"No. I don't believe I have, really. I only remember the parts we learned about in school. As you can imagine, World War II was quite an extensive subject."

"I imagine so," said Anne. "I was only curious. The girl Anne has a boyfriend in the diary. But it looks like it is going to be an ill fated affair, like most teenage romances," Anne added.

"Ah. You are a skeptic of love?" Jarred asked.

"Let's say I am a realist." Anne replied. "And this girl has picked the wrong time to fall for a guy."

Jarred noticed that the tense was wrong in her statement. He wondered for a moment if she was speaking about herself or the Anne in the diary.

:

The Department for Culture, Media & Sport was housed in a typical large building, with huge white columns out front. They joined the countless other pedestrians who walked between them to enter the ministry, and Anne felt like a mouse scurrying from hole to hole, looking for bits of cheese.

They passed through a metal detection machine and were directed to the second floor, which housed the Arts Ministry.

Jarred spoke over the echo's of the footsteps walking up the marble staircase.

"So, what are we doing here, exactly?" he asked.

Anne took out the folded piece of paper in her purse and handed it to him. It was entitled: *Treasure Act, 1996*. He looked at her.

"Treasure Act?"

"In 1996 your government signed on with the UNESCO Convention on Illicit Cultural Trade. Seems the pilfering of national art treasures was not limited to the forties." Jarred assumed she was referring to the Antiquities found in numerous British Museums around the country.

"Part of the Act allows for a registration of certain artifacts, which make them easier to be traced, found and returned to their rightful owners."

"OK. And you plan to register the cross?" Jarred asked.

"On behalf of the Georgian Government, and with their support." Anne pulled out an envelope from her purse and handed it to Jarred. It contained several descriptions and pictures of the cross, as well as a letter from the Ministry of Culture, Republic of Georgia, and a letter from the CBA, the Council for British Archaeology.

"When did you have time to do all this?" Jarred asked.

"My boss loves me because I know how to get things done. I only *loo*k like I don't know what I'm doing," Anne said, as they entered the office.

"I'll wait out here," Jarred said, "I need to make some phone calls anyway."

Anne returned about thirty minutes later, and Jarred was across the hallway still speaking on the phone.

"I need to call you back..." She heard him say as he put the handset in his pocket and walked over to her.

"Done," Anne said.

"So, let me ask you. What makes you think that the cross is going to come up for auction in Britain?" Jarred asked. "I mean, if you do all this work and it doesn't...then it seems a bit of a waste...."

"Well, that is, in part, true. The UNESCO convention was signed on by most countries. But it works best if the piece is registered willingly by the owners, and in a country where the registration is respected. Still, having England recognize it as a national art treasure would be helpful in any extradition proceedings, and we also have done the equivalent in the US. Or I hope Harry has finished with it, at least. Besides, I don't really expect the cross to go up for auction here, but rather in one of the former British territories. Oh…and one more reason: the insurance company will accept the registration instead of a commercial appraisal, which saves our client both money and time."

"Should I ask where you expect this to happen?" Jarred asked.

"Probably not," Anne said, and smiled. She liked a little mystery.

"By the way. I put your office address and number as a local contact for the registration," she said, as they started down the stairs.

"Great. Should I be worried about that?" Jarred asked.

"Only if you are hiding something. They might want to do a background check to see if you are a known dealer in black market antiques. Perhaps they'll come by and check out the office to make sure it's a legitimate business. You do really work for a barrister firm?" Anne looked up at him with a grin. But he looked straight ahead and was not smiling.

"I'm kidding, Jarred," Anne said. "I'm sure it's just routine paperwork."

Jarred broke into a smile. "I just hope they don't find the sarcophagus behind the office supplies."

They walked back to the office at a good pace. By the time they returned, it was nearly 4:00 p.m. and Jarred excused himself for a meeting with his boss.

Anne organized her desk, and cleaned up. She was pretty much finished here and didn't know if she would be returning or not the next day.

She left a note for Jarred, in case he looked for her, and took a slow stroll back to the hotel, stopping at a store to pick up a banana and an apple. It had just started to drizzle when she reached the hotel.

Once in her room, she changed into a comfortable set of pajama's, sat on the couch, and picked up the diary.

Chapter 23

May 6th 1939 – Cornwall Estate, Kent

Anne awoke to the sounds of the birds and her sister singing in the next room. There was something different about the house and she got up out of bed in her long nightgown and walked over to the window. There were only two cars in the driveway. She hadn't seen that few in weeks, no boots, no walking around, no sounds of male voices, no clanking of tools.

Anne walked barefoot to her door and opened it up to peep out. She could see her sister's door, still closed, and walked past it, partway down the stairs to the point where she could see into the drawing room. The doors were wide open, and she could see a man lying down on a couch, though she couldn't tell who it was.

Anne fingered her hair to remove the knots and quietly went into the room. It was John, and she sat in a chair and watched him sleep for a few minutes.

A dog barked and Anne looked up toward the window that opened into the inner courtyard, but didn't see anything. She pulled her legs up under her nightdress and turned back toward John. She jumped and let out a sound when she realized that he was looking back at her. He was still on his side, his face on the pillow.

"Hi," he said.

Anne removed her hand from in front of her mouth.

"Hi. Sorry. I didn't mean to wake you," she said.

"How long have you been there?" he asked.

"Um. Not long. I thought you might be Poppa. I just saw a body lying on the couch, so I came downstairs," she said.

"Where is everyone?" she asked.

"I think most are in London. Your father and mine should be here sometime this afternoon, maybe tomorrow." He pushed himself up to a sitting position, and a blue wool scarf fell to the floor. He didn't see it, but Anne did. She noted there was a dark stain on the fringe.

"I guess I should be going as well," he said.

"No!" Anne surprised herself at the outburst and looked up at his face. "No. I mean. You can stay and rest. You look tired." John got up and went to the mirror on the wall behind him and peered at himself for a moment. He had a dark shadow across his face and his hair was a mess. He pushed back the most egregious blonde locks and turned back toward Anne, who remained seated.

"I'm OK. It's just been a long night. What time is it anyway?" They both looked toward the wall clock.

"Nine." They said it simultaneously and Anne laughed nervously.

"Are you hungry? Can I get you something to eat?" Anne asked.

John looked as if the thought had not occurred to him until that moment.

"Yes, actually—I'm famished," he said.

"I'll go get something." Anne hopped up to her feet and then realized, when she felt the cool wood floors, that she wasn't dressed. She looked down at her feet and John followed her gaze. Her gown went down to mid calf, where it ended in a bit of cream lace. Anne looked up, and blushed.

"Uh. I should put something on. I'll be right back." Anne took off without saying another word, and John heard her rapid footsteps on the stairs.

A minute later he saw a glimpse of her in a housecoat and slippers as she passed by on her way to the kitchen. He went over to his jacket that hung on the coat rack and looked for the envelope, which he needed to give to his father later that day.

"Looking for this?" The voice was not one he wanted to hear. John turned around and found Michael standing in the doorway. He held the brown envelope in his hand. It had been opened. Michael wore the same clothing that he had the previous night, except his shirt was ripped by his shoulder, and there was a scratch on his forehead. He saw John looking at his forehead and touched the cut.

"Had a bit of mishap in the woods last night," he said.

"You look like crap," John said.

"So do you, old boy. You should try getting some sleep," Michael said.

"So, what kind of report is this, John? You into something you should be telling your partner about?" He threw the envelope on the desk and John looked at it.

"It's just for my father, Michael. No need to be concerned," John said.

"Of course it is a concern to me, John. You are a bit critical of my …. methods. That is always a concern to me." Michael's voice rose.

"Well, then perhaps you should reevaluate your methods. In fact, you should reevaluate your whole life. What is the matter with you anyway? The country is going to war. No. The world is going to war, and here you sit as if all that matters are your own private little games," John said.

"Games? Johnny? I do not play games. Well, actually I do, but they are none of your concern. I must amuse myself as I find this whole thing…" Michael swirled his right hand in the air, "boring. There is so much more to life than Queen and Country. That said, you *will* change your report. Not that it would have an effect given the low office your father holds. But still, why muddy up such a promising career? You will change that letter!" Michael pointed to the envelope again.

"Or what, Michael? I'm not one of your floozies you can manipulate with hollow threats and promises…" John stopped speaking as he noticed movement behind Michael, and Anne came into view.

"Oh! I'm sorry..." Michael turned around and faced his sister and she immediately took a step backwards.

"Why, Anne, what a pleasant surprise. What are you…" Michael looked at John and then at Anne again, "Oh… I see. Does poppa know about this?"

"There is nothing to know about, Michael. Leave your improprieties in your own mind! This is none of your business," John said, his face flushed.

Michael walked over to Anne, who was holding a tray with some bread and other food on it. He reached up and caressed her cheek.

"This is my business, John. She is my little sister and I must look out for her innocence." Anne pulled her head away but didn't move.

"Michael, I'm warning you. Leave her alone. She was just getting me some food." John walked over to where Anne stood and took the tray from her.

"Thank you, Anne. I'll see you later." He gave her a tender look and smile and Anne turned to leave. She glared at her brother, who had taken out a cigarette and lit it.

Anne left, but John noticed that he did not see her walk back up the steps toward her room.

"John. Back to the matter at hand. You will change that letter, or I'll make things very uncomfortable for you both—you in particular." Michael moved over to where John stood, picked a piece of bread off the tray, and took a bite.

"You would, wouldn't you?" John said. "You really would sully your sister's reputation over this stupid letter." John picked it up and held it.

"Perhaps. But I don't really need to... remember our little secret?" Michael drifted off and walked over to the couch where John had been sleeping. He picked up the blue scarf and smelled it. John was furious as he tried to think of something to say. He couldn't believe Michael was intent on blackmailing him with something that had happened when he was thirteen, six years ago.

"Isn't this Theresa's?" Michael said, as he walked out the room. He let the scarf run through his fingers and fall to the floor. John heard him laugh and the door closed.

John walked over to where the scarf was and picked it up.

"John?" Anne had reentered the room and saw him holding the scarf.

"Anne." John threw the scarf behind him and walked over to her. "I'm sorry about that. Don't worry, he won't say anything. I'll make sure of it." He reached up to her forehead and gently moved a lock of auburn hair from her eyes, wrapping it behind her ear. He said something in French and Anne looked up at him, puzzled, but remained silent. It was the first time he had touched her and her skin burned.

"The worth of a man is in the company he keeps." He translated but she didn't hear what he said, she only felt the loss of his touch as he pulled his hand away.

"You better go. Thank you for the breakfast. Perhaps I'll see you later today." He turned around and Anne watched him walk back toward her father's desk, and then she turned around and walked up the stairs to Lizzy's room.

"Lizzy, you ready for breakfast?" John heard her voice from on top of the stairs as he looked out upon the courtyard. He lifted his hand to his face and took in a breath. He could still smell the light scent of Anne's hair upon his fingers. He would not allow Michael to hurt her again.

Chapter 24

London, 2004

Anne heard the knock on the door. She looked up from the diary at the clock. It was a little after six.

"I don't need a turn down!" She tried to speak loud enough to be heard through the door. But the knock came again.

Anne got up and spoke to the peephole. "I don't need a turn down. Thank you!" She turned away to go back to her seat.

"Anne?" It was Jarred. She looked down at what she was wearing and thought about changing into something else, then decided it would take too long.

He looked a little surprised.

"Oh, sorry. I didn't mean to bother - you just took off and I didn't get to ask you if you wanted to catch a bite to eat?" "Well, I picked up some food on the way home…"

"Oh? Well, what about a play?" He showed her two tickets and her face lit up.

"Twelfth Night," he said.

"What?"

"Shakespeare," he said. "It's a love story, a story of mistaken identity and jumping to conclusions."

"Oh. Yes. Sorry. When I think show tickets I'm thinking, Lion King, Phantom…but I'd love to go," she said.

"Perfect. I rather hoped you would say that," he said.

"Um… want to come in? I think I should probably change." She opened the door and he walked in. He went over to the sofa where the diary lay and sat down beside it as she went into the bathroom.

"I guess I should ask." Anne popped her head out, and obviously surprised Jarred, who had the diary open on his lap. "...what I should wear…" She looked at the diary and didn't quite know how she felt about him reading it.

"I'm sorry!" Jarred flipped the diary closed and put it down. "I didn't mean to pry. It was just sitting there… Oh. The play is informal. Anything is fine." He stood up. "Perhaps I should wait outside?"

"Oh. No. It's no big deal. Just kind of surprised me… I'll be right out." Anne disappeared again and Jarred started pacing with his hands behind his back.

She reappeared in black slacks, a cotton blouse and her hair tied back with a colorful scarf.

"Shall we?" she said, as she put in some ruby colored earrings. Jarred stood in the same place she had left him a few minutes before.

"Good!" he said, and walked over to the front door to open it for her while she put on a black mid length coat and a pair of matte black leather shoes. She headed out the door but then looked back at the diary, which lay exposed on the couch.

"I'm sure it will be fine," he said, and she took a step forward, then turned around and went back in.

"I'd hate for something to happen to it. After all, it is on loan to me. She picked it up and went to the closet, where he placed it inside her suitcase and zipped it back up, then smiled as she passed through the door.

"You have your hair, um…in your jacket," he said as she passed.

"Oh. Thanks." Anne reached back and pulled out the modified ponytail so her locks fell over the coat collar. "I do that all the time."

The Shakespeare Globe theatre was located in Southwick, London and they caught a taxi to save themselves the walk in the drizzle. It dropped them off in front of the entrance, where a line had formed, and Anne and Jarred ran over to the awnings.

"This building has a colorful history." Jarred pointed to a plaque on the stone façade. A recorded message droned in the background for the benefit of the people waiting in line, and they listened to it in silence.

"This theatre was originally built in 1599 by Cuthbert Burbage. As the Globe Theatre it became the preferred location where many of Shakespeare's most renowned plays were first performed. In 1613, three years before his death, an unfortunate incident occurred during the firing of a canon in a production of Henry VIII. The cannon set the dry thatched roof of the theatre on fire and completely destroyed the original building.

"The Globe was rebuilt within a year but was almost immediately closed by Oliver Cromwell when the self proclaimed 'Lord Protector,' assumed control of Parliament and removed the king from power. Cromwell professed that theatres promoted sinful behavior and ordered his loyal puritan army, appropriately known as the 'roundheads', to close down every theatre, including the Globe (which was as most theatres were, 'round' in shape). It was subsequently destroyed to make way for tenements.

'In 1989 remnants of the foundation of the Globe were discovered and the Globe Foundation commenced construction of a building that would, in every way possible, be identical to the one originally built for the world's most famous bard. On April 4, 1997, Mark Rylance, artistic Director of the Globe Theatre, formally launched the Opening Season on the Globe site which you are looking at today. It is in part supported by voluntary donations. You will find receptacles placed throughout the theatre."

Anne enjoyed the story, and she had grabbed Jarred's forearm halfway through.

"1599!" she said.

"Yes. I know that is unusual for you to think about. I've been to America, where a chair is considered an antique when it is a hundred years old. But we would use it for a child's playhouse."

The ushers had opened the doors and Anne and Jarred soon found themselves in the lobby.

"Imagine, four hundred years ago, Shakespeare sat at this site and watched the very first Henry VIII, Winter's Tale, Twelfth Night." Jarred whispered to her.

Anne grabbed his arm tighter and they walked in and were seated seven rows from the stage, front and center.

"Oh. I forgot. I'll be right back." Jarred left, and Anne mused at the slates in the wooden stage and the voices that she could hear from behind the drawn curtain.

"Here." Jarred handed her a theatre brochure of the *Twelfth Night*. It contained the entire text of the play.

"In case you want to follow along. Sometimes it takes a while for the ear to grow accustomed to the, as you would say, King James English," Jarred said.

He was right. Anne couldn't understand a thing for the first fifteen minutes or so, but then her ears attuned to the sounds and she was carried away with the rest of the audience. Jarred noticed several times during the first several acts that she grabbed his arm. It was not an unpleasant sensation.

The clown ended the Act and intermission was called.

"So. I take it that you are enjoying yourself?" Jarred looked at Anne. She brushed away a lingering tear.

"Yes. Very much. Thank you for taking me," she said.

"And what was your favorite part?" he asked.

"Hmm. I don't think I had a favorite part. I do love the funny but wise words of the Clown. How about you?" Anne asked.

Jarred took the play text from her hand and unrolled it, reading from Act I, Scene V.

"Tis beauty truly blent, whose red and white,
Nature's own sweet and cunning hand laid on:
Lady, you are the cruell'st she alive,
If you will lead these graces to the grave
And leave the world no copy."

:

"Ahhh," Anne said, and smiled. "A romantic. I should have guessed."

"We Englishmen are quite comfortable with our feminine side!" Jarred grinned and stood up.

"Would you care for a drink or something?" he asked.

"No, thank you. I'll just wait here—but go ahead," she said, and he left.

A few minutes later she thought she might as well use the restroom before the play started again, since she had no idea how long it would be. She meandered through the theatre, saw a line at the end of a corridor, and figured that must be the ladies room. There always seemed to be a line. As she approached it, she saw Jarred with his back turned away from the noise, speaking into his cell phone.

She walked up to him and stood there for a moment to surprise him when he turned around.

"No. I'll be out for awhile." With her proximity she could hear his side of the conversation.

"She is here with me. We're at The Globe…Yes, in SouthWick... A good thirty minutes at least…well, I suggest you do it quickly."

Anne started to feel uncomfortable with her eavesdropping and tapped him on his shoulder. The herringbone sport jacket had a gunnysack kind of feel to it. She smiled and waved when he turned around.

"Oh!" He spoke into the phone, "I'm going to have to call you back... I know... I'll call you back. Anne is here right now. OK." He hung up.

"Hey. I thought you were absorbing the actor's aura," he said. She noticed he looked a bit flushed, and it really wasn't that warm.

"Well, I decided to visit the ladies room and saw you, so...." she said, and shrugged.

"Ah. Yes. The 'I better go while I have a chance' thought. I am familiar with that, especially during very long staff meetings." She looked at the cell phone in his hand, but didn't say anything.

"My mum," he said.

"What?"

"My mum." He waved the phone.

"Oh.... And she knows who I am?" Anne asked. She wasn't sure how she felt about this revelation.

"Well, not really. I mean... a little. I've mentioned my American friend from Chicago..." He drifted off.

"And you always call your mum at night?" She smiled.

"Not really. Well, sometimes... is there a correct answer to that question?" They both laughed.

She left him and walked over to the line, and he waved and went into the men's room. They met at their seats as the second half was starting.

She grabbed his arm as they sat down and let her hand remain there during the first scene.

:

It was late when they finally reached her hotel.

"Shall I see you up to your room?" he asked, as they pulled up to the front door.

"Um. No. That's OK," she said.

He looked a little disappointed and she added: "I'll see you in the morning?"

"Sure," he said.

"Nine a.m., here at the restaurant?" he said as he leaned over and kissed her on the cheek. "I had a great evening," he whispered in her ear. Anne could feel her cheeks blush and was thankful when the valet opened the door.

"Me too. Thank you for the invitation." She stepped out of the car and didn't look back as she entered the hotel. Her heart was hammering and her palms sweaty. She didn't feel ready for this. It was all too much.

She took the elevator up to her room and opened her door.

The feeling was immediate. Someone had been in her room. She looked around, but nothing seemed out of place. The bathroom counter was a mess, just like she had left it. Her pajamas were hanging on the washroom door. The closet was ever so slightly open, and so she slid it to one side. There were two sweaters and three blouses hanging up. On the floor her single carry on bag was sitting in the same position she had left it. She reached inside and pulled the case out, setting it on the floor while she knelt beside it. Then she noticed the unlocked front door, so she got up and latched it, then sat back on the carpet and unzipped her bag.

Anne dug through the clothing till she felt the hard binding of the diary and removed it. It looked the same as when she had put it in. She opened it, and it fell open to the entry one night past the one she had last read, April 22, 1939. She was going to read that tonight anyway, so she left it open and got up and put it on her nightstand. It was then that she noticed the bed had been turned down. The maid must have come in! She laughed at herself, and took off one earring. Her hand brushed the cheek that Jarred had kissed, and her fingers lingered there for a moment. It still felt warm to the touch. She took a deep breath and walked over to the bathroom mirror, where she gazed at her face while she removed her scarf from her hair and the rest of her jewelry.

She wasn't ready for this. This feeling scared her. Tomorrow she needed to talk to him.

Anne brushed her teeth and took a shower, then dried her hair. It was nearly midnight by the time she crawled into bed.

She would just read one entry in the diary, then go to sleep.

Chapter 25

May 9, 1939, Cornwall Estate -Kent.

Father has been home for three days now. He and Sir Percy Harrision, John's father, have been spending a lot of time talking. They seem much happier now. When I bring them food I can see they have a lot of papers on the floor. They look like maps and plans of some sort.

John has been here too. Every day he makes it a point to find me, whether in the garden or kitchen. Sometimes he will ask me to play the piano as he watches. This is a peculiar feeling. I'm scared and happy at the same time. No one noticed that I turned eighteen two weeks ago. I think they are too busy and, with Momma sick, I guess it doesn't really matter. There are more important things to do. Lizzy and I have been spending a lot of time talking. She misses mother a lot and I guess I have become like one to her. I don't mind. I guess I feel much older than I am anyway. Michael has been around too. He has often come to my room at night but I will not let him in. When I see him during the day, he just stares at me. I wish Poppa would send him away. All the men are down in the drawing room talking about something. I was told not to disturb them until lunch.

"Has anyone seen Theresa?" Lord Cornwall asked. Sir Percy, John and Michael were all seated in chairs reading documents, and they all looked up at the change in subject.

"That useless girl is always missing," Michael said, as he looked intently at John.

"That may be so, but the head mistress said she hasn't reported in two days for work, and we'll need to replace her if she doesn't show up soon," Lord Cornwall said.

"I'll look into it," Michael offered.

"Fine," Lord Cornwall said. "If you will all turn to page ten of the plan, let's keep going."

After the meeting, Lord Cornwall and Sir Percy went to the dining room, and John approached Michael.

"Where is she?" John asked.

"She? Who?" Michael smiled.

"You know bloody well who," John said.

"Oh. You mean the little missing maidservant? What did Rad call her? Hmmm. Oh yes, 'the skirt.' I believe he was under the distinct impression that he thought she was *your* skirt," Michael said, as he lit up a cigarette and blew the smoke into John's face.

"Michael, answer the question. Where is she?" John didn't budge.

"Let's just say she is on a sabbatical. But I'm sure she will show up some time soon." Michael turned and walked to his father's desk.

"And how is my little sister, Johnny? Are you taking good care of her? Tell me, does she like to be fondled?" Michael stood with his left palm cradling the elbow of his right arm as he held the cigarette next to his face.

"Michael. Nothing is going on between your sister and I. You didn't *see* anything that morning," John said.

"So you keepth protesting!" said Michael. "But he who protests too much is certainly guilty." He laughed, and walked by John to join his father in the dining room. John followed him with his eyes and then his feet.

The table was set for lunch. Lord Cornwall and Sir Percy sat at the table ends, with Michael and John on one side and Lizzy and Anne on the other. Anne's seat was empty, as she was still helping the cook serve the food.

"Sure would be nice if Theresa joined us," the cook said.

"Michael is going to look into it," Lord Cornwall answered. The cook stopped for a moment and looked at Michael, then back at his father.

"If you say so," she said, and went back to the kitchen. Anne reappeared a moment later with drinks. She went around the table and poured a glass of water. As she filled Michael's glass, John watched him stare at Anne's chest. It made him sick.

"Michael, when are you going to look for Theresa? I'll come with you." The comment drew Michael's attention from his sister to John.

"Today. We'll go today," he said.

Anne took her seat across from John and smiled at him. Michael noticed it.

"So Annie, do you have some news for us?" Michael asked. She looked up at him and blushed.

"No. Not really." She looked up quickly at John, then at her father who was also looking at her.

"Oh. My mistake. I thought Johnny here mentioned you were going to tell us something," Michael said.

"No, Michael. I said Lizzy. Your other sister was going to tell us something." John looked up at Anne, then at Lizzy, her ten-year-old sister.

"What do you have to say, Lizzy?" Lord Cromwall asked.

Lizzy stood up. "I want to be called Elizabeth, not Lizzy. I'm too old for Lizzy," she said.

"Very well, Lizzy," Lord Cromwall said. "We'll try and call you Elizabeth, like our Queen." He smiled at the table. John looked at Anne and smiled.

"Whatever," Michael said.

After lunch Michael and John met outside.

"Nice catch at lunch old man. Quick thinking," Michael said.

"Let's get on with it," said John.

"Just a minute. I need to get something from my room." Michael ran off and left John by himself. John looked around at the evidence of spring starting to awaken, and wondered what he was going to do with this maniac all day.

Michael returned with his rifle and John looked at him.

"What do you need that for?" John asked.

"Protection," Michael said. "You never know when you are going to need it." John stood there and looked at him.

"Well, let's go. I figure we'll go visit the Stamwell's and the Horace's. She has friends there. Then we'll go into town and check out the bars, or maybe take a walk in the woods. Michael had loaded the shotgun with two shells and had snapped it shut simultaneous with the last statement. John didn't react and Michael looked disappointed.

Up above them, Anne watched from her room in a panic. She wanted to yell down to John to not go, but she couldn't. If anything happened today she didn't know what she was going to do.

Theresa was not at the neighbors, nor in the town, and on the way back to the estate, Michael pulled off onto a back road.

"Where are you going, Michael?" John was tired and he was sick of the company.

"Just for a drive through the woods. Perhaps we'll see something," Michael replied.

They stopped a few hundred feet from the house where the woods had been cleared and they got out.

John walked three feet away and spoke.

"This is stupid, Michael. I know that you know what happened to her. Why are we wasting our time?" John said, as he looked out over the pasture.

"Because I can," Michael said. John turned around and was staring down the barrel of Michael's gun. He reflexively put his hands up and took a step back.

"What are you doing, Michael?"

"Anything I want to, John." Michael kept the gun level at him, and pretended to pull the trigger.

"Pow. Game over," said Michael. "See how easy it would be, Johnny boy?"

"Don't be a fool. You'd never get away with it—everyone knows I'm out here with you."

"But I already have, John," Michael said.

"What do you mean?" John stuttered just a bit.

"Nothing," Michael said, and started lowering the gun. John released a breath and lowered his arms in response, but stood there.

"You just remember, I could have pulled the trigger... Maybe it was suicide. Perhaps remorse over some past misdeed. I struggled with you for the gun..." Michael mimicked a struggle, dancing around the broken twigs, " but you took it from me and blew your brains out. Remorse is a terrible thing, John."

"Are you finished with your little drama, Michael? Because I'm tired, and just want to get the hell away from you." John took a step forward and Michael didn't raise up the shotgun, so he continued slowly to the car and got in. Michael laughed like a hyena.

"God, John, you looked like you believed I would have actually done it!" He slapped John on the knee as he got in the driver's seat. John noticed he put the gun between the door and himself.

"I was just joshing, John! Have a sense of humor. That's the problem with this world. It needs a better sense of humor." Michael laughed as he started the engine and floored it, throwing rocks and sticks behind the car as he sped off in the opposite direction. John had to grab onto the door to hang on.

When they returned to the house it was almost dark, but Anne watched as John got out of the car and walked toward the front door. She continued watching as Michael got out of the opposite side with his gun and aimed it at John's back. She saw him jerk it up in the air like he had fired a shot, and saw the smile on his face as he walked around the house toward his room. She shivered uncontrollably as she walked over to her bed and crawled under the covers. Her diary lay open on her bedside table with a pencil marking the page, and she pulled the book to her and started to write. Her hand was shaking.

Chapter 26

London, 2004.

Anne shivered as she read the last entry and put down the diary to go to sleep. She turned off the lamp, and lay tucked under the covers, acutely aware of the stillness of the room. She closed her eyes and tried to picture something peaceful and she replayed the evening at the theatre with the actors and sets, and the smell of the wood floors. She could hear Jarred's voice as he read to her the words from Viola…

"Tis beauty truly blent, whose red and white,
Nature's own sweet and cunning hand laid on:
Lady, you are the cruell'st she alive,
If you will lead these graces to the grave
And leave the world no copy."

The alarm went off at 8:00 a.m., and Anne awoke refreshed and looking forward to the day. She hopped out of bed and warmed herself a cup of tea, then opened the door and picked up the London Times from the hallway and sat at the table holding onto her cup, sipping, and flipping the pages until 8:30. She got up, pulled the curtains fully open, and looked outside. It was quite a spectacular view with the sun interspersed with fog banks rolling in from the Thames. Her room faced southeast, over the city, and the town looked like a medieval monochrome picture, which had been hand rubricated with color. It was a collage of silver and gray and black, all wrapped in bursts of orange. She wished she had a camera to take a photo.

Anne showered and wrapped a yellow towel around her while she used the blow dryer on her hair. She looked at her dark, auburn hair against her opaque skin and hazel eyes, and traced the outline of her face down to her collarbone with her fingers. She had never considered herself beautiful, at least compared to the movie stars and celebrities she had seen. Her mother was always trying to get her to do 'more,' as she put it… more make up, more time on her hair, shorter skirts, tighter pants. It was not that she minded looking nice, but just that she felt she had a lot of other things to offer, so she yielded to her mother's wishes only on occasion, the rest of the time preferring to appear 'natural'. As she looked at her eyes, she wondered what Jarred thought as he looked at her.

She finished with her hair straight down and applied some lipstick with a little blush on her eyes and cheeks. She put on a yellow chiffon short-sleeved top and a pair of nicely fitting blue jeans with a brown belt. She turned around to look at her rear in the mirror and thought that perhaps she should really go down to the gym and do a workout, but soon dismissed the thought. She grabbed her purse and her black coat, and walked out the door, placing the do not disturb sign on the outside handle.

Downstairs, she sat in the restaurant and ordered a glass of orange juice while she waited for Jarred. At a little after 9:00 a.m., he showed up.

"Good morning," he said, as he sat down. He was wearing a cobalt blue polo type shirt and a pair of blue jeans with loafers. She was glad that he was not dressed up. His hair was a little disheveled, undoubtedly by the constant London wind, and he wore a silver watch on his left wrist. She could just smell his cologne as he settled in.

She looked at him for a moment. And he looked back with a puzzled expression. He reached up and finger combed his hair, and she smiled.

"Good morning. I was just thinking that I've spent more time with you than working," she said.

"And that's a bad thing?" he asked.

"Well. I can't really decide..." The waitress who asked for their order interrupted them. She was a pretty blonde girl, about Anne's age, and Anne noticed that the girl looked at her hands before she spoke.

Jarred ordered flapjacks and she ordered a bowl of fresh fruit and a bagel.

"You do realize it's fall?" he asked.

"Hmm. You don't think I should have ordered the fruit?" she asked. "It doesn't really matter. I usually just pick out the cantaloupe anyway. The honeydew is always hard…" she paused for a second and looked up at him, "Jarred?" Her change in tone was unmistakable.

"Yes."

"I need to talk to you about something," she said.

"Uh-Oh. This doesn't sound like a good conversation to have, given the day I had planned. You do realize it is a Saturday… fun day… no work kind of day?" He paused, and she smiled, even though she didn't mean to.

"I know what day it is." Actually she didn't, but that wasn't the point.

"This… thing…" she motioned her hand between them.

"Thing?" he asked, innocently.

"You know. This… whatever. This connection, I guess, for the lack of a better word," she said.

"Connection? OK. Sorry. Yes. I think it is noticeable to the generic passerby that we 'click' as you Americans say." Jarred waited.

"I'm…. uneasy… with it," Anne said, and looked at him. He wasn't smiling. "It's just that I have to say I don't know how to define it, and that makes me uncomfortable." She struggled with the words.

"You want me to define it?" he asked.

"No!" she answered too quickly.

"Look, I have to be honest and say I've never quite experienced this before, and I'm not sure what that means," she said.

"In other words, if your parents met me or your friends, and they noticed this... chemistry…" He motioned between the two of them like she had done, "you would be embarrassed?"

She thought for a moment. "Yes. I guess I would."

"And why, exactly?" She hadn't thought about that part.

"I don't know. Perhaps I'm… scared of it." She paused a little too long before saying 'scared'.

"Do I have a say in this?" Jarred asked.

"Hmm. I don't think so…" She looked at him and hoped he would stop asking questions.

"OK. Well. Let's see. So you don't want to work together or see me?" he asked.

"No. Not at all. I'm an adult. I can deal with this. I just need some boundaries. Unfortunately, I don't know where I want the boundaries," she said. "God… I sound like a typical female. I really hate that." She closed her eyes and massaged them for a second.

"Anne. Look. I don't like the thought that I make you so uneasy, and I do acknowledge that we get along well. In fact, I would also say that I've never met anyone like you," he paused.

Anne thought she should not have enjoyed hearing that last statement as much as she did. She also knew part of her resistance had to do with the relationship that she was just in, but didn't really want to open that can of worms with Jarred.

"So. I guess we can—what's the old 'cliché'—be friends? I have to say that I'm a bit confused as to the lines that you allude to, but what do you say we figure them out along the way?"

The waitress put their food on the table as he was finishing up the last sentence, and Anne appreciated the distraction.

She took a bite of the fruit and winced a bit.

"Ha! Fresh fruit!" He laughed as she delicately removed it from her mouth and put it on the side of the plate.

She wasn't sure what the conversation had accomplished, but she felt better.

"So, is there something in particular you would like to do today?" he asked.

"Well, now that you mention it, I was thinking it might be fun to stop by the British Library, and then..." she took another bite of a different fruit and chewed it tentatively.

"Then?" He prompted her.

"Would you mind heading back out to Betty Theison's?" she asked.

He looked kind of surprised.

"You're really getting into this story, Anne. Well, I suppose no harm. Actually, it is probably a good day for a drive. I know of a couple of wine tasting places out in Kent, if that interests you," he said.

"Yes, please!" she answered.

"Would you mind if we turned around the itinerary and went out to Kent first? I'm thinking it would be nice to do in the morning."

Anne shrugged her shoulders as she took another bite.

After breakfast they left the hotel and walked a couple of blocks to where Jarred had parked his car. He opened the door for her and held it there for a second, then left it without waiting, and walked to the other side of the car and got in.

One of those confusing boundaries, Anne thought.

There was a single orchid on the dashboard and Anne looked at it.

Jarred saw her.

"Um… well that was a gift, prior to the conversation this morning. If you don't want it, I can take it home and do all kinds of horrible things to it… make it wish it had stayed in the florist shop." He reached over to grab it but she picked it up.

"Oh, no. We wouldn't want to lose innocent lives due to my state of confusion." She took it and held it in her lap.

"Buckle up," he said, and she pulled the shoulder harness over her body and inserted it into the clip, at which point he shot out into traffic, eliciting a yelp from Anne. He turned on the radio and pressed the CD. Nora Jones, *Come Away with Me*, came on and Anne sang along, moving her head to the rhythm.

The drive out to Kent was like driving through Universal Studios. As if on queue, every ten minutes the weather changed. Sun, hail, rain, more sun, drizzle, then fog and then finally unabashed sunshine as they entered the countryside.

"Can I drive?" Anne said, after a period of silence between tracks on the CD.

"What?" Jarred looked at her playful face.

"You know… drive." She put her hands out in front of her and demonstrated on a fictitious wheel.

"Really? Why?" he asked already slowing down.

"Just because. I've never driven on the wrong side of the road," she said.

"Wrong side? Who made it the right side? You Yanks have been doing this road thing for only a couple of hundred years. We've been at it for over a millennium!"

"Whatever…" Anne said, " I want to drive."

"OK then. The lady wants to drive. Should I ask if you have a valid license? You know what… I don't want to know." He had pulled over onto the gravel shoulder and she got out of the car before he had fully stopped and ran over to the other side. She held the door open for him and hopped into the driver's seat as soon as he had vacated it.

He got in and they both buckled up.

"OK. Just tell me how to start this thing." She was looking all over for the key on the dashboard.

He started laughing so hard he was crying. In between gasps for air, he pointed it out and she started the car up.

"It wasn't that funny," she said as she threw it in first gear and peeled out of the gravel onto the road. Jarred went silent for a moment and looked at her. She was smiling as she shifted adroitly with her left hand and steered with her right. She worked through all five gears.

"Now, up here you want to take a left." Anne slowed down a bit and waited for some traffic to clear then took the left turn and panicked. She couldn't figure out what lane she needed to be in after the turn. Right lane, left lane. There was a truck coming head on in the distance and she was still mentally trying to figure it out.

"Left! Left!" Jarred was pointing to his left and she swerved into the lane just as the truck passed them blaring his horn. Jarred was still holding onto the 'oh God' handle with both hands and Anne had a death grip on the steering wheel. Her heart was beating so hard she thought Jarred could hear it.

"Uh. Perhaps you should drive," she said after a moment.

"Perhaps." Jarred started chuckling again, and pretty soon they were both laughing. Anne pulled over to the side of the road and, after composing herself, they swapped places again.

"Thanks," she said.

"No problem," he said.

"That was fun," Anne added, as she started to laugh.

"Yeah, if you're into that sort of thing." They both started howling again.

After a minute or so, Jarred caught his breath.

"Whew. My gut hurts." Anne still held her stomach and couldn't reply. She just leaned, rolled down the window, and stuck her head out for oxygen.

It occurred to Anne, as Jarred was driving, that she probably should have called Betty. But, either way, it was nice to get out into the county.

As they neared the Cornwall estate they passed a huge castle-like stone structure in the distance. The entrance to the extended driveway was decorated with a ten-foot high wrought iron gate. Above the gate, also in black iron, was the family name "Stamwell." Anne looked at it as they passed.

"Something of interest?" Jarred asked.

"No. Well, yes. Just a family name that was mentioned in the diary," she said.

"The Stamwell's have been out here at least as long as the Cornwall's. The family can be traced back to the rule of Bloody Mary in the sixteenth Century."

A few minutes later, they passed another equally impressive entrance.

"The Horace's," Jarred said.

So, these were the two estates that John and Michael had visited that day, Anne thought.

"I don't know a lot about the Horace's. I think they came here from Scotland around the seventeenth century. Either way, an old family."

Anne recognized the next driveway. Though the Cornwall estate had gone into disrepair you could see that at one time the family had been quite prominent. Jarred got out of the car to move the gate and then drove through it. This time he just left it open.

He again pulled up a little way from the cottage and made no attempt to get out.

Anne opened her door and, then turned to him.

"Why don't you come in? She's a friendly old lady, and I'm sure she would enjoy seeing a handsome man." Anne realized the inadvertent compliment she had given, and felt her cheeks getting warm again.

Jarred paused for a second.

"Well, since you put it that way, how can I refuse?" He joined her on the other side of the car and they walked up the cobble stone walkway together. Anne had a strange sense of déjà vu as she knocked on the door.

"Just a minute!" She could hear a chair creak and some footsteps as Betty came to the door. "Oh. Hello dear!" she said.

"Hi Betty. I'm Anne, if you recall, and this is Jarred." She pointed to Jarred.

"I know who you are, dear. You were just here a few days ago." She opened the door and they walked in.

"Jarred. Are you American as well?" she asked.

"No Mum. I'm good Ol' English," he said.

"Oh. That's nice. Are you from around here? What is your surname?"

Jarred paused for a moment.

"Mulberry, Ma'am."

"Hmmm." Betty turned to look at him. "I used to know some Mulberry's... did you say you were from around here?" Betty asked again.

"No. I'm from London. My family all lives there. Mulberry is a pretty common name," he said.

"Yes. You're right of course. Please, sit down." Betty took a seat in her rocking chair, and Jarred and Anne sat on two wooden stools. The fire was going, and Anne wondered who cut her wood for her. The smell of baked apples came from the adjoining kitchen, and it made Jarred's stomach rumble. Anne looked at him, and smiled. He rubbed it and shrugged his shoulders.

"What brings you back out here, Anne? Have you finished with the diary?" she asked.

"No. Not yet. But thank you for sharing it with me. It is a very intriguing story," Anne said.

"Where are you at in it?" Betty asked.

"May 1939," Anne replied. Jarred looked at her when she said the date but she didn't notice.

"Anne—the girl in the diary—was talking about some incident that happened here around then. A missing girl, or something," Anne said.

"Hmm... well, it has been a long time since I read it, but I seem to recall something like that," Betty said.

"I was just wondering if you would mind if I looked inside the old house? She writes so much about it. I would really like to see it," Anne said.

"My. This story has *really* caught your attention, Anne. That's good. I think we should all have an adventure when we are young—at least one. I remember when I was..." Betty gazed off into the fire and then turned back and smiled.

"Summer's lease hath all to short a date... William Shakespeare," she said, and slowly got up to walk them out.

"It goes by all too quickly, Anne. Like a single season..." Betty turned away from them toward the front door.

"The house is open. Take your time, but I don't think much is left in there anymore. The estate people have pretty much stripped her of anything valuable. " Betty grabbed the handle and a little bell tinkled as the door opened, and Jarred and Anne went out into the sunshine.

Anne stood a moment in the courtyard and looked around to orient herself. The cottage, where Betty lived, was either one of the servant's quarters, perhaps Theresa's or even Michael's room. Straight ahead of them was the back entrance to the main house, and they walked the hundred feet over the weed-infested gravel. The car was parked to their left as they walked, and the driveway continued past the cottage, out of the courtyard to the back of the property. The inner courtyard had three small cottages in it, and a couple of sheds.

Jarred followed Anne as they approached the back door. Anne brushed away some spider webs that had covered the weathered brass handle in order to release the lock with her thumb, and the door swung open. The room was a pantry area, with the kitchen off to the left, and they walked straight ahead through a short corridor and a passage door out to the dining room. From there Anne could see what had to be the drawing room, about forty feet away to her right. The double doors were open, and she could see a large desk in at the far end of the room. Directly in front of them was the main entrance, and off to the left a large sitting room that contained a covered grand piano. Past the sitting room an open staircase went up to the second floor, at the top of which were a series of doors that had to be Anne and Lizzy's bedrooms. There was a hallway, which stretched off the dining room in the opposite direction to another wing of the house. Anne couldn't remember ever reading about that part of the house. Perhaps it was where Anne's mother lived.

The house was empty, in a strange almost lived-in way. Anne remembered when she was a child there was a family that lived on the same street that was killed in a car accident. After their funeral, the family came and took the things they wanted, and the house was left unattended. One day after school, she went inside on a dare, with her sister. The house didn't feel vacant but it was also obviously not occupied. It was like a house waiting for someone to come home. But the people never returned. That is what this house felt like. It was as if the family left for a vacation, and then, for some reason, never came back.

Jarred had moved over to the drawing room and Anne followed him, her footsteps leaving an imprint in the dust, which had accumulated to the point that it almost looked like a layer of frost on the wood floors. The floors were solid and didn't creak. Anne noticed that the wood paneling was in almost perfect condition.

She entered the study and could picture John and Michael having their argument inside the doorway. She could see where Anne could have stood unseen by both of them, right outside the door but well within earshot. From the entry to the study she looked back, and the staircase loomed off the main floor, then disappeared from that vantage point like stairs to heaven. Anne must have been halfway down when she had observed John lying on the couch that morning. The study had many more bookshelves than she had pictured. The entire room was lined with them, starting at about four feet off the floor. Most of the shelves were empty now, but Anne could picture the rows and rows of volumes, which had lined the bookcases for who knows how long. At the far end of the room was a huge mahogany desk. Anne joined Jarred by it and looked at the top, which was unprotected.

There were cuts and abrasions where writing utensils had penetrated the wood, and there were scars from unkindly patrons or errant drops of heavy objects. She moved to the backside of the desk and looked out the windows, which showed a clear partial view of the courtyard, as well as the road that departed the property to the rear. The desk had two rows of drawers in it, and Anne pulled on several of them, but they were all empty. As she walked out of the room she could see light colored spots on the wood floor where the legs of chairs or sofas must have stayed for a very long time.

"Do you want to go upstairs?" Jarred spoke quietly and pointed at the staircase, and Anne nodded her head. It was almost as if words would disturb the waiting house, that if they spoke too loudly, they would force it to recognize that it was no longer the stately manor it had been, but rather, that it was merely an empty vessel, standing in another time, awaiting an undeserved end.

The stairs were substantial and felt as if made of the trunks of ancient timbers. There was no creaking, no emptiness to the sounds of their footsteps as they made their way upstairs.

At the top of the stairs there was a door off to the left, and Anne could see the outline of a name or word on it. She rubbed the spot and could make out the name 'Elizabeth' on it. She hesitated for a second. It felt as if she should knock, that if she listened hard enough she could hear a little girl playing with her toys inside. Anne grabbed the crystal knob and turned it. The door opened easily.

It was a smaller room, about fifteen feet by fifteen feet square There was some kind of wall paper with horse prints that had started to fray but was still in remarkable condition—mustangs, gray mares, Clydesdales, Arabians. Anne walked around the room and found a name written in childish writing. It said 'Oddfellow'. Anne seemed to remember reading about that horse somewhere.

The room still had a single bed in it, and a nightstand. The bed cover was still on it. Anne was sure it used to be a pretty yellow, but now it was more faded chiffon.

They left the room and continued to the next door. Anne already knew whose room it was, and her name appeared on it, painted in white. There was a rose at the end of the name. Anne paused to gather her thoughts and Jarred almost ran into her. She felt the bump and heard his apology but took her time and traced the name with her finger, as she had done with the inscription in the book so many times. It was, without a doubt, the same handwriting.

Anne grasped the knob and slowly turned it. As it swung open she half expected to see a young girl in her nightgown sitting in her bed, writing in her diary. She gasped as the door swung open and, with a small tap, hit the wall. The room was in almost perfect condition. It eerily reminded Anne of those TV shows where a son or daughter goes missing, and the parents don't touch a thing in their child's room so that they can come back to it exactly the way they had left it. But this room hadn't been lived in for what had to be over fifty years. And though everything was covered in dust, it was perfectly preserved. Even down to the pictures on the walls. Jarred had made his way over to one of them.

"Anne, come here. This must have been her." He pointed to a picture of a girl about seventeen. It was taken without her knowledge, as the girl was half turned away from the camera, looking at something in the distance. There was an inscription on the bottom of the page. *"To my lovely Anne, forever hopeful. Love, Mother."* Another picture of Anne, several years later, was next to it. She was holding what had to be her sister's hand as they walked down an aisle. Anne couldn't tell if it was a wedding or a funeral. The younger sister was crying. The last picture Anne recognized immediately. It was of a beautiful young girl at the piano, with a room full of people. There was a young man sitting beside her with the most enamored look on his face. It could only have been John.

Jarred peered at the picture for the longest time. She couldn't tell if he was looking at the girl or someone else but it obviously captured his attention.

Anne whispered in his ear. "Do you recognize someone Jarred?" He was a little surprised and pulled back.

"What? I'm sorry, I didn't hear you." He looked at her questioningly.

"Never mind. I was just kidding. It is a beautiful picture, isn't it? Do you see that young man there?" Anne pointed to the young man in the tuxedo.

"Yes," said Jarred.

"That is John… John Harrision," she said.

"The book I have was a gift from her." She pointed to the young girl. "To him." She pointed to John. "What an amazing shot. I can't believe this is here. It is like looking at a window into someone's heart." Anne left his side and went over to the fully made-up bed, and sat down. There was a small, yellow nightstand by its side, and she traced her fingers on the top of it through the dust. The motion left three small snake-like tracks behind. There was a single drawer that was closed and she tugged it open. Inside, there was an eraser, a pencil that was still sharp, a couple of scraps of paper and a hair ribbon. Anne picked up the pencil and the hair ribbon, and held it in her hands as she absorbed the surroundings.

"I'm going to go downstairs. Take your time." He left the room, and she heard him walk softly down the stairs. She got up, still holding the ribbon and pencil, and walked over to the window to pull open the sheer curtains. She could see below to the main driveway as Jarred walked out the front door and pulled out his cell phone to make a call. It must have been a similar scene that Anne had watched in 1939 as John came in from the trip with Michael. The thought made her shiver, and she rubbed her arms.

She looked down at the objects she held and went over to the nightstand and put them away, closing the drawer. She exited the room with one final look, shut the door, and made sure it latched. Then she walked down to the main floor. Jarred stood at the bottom of the staircase.

"Just one more minute." Anne held up a single finger and pointed to the piano. Jarred walked over and joined her, and they lifted up the cloth cover from the front of it. Under the cover, and on top of the soundboard, there was a metronome that had been laid on its side, and Anne set it upright to let the arm loose. It swung back and forth with the familiar tick, tock, tick, tock. The piano was beautiful and ornate. It was made of a dark wood, and was heavily stained for a deep ember appearance. It looked in remarkable condition. Anne uncovered the keys and ran her fingers over them without making a sound. They felt like silk petals under her fingertips. The ivory was yellowed but there were no keys missing. She saw something inside the lid of the piano, between the music stand and the strings, and she reached in and removed it. It was a copy of sheet music for Beethoven's Sonata No. 1. Anne knew the particular piece well, as it was also written for cello.

They put back the music, and replaced the cover on the piano as if someone might want to play it someday, then walked out the back door into the sun of the courtyard. Anne turned around and looked at the old house. Jarred could see her eyes were moist and watched as a single tear fell. He grabbed her by the hand and led her back to the car, where he opened the door for her and then got in the other side. Without saying a word, he drove out the driveway and down Fleming road back to London.

Chapter 27

May 10, 1939 Cornwall Estate, Kent

The head maid discovered the blue shoe as she emptied out the morning dishwater. One of the dogs had been chewing on it and she shooed him away to pick it up. It was a woman's shoe, suitable for a servant girl, and it was badly torn and covered in mud.

Lord Cornwall was in the study along with John and Sir Percy. "Excuse me sir, but I need to show you something," she said.

"What is it, Mrs. Cohen? We are rather preoccupied here." Lord Cornwall looked up from the paper that he and Sir Percy had before them on the desk.

"I'm afraid the dogs have brought something in." Mrs. Cohen presented the shoe held over a rag so that it didn't sully the house.

"Mrs. Cohen, it's a shoe. Throw it out, woman." He waived his hand.

"But Sir, I think this belonged to Theresa and, as you know, no one has seen her in going on four days now. I'm afraid this is not a good omen," she said.

All three men in the room stopped what they were doing and went over to the shoe. It was made of cloth, which was nearly torn off. Sir Percy grabbed it with his thumb and forefinger, and held it up. There were dark stains on it that could have been blood, or just soiled dirt.

"Where did you find this, Mrs. Cohen?" Sir Percy asked.

"Just out in the courtyard." Mrs. Cohen pointed out the window to the back of the house. "One of the dogs was chewing on it, and I shooed him off. I don't know where he got it from."

Sir Percy turned to John.

"What was the result of your search yesterday, John?" "We found nothing, father. No one at the neighboring estates had seen her, and we found no one in town either...." He looked down at the shoe again and felt his heart skip a beat.

"How long has it been since you've seen her, John?" John paused a little too long, and his father narrowed his eyes.

"Umm. I saw her the day we took the last shipment to the port. That would be four days ago, as Mrs. Cohen said."

"Do you know anything about the girl, John? Was she seeing anyone, or involved in anything that we should know of? Did you hear anything on your search?" Lord Cornwall asked.

John and Mrs. Cohen looked at each other, but no one answered.

"Answer me! That wasn't a request!" Lord Cornwall's tone caused Mrs. Cohen to jump, and she looked again at John.

"Michael. She was seeing Michael." John interrupted the interrogation and looked down when he said it.

"Michael? Why would he want anything to do with this servant girl?" Lord Cornwall's voice got softer as he realized his rhetorical question.

"Where is he?" Lord Cornwall asked.

"Who? Michael?" John asked.

"Yes. Michael! Who do you think I mean? The crown prince?!"

"Sorry Sir. I'm not sure, but perhaps in his room out back." John looked at Mrs. Cohen, who shook her head vigorously up and down.

"Tell him to get in here!" Again, Mrs. Cohen and John looked at each other.

"I'll get him." John turned around and quickly left the room.

"You can go now, Mrs. Cohen." He heard Lord Cornwall say.

John approached Michael's cottage like he was stalking an animal. He stood in front of the door and could see a light on inside, and took a deep breath, then another, before steadily knocking on the door.

"Yeah? I'm kinda busy in here right now!" Michael's voice was groggy, and hard to understand.

"Michael!" John said, with no response.

"Michael!" he said it a little louder. When he still got no answer, he tried the door. It was open and John held it just wide enough to yell inside.

"Michael!" He finally heard some sounds and waited with his hand on the cold metal handle, his feet still well outside the threshold.

"What the hell do *you* want?" Michael came out without a shirt and only his long undergarment on. His eyes were bloodshot and his hair completely disheveled.

"The dogs found a shoe," John said.

"So what?"

"It's Theresa's," John said. That got his attention and Michael broke out in a smile.

"Ah, I see," he said. "Sounds like we may have the beginnings of an exciting day, John. What did you tell them?" Michael asked. John noted that he didn't specify who was 'them'.

"Mrs. Cohen brought the shoe in to the study. Your father, myself, and my father were there," John said.

"So, what did you tell them?" Michael asked, again.

"Nothing. I didn't say anything," John said. His hand was getting so slick he could barely hold onto the door handle, and he let it go to wipe it off on his pants. Michael saw the movement. The door swung all the way open and knocked something over, which made John jump.

"What did Mrs. Cohen say?" Michael asked. John hesitated.

"*I* said that you and Theresa have been 'seen' together," John said. "Your father wants to speak to you right now." John turned around, and walked hurriedly back across the gravel drive. He could feel Michael staring at him.

A few minutes later Michael walked into the kitchen and found John standing by the piano. He had put on a pair of blue gabardine pants and a white shirt that was buttoned down the front, but the cuffs were open. He went over to him and put his mouth up to John's ear.

"Remember two things, Johnny. The guards think that she was *your* girlfriend. *She* said she was your girlfriend. And let's not forget about the other problem. Now, what would Anne think about all of that?" He pulled a few inches away and added. "Follow my lead and you'll be fine."

Michael spun on his heels and walked into the drawing room. His father and Sir Percy were still there.

"Where is John?!" Lord Cornwall's said, and John quickly entered and stood by the doors.

"Michael. I assume John has told you about the shoe?" He didn't wait for a reply but Michael nodded. "Did you have a relationship with this Theresa?" Lord Cornwall asked.

"No, sir. I mean yes, sir. We were friends, that's all." Michael looked his father straight in the eyes.

"Friends? What are you talking about? Friends with one of the servant girls?" Lord Cornwall was not going to be as easy as Michael thought.

"Not exactly friends, father. She was just a distraction. She was known to be a... companion to lonely men," Michael said. "I was not the only man she enjoyed keeping company with here."

Lord Cornwall's face was like steel. John couldn't read anything in it.

"Do you know where she is?" Lord Cornwall asked.

"No, father. I have no idea. Last time I saw her was with John, about four nights ago when we went to the port."

John could feel his ears burn, and his father turned to him and looked. Michael's comment made it sound like John and Theresa were together and there were enough people believing that lie.

"No that's not correct—" John started.

Michael looked at Sir Percy and smiled. "Whatever. We saw her before we left. We were together out in the back, weren't we, Johnny?" Michael turned to John and smiled.

"Yes. We saw her before we left," John said. Michael interrupted him again.

"Like I already stated," Michael added, and stared at John.

Sir Percy looked at John, and then at Michael, like he had missed something.

"So, when the inspector comes, that is what he is going to find out then. Yes?"" Lord Cornwall didn't wait for an answer.

"We are going to be calling the police today. Sir Percy?" Lord Cornwall said.

"I'll take care of it, sir." Sir Percy rarely called him that in private company, and John and Michael took due notice of the formality.

The conversation was over and John did not feel it would be wise to give Lord Cornwall anymore reason to be upset today. He would just have to wait for a better opportunity to clarify things.

Michael left, and John followed him after receiving a stern look from his father. John watched Michael as he left through the kitchen, then he went over to the sitting room at the front of the house. He sat and thought about what he was going to say should this investigation take the turn he was afraid it was going to.

"John? Am I disturbing you?" The voice immediately calmed his nerves and he turned around to face Anne.

"No. Never. What are you up to today?" His voice was as soft as his heart felt.

"I heard some kind of commotion, so I peeked down the stairs, but it looks like everything is over now." She smiled.

"Are you alright?" she asked.

"Yes. I'm fine." He pondered whether he should tell her what was going on.

"Look, Anne. I need to tell you something." She sat down across from him, her knees together, and placed her hands on her lap. She had the most beautiful hazel eyes.

"You know that Theresa is missing?"

She nodded.

"I fear that something very bad has happened to her," he said, and her eyes opened wide.

"What do you mean, John?" she asked.

"I fear she may have been... harmed," he said. She reacted by putting her hand to her mouth. He was thankful she remained quiet, as he could hear their fathers still talking in the study.

"And... I fear Michael is involved," he said the words slowly and watched her reaction.

"I am afraid that Michael is not a very good man," she said.

"Yes. We both know that for a fact." His teeth were clinched as he spoke.

"Inspectors are coming today and they will be asking many questions. They may talk to me as well. Please do not let it concern you." At hearing this, she grew very solemn.

"What do you mean, John? Has Michael involved you somehow?" John wasn't sure how to answer that question.

"I don't quite know, Anne. I don't understand him," John said.

"John, can I speak to you a moment? Hello, Miss Anne, Good morning." Sir Percy had appeared behind Anne, and she turned around and smiled at him.

"Yes father," John got up and walked away toward the study with Sir Percy.

Chapter 28

May 11, 1939 Cornwall Estate, Kent

BY the next day it was not really a great surprise to John when they discovered the body of Theresa. They found her in the woods, about a half-mile from the house, lying on her side, her arms flung wide open in a gesture of helplessness. She had deep gashes across her forehead, face and neck. John noted that it was almost a direct path from where he had last seen her and Michael the night she disappeared. Her feet were bare and her blue dress and bodice ripped. There was little doubt to any of the men that she had been raped. The only question was, did she die before or after?

John was drawn to look at the body in order to better understand what he was dealing with. From what he saw, this was not a crime of passion. It looked premeditated and staged. Michael *wanted* them to find the body. So the question was why. John knew by now that he would be pressured to back up Michael's story. That path had been determined the day before. Actually, on reflection, Michael had set him up six years ago, the night he had unwittingly helped in the molestation of Anne. He felt like a marionette, on glass strings, dancing over daggers, and needed to find a way to sever the connection.

"Gentlemen. As it appears, you two are the last persons to have seen Theresa alive," Inspector Roarke said. He was in the sitting room along with Michael and John. The inspector seemed to favor this room because of its proximity to the front of the house. "Now that you have had time to reflect, can you more precisely pinpoint the time when you saw her?" he asked.

"It was around eight in the evening, inspector. I'm sure of it, because we had finished supper and John and I were out in the courtyard talking about the evening's assignment for the Crown." The inspector didn't even look up at Michael's obvious attempt at impressing him. He was writing in a small notebook.

"John?" He looked at John and received a tentative nod.

"Well, that's good because several others have indicated that they saw her around six. So that helps provide a timeline. Did either of you see her after eight?" John noticed the minute change in the question and opened his mouth to speak, but Michael cut in.

"Inspector, since we already said that was the last time we saw her, if we had seen her after that time, we wouldn't, then, have seen her for the last time at eight, now would we?" Michael had his feet on the couch and his head was leaning against a pillow.

"Yes. That would be so then. Ha!" the inspector said. Michael silently mimicked him and John looked at him sternly.

"Where were you two that evening?" The inspector flipped some pages then added: "the evening of the sixth, I believe?"

"I'm afraid we can't tell you that, inspector. It was a matter of national security," Michael answered, and lit up a cigarette.

"John?" The inspector turned to him. John was seated as far away from Michael as he could while still facing him.

"I'm afraid so, inspector. You'll have to get clearance for us to answer that," John said.

"Hmm." The inspector made a note.

"What was she wearing that night… John?"

John looked up at him, and then at Michael, who smiled and took a drag.

"Uhmmm. I'm trying to recall… I think she had on a coat. A long coat. A dress, like the one she is …uh, *was* wearing…." John stopped and looked at Michael again.

"She had on a scarf, a blue scarf, and matching gloves. Remember, John? It was a tad chilly, and she had on a scarf," Michael said, and then took another drag.

John paused for a moment, and recalled the scarf she had on in the car when she tried to cover herself.

"Yes. That's right. She had a scarf. It was long, wide," John measured his hands apart. "About this wide. I think it was blue…. like Michael said." The inspector stood between them with his back to Michael, and Michael mimed something to John. It finally occurred to him that he was referring to the morning that he had seen John and Anne together in the study, and John had found himself with a blue scarf with a stain on it. John's eyes got wide and the inspector quickly turned around to Michael, but Michael had leaned his head back and was feigning sleep. The inspector turned back to John.

"So there was a scarf?" he asked.

His jaw felt so tight that he didn't think he could open it, but finally spit out.

"Yes."

Outside the room, Anne had been listening to the interview. She, too, remembered the scarf but did not see the interaction between Michael and John. She panicked and ran as quickly as she could, without making a sound, into the study and looked frantically for the scarf. She remembered seeing John stand up with it in his hands, and she recalled the dark stain on it. Anne looked around the couch and chairs but found it nowhere. She got on her hands and knees and lifted up the skirt of the couch that John had risen from, and reached into the darkness. Her hand touched something thick and light, and she pulled it out. It was a blue scarf. In the middle of it was a large dark stain, and she touched it with a finger. It was dried and crusty.

"John," she said, under her breath. Her heart pained her as she held the material in her hands, and she felt lightheaded, her mind refused to comprehend what she held in her hands, but she had no time to think about it, as she heard footsteps coming. She looked around, frantic for someplace to put it, and ran to her father's desk, where she saw the humidor on the front edge. She opened it up, grabbed the few remaining cigars and put them in her dress pocket, and stuffed the scarf in before shutting it tightly again. She was thankful that it closed completely.

"Anne?" Her father was behind her, blocking his view of the humidor. She took a deep breath and turned around. All the blood had drained from her face.

"Are you alright, Anne?" Her father asked as he walked toward her back.

"Yes, father. I'm sorry. I just got a bit dizzy," she said. He took her by the shoulders and helped her to sit down.

"Are you feeling well?" he asked.

"I think so. There is just so much happening today with the police and Theresa. I don't like this," she said.

"None of us do, Anne. It will be over in a day or two. Perhaps you should go lay down for a while," he said.

"I think so, father. I need to check on Lizzy anyway." Anne got up and walked slowly out of the room. She prayed that no one would open the humidor.

The inspector had finished with John and Michael and they looked at each other as they left the room and, then both looked at the study as they passed by. Michael smiled and pretended to throw a scarf around his neck as he walked away. He knew John wanted to look for it but he dared not do so until later.

:

No one saw Anne come down into the study that night after everyone had gone to sleep. As she didn't want to touch the scarf again, she grabbed the whole humidor and removed it from the study. It made her feel guilty but she fought back the feeling. She told herself that, if she didn't take it, Michael would only continue whatever sick web he was weaving. And whatever that was she knew that he would not be the one getting blamed. As long as she could remember he never got punished for anything he did. If her father asked about it, she would tell him that she didn't like the smell and had put it away. He knew it was true and wouldn't care, as he had stopped smoking several years before. She took the small box upstairs, placing it in the drawers that were hidden in the bottom of her bed.

Some time after midnight, John entered the house and walked silently into the study. There were no lights on and he pushed the switch on the flashlight he had brought and shone it around the furniture. As he moved the light around the room, he came upon a pair of shoes and his heart leapt up into his throat and hung there like a giant ball of lead.

"Hello, Johnny boy. I knew you'd show up." It was Michael.

Chapter 29

London, 2004

Jarred took Anne to the Hotel early. The tour of the house seemed to have drained her and she was very quiet on the drive back in to London. Normally he would have been disappointed, but he needed to attend to some things as well.

"Can I check in with you tomorrow?" he asked.

"Yes, thank you. I'm sorry I killed the day. I don't even know why this story is affecting me so much. Let's see, tomorrow is Sunday. Is there such a thing as a Sunday brunch? I'd like to treat you for all your kindness." She looked at him.

"I think I can handle that," he said. "How about I meet you at eleven? I need to go visit my mum in the morning anyway."

"You could bring her along if you want," Anne said it without thinking, and immediately regretted it. "Or not....I'm so tired, I don't know what I'm saying." The valet opened the door, and Anne got out. She turned around and gave Jarred the best smile she could muster.

"Thank you. I'll see you tomorrow," she said.

"Good night, Anne," Jarred said, and then realized it was only 2:00 p.m.

She pretended not to hear and he drove off.

Anne was very tired but, when she got back to the room, so many questions had come up in her mind that she pulled out the diary and skipped a couple of pages till she thought she found what she wanted to know.

May 11, 1939

It has been a terrible day. The inspector has been asking everyone many questions about Theresa, and I was too nosey, and listened to the interview with John and Michael. I feel terrible that I have taken evidence and hidden it. My heart hurts and my conscience is screaming at me, but I am positive that Michael was up to no good. I think that he was trying to frame John, and I don't understand why. I even have some doubts as to whether John has been telling the truth, but my heart tells me to believe him. I have prayed for forgiveness but I am heavy with sadness. It is very late, and yet I cannot sleep. I think I can hear voices from downstairs, but I am fearful of what that might mean. I have locked my door and am in my bed with all my covers. I will be happy when morning has arrived.

"I knew you would come, Johnny." John could only see a silhouette of his antagonist as he stood in front of him, and beside the sofa. "But it's not here. I am afraid someone has beaten you to the game, Johnny," Michael said.

"What have you done with it?" John demanded.

"Quiet John, you wouldn't want to wake up the children." He pointed upstairs.

"Sit down, we need to get some matters straight," Michael said as he sat down, and John could finally see an outline of his face in the glow of his flashlight. His eyes were wide and dilated as if he had been taking narcotics. John would not have put it past him.

"Just for the record, I did not take the scarf. But it makes for an interesting twist, don't you think?" Michael said.

"Michael, this whole thing is ludicrous. Do you really think you are going to get away with this? They will hang you!" John leaned forward to keep his voice down while still stressing his point. It pleased him to put his hand around his own throat to highlight the consequence.

Michael paused before answering, and without a change in his stone like expression said: "Or *you*."

John froze and thought about all the things that he had said that day even though he really had no choice, then looked up at Michael.

"Is that your intent? To frame me for this?" He was surprised at how calm his voice was, but his hands were clenched in the dark.

"Only as a last resort. You see, Johnny, if we keep to our story nothing can be proved. We were with each other most of the night. No one saw either of us with her, except for Rad and his buddy, and the inspector doesn't know about that anyway. Remember - it was a secret mission and he doesn't have any idea of where to even start asking questions. The police can investigate and speculate all they want, but they cannot prove anything," Michael said.

"And, other than my own skin, what is my motivation to help you cover up a murder, you sick bastard?" John had his teeth clamped down.

"Well, I would expect that is incentive enough, however there is always the other matter …"

John was getting sick of his reminding him. "That happened SIX years ago! What is there to gain by telling your sister anything at this point?"

"It isn't what I have to gain, it's what *you* have to lose. Do you love her, Johnny? Can you let her go? We could just go upstairs right now and tell her everything. Do you think she will believe you? Do you think she would even care to hear your explanation as to why you were guarding her door that night?"

John had heard enough. He was right. He hated Michael with every fiber of his body, but Michael knew he was in love with Anne. He held all the cards. Michael's time would come, but he would just have to be patient.

"We have an understanding then?" Michael asked. He didn't wait for the answer as he left the room. John waited in the darkness for his anger to subside. What next? He thought. What next?

:

The next day the inspector returned, and he requested that Lord Cornwall, Sir Percy and the two boys join him in the study. Lord Cornwall was behind his desk, Michael sat in one of the wing chairs, and Sir Percy stood while John sat in the wing chair opposite Michael. None of them could see Anne at the top of the stairs as she strained to listen.

"Gentlemen, we have a couple of problems that need to be handled," the inspector started.

"You said that you saw Theresa with a scarf and gloves on the night of her disappearance. Is that correct?" He looked at Michael.

"Yes, that is what she was wearing," Michael said.

"And yet when she was found, neither the scarf nor the gloves were with her. Yet the rest of her attire was as you saw."

"I'm sorry, but I don't see the point. She could have lost them, the killer could have taken them, the dogs could have removed them." John spoke up, much to his own surprise.

"True. True." The inspector nodded, and stopped to take a sip of water. "However, given the chilliness of the night, it is unlikely she lost them. So, either the dogs had removed them, or the killer took them or *misplaced them*. Now, we have men searching all over the house and around the grounds, but none of the three missing pieces have been found. I think that unlikely, especially given the seeming predilection of the dogs to bring their treasures back here, as they did the shoe."

Lord Cornwall spoke up. "So what are you saying, inspector? Certainly it is not unusual for a criminal to take items from a victim?"

"No. You are quite right, Lord Cornwall. However, that is not quite the case here. You see, in one of our many searches around the grounds we found what appear to be her gloves." He pulled out a pair of blue, well-worn gloves from his jacket pocket.

He turned to Michael. "Are these the gloves you saw her with?"

"Yes. I think they were. They were certainly hers. I had seen them many times during the winter," Michael said, without hesitation.

John froze and he could feel the acid inside his stomach start to rise fast.

"Oh, pray tell, inspector, where did you find them?" Michael mocked.

"Well, now that is the problem. They were found in young Mr. Harrision's automobile. Under the front driver's seat," the inspector said.

John looked up at his father who had a blank stare on his face.

"John, what can you tell me about this? Was the girl in your car that evening?" The inspector asked.

The question had so many implications that John couldn't get himself to answer. His mouth was dry and he needed more time! Michael sat across from him with a shocked look on his face.

"Sir. I don't know how those got there," John said. It was the only truthful thing he could think of to say.

"Inspector. Is there something else that we should know before deciding whether to end this interview or not. If you are prepared to make a formal charge against my son, perhaps we should consult with our family barrister." John was relieved to hear his father's voice.

"I'm afraid there is, Sir Percy. With Lord Cornwall's permission this morning I spoke to someone named Rad…" the inspector flipped pages looking for the name, then gave up, "well, Rad something..."

John closed his eyes. Michael must have seen this coming! He stood up and looked at the inspector. Michael started to protest, and he put up his hand.

"Inspector. The girl was with us. I suspect you already know that," the inspector nodded and took a seat.

"However, she was not with me. The household staff knows that she was Michael's... friend. She returned with us to the house very late, and I dropped her and Michael off on the road before the house. That is the last I saw of them," John said, staring at Michael. It was all out now.

Michael immediately got to his feet and turned to his father instead of the inspector.

"Father I already told you that it was over between myself and Theresa and that I gave her to John." John hated the sound of the comment. "You also know that I'm the one who encouraged you to allow the inspector to talk to the guards, and they can testify that Theresa was with *him*."

"What did the guards say, inspector?" Lord Cornwall asked.

"Michael is correct, Lord Cornwall. The guards did say that Theresa indicated she was with John."

"So, Johnny here is just trying to lie to cover his rear. No one saw Theresa and I get out of the car late that evening. The facts are that he dropped me off where he said he did, but Theresa was with him, not me. I went to bed," Michael finished and sat down, glaring at John.

"John?" the inspector asked.

"He's lying," John said.

"I think this interview is over inspector. Unless you have other evidence I don't see anything to controvert what Michael has stated." Lord Cornwall stood up.

"Or what John has said," Sir Percy said, softly.

"Indeed," the inspector said, "until later gentleman," the inspector left the house.

Anne was up on the stairs crying and shaking uncontrollably. She held on to the vertical bars of the railing with both her hands and did not know whom to believe. She needed time to think. She managed to pull herself up to her feet and open the closest door, Lizzy's room, stumbling into it before anyone could see her.

"What's wrong, Annie?" Lizzy sat on the floor with her dolls, playing. Anne laid face down on her sister's bed, and wept. Lizzy got up, and sat beside her to run her fingers through her sister's hair.

"It'll be alright, Annie. It'll be alright."

Downstairs, Sir Percy and John walked out to the front of the house.

"Father. I swear. I didn't have anything to do with it," John said.

"I have no doubt, son," Sir Percy said, as he led them out to the front of the house to Sir Percy's automobile.

:

Later that day, Sir Percy, along with John and the family barrister, met up at the Police Station. Their station in life did not allow them the privilege of having the interview in the comfort of their home unlike the Cornwall's. They were seated in a square room about ten feet wide with a single glass wall, four chairs and a table.

"Sit down, son." The inspector pulled out a chair and John sat down. He had put on a fresh shirt and new pair of shoes, but looked like he had been awake for days. The inspector placed a glass in front of him.

"Tell me what happened that night, John," the inspector said.

"I'm sorry, sir. I did not reveal the complete truth before."

"Why not, John?" the inspector asked.

"Because Michael threatened someone I care about if I didn't go along with his story," John said.

"What did he threaten to do?"

"I don't really feel I can divulge that information. It is of a personal nature and happened a long time ago."

"So when you said 'threatened' you didn't mean with physical harm?"

"No. He threatened to reveal something about someone that I care about," the answer seemed to placate the inspector. He had been involved in enough Royal intrigue to not ask anything further.

"Let's go over what happened that night again, John."

John told him the story from the beginning to end.

The inspector finished writing something in his journal and looked at him.

"John. Is there anyone else who can confirm your story?"

"No. Michael made sure of that," John said, resigned.

"OK. Thank you for coming in. You are free to go, for now," the inspector said.

John hesitated. "I'm sorry. Do you believe me?" he asked.

"Look, John. You don't seem the type to do something like this. However, there are some problems with your story. Specifically: your first statement to me, the gloves in the car, the fact that two witnesses say that Theresa said she was with you and the fact that no one can offer testimony to refute what Michael has said. As of now I'm afraid you must be the prime suspect. If you think of anything that would help us, please let me know. Until then, you are to stay at the estate until further notice." The inspector left the room.

"Father. I'm sorry. I know this is embarrassing for you," John said.

"Yes, son, it is. You should have told the truth. I do not know what this secret is that keeps you bound to Michael but it cannot be worth this," Sir Percy said.

John remained silent. He was having his doubts as well.

:

John returned to the Estate with Sir Percy late that evening and sat alone in the sitting room.

"John?" John turned and saw Anne standing in front of him. Twenty-four hours, he thought as he remembered the exchange they had had in that very room the day before.

"Hi, Anne." She looked sad, as if she had been crying.

"Are you OK?" She sat down, he noticed, a little farther away than the day before.

"Yes…No. I don't know, Anne. I'm in a lot of trouble." John pondered if he should say anything.

"I think I'm being framed for the murder of Theresa," he spit out. He was surprised when she didn't react.

"Is any of it true?" Anne asked. John didn't know how much she knew. He suspected that Michael had told her something.

"It is true that Theresa was with us that evening," he started.

"Then you lied?" Anne looked hurt.

"No. Yes. But –" he stopped himself. This was his decision and he would have to accept the consequences. What could he tell her anyway—that Michael had blackmailed him with threats of revealing her attempted rape?

"Yes, I was pressured by Michael. I should not have let him do that to me. I'm very sorry, Anne. I don't lie." He looked at her but didn't know if she believed him.

"But why?" she asked.

"Because he threatened someone that I love," John said. It was the best answer he could give her.

"Have you lied about anything else?" Anne asked. Her hands were on her lap, her back straight. She had a tear falling down her cheek.

"No. Anne. NO! I will never lie to you. I'm so sorry. Please…" he said, looking at her eyes. She looked away and wiped the tear away.

"Do you believe me?" he asked, tentatively.

"I don't know, John. I believe that you didn't murder her, but I don't understand everything. My father is embarrassed that this has happened here. He is upset that the family has been affected. I don't know what is going to happen." Anne got up and looked down at him, her face soft with pain.

"I know, Anne. I have caused a lot of grief for both our families. I wish I could undo what has been done," John said.

"Perhaps time will help." Anne turned away with a sad smile and left the room. John sat in the chair looking out to the driveway. He had not killed Theresa but he did want to kill Michael. A few minutes later he had his chance.

"What did you tell them?" Michael asked, before John even realized he was not alone. The voice made John angrier that he had ever been and he spun up on his feet and lunged at Michael with a flailing fist. Michael stepped aside easily and laughed.

"Wow. John. I didn't know you had it in you!" he said, as he watched warily. John gathered himself and walked up to Michael and stood with his face within a few inches of him. Michael stood his ground.

"I swear. I'll kill you if you try anything else," he said.

Michael backed away and laughed again. "Like what, John? What could I possibly do?"

John realized he had an opportunity with Michael and his demeanor changed. "I need you to do something for me. Given all that that has happened…" he said.

"What? Like you trying to make me look like a fool in front of my father? Like trying to stick the murder of that tramp on me? Why would I help you? In fact, I'm thinking of talking to little Annie tonight… or doing something…" Michael stopped and looked at him closely, "on the other hand. If you scratch my back, I'll keep that little secret quiet and tell your precious Annie that you were the good guy."

John tried to ignore the threat but inside he had to admit that he was concerned. He decided to play along.

"What do you want?"

"Take a ride with me tonight?" Michael lit a cigarette.

"So you can kill me?"

"Use your brain, John, if I did that they would suspect me first. No. I need some help doing something. It won't take more than an couple of hours," Michael said.

John thought about it for a moment. This could be his best chance to catch Michael red handed. He had no doubt that whatever Michael wanted his help for in the middle of the night was not legal.

"Fine. You give me a letter for Anne and I'll meet you."

"Midnight. Bring your car and wear something dark," Michael said.

"And bring the letter or I don't go anywhere," John said.

Michael waved as he walked off and out the front door. John watched him disappear around the corner then went into Lord Cornwall's office. Thankfully there was no one around. He picked up the telephone and dialed a number.

"Hello? May I speak to inspector Roarke please?" John waited while they located him.

Chapter 30

London, 2004

Anne sat on the bed with the diary open in front of her. She sipped on a cup of chamomile tea and put it down long enough to dial a phone number.

"Hello?" she asked.

"Anne?" Jarred asked.

"Yes."

"I'm surprised to hear from you. It's, what…only been a couple of hours since I dropped you off. Are you feeling better?" he asked.

"Yes. Much. Thank you. Say, you mentioned you had a friend in Scotland Yard?" Anne sensed the hesitancy on the other end of the line.

"Yes, I do. I went to school with her," Jarred finally said.

"I was just curious about something I read about in the diary, about the murder of a girl on the Cornwall estate… anyway, I'd like to talk with her if possible. Do you think you could arrange it?" Anne said.

"Uh…sure. I think so. Can I get back to you? I'm in the middle of something right now," Jarred said.

"Of course," Anne said, and hung up. She lay back on the bed and stared at the ceiling for a moment, and her stomach growled. She rubbed it with her hand and thought about Anne. She wondered how she would handle being lied to by someone she cared about. She valued honesty and didn't even like feeling like she was keeping something from her parents, let alone someone with whom she was in love. She thought it would likely kill her if she was forced to. But she had to acknowledge that, at times, keeping something private was not the same as a dark secret. She just didn't like the feeling that she was hiding something. Still, she had no doubt that John had made a decision, right or wrong, to keep something from Anne, and that was a decision that only he could make. There was no way to judge what he had done.

She thought about Tony. What went wrong there anyway? Besides the fact that he was a jerk, and selfish, and had no class. That was it, actually. He didn't treat her like a lady. He had never even opened the door for her, not that that was such a big deal, but still, it was nice to feel appreciated. Her stomach rumbled again and she laughed, and stood up. She needed to eat something so she grabbed a sweater and a room key and went downstairs.

The lobby was very busy, and Anne went into the restaurant where the hostess greeted her.

"One, please," she said. She thought that perhaps she should have just ordered room service, but then decided that being around people would be good.

She was seated at a table for two against the far wall of the restaurant, and selected the seat that faced the room. From her vantage point she observed several couples that were obviously not just business associates.

The unspoken communication between a man and woman intrigued her, and she found herself thinking about the way she dealt with Jarred. Was she misleading him? He certainly didn't seem to mind. Did she like him? Yes, very much, and when she was not with him it was much easier to think clearly about the things she should or should not do. But when she was around him all those pacts she made with herself went out the proverbial window, and she found that she just enjoyed the time. He made her feel so... unique.

She ordered her meal, a Caesar salad with grilled chicken, and ate it slowly while watching the couples interact.

Had she bothered to look, she would have seen the man seated six tables away from her in the black sport jacket and turtleneck sweater. She would have seen him speaking into the dangling microphone that hung from his left ear for the better part of thirty minutes. He got up, left some money on the table, and walked out of the restaurant into the lobby, and then out the front door where he met up with another man.

"She came downstairs about thirty minutes ago and is just finishing up a salad. Do you want me to keep waiting for her?" the man said.

"Yes. Stay with her until we are sure she isn't being followed," Jarred said.

"Do you have any indication that she is?"

"No, but I'd like to make sure. I can't stay with her all day and night," Jarred said, though he thought he wouldn't mind doing so if she would allow it.

"Fine with me, I can use the overtime," the man said. He walked back in and sat down in the lobby.

A few minutes later, Anne walked out and the man watched her get in the elevator and head upstairs. He saw no evidence that anyone paid attention to her.

Anne took the night off from the diary and made some notes on a writing pad, then watched a movie on Pay Per View. Before going to bed that evening, she didn't set the alarm, and pulled the heavy curtains closed.

When she awoke it was almost 10:00 a.m. She sat up in bed and looked around at her room, then pressed the power button on the TV and lay back down to attempt to get herself mentally awake. In a few minutes she got up and went to the bathroom, and looked at herself in the mirror. Her hair was a mess. She was wearing a tank top and shorts, and the top showed her collarbone and neck. She took off her clothes and looked at herself, full length, in the mirror, then quickly got embarrassed and turned on the shower and stepped in.

She met Jarred in the lobby at a few minutes after eleven. Her hair was still a little damp, and she wore a simple beige T-shirt and khaki pants with open toed sandals.

"Hi," she said, as she walked up to him.

"Good morning." Jarred looked at her a little longer than normal.

"What?" she asked, as she tilted her head to one side.

"Nothing. You just look a little different…nice necklace," he said.

She reflexively reached up and fingered the pink crystal necklace. She had purchased it on the trip to New York.

"Thank you," she said.

"So, I was thinking brunch or tea."

"What do you want?" she asked.

"I thought I would go for brunch, but I can change," he said.

"That's fine with me. I'm starving," she said.

"Shall we?" He got up and gestured with his hands. He held open the front door and she smiled to herself.

The streets of London were empty compared to the last several days. Jarred turned right and touched her back as he guided her in the correct direction.

"I'm sorry to have bothered you last night. It sounded like you were busy," she said, as they walked on the sidewalk.

"No. Not really. I was just a little surprised," he said.

"So, if your friend is available, I would like to meet her," she said.

"Oh, yes. We can stop and see her later if you want. She doesn't live too far away."

"So, how's your mother?" she asked.

"She's fine. Pop too. I try to see them at least once a week."

She liked that and thought that she needed to call her mom today as well. She made a mental note.

The brunch was at Shenanigan's on the waterfront. She noticed the award 'Best Champagne Brunch' in the window as they went in. It smelled heavenly.

Jarred had obviously called ahead, as they were seated ahead of several other parties waiting for service.

"You can help yourself whenever you want to. It's a buffet." The hostess indicated the long line of very happy people off to her right. The place was alive with chatter and conversation. Food makes people so cheerful, she thought.

"I can wait here if you want to get something," she said, as she put her purse and sweater down on the seat. Jarred looked a bit nonplussed.

"Absolutely not. You're coming with me so I can watch you choose your food. You can learn a lot from the way a person eats at a buffet. Besides, I hear they have mulberry jam here."

She blushed. "That's not fair! You can't bring up faux pas after a week!" she said.

"Anne's rules of etiquette?" he asked.

"Absolutely," she said.

"OK. Glad we have that cleared up." He reached over and grabbed her purse, and slung it over his shoulder.

"What are you doing?" She laughed.

"Helping you. In case you need both hands," he said, and waved her in front of him. She laughed and went in front of him.

They returned to the table laden with food. Jarred took off the purse and set it down by her side, then took a seat opposite her and took a bite of something that Anne had passed over at the buffet.

"What is that?" She pointed to it.

"Sweetbread," he said, with his mouth full.

"Sweet what?" She had a wary look.

"Oh," Jarred swallowed, "do you have a sensitive stomach?" he asked.

"Maybe I shouldn't know," she said.

"Probably a good idea," he said, as he took another bite. "So, what have you discovered in that diary of yours that you are so curious about?" Jarred asked. Anne had just taken a bite of an omelet.

"Umm," she said, and looked at him with her mouth closed, her eyes wide.

"Sorry, Jarred's rule number one. How to impress a girl. Ask her questions right after she has taken a bite... of anything," he smiled.

She pulled the napkin up to her mouth and finished chewing.

"Yes, very impressive," she said, smiling, careful not to expose her teeth as she spoke. She took a drink of orange juice and then settled back in her seat.

"There is this girl in the diary. She was a servant at the Cornwall Estate and she was found dead. I think they suspected John, you remember him, right?" she asked.

"Yes. Anne's beau," he said.

"Correct. So they questioned him, but I'm not sure what happened." She stopped to take a bite of a piece of watermelon.

"So, the diary doesn't say what happened?" he asked.

"Yes, it does, but I don't think anyone was ever convicted. I'm curious if anything happened later," she said.

"Hmmm. I see," Jarred said, as he took a bite of what looked like salmon.

"And there is something else I wanted to ask your friend." Anne had her head down appraising her plate while she spoke.

"And that would be…?" Jarred looked at her but she didn't' look up.

"I was wondering if she could tell me who currently owns the Cornwall Estate. I'm just curious. I was thinking…." She drifted off.

"Do you know you don't finish a lot of your sentences?" Jarred said.

Anne laughed. "I'm sorry! My sister is always saying the same thing. Bad habit. I guess I figure if I never finish the sentence I can't be convicted of anything I might have said."

"Quite strange reasoning," Jarred said.

"I know. I'm a bit strange about some things. But some men find that charming…" Anne said, as she played with her food.

Jarred started laughing. "There you go again!" Anne blushed and nervously picked up her glass of champagne and took a gulp. The bubbles tickled her throat as she swallowed, and she let go a little burp.

"Oh, God!" She held her hand over her mouth and looked like she was going to cry, or burst out laughing; Jarred couldn't tell which.

"Nice," he said, "you realize the Chinese would view that as a compliment." She turned bright red. "However, the English, refined as they are, well they…" He stopped mid sentence and cheered her with his champagne glass, then took a sip.

"Well, there you have it," he said, with a very large grin.

"Oh, God," she said.

After an enjoyable brunch, Jarred escorted Anne to the waterfront and they spent about an hour walking along the boardwalk. The sun broke out periodically and warmed them, and the cool breeze off the water kept them cool. It was a perfect afternoon in London.

Jarred hailed a taxi and gave him an address. He then pulled out his telephone and dialed a number.

"Hello? Ginger?"

"It's Jarred… Yes. I was wondering if you might have a moment to meet a friend from the States… we're about fifteen minutes away. Great. We'll swing by." Jarred hung up.

They were let out on a row of small houses like Anne had seen in magazines and movies. In fact, she thought this might have been in that Hugh Grant flick.

"Was this…?" She pointed down the street.

"Notting Hill," he said.

"Cool," she said.

"Now, there is a truly American term," he said, but she was too busy looking up and around at the famously colored houses.

Jarred went up to one and knocked.

"One minute!" They heard a voice and then the stomping of shoes going down stairs.

"Hi, Jerry!" she said, and Anne looked at him funny.

"Hi, Ginger. This is Anne," Jarred said.

"Hello, Anne." Ginger stuck out her hand and they shook.

"Come on up." Ginger took off up the stairs and Anne followed with Jarred behind her. The flat opened into a small one-bedroom apartment, nicely furnished, with contemporary furniture.

"Have a seat anywhere. Tea?" Ginger asked. Anne and Jarred sat on the sofa, a few feet apart.

"Sure," Anne said.

"No, thanks," Jarred said.

"Tea for two." Ginger turned away and reappeared with two cups, saucers and a selection of tea.

Anne picked Chamomile.

"So, you are from the States, eh?" Ginger said.

"Yes. Chicago," Anne said.

"And what brings you here—to London, that is?" Ginger asked as she sat in a well-worn armed chair.

"Work. My company sent me over to work on some legal matters with Jarred's firm. That's how we met," Anne said.

"Well. Good! Jerry and I went to school together but, once in a while, we get to work together…what with him being in law and me being at Scotland Yard. Jerry said you had some questions about Scotland Yard? Mind you, I'm just an investigative clerk. That means I mostly do research, and such," Ginger said.

"I think that's perfect," Anne said.

For the next ten minutes she explained the diary that she had found, and Ginger and Jarred paid close attention.

"That is quite a story you have found, Anne. You know the Cornwalls were once a very powerful family. I don't think Lord Cornwall is alive, but I think I heard his son was living somewhere in one of the colonies," Ginger said.

Anne found it funny that they still referred to them as 'colonies'.

"Yes. I believe Hong Kong," Anne said.

"Yes! That's it. Anyway, the family, if they are around, may not like it very much to have someone poking into such an old case. You do realize that diaries are not the most reliable sources of information? There could be a lot of conjecture or fantasy…but if it happened we should have something about it in the computer system. I doubt it would do any harm to have a go and see. Do you know what happened to Anne... I mean the one in the diary?"

"Nothing very good. It seems that she led a difficult life," Anne said.

"It was hard being a Royal back then, as it is even now. You have the titles but not nearly the power as the families did in days past. Still, the pride is born into the children, and some find it a difficult cross to bear. Just ask Jerry."

"What?" Anne said, and looked at Jarred, who stared at Ginger.

"Oh, sorry. Just thought you knew. Perhaps you two should have a talk later," Ginger said, and smiled.

"We will," Anne said, and she looked back at Jarred, who shrugged his shoulders and remained unusually quiet.

"Do you know anything about the Cornwall Estate out in Kent?" Anne asked.

"No. Not really. It's not my neck of the woods out there. But Jerry should know something..." Ginger said, and Anne looked at him again.

"I'll explain, Anne. It's really not a state secret. My dad married into some very, very distant royalty," Jarred said.

"Anne, give me your number and I'll give you a ring tomorrow with what I find out. Either way, it sure has made your visit an exciting one, eh?" Ginger said.

"Thank you, Ginger." Anne turned and looked at Jarred. "Shall we go? You can show me the house where that funny man in the underwear answered the door for Julia Roberts."

Ginger laughed. "Ya. I think a lot of the Yanks look for that place. I'm not sure it's really here. Never saw the movie. Don't like Hugh Grant."

Jarred and Anne excused themselves and left the flat. As soon as they were out of eyesight Anne grabbed Jarred's arm and stopped. He knew what was coming, and winced.

"Royalty?" she asked.

"No. I mean yes. But it's like being the tenth cousin by marriage and a couple of in-laws to President Bush. It's really not worth mentioning, and I've never met anyone important. Truly," Jarred said.

"But still, that is a bit of an omission," Anne stopped herself. "But it does explain how you know so much about the Cornwalls and the other families out in Canterbury." She looked at him again. He had both his hands in the air.

"I surrender! It was not intentional. Next time I meet an American I shall dutifully introduce myself as Sir Jerry Mulberry, Lord of my Dockland's flat, Jester to the Queen, by marriage." He laughed at himself and she hit him as hard as she could on the arm.

"Ouch. Vicious woman!" He mocked like he was hurt and rubbed his forearm. Two tourists passed by them and walked out into the street to give them a wide berth, and Anne turned candy apple red.

"Jarred!" She looked around for anyone else who might have noticed.

Jarred bent over and whispered in her ear.

"I'm also a secret agent for Her Majesty's government," he winked at her but didn't smile.

"Knock it off, Jarred." Anne turned around and started walking down the street. Jarred quickly caught up, but she didn't look at him.

"I'm in the mood for something," Anne said.

"Like food?" Jarred asked. But we just—" Jarred started and she cut him off with her hand.

"Like ice cream, dessert, tea?" he asked.

"Any of the above. Your choice," she said.

"Fine. I know just the place." He grabbed her arm and continued in the same direction. She didn't resist.

:

That evening, at the hotel, Anne was in a funny mood. She was both happy and anxious at the same time. She wanted to read the diary but was almost afraid to learn anything more. Maybe Ginger was right. Maybe it was fanciful fantasy. She finally picked up her cell phone and called her parents. Her dad, whom she adored, answered, and they talked about her trip and the missing cross, the weather, and the places she had visited. After she hung up she felt better, almost like she had confessed her sins to a priest.

Anne turned back the cover on her bed and sprawled out on it, still dressed in the clothes she had worn. She took the diary, placed it in front of her, and turned it to the last page that she had read, which was marked with Betty's last letter.

Chapter 31

May 11, 1939 Cornwall Estate, Kent

Something has awakened me from my disturbed sleep. My clock says it is midnight. I am writing this while sitting at my window to capture the light of the moon, because the footsteps I heard have come from the front of the house, so I dare not turn on my light. I saw someone leave. I think it may have been John. I am so sad. My heart aches and I have cried until I have no more tears. Lizzy must think I am mad. I cannot possibly explain to her what I feel. I want to believe John so badly, but can I be certain he is telling the truth?

"Good of you to join me, Johnny." Michael was dressed in all dark clothing, and he opened the driver's door.

"I'll drive," he said. John got out and held out his hand.

"The letter first," he said. Michael smiled and pulled out a folded piece of paper from his pocket. John took it and walked over to the headlights in order to read. He returned a minute later and without a word opened the rear door and sat down.

"Beautiful night for a drive, Johnny. You could almost drive by moonlight." John remained silent. Michael started up the automobile and drove down the road without his lights on. They could see the road clearly until they drove through a shelter of trees.

"Turn them on, Michael. Don't be stupid," John said.

Michael turned on the headlights, and started singing a bar song.

"Where are we going?" John asked.

"The port," Michael said.

"What for? Everything's gone."

"Not quite everything," Michael turned around and smiled.

"So, Johnny. Here's how it goes: We need to make this a bit quick. Rad, my man, will be there, and he is going to send off the other guard for some eats. That should give us about ten minutes to remove the boxes," Michael said.

"Boxes?" John remembered only one thing in boxes at the port.

"Yes sir!" Michael was in an especially good mood.

John watched the speedometer as it passed seventy. The car shook violently when Michael hit ruts in the road.

"Slow it down, Michael," he said.

"Oh. You *are* paying attention," Michael slowed down a little. "Just making sure. These details are important now. The Devil is in the details, you know."

"Listen, Michael. Let's get this straight. You are blackmailing me to do this. I neither want to be here, nor should I be. Just get us there so we can finish this and go home, then I can stop hearing your revolting voice," John said.

"OK by me," Michael said, as he started to whistle between puffs on his cigarette.

John rolled down his window to clear the smoke out of the car. He looked out at the rolling hills as they drove by and wondered if he had the guts to kill him. It would be doing the world a favor.

"What the hell?" Michael exclaimed. John looked up and saw him looking in the rear view mirror.

"What's wrong?" John said.

"A car just pulled out behind us, out of nowhere…" his voice got hard, "you wouldn't have tipped anyone off to our little expedition now, would you?"

John took a deep breath before answering. His voice needed conviction.

"Why in the world would I do that? I'm sure that we are about to do something unlawful. I certainly don't want anyone having any new reason to suspect me," John said. He had turned around and looked out the back window. About two hundred yards behind them a car followed.

Michael floored the pedal and the car jostled around so violently on the rutted road that John had to brace himself so that he wouldn't be thrown around like a rag doll.

"Slow it down, Michael!"

Michael ignored him and took a hard right, which threw John against the opposite door.

"Dammit, Michael!"

Suddenly Michael made one more turn into a grove of trees and shut off the lights. John could still see the ember of the cigarette he held between his lips reflecting in the windshield.

"Keep quiet!" Michael said. He held something in his right hand as he turned toward John and watched. After the car had passed Michael got out of the car and opened John's door.

"You're driving," he said, and motioned with the object in his right hand.

"Why should I do that?" John was trying to stall for time.

"Get out and drive! This isn't a negotiation!" Michael pointed the object at John and his fears were confirmed. It was a gun.

"Fine," John got in the driver's seat and Michael sat directly behind him.

"Start it up and let's get going. You know the way. If you get any ideas I won't hesitate to use this," Michael said. John knew it was true.

After about another thirty minutes of silence they arrived at the port. John was directed to turn the headlights off well before they reached the gate, and a figure came out of the shadows, and allowed them in. The car continued as far as it could go, and John turned it around and backed it up to the nearest loading area.

They both stayed in the car, Michael rolled down his window and Rad came up to him.

"You've got something for me, Michael?" he asked, with his black gloved palm extended.

Michael reached into his jacket and pulled out some vials and handed them to Rad. Now John knew for sure where the wild looks of Michael had come from. He ignored the exchange.

"Ten minutes. That's it," Rad said, and disappeared into the darkness.

Without the lights on, the building was almost completely dark. It was hard to even recognize it from their prior visits. Michael took out a flashlight, turned it on, and signaled for John to follow him. They went past the outside warehouse and passed the doors where Michael had pressured the guards to let him in. Unlike the time they had been there before the interior room was empty. There was a single empty cart with wheels on it about six feet long and two feet wide. It had two shelves on it, and Michael rolled it in front of him to the far side of the room, then started stomping on the floorboards till they both heard a change in resonance. He held the gun loosely in his right hand always making sure that John was at least a few feet from him.

"Here. Hold on to this," Michael said, and handed John a bulky portable light. John took it and directed the light to where he was standing. Michael took a small cat's paw from his jacket and removed a few loose nails, then pulled up several boards, took the flashlight from John, and shone it down the dark hole.

"Here," he handed it back to John, "you're going in." Michael backed away from the opening and signaled him.

There were some boxes, about five feet down, and he sat on the edge of the opening and used the top box as a step. It smelled like the crawl space of the house he had grown up in. When he had played hide and seek with the neighbor kids, it had been the best place to hide, because no one except him would ever go there.

John lifted up the first box and swung it up with a thud to the floor where Michael was standing, then pushed it till it was out of the way.

They both heard the car drive up, and John froze. Michael turned off the light and ducked to the floor where John's head was.

"I'm not covering for you, Michael, if this goes bad," he whispered.

"If we get caught, Johnny boy, we'll *both* hang. This is treason." Michael's voice was seething as John pulled himself out of the hole. Michael held the gun at John and signaled for him to be silent, then went over to the window where the car had pulled up. John went with him and looked out.

There was another guard speaking to Rad, who was obviously trying to get him to move, but the guard sat down and stretched his feet out in front of him.

"Rad, I'm not going anywhere. The garrison will be here in thirty minutes, and then I'm going back to the barracks to catch some shuteye. I'm going to eat my chicken, have a drag, and wait," the guard said.

Rad looked up toward Michael, shrugged his shoulders, and walked off.

"You dumb ass!" Michael said, under his breath. "He's high." John had never heard the term before, but he gathered the connotation.

"What are you going to do?" John turned to Michael.

"Only one option left… I'm not going to get caught, and we are out of time." Michael started to walk toward the door.

John grabbed his arm and hissed. "Are you crazy?!"

"I thought you already knew the answer to that."

Michael yanked his arm away. "And what do you want to do, go out there and give yourself up? How are you going to explain to the police, your father, and *my* father what you are doing on government property at this time of night?" John was silent.

"That's what I thought, Johnny. All talk—no guts." Michael went to open the door and John grabbed him by the arm holding the gun.

"No!" he yelled. The guard immediately reacted and spun up on his feet. His revolver was pointed toward them.

"Stop it!" Michael yelled as he kneed him in the groin, which sent John to the floor, moaning. "You screw up!" he added, as he kicked him then turned toward the guard who was now running toward them.

"Hold it! Don't move!" John heard the guard's voice simultaneous with two shots. He turned on the floor to look where Michael stood, and then stumbled to his feet. He could see through the door to the outside. The guard lay face down, sprawled on the concrete ramp. A dark pool of liquid was forming around the man's left side.

Rad came running up the driveway and saw Michael with the gun drawn, and the fallen guard.

"Wha-t, Wh-at have you done?" he stammered.

Michael walked up to him and lowered his gun.

"Calm down, Rad. Calm down. There was nothing else I could do. He saw us. We would have all been caught. You didn't want that, did you?" Michael said.

"N-o. N-o. But what am I going to say?" Rad's eyes were wide, and panicked.

"Nothing, Rad. You're going to say nothing." Rad looked up at Michael as the gun fired again, and Rad looked down at his stomach. He kept backing up until he finally fell on the ground, back first.

John was mortified, and stood watching as the whole scene unfolded. It was like a dream, a devil's nightmare, and he was transfixed.

Michael walked up to him gestured with the pistol.

"We've got work to do. Let's move," Michael said, and followed John back to the hole in the ground.

With the six boxes safely in the trunk of the car, Michael was in a very good mood. He took a seat in the back and told John to drive. John was appalled at what had happened in the last few minutes and it took every fiber of his will to calm down.

:

About twenty minutes later the man watched the speeding car as it passed him. It was 2:30am. This time he was a little more cautious and waited until they had almost disappeared before pulling out to follow them. With the moon high above, he turned off his lights and sped up until he was within hailing distance. John had watched the car close the gap in the rear view mirror, and tried to keep Michael talking.

"So, why steal the gold? You have enough money of your own. What are you going to do with it?" John asked, as he glanced again in the mirror. The inspector's car was less than fifty yards back.

"Anything I want, the point is that I was able to take it and no one will ever know," he paused, and pointed the gun at John, "except you of course. And you're in this past your neck anyway." Michael laughed and looked out the window at the passing hills.

"What about the men that you just shot? You don't think there will be an investigation?" John asked.

"I expect there will be. We'll have to see…" Michael stopped and John looked at him in the mirror, "What—" he had turned around and was looking out the back window, the inspector's car was hurtling toward them.

"Step on it. Now!" Michael pushed the revolver into John's shoulder and John yanked the wheel to his right flinging Michael against the opposite door. Then he stomped on the brakes, which propelled Michael forward into the back of the front seat. There was a string of obscenities and a loud crash as the inspector rammed the rear of John's car and spun it sideways. Both cars came to a stop amid a shower of gravel and the next moment was eerily silent, like the proverbial calm before a storm. John released his death grip on the steering wheel, yanked open the door, and ran a few feet before he heard the glass shatter and the sound of the gunshot. He froze and put his hands in the air, his back was toward Michael.

"Where are you going, Johnny?" Michael's voice was calm, steady.

"Throw out the weapon and get out of the automobile!" The voice was unmistakably Inspector Roarke. He was walking in their direction, from behind them.

"Inspector! What are you doing out at this time of night?" Michael yelled from where he was sitting.

"Michael! Throw out the gun and get out of the car. Whatever you're up to, it's over," the inspector said.

"OK. Alright."

John was relieved to hear a thud as Michael threw a dark object out of the broken window. He heard his car door open and he turned around with his hands up and took a few steps over to where Michael was now sitting. He could see the inspector standing about ten feet away his gun pointed towards both of them. As he started to stand up, John saw the intense look on Michael's face and glanced toward his feet where he thought the gun had landed. The cat's paw was lying on the ground.

"Inspector!" John yelled, and reached for Michael's arm as he raised it in a smooth motion. Michael was stronger than he expected and he could feel the kick of the revolver as the trigger was pulled. Two shots rang out and John watched in horror as the inspector was propelled back by the bullets. He crashed against his own car and fell to the ground holding his chest. Michael wrenched his arm away from John and walked over to the inspector while he kept the gun pointed level at John. The inspector's eyes stared vacantly at the sky and he made no movement. Michael turned back.

"What were you up to, John? Did you set this up?" His voice was again strangely calm. There was no hint of panic or stress.

John stood facing him, his car partially blocking the line of sight. He thought about trying to escape but it would have been a fool's run. He took a couple of breaths and tried to calculate what Michael would do with him.

"I could just kill you," Michael lowered the gun and held it at his side. You could run. That would make it a bit more exciting," he pursed his lips and stared at him.

"No. I think it would be better that you live. Get in the car."

John obeyed. At least it would buy him some time.

"You realize we have to leave," Michael said, as he lit up a cigarette. They were twenty minutes or so to the estate.

"Leave?" John asked.

"What? You don't think they won't find your damaged car and link it to what happened? We're the prime suspects. Well that's not quite true. *You* are the main suspect… again." John hated the inclusive pronoun.

Michael was silent for a few minutes.

"You're going to drop me off at the estate so I can gather some things. You will take my car and meet me at a place I know," Michael told him the London address.

"And in case you get any bright ideas, remember what I'm capable of," Michael added.

John thought about his options. There weren't many. He could go to the police and try and explain his way out of everything. That very well could end in disaster for him. Or he could run. Neither choice was acceptable.

"Fine," was all that he said.

They returned to the estate by 3:00 a.m. and Michael had John get out at the road and then took John's car around to the rear of the estate. John walked up the driveway and around the back to the panty entrance, and entered the kitchen. There was a small table on the far side of the kitchen where the staff took their meals. John went over, sat down on a chair, and put his head in his palms with his elbows on the table. His hands shook so badly they scratched his scalp. He willed himself to calm down. He desperately needed a clear head.

"John?" The voice was soft, like an angel's, and the last voice he wanted to hear at that moment.

"John?" Anne walked over and sat beside him. She could see he had tears in his eyes. She reached out and touched his shoulder, then withdrew her hand and rested it on the crook of his elbow. She could feel him shaking. "What's wrong?" she asked.

John looked up from his hands, his face in pain, and tried to speak, but his jaw was frozen and would not move. The tears kept coming, but he no longer cared.

"John, you're scaring me. What's wrong?" she asked.

He forced himself to take several deep breaths, and was finally able to speak.

"Very bad. It is very bad."

Anne left her hand where it was.

"Please tell me, John. Please!" Anne pleaded.

"I can't, Anne. Please don't ask. I can't say anything." John steadied himself and looked at her.

"I love you, Anne. Never forget that," he said.

Anne looked at him, her face awash with emotion and she started to cry.

"Ohhh, isn't that precious," the voice made both of them jerk their heads to the pantry door.

"Oh, Anne. I forgot. I'm supposed to tell you something. That little detail about Theresa being with Johnny on her fateful night. We'll, that's not quite true. She was actually *my* little play thing." Michael went over to the kitchen sink and washed his hands.

"Oh, and one more thing, if either of you think about telling what I just said to the police, I'll deny it, and I'll make sure Johnny here goes to the gallows for her murder. And that would leave Annie with only me to comfort her. See, Johnny? I told her, just like I said I would. I do keep my word. So let's just keep this a little secret amongst us three. What do you say?" Michael looked at them both and nodded.

"I'll take that as an agreement. Don't stay up too late, you love birds. Wouldn't want you to get caught in an inappropriate situation. That could just *ruin* the reputation for such a promising young lady," he said, as he shut the panty door.

"John, what has he done?" Anne asked.

"Things I can't even believe."

"Like what?" she asked.

"Anne, he's truly wicked. He's done it again," he said.

"Murdered?"

He looked at her and nodded.

"Go to the police John. Tell them."

"I would like to, Anne. I will if you want me to," he looked at her.

"What do you mean if I want you to. Isn't it the right thing to do?"

"Yes, it is. But I don't think they will believe me. They would more likely arrest me."

"I don't understand… for what?"

"Anne, I don't know. It's all a blur. He has involved me… again. I tried to stop him. I tried, but you know how he is."

"But if you don't go to the police, what else can you do?" her voice was pleading.

"I can leave," he said.

"Leave? Where to? They'll find you, wherever you go."

He wasn't sure she understood the consequences if he stayed.

"Anne. If I stay I could hang," he looked at her again and held her eyes. She started crying.

"No. No. They wouldn't. You didn't do anything, right?"

"But it *looks* like I did. Michael has made sure of that."

"But it's his word against yours…" she tried to wipe the tears away from her eyes.

"Yes. But your family is very powerful. I think it is likely that both of us, but certainly I, would go to the gallows."

"No…" Anne said, as she forced herself to think,"but where would you go?"

"A long way away, Anne, maybe America." He grabbed her hands and held them. "But if you want me to stay and try to fight this, I'll do it. To me, either choice is wretched."

"I – I can't make that decision…" Anne's eyes were wide and her hands were shaking.

"I have no time Anne. I have to make a choice tonight, right now. I either wait for the police, or leave. I'm sorry, I shouldn't be asking you to make my decision…"

"I don't want you to die… I couldn't take that."

"Then I will leave."

"But when will I see you again?" Anne's words came out in shudders.

John got up from the chair and kneeled beside her like he had always imagined he would do when he proposed.

"Anne. I don't know. Maybe never… if I run they will always be looking for me. I will never be able to return here."

"I can't do this, John. I can't…"

"You…" John started saying something.

"What?" Anne stared down at him their hands clasped together on her lap.

"No. I can't ask it of you," John stood up and willed away his emotions.

"Please. What?" she asked.

"No. It is not fair," he said.

"*Please,* tell me."

John reluctantly decided to proffer what he viewed as his last chance at any kind of happiness in his life.

"You could come with me."

Anne's eyes widened with the words and John's heart soared. And just as quickly his hopes were whisked away as her eyes showed the realization of what such a radical decision would mean.

It wasn't a fair question at all and he stood up, walking toward the door. He could hear Anne's sobs behind him.

"John?" he stopped and turned around. He could make out her hazel eyes, even from that distance.

"Anne. I love you. Please don't forget me."

John walked out of the room, leaving Anne at the table watching him. Her breaths were shallow and rapid, and her body was shaking uncontrolled. Still, she watched him till he disappeared.

He had wanted to tell her so many things in those last few minutes. He wanted to pour out his heart. Confess to what had happened when they were thirteen. But it would have been unfair to her and if Michael found out who knows what he would do to them both. No. His bad choices would be his cross to bear.

John kept going until he passed through the front door, and out onto the driveway. He got in his automobile and sat there for a moment before Anne heard the engine start and the gravel move as he drove off. It was the last time she would ever see him.

May 12, 1939 Cornwall Estate, Kent

He left. He left. I should have gone with him but I couldn't. I couldn't. Lizzy needs me. My family is here. What would we have done in America? It isn't fair! I hate Michael. I hate him like I hate the Devil. I hate myself. Should I have asked him to stay here to die on the gallows? Can I be happy with the knowledge that he is alive somewhere else? What of me? I'm sorry, John, I'm so sorry.

:

London, 2004

Anne awoke to the sounds of a seagull outside her bedroom window. She was still dressed in the clothes she wore last night, the diary open in front of her. She read the last entry again, and it once more brought tears to her eyes. She wondered what she would have done if she had faced the same situation. What if she lost trust in someone she cared about? Was she strong enough to take a leap of faith? To hell with what other people might think!

Anne showered and dressed, then grabbed a muffin and latte on the way to Turnberry & Sons. When she arrived, Jarred was not there, and the office was mysteriously quiet. She looked on the computer and confirmed that it was indeed Monday. Perhaps it was a legal holiday? But, then again, the doors were open, so everyone probably was just running late.

She ran down to the fax machine to check and see if the fax had come in from the Department of Culture, Media and Sport. Cindi, was in the communications room

"Hi, Cindi. Did I receive a fax over the weekend?" Anne asked.

"Good morning, Anne. Yes. I have one here for you." Anne walked over and picked up the two pages.

"Did Jarred come in yet?" Anne asked, then immediately felt self conscious, but Cindi didn't blink an eye.

"No love. I don't believe he is coming in. Something about needing to handle some personal things," Cindi said.

"Oh," Anne said.

"I'm sure I could reach him if you need something, dear." Anne thought she was a little young to be using all those pet names.

"No. No big deal. I can call him if I need something," Anne said, and walked back down the hallway.

She looked at the fax as she walked. The Ministry of Arts had approved their application to have the cross, identified as a registered treasure of the Republic of Georgia.

Anne sat down at the computer station and started typing an email to Harry, but then changed her mind and instead picked up the phone and dialed his mobile number.

"Hello?" There was something wrong with Harry's voice.

"Hi, Harry. It's Anne," she said.

"Oh. Hi, Anne…" She heard something drop, and Harry let go an expletive, then someone else asked what was going on.

"Is something wrong?"

Harry came back on the line.

"No…"

Anne paused for a second and realized what she had done. It must have been 2:00 a.m. in Chicago. "I'm sorry, Harry! I forgot about the time difference! I'll send you an email."

"No. That's quite all right. I always get up at this time to let out the dog anyway," Harry said.

"What's up?" he asked.

"Well…. We got the application approved for the registry, that's all," she said.

"Oh. That's great, Anne. Nice work," Harry said, obviously falling back asleep.

"Goodnight, Harry. I'll call you later. It's good to hear your voice," she said, and hung up the phone. She heard him say goodnight right before the receiver hit the cradle.

"Oh God, Anne, where is your brain at?" she said, to the telephone. But hearing his voice did make her feel better. She thought that perhaps she was getting a bit homesick.

The rest of the morning she finished up paperwork for the extradition of the cross if it ever came to fruition, and checked on the Internet for upcoming auctions from the major houses. There were several dates that were now being published for sales of Eastern European religious artifacts and treasures. Anne wrote down the list on a pad of paper. One looked of particular interest, coming up in a few weeks, in November.

Anne wrote an email to Harry, apologizing for the phone call and letting him know what she was doing. Then sent one off to her mom and dad, and a girlfriend in Chicago.

There were two emails in her inbox from her 'private' list'. The first one was from her sister Jen, and the second from Tony. She made a mental note to remove him from her 'private' list. Maybe the spam filter would screen him off she mused. That would be appropriate.

She deleted the email from Tony without even reading it, and read the one from Jen, who just wanted to know about her love life, her favorite topic of conversation.

Dear Jen,
Did I mention I was going to London again? We'll, I'm here. I've been working on that cross situation. I'm sure you have no problem recalling that! I think I've pretty much gone as far as I can go for now. OK. So, in the meantime, I've been having fun learning about some history, and such. I think I told you about the book I found in Chicago with that inscription in it from 'Anne'?! We'll, I actually went to her house yesterday. What an absolute kick, AND I have her diary. A nice old lady now lives in the house. She kept it all these years - what a sad story. Remind me not to live this poor girl's life. I did discover a 60-year-old murder though! Jarred, (remember him), introduced me to a friend of his who is doing some research for me. I'm really getting into this story. I feel almost like she is thanking me. Someone is finally hearing her story and finding out what happened (not in a weird way – you understand?!). I'm having the time of my life.

Love,
Anne

P.S. Yes. I'm enjoying Jarred's company as well. That is all you're going to get out of me!

Anne looked at the email and thought to herself: I really am enjoying this. Though heartbreaking, learning about this story has made me feel more alive than I've ever felt. There was Jarred as well.

She looked at the phone, and almost called him, but thought better of it.

Anne took off for lunch and walked around the neighborhood looking for a suitable place. She finally settled on a café with an outdoor patio, ordered a sandwich and a glass of water with no ice, and people watched for the next hour.

Upon returning to the office there was a message on a Post-it note on her computer.

"Call Ginger 020 5555 1212." She still wasn't used to all the numbers over here.

She sat down at her desk, settled in her wooden seat, pulled out her pad and pen, and picked up the receiver. She got voice mail.

"Hello. You've reached Ginger at Scotland Yard. Please leave your message at the tone."

"Hello, Ginger. This is Anne. Looking forward to your call. I'm back at the office. Turnberry… oh you have it." Anne hated leaving messages.

She stared at the phone for five minutes and then thought about calling her again, but refrained. She decided to use the restroom, and ran out the door and down the carpeted hallway, nearly running over some short, bald man with a briefcase.

"Watch out, Love! What's the 'urry?" he said.

"Sorry!" She cringed, and waived to him, then exited to the bathroom.

When she returned down the hall she could hear a phone ringing, and ran into her office, grabbing the handset.

"Hello? Hello?" she asked.

"Hello? Anne?" A woman's voice asked.

"Ginger?" Anne asked.

"Yes! Good. You remember," Ginger said.

"Of course I remember, Ginger. Thank you so much for calling back," Anne said.

"Well, I did a little poking around here on the computer, and I'm afraid I don't have too much news," Ginger said.

"Anything would be great," Anne said, and picked up her no. 2 pencil, moving her pad to where she could take notes.

"There are some strange things about this Anne." Ginger's voice was very soft, almost as if she was trying to not be overheard.

"What, Ginger? I can barely hear you?" Anne said.

"Sorry. Can I call you back in a minute?" Ginger said.

"Uh… sure, of course," Anne said, and hung up.

A few minutes later the phone rang again.

"Hello?" Anne said. She heard cars and trucks in the background.

"It's me, Anne. Ginger. Sorry about that but there is something strange about this case," Ginger said. "I'm not sure it's a good idea to dig too much into this."

Anne could feel goose pimples began to form on her arms, but she couldn't resist.

"Why Ginger? What's so strange?" Anne asked. There was no reply.

"Ginger?"

"Well, first of all it is strange that the case is still active. I mean, not like it's just never been solved, but that *someone* is holding it open for investigation or for some other reason. You see, when a case is unsolved it remains technically active, but no one is assigned to actively monitor it. But, if someone is working the case or is monitoring its progress, they can tell when anyone else has made inquires about it. And I'm afraid they know I've looked at the case," Ginger said.

"Has that caused you any problems? I'm so sorry if it has, Ginger. I certainly didn't mean to cause you trouble," Anne said.

"No. I don't think so, at least. But there were a couple of other things that tell me you should stop asking about this. One, MI5 has this case assigned to them. That is quite unusual," she said.

"I don't understand. Why would an intelligence agency be monitoring a murder case?" Anne asked.

"Well, that's it love. I don't know. Normally they don't get involved unless there is something about national security. Another unusual part is that the MI5 security clearance is very, very old. I'm thinking someone from the original investigation took this case into MI5 a long time ago. Just for curiosity's sake, is anyone else mentioned in the diary? Any men?" Ginger asked.

Anne thought for a moment then listed them off. "Lord Cornwall and his son, and Inspector Roarke, Sir Percy and his son. Wait. Sir Percy Harrison was his whole name, I think, that's it."

"Say again? What was that last name?" Ginger asked.

"Harrison. Sir Percy and John Harrison," Anne said.

"Are you certain?" Ginger asked again.

"Yes. I'm positive, their names are all over the diary," Anne said.

"Does Jarred know about this?" Ginger asked. Anne thought it was a strange question.

"Well… I think so. Yes. I think I've mentioned it," Anne said.

"And he didn't say anything?" Ginger asked.

Anne started to feel very uneasy.

"No... Why, Ginger? Why would he mention something about someone who lived sixty years ago?" Anne asked.

"Sir Percy Harrison *is* MI5, or was, I should say," Ginger said, but Anne felt the answer was incomplete.

"And Jarred should have known this?" Anne asked.

"Yes. He definitely would have. You see, Sir Percy Harrison was Jarred's great uncle," Ginger said.

Anne nearly dropped the phone.

"Wh-at?" she asked.

"Yes. Jarred's mother's maiden name is Harrison. Her mother's uncle was Sir Percy. I thought he would have told you this after our last conversation. Sir Percy later became a cabinet minister of finance, succeeding Lord Cornwall. He became a very powerful man. Jarred is related by blood, albeit very little blood, to that royal line," Ginger said.

"I'm not sure... I don't know why he didn't tell me," Anne said.

"I don't know, dear, but he probably had good reason. One more thing: I did receive a call about my query into this case, a bit ago, but not from MI5. I'm not sure who he was, but he wanted to know why I had queried the system about it. I feigned a mistake and hung up on him. But I don't think I'll be doing anything else on this. I hope you understand," Ginger said.

"Absolutely. I'm sorry I've caused you so much trouble as it is," Anne said.

"Oh. I'm sure it's nothing. No worries," Ginger said, and hung up.

Anne sat in her chair trying to understand the meaning of this last revelation. Her immediate reaction was to call Jarred, but she thought better of it and decided to keep it to herself for now. She needed to figure some things out.

Chapter 32

Anne spent the afternoon handling queries about various ongoing and unrelated subjects from the Chicago office that had accumulated in her email. A little after 4:00 p.m., her eyes were dry and exhausted from working on the computer and she shut everything down and took a circuitous route back to the hotel. A typical afternoon drizzle started and her hair was damp, her sweater wet, but she was lost in thought, and didn't really notice. As the hotel came into view, Anne saw the familiar black Merkur sitting outside, and hesitated for a moment before proceeding in. Jarred sat in the lobby and got up when she came into view.

"Hi there. You look like an Afghan I used to have as a child. Ever hear of something called a brolly?" Jarred said, and smiled.

"A brolly?" Anne asked, not sure whether to smile or not.

"Oh, that's right, you Yanks call it an umbrella. Such an ignominious name." This failed to get the expected smile and Jarred quickly added. "Do you want to dry off? We can go up to the room."

"Umm. No, that's alright. I left it a mess..." Anne drifted off, but Jarred thought better of commenting on the habit. Anne sat down on the seat kitty-corner to him.

"So. I'm sorry I didn't come in today. Some pressing matters came up. Family things," Jarred said.

"Well, actually it ended up being a good thing. I got a lot accomplished, things I had been neglecting. So, is everything OK with your family?" she asked.

"I think it will be." Jarred paused for a moment. "One of my uncles was having some issues that needed my attention." He looked at her again, puzzled.

"Is everything OK, Anne? You seem a bit—well, distracted," Jarred asked.

"Sorry. Just have some things on my mind. So, what uncle is this? The Royal?" Anne asked

"Well... I guess you could call him that. But really, there are so many titles running around this country it's hard to keep track of them all," Jarred said.

"Ginger called me today," Anne said.

"Who? Oh. Yes. Ginger... and did she find out anything useful for you?" Jarred said.

"Just that someone was monitoring this sixty year-old case." Anne looked at him for any reaction but didn't get any.

"That seems a bit strange," Jarred said.

"She thought so," Anne said, "even so, she did mention a couple of other interesting aspects about some of the people involved in the original incident. She said that this case was giving her some unusual vibes." Anne couldn't think of any clearer way to give Jarred an opportunity to fess up.

"Well, Anne. Perhaps it is better this is dropped. You know, some people get quite put out when others meddle in their business. If Ginger was concerned, it sounds like it would be wise to drop it. It certainly isn't worth getting into any trouble over," Jarred said.

Anne shook her head. "I might...."

Jarred looked at his watch. "Listen, I'm kind of tied up tonight on the same family matter, so I just wanted to stop by and make sure you were fine. The office said you had left a while ago, so I just took a chance and came here. I'm sorry I disappeared on you today." He stood up and looked down at her.

"Shall I see you in the morning then?" he asked.

Anne tried her best to smile and nod her head, at which point Jarred turned around and walked out the front door. Anne watched him through the glass as he got in his car and drove away. He was talking into his cell phone as he disappeared from view.

Anne looked around the lobby, then got up and took the elevator to her room. The man in the corner had watched Jarred leave, and he followed her with his eyes till the doors closed.

When Anne entered her room she went into the bathroom and looked in the mirror. She smiled as she turned her head one way, and then another, her hair sopped together and moving as one, and thought that she indeed looked like one of those Afghan dogs with wet hair.

She was disturbed by Jarred's lack of disclosure, but she reassured herself that he must have a good reason and decided to give it time. With the blow dryer turned on, she didn't hear the telephone ring, and didn't see the message light flashing until some time later. When she finally retrieved the message, she wished she had caught the call.

"Hello, Anne, this is Ginger again. Say, I was just wondering if you mentioned to Jarred that we had talked. No biggie, so I'll just catch up with you when I can."

Anne looked at the clock and it was almost six, too late to call. And besides, Anne didn't have her phone number, at least not her home number. She walked over to the window and looked down to the street. The drizzle had turned to rain and the water running down the pane obscured her vision, but she thought she saw a car like Jarred's down below, and put her palm up to the glass. She could feel the coldness of the rain.

Anne ordered a spinach salad and a bowl of chicken soup from room service and settled down for the night. The diary awaited, and although she had a bad feeling about the direction it was going, she knew she had to find out. She sat on the sofa and opened it.

May 12, 1939 Cornwall Estate, Kent

I think I shall go insane. Should I have agreed to go? Should I have asked him to stay? I miss him terribly.

Father has been very agitated and told Lizzy and I to stay upstairs, which is fine with me. I do not know what I should do about John. The night has offered up no solutions, and he has not returned. I think that, if he did return, I would do anything he asked. I am scared that I shall never see him again.

Sleep has escaped me. I think I shall faint from exhaustion but, when I close my eyes, mad dreams and visions make my heart panic. I have not eaten anything but some bread, but I must not show my pain to Lizzy. She has much to worry about as it is.

I pray all day long for relief but I feel none. Perhaps God himself has abandoned me. If this is to be my life, why oh God, was I born?

:

Anne put down the diary and stared out the window at the pouring rain. She tried to imagine what this poor girl went through: the self-doubt and self-loathing punctuated by despair, the doubt whether she wanted to live or not. A single event not of her making that had turned her life into chaos.

She had no idea how long she had been gazing at the window when the knock on the door came. It made her yelp and jump out of her seat. She just barely caught the diary as it fell to the floor.

"Room service!" the voice said.

"One minute please!" Anne said. She ran to the bathroom to look at her eyes. They were red and she splashed some cold water on her face and rubbed them, then wiped off with a towel and answered the door. The young man looked at her, and she turned away and pointed to the area by the sofa, where he set the trolley up and uncovered her meal. She signed the receipt, giving him a nice tip, and he left. She hoped the tip would make him forget her appearance.

The chicken soup was lukewarm, and the spinach salad was missing the almonds, but it was food, and she ate it while she stared out the window. The diary lay closed on the seat beside her, where it remained for the night.

Chapter 33

Jarred left the hotel and drove around the block a couple of times, then re-entered the driveway and parked. The man in the brown herringbone jacket remained seated in the same chair he had been in before. He was eating some nuts in the bowl in front of him, and Jarred declined his offer to share.

"Did she go to her room?" Jarred asked.

"Yes. Do you still want me to stay?" the man asked.

"Definitely. At least till midnight or so. Make sure she doesn't leave, and if she does, follow her."

"Do you expect anything to happen... just curious... and if something does, what do you suggest I do?" the man asked.

"If it's going to happen. It'll be in the next day or two. We have to presume that they know she has made inquiries and I am unsure of the possible consequences because of it. I want her kept safe, whatever it takes."

Anne got up early the next morning and put on a blue Lycra top, and a pair of body-fitting exercise pants with her favorite running shoes. She put her hair up in a ponytail and walked out the room to the fitness center, her hair bobbing behind her. The fitness room was two floors down. It was small, and had a stairstepper, treadmill, elliptical trainer as well as a multi-use plate weight machine. There was the requisite TV in the corner, with a local news station on it, and a water cooler. Anne went over and drank three glasses of water, then got on the treadmill. She programmed it for thirty minutes of aerobic exercise and started the warm up cycle.

After about twenty minutes, another woman, about forty and slightly overweight, came in and got on the stairstepper. She started her way to the top of wherever she was going, and Anne smiled at her, commenting that she was almost finished if the woman wanted the treadmill. She acknowledged the gesture, and Anne upped the speed to seven kph for the last ten minutes. The monitor said that her heart rate had hit its target range, and Anne felt the familiar cadence of her feet hitting the belt, and deep, even breaths. It was a great feeling, and often made her lose track of where she was or what she was doing.

The TV monitor was showing a local rugby game, or something that looked like it, and after that, the local weather broadcast came on. It was of no interest to her and she looked straight ahead out the glass partition to the swimming pool, where she reminisced about her childhood and the neighbor's pool. She remembered begging the boy, whose parents owned the pool, for an invitation. He had acquiesced after she agreed to let him kiss her on the cheek. She was ten at the time.

Anne totally missed the next news segment about a woman who was found murdered in her flat in Notting Hill. The police thought it was a routine robbery that went bad.

After she was finished, Anne drank three more cups of water and left the fitness center, heading back to her room. Her outfit was stained from her exertions, and she threw a towel over her shoulder to make herself feel a little less conspicuous along the way.

The *London Times* was outside her room, and she picked it up and looked at the front page as she unlocked the door. Tony Blair was saying something about the Tories, whatever that meant. Anne laid the newspaper on the sofa, and wheeled out the room service tray from the last evening, then undressed and took a shower. By the time she had finished with her make up, hair, and clothing, it was 8:00 a.m.

The telephone rang. A man's voice that she didn't recognize started talking.

"Have you watched the news?" he asked.

"What? Who is this?" Anne asked.

"I said. Have you seen the news, Anne?" Hearing her name made her both curious and nervous.

"No... why?" she asked no longer interested in knowing who it was.

"You need to watch the news. I will call you in one hour's time." The man hung up, and Anne went over to the TV and turned it on. She flipped channels until she found the one from the fitness center and they were showing excerpts from a speech from Tony Blair. They then went to commercial and Anne took the opportunity to try and call Ginger back from the day before. The phone rang and Ginger's voice mail came on.

"Hello. You have reached Ginger. It is Monday and I'm in the office. Please leave me a message." Anne immediately noticed that the message was old, but it was still early in the day, and she dismissed it.

"Hello, Ginger. This is Anne…" Anne stopped speaking and dropped the phone as she saw pictures of Ginger's flat on the news. She turned up the volume to hear what the newscaster, who stood outside her home, was saying.

"A young woman was found dead this morning from what looks like a break-in gone wrong at her flat in Notting Hill. An anonymous tip was called in to the police at three a.m. this morning that something was amiss at this address. When they arrived, they found the young woman, described as in her late twenties, dead by a knife wound to the abdomen. Her name has not been released, but according to the tax records the flat is owned by a Miss Ginger Thereaux."

Anne's breathing was ragged and her palms clammy, the thumping of her heart felt so intense she thought it might pop through her chest onto the carpet and she pressed her hand against her left breast to slow it down. She could feel it pulse under her hand. The phone receiver lay on the floor, and she sat down beside it, oblivious to the sound it was making. The news channel went on to another story but Anne's mind was still digesting the death of this woman that she had just met two days before. At first, she dismissed any possible connection with her conversation with Ginger. She rationalized that it was just a terrible coincidence, but then gave in to doubt because of Ginger's reservations the day before. What had she done?

:

May 13, 1939, early morning.

Before going to meet Michael, John stopped by his father's London flat and let himself in with his key. He knew his father wouldn't be there until the next day or two. He gathered up some spare clothes and put them into a satchel, ate some left over chicken and sat down at his father's desk.

He took the better part of an hour writing the letter to his father and put it in a sealed envelope in the top drawer. After he finished the next letter he addressed the envelope, affixed a stamp, and left the flat, depositing the letter in the outgoing mail receptacle. Anne should receive it in a day or two.

John arrived at the London address that Michael had given him slightly before dawn. He parked his car in an alley off of the main street and walked past an iron gate and down an unkempt sidewalk. It was a dilapidated old house at the end of a cul-de-sac. He knocked on the door and walked in without waiting for an answer. The room was dark.

"Hello, Johnny boy where have you been?" It was the voice he hated more than anything in the world.

"Nice entrance. Planning on doing something?" Michael said, as he turned on the kitchen light, temporarily blinding John. Michael laughed, as the object in John's hand became visible. It was his satchel.

"I should have known better. No guts." Michael sat down at the kitchen table and signaled John to do the same. "Nice of you to show up. We have lots to discuss."

"Let's get it over with then," John said, as he pulled a chair away from the table and sat down facing him. He put his satchel down on his right.

"I've made arrangements for you to catch a ship in a couple of days," Michael said, as he drank a bottle of ale.

"Where? Maybe I'd like to make my own arrangements," John said.

"Like you could… fine with me. But, just in case, the ship is called the *Magdalene*," he pushed a London Times page over to John and pointed to the ship departure listing. "It leaves on the sixteenth to Halifax. From there I'm sure you can figure out your own way to America, or wherever you want to go."

John looked at the listing. Nova Scotia, Canada. It was as good as any place.

"The first mate is Charles. He's your contact," Michael said.

"And where are you going?" John asked.

"I haven't decided yet, maybe South America. I've always liked Spanish women,"

John didn't bother commenting on the statement.

"Where do I sleep?" John asked, as he stood up.

"Anywhere you want," Michael replied.

May 14, 1939

Michael purchased the daily *London Times* at the corner newsstand. The majority of the newspaper was dedicated to the prospects of war and he flipped through the pages until he found what he was looking for. There were two brief articles. Michael sat at a small café in Canterbury dressed in a heavy sweater, his favorite blue gabardine pants, and military boots along with a wide brimmed hat. The awning kept him dry from the light rain. He hadn't shaved in two days and he kept his head down when cars passed by.

> *Military wire. Two guards were found shot at an abandoned Port building. One survived multiple gun wounds and is listed as in critical condition in the Army barracks hospital. The other was pronounced dead at the scene. The military has neither revealed the identities of the men nor why they were guarding an empty warehouse. The motives behind the shooting are not known. Wanted for questioning are two men in their mid twenties. Considering the overtures of war in Europe, the military has designated this as a matter of national security and MI5 is coordinating the investigation with local authorities.*

On the same page there was another story.

> *Canterbury: Local constables are investigating the shooting death of one of their own. Police Inspector Roarke was found shot to death outside his automobile in the early hours of yesterday morning. The authorities suspect at least one other automobile was involved in the incident and an unknown number of assailants. Asked if whether they had any leads, the local station reported that they were intent on tracking down several suspects.*

Michael left the page open and lit a cigarette. He ordered a cup of coffee from the waitress, flirted with her a little, then read it again, while strategically holding his butt above the first article and allowing the ashes to sear the paper. By the time his coffee was served to him the article could no longer be read.

He returned to the flat and found John sitting at the kitchen table drinking a cup of coffee. He threw a copy of the paper on the table and opened it to the desired page.

"Read it," he said, and sat in the opposite chair waiting for John to finish.

"Nice articles, eh?" Michael said, and sat down.

"One of the guards is alive," John said.

Michael looked at him. "Mixed emotions eh, Johnny? Happy we didn't kill both, scared that he knows who we are and will tell the cops." John wanted to correct the 'we' part but knew it was worthless to try.

"Which one lived, Michael?" John asked.

Michael thought for a moment, wondering if John had indeed read the article because, if he had, he should have realized that the one that was shot once, and was dead, was Rad. The first guard Michael had shot twice, and that is the one that lived, according to the article. This meant that he might have seen their faces, but didn't know their names.

"Well, Johnny. Seems like we have a bit of a puzzle. For if it was Rad, he knows the both of us. If it was the other guard, well, who *knows* what he saw." He waited to see if John corrected him.

"So you don't know," John said, and bowed his head.

Michael pondered this unforeseen gift for a moment.

"Look at it this way. Best case scenario is that the guard can identify us by our faces – *if* he lives." John looked at him and narrowed his eyes. He didn't like the sound of Michael's tone. "On the other hand, worse case scenario is that Rad has already told them who we are, or will tell them as soon as he can. Either way we still only have one choice."

John looked at him with a blank stare.

"Either way. You shouldn't be seen. NO contact with anyone, *Comprende?* In a couple more days we're gone."

Michael went back to his bedroom and lit another cigarette while he lay on his bed. He watched the smoke rise to the ceiling, and smiled. It was just *too* perfect.

I'm Sorry… Love, Anne

May 15, 1939 Cornwall Estate, Kent.

Anne awoke early the next morning. The sun was coming in through the curtains and it enveloped her like a warm hug. She stayed there, motionless under her covers, until a cloud disrupted the light, and she got up and sat on the edge of her bed. Her diary lay where she left it the night before, the pencil still marking her last entry. She contemplated the day in front of her. It had been three days since she last saw John. Though she felt despondent and reclusive she had refused to show her pain to her little sister, and she was proud of that. Still, each day a clearer picture of her future was opening up in front of her. She could not go back in time, she must accept the life she had to live.

Anne put her left foot in her slipper without looking, but couldn't find the right one, so she looked at the floor and located it about two feet from the bed. It must have fallen there when she had kicked them off last night. The corner of her eye saw the small white envelope, and she involuntarily sucked in her breath and looked at it. She got up from the bed her eyes fixed on it as she drew nearer, like it might scamper from whence it came. Her mind was tempering her hopes with the knowledge that it was probably something from Lizzy. She knelt next to it, her clean gown gathering on the floor around her feet, and picked it up. It was not Lizzy's writing. It was a letter. The maid must have slipped it under her door that morning. She immediately sat on the cold wood floor and opened it up. With the first two words her eyes welled up and she blinked back the tears.

Dearest Anne,

I don't even know how to write this letter. I cannot begin to explain how this whole situation happened. It is of no consequence at this time anyway. My fate has been drawn and I must live with it. I am so sorry for the pain I have caused you, the doubt. It was never a part of my dreams to be sitting here writing to you – like this. I always thought we would be together. What a mess I have made of our lives.

I want you to know that each and every minute that I live, you will remain in my thoughts. I will hear your voice in my mind in every bird's call, your eyes in every sunrise, your laughter in every rainbow. I will feel your spirit in every creature I see and your touch in every ocean I travel. I want you to know that I will always remember you.

"Tis beauty truly blent, whose red and white,
Nature's own sweet and cunning hand laid on:
Lady, you are the cruell'st she alive,
If you will lead these graces to the grave
And leave the world no copy."

My dear Anne,

Please don't forget me. With all my very being, Love John.

Anne sat on the floor unaware of the cold or the hardness of the wood. The streams of tears fell without a sob onto her lap where her hands held his letter. Her head throbbed with the knowledge that she had let him leave—alone. It was a choice that she knew she would doubt for the rest of her life.

A light knock awoke her from her unfocused gaze.

"Annie? Can I come in?" Lizzy's muffled voice came through the door.

Anne wiped away the rest of her tears and stood up, she put the letter in her diary and unlocked the door. Lizzy ran into her arms.

"Annie. I had the most terrible dreams," Lizzy said.

"It's OK, Lizzy, you're awake. The nightmares are over," Anne said, as she fiercely hugged her little sister.

If only she could believe the words that fell so easily from her lips.

She took Lizzy downstairs and ate breakfast. Her father came over and kissed her and Lizzy on the forehead before he departed to London. She wondered if he noticed how quiet she had been, but he said nothing.

She was surprised to see Michael in the study speaking to her father. It was all she could do to walk away and take Lizzy to the piano, where she gave her little sister a lesson—her third one this week. She wound up the metronome and it began its incessant tick, tock, tick tock. Anne counted aloud as Lizzy practiced *Fur Elise.* She couldn't think while she did it. It was a relief.

That afternoon Lizzy took a nap and Anne went to her room and shut the door behind her. She took out some paper, and sat down at her desk to write the hardest letter of her life.

Chapter 34

2004 London

The telephone rang almost exactly an hour later. Anne found herself still sitting on the carpet her hands splayed behind her supporting her weight as she leaned on them. The fibers were making imprints on her palms. She looked up tentatively at the television, afraid to see some additional development, and was relieved to observe a newscaster on some ship in an obviously far away locale. It was somewhere tropical.

Anne looked at the phone as it rang for the third time but she couldn't get herself to answer it. The call finally went to voice mail, and she got up from the floor and went to the bathroom to fill a glass of water. She saw the envelope immediately. It had been slipped under the door in a business size envelope and had her name printed on the front. Anne picked it up and shook it. A single card or piece of paper moved inside, and she ripped one side of it open and turned it upside down. The card fell to the floor and she stared at it from where she stood but it was upside down and nothing showed.

Anne left it there, filled her glass of water, looked at her red eyes in the mirror, then returned to the note on the carpet and took several gulps from the glass. She then put it down on the marble counter, and bent over and picked up the piece of paper with two fingers as one would fetch a piece of trash from the garbage. She flicked it over with her wrist and it fell face up so she could read it.

> *Anne,*
> *You may hear some disturbing news today. I will explain soon, but am unable at this time. Please be patient and I will contact you. Be careful, and try not to leave the hotel. It could be dangerous.*
> *- Jarred*

Anne bent over and picked up the note, and moved back to the bed where she sat down and placed the card beside her, staring at the TV. The note raised more questions than it answered, and she considered just calling him, but couldn't get herself to do it. She tried to evaluate her feelings toward him, but they were as ambiguous as the predicament she found herself in, so she finally gave up.

The ring of the telephone awoke her from her daze. She rolled over and picked it up.

"Hello, Anne." It was the same voice as earlier. "I assume you have seen the news?" the voice asked.

"I refuse to speak to someone who does not identify themselves. Who is this?" Her shaking hands belied Anne's firm voice.

"I'm terribly sorry, Anne. This is Sir Alex Reinquist. I apologize for the earlier mysterious call, however, I needed you to understand that you are involved in a potentially dangerous situation." Just great, thought Anne, two warnings in two minutes.

"I don't know you from Adam, *Mr.* Reinquist. Why in the world would I believe anything you had to say to me?" Anne asked.

"Are you watching the news, Anne?" Sir Alex asked, his voice still patient.

Anne hesitated as she saw the news stories rotate back to the Notting Hill murder.

"Yes," she said.

"Keep watching," Sir Alex said.

Anne turned up the volume so she could hear what the newscaster was saying. Most of the information was old, and she was about to turn it back down until they showed a picture on the screen that she immediately recognized. Anne gasped.

"Ah, I see you recognize the face," Sir Alex said.

The TV had an older, but clearly recognizable, picture of Jarred. It looked like a government ID photo.

"We just released that," Sir Alex said.

"I... don't understand..." Anne said.

"Listen, Anne, I can't speak about this matter on the telephone. It is too sensitive. I'm going to send a driver by to pick you up for your own protection. He'll be there in about thirty minutes—" Anne cut him off.

"I don't think I'm comfortable with that. How am I even expected to know that you aren't involved in this...situation? After all, Ginger worked for Scotland Yard, and now she's dead. I have to assume not from a burglary, as the news indicates," Anne said. She sat up on the bed with feet on the floor and tried to take deep breaths to slow her heart down.

"Yes. Good question. Well, for one, the place where I want you to come is the Palace of Westminster," Sir Alex said.

"Which means nothing to me," Anne said.

"Oh, sorry, you may know it as Parliament. I work at the House of Lords. You can look it up on the Internet, if you wish," he said.

"I'm sorry, Sir Alex, but that doesn't make me feel much better about the situation," she said.

Sir Alex's voice became more serious.

"Really, Anne. What choices do you have? The girl, as you said, is deceased, and she worked at police headquarters. Jarred is wanted for questioning by the police and you don't know anyone else in London." His voice became a bit calmer and he added: "I'm really trying to help here, Anne. We need to ask you some questions to get to the bottom of this matter. You can bring a cell phone with you, and you will be picked up in a car with a driver. You will be by yourself in the back. If he does not take you to Parliament, you can call the police."

Anne knew he was right, to an extent. She didn't have many choices. She didn't feel the police could protect her if they couldn't protect their own and, other than Jarred, whom had not been very forthcoming about his family, she didn't know anyone else in England that could be of help.

"OK. What's the address that I'm going to?" Anne asked.

"Unlike in America, our Parliament is just referred to as the House of Lords or House of Commons. You are going to the House of Lords," Sir Alex said. "Look, I hate to concern you anymore, however, for your protection I suggest that you leave the hotel precisely at 10:00 a.m. You will see a blue Rover sedan, with tinted windows, and a driver. There will also be another automobile behind the blue Rover. That is there for your protection. Wait in the lobby until you see both vehicles, then go immediately to the blue Rover and enter the back seat. It is very important that you do this quickly, in the event that you are being watched. I will personally meet you at the House of Lords."

Anne hung up the telephone and called the concierge.

"Can you give me the telephone number to the House of Lords please," she asked.

"Sure, ma'am, one minute." The woman returned a moment later and gave it to her.

Anne called the main switchboard and asked for Sir Alex Reinquist.

"Just one moment please. I will connect you to his office," the voice said. Anne hung up.

She got up and brought her purse over to the bed and took out her cell phone to retrieve Jarred's telephone number from her purse, then sat down and dialed it on the hotel phone. She took a deep breath before the first ring. She waited for him to answer, and found herself anxious to hear his voice. That concerned her almost as much as the need to speak to him.

"Hello. This is Jarred. I'm obviously not available. Please leave your message at the tone." Anne hadn't contemplated this event, and hesitated.

"Uh… Jarred. This is Anne. Please… Oh. I'll call you later…" Anne looked at the phone, then added. "I hope you are OK."

Next she went over to the desk and removed a piece of paper and a pen, and sat down at the chair. She wrote the date, time, and place of her meeting with Sir Alex, as well as her personal information, on a piece of paper, then repeated the same thing on another piece of paper and put that copy into an envelope and addressed it to her sister in New York.

She took the diary, and the first note, and put it into the closet safe. At least if something happened to her someone might figure out where she had gone.

Anne changed into a light business suit and a pair of flat shoes, gathered her purse along with her cell phone and the letter, and walked downstairs to the lobby, where she purchased postage for the letter and mailed it in the office lobby. She sat down in a chair facing the front doors and waited for the blue car.

She had no idea what this meeting was about, or how she found herself in this mess. She found herself both frightened and wanting justice for Ginger. Obviously something had been uncovered that was very important to someone and, despite her fear, she found herself recklessly wanting to know what it was.

The man in the corner of the lobby observed her mailing the letter, and then taking her seat. It was obvious Anne was waiting for someone, and he made a phone call with an update to his superiors.

At exactly 10:00 a.m., a blue sedan with tinted windows pulled up outside the front doors, and an identical white car was behind it.

Anne got up from her seat, put her hand in her purse to grasp her cell phone, and hastily walked across the lobby, through the front doors to open the right rear door behind the driver. The car was empty, just as Sir Alex said it would be. She got in and was immediately pinned to the seat as the driver accelerated. He didn't look at her or say a word.

She didn't observe the white car behind them, which blocked the driveway and prevented the very irate man who had been watching her from following. The driver of Anne's car smiled as he observed what had happened in the rear view mirror.

Anne looked around the inside of the car. It smelled new and, other than the tinted windows and the privacy glass that was between her and the front seat, there was nothing special about it. She reached up and inconspicuously unlocked the door. She was relieved to see that the locking mechanism worked.

The streets of London were packed, and Anne had no idea where she was being taken. She looked out the window and found herself passing Buckingham palace. At least she could check that off her tourist list. The guards with the big hats stood outside the gate, just like she had seen in the movies.

The driver passed an official looking building and took a turn into the back parking lot. He pulled into a reserved spot, got out of the car, and then opened the door for Anne. She tried to look at his face but he never looked up and the brim of his hat prevented her from seeing anything other than his chin, which was covered in a faint layer of stubble. She also noted that he wore gloves and army type boots. She got the feeling that he wasn't a full-time driver.

He pointed up a set of stairs and Anne felt better as several people, men and women, joined her as they entered the building. She was surprised to see a security check point where the people were lined up in order to put their belongings through the metal detector. Most of them wore badges and the ones that did not, such as herself, were asked to sign in by a short, dark woman that she could barely understand.

Anne wrote her full name on the sheet of paper, and then got in line with the rest of the people. She put her purse on the conveyor belt and walked through without incident. On the other side, she paused where everyone was picking up their belongings. A man came out and took her purse and walked toward her.

"Is this yours ma'am?" He was about twenty-five, thin, with an ill-fitted uniform.

"Yes. Could I have it please?" she asked.

"I'm sorry ma'am. Since you are a visitor we need to hold onto this until you leave the premises. Here is a receipt for it. Please pick it up over there when you exit the building." He pointed to another table about ten feet away.

Anne was about to protest but the man just turned around and walked over to a locker, put it in it, and came back and handed her the key.

"Give us the receipt and the key when you return, and we'll get your purse back for you." He then turned to another woman behind her and repeated the spiel.

Anne stood there for a moment contemplating if this was a normal procedure until she saw the man take the woman's purse and go through the same motions. Anne turned around, unsure of where to go, and another man, about seventy-years old, quite pale, in a gray suit, white shirt and red bow tie, walked up to her.

"You must be Miss Compton?" he said.

"Are you Sir Alex?" she asked, and he smiled. He looked innocent enough, she surmised.

"Welcome. Sorry for all covert routines, however we felt that it was necessary. Please follow me." Sir Alex took a few steps and made sure she followed.

They walked down a flight of stairs and through three hallways. Anne soon lost track of the number of twists and turns, which made her start feeling uneasy again. They reached a door, along a corridor of identical doors. It had no designation on it just the number 14532. Anne tried to memorize it, and followed Sir Alex into the brightly-lit room.

She was surprised that it opened into more of a study than an office. It was about twenty or so feet square, with paneled walls and a floor to ceiling bookcase that ran along the back wall behind a very large desk. In front of the desk were two oversize leather armchairs. There was a door off to her right and a man walked through it. He looked to be about the same age as the first man, and he moved over behind the desk and sat down. The room smelled of cigars.

"Hello, I'm Lord Ashley. I believe you have already met my aide?" Lord Ashley said.

Sir Alex moved to her left and into her view. It made her feel better, and she sat down.

"Yes. We've met," Anne said.

"I apologize for all the clandestine actions, Ms. Compton," he said. "But I'm sure Sir Alex explained we have a potentially unfortunate situation here." Anne thought to herself that 'unfortunate' was an understatement to the deceased Ginger.

Anne looked around the room and saw a picture of a country estate. It looked familiar and Sir Alex noticed her gaze.

"Anne," he stepped in front of her, "we wanted to discuss what relationship you had with Ginger," he said. The use of the past tense made her fidget.

Anne thought about this for a second.

"First: how do you even know about me?" she asked.

"Good question," Lord Ashley said, "Sir Alex." He motioned toward Sir Alex with his hand.

"The simple answer for that is Ginger," Sir Alex said.

"But I thought she was dead?" Anne said, suddenly hopeful.

"Yes, I'm afraid she is. However, before she died she managed to mention Jarred Mulberry and yourself, an American," Sir Alex said. "We were able to trace you through your hotel registration."

"So… why was she killed?" Anne asked. "And why are *you* involved. Who are you anyway?"

"That's rather complicated, Anne," Lord Ashley said.

"I think I can understand it. Try me," Anne said, as she crossed her legs.

Sir Alex looked at Lord Ashley and he nodded, at which point Sir Alex turned back to Anne.

"First of all, we are a Special Branch of intelligence having to do with war time crimes. The matter, which Ginger was investigating and Jarred's family is involved in, has to do with crimes that were committed during World War II. We understand that was a long time ago, however they are still considered open cases and are a matter of national security. Ginger's unofficial investigation triggered a reaction from someone that would prefer that certain things be kept where they have been for sixty years. Buried."

"So you are MI5? MI6? Someone else?" Anne asked.

"We are related to all those intelligence agencies. But are with none of them specifically. I'm sorry, that is all we are at liberty to say," Sir Alex said. Anne noticed a bit of perspiration on his forehead and he turned away, wiping it off with a handkerchief.

"Look, Anne. We really need to know what it is that you have uncovered about this murder in 1939, as well as what Ginger told you. We obviously think we know who is involved, but your help may give us the assistance we need to solve this case and put it to rest," Lord Ashley said, when Sir Alex turned away.

Anne was unsure if she wanted to help them make a case against Jarred, if that was what they intended to do. She was not happy with him, but didn't believe he was involved in this matter, and her heart told her that a betrayal like this would be the end of their friendship, or whatever it was, and she didn't want that. She owed it to him to at least talk to him and find out why he had failed to reveal his relationship to the story in the diary.

The extended pause on her part caused Sir Alex to turn back around.

"Anne. We know you and Jarred are friends. So this is difficult for you to do. However, you saw that he is already wanted for questioning by the police. I guarantee it would be better for you to tell us what you know than for him to be questioned by Scotland Yard. They don't take kindly to the loss of one of their own."

"I don't believe Jarred had anything to do with Ginger. There is no way that he could do that," Anne said.

"I wouldn't be so... " Sir Alex started saying. Lord Ashley got up from his chair and moved around the desk. He signaled to Sir Alex that he wanted to speak and sat down in the chair opposite Anne. She could smell the faint scent of cigars on him, and it confirmed that this was his office. She wondered where Sir Alex worked.

"I know that this is hard. We don't want you to incriminate your friend. We just want to know what Ginger told you. Let's start there." His voice was soft, and reminded Anne of her grandfather.

She thought for a moment and didn't see anything that she knew that could possibly implicate Jarred of murder.

"Fine," she started, "I told her..." Lord Ashley cut her off.

"Did Jarred introduce you two?" he asked.

"Yes." Anne started again. "I told her that I had found a diary from Anne Cornwall. Do you know who she is?" Anne asked

"We are familiar with the Cornwall family in Canterbury, correct?" Sir Alex offered.

"Yes," Anne said. "Lord Ellias Cornwall's eldest daughter. Anyway, I told her that the diary spoke about the murder of a servant girl, Theresa… I don't know her last name; the diary doesn't mention it. I just wanted to know if anyone was ever prosecuted for her death. That's it."

"I see…" Lord Ashley said. "This diary, does *it* speculate as to who Theresa's murderer was?"

Anne found the question a little suspicious. She thought this was about Ginger, not Theresa.

"Uh. Yes. No. Kind of, I guess. It has some conjecture, that's all." For some reason she didn't feel like revealing that Michael Cornwall murdered Theresa. It seemed a wise thing to do at that moment. Her initial misgivings were growing. "So, are you interested in solving the murder of Theresa or Ginger?" she asked.

"Well, I suppose both. They seem to be connected at this point in time," Lord Ashley said. He crossed his legs so that she could see the bottom of his shoe. It was leather, and looked new. "Where did you get this diary?"

Anne hadn't anticipated this question.

"I. Umm. I… it was given to me by someone that I met." Anne knew the answer was not satisfactory.

"And do you have a name of this person?" Lord Ashley asked.

"I think it was Betty… something…" Anne was thankful that she didn't remember her last name at the moment. She also noticed the reaction in both the men at hearing the name, and she added: "Do you know her?"

Sir Alex again looked at Lord Ashley. It was Lord Ashley that spoke.

"Betty is a fairly common name. I think Sir Alex and I were thinking about a person in Parliament, that's all. Unless, of course, you *did* receive the diary from a government official?" Sir Alex chuckled.

"No. I don't think so," Anne said.

"So, back to Ginger. Did she agree to investigate this matter for you?" Sir Alex asked.

"Yes. She said she would call the next day if she found out anything," Anne said.

"And what did she say?" Sir Alex asked. They both paid rapt attention to the question.

"Not much. She said that the case was still being monitored and that whomever was watching the case knew she had inquired into the file... Oh... she also mentioned that someone had called her and asked her why she was investigating it. The last thing she said was that she wasn't going to look into it further, because she felt something wasn't quite right."

"And that was the last you heard from her?" Sir Alex asked.

"Yes," Anne said.

"And did she mention who it was that called her? Did she recognize the voice?" Lord Ashley asked.

"No. She didn't," Anne said. "That's all I know, gentlemen. Can I go now?"

"Just a few more questions, Anne," Lord Ashley said. "Did you tell Jarred what Ginger had said?"

"As I said before, I'm not comfortable talking to you about Jarred. I need to speak to him first," Anne said.

"Did Jarred tell you that he was with MI5?" Sir Alex asked.

"MI5? You mean Sir Percy?" Anne immediately realized the mistake she made.

"Sir Percy?" Lord Ashley asked. "Where were you told about Sir Percy?"

"Uh... the diary might have mentioned him," Anne said." Her mind was working furiously to try and figure out an answer to the question she knew was coming. Her heart rate was ratcheting up.

"And how do you know that Sir Percy was MI5?" Lord Ashley asked.

"I think the diary mentioned it," Anne said, her eyes down toward the floor.

"The diary mentioned it? Are you sure? That would mean that Lord Cornwall's young daughter knew that Sir Percy was a government agent, and unlikely fact." Lord Ashley stared at her.

"Uhh... I could be mistaken," Anne said, her hands clenched together in her lap. "Perhaps it was... Ginger." She finished.

"Ginger?" Lord Ashley said. "Ginger mentioned that Sir Percy was MI5?"

Anne threw up her hands and looked at him.

"I don't remember… perhaps. I'm really nervous here. I don't like this interrogation and would like to go back to my hotel." She stood up and straightened her skirt.

"Just one moment, Anne. I need to speak to Sir Alex in the other room."

The two men went out the door to her right, and she could hear them speaking. Her first inclination was to leave the room and exit the building but she had no idea how to get back to the entrance, so she waited. The picture that Sir Alex had blocked earlier caught her attention, and she walked up to it. The wrought iron gate, stone pillars and driveway were all in perfect condition, unlike when she had seen it a few days ago, but she recognized the estate. It was the Cornwall's. She wondered why Lord Ashley would have a picture of that on his wall?

The two men reentered the room and the noise spun Anne around. She felt her cheeks blush, as if she had been caught doing something she ought not.

"Anne, we've discussed this and I'm afraid, for your own protection, we need you to move out of your hotel. We have a safe house just outside London where we can protect you until this matter is resolved."

Anne stood there, mortified. The thought had not occurred to her that she would be requested to stay with these strangers.

"But… I… all my stuff is at the hotel. I'll go back and pack it up and then we can talk about where I can stay that is safe," she said. All she wanted was to get out of this building.

"We're going to take care of that, Anne. We'll send someone over to pick up your things. We've already made the phone call," Sir Alex said.

Anne almost mentioned the safe but decided against it.

"Look, I don't want this. I'll take my chances by myself. This whole situation is making me very uncomfortable," Anne said. Her hands were so clammy that she was afraid if she made a run for the door that she wouldn't be able to grab the doorknob. And besides the fact, she didn't have her purse or her cell phone. She was stuck, and they knew it. She felt like a hamster in a cage with two hungry cats.

"I know how you feel, Anne. But we can't afford to take the chance. Imagine the headlines if an American was *murdered* in our city and we allowed it to happen." Anne couldn't tell if it was a threat or a statement of concern. She struggled for a reason to contact anyone to let them know where she was, and who she was with.

"OK, if we are going to do this, I need to make a phone call and notify my employer. They are expecting me to report." Anne looked at her watch. "Actually, I'm already late." Anne moved over to the telephone, but Sir Alex met her there and put his hand on the handset.

Anne looked down at his hand and the telephone.

"We've already notified them that you are detained on official business," Sir Alex said.

Anne could feel the panic start to rise, and raised her voice.

"So they think I'm being investigated as a criminal? I absolutely *insist* that I speak to my superiors. I could lose my job over this!" she said.

"No, Anne. We've made sure they know that this is for your protection. They were very understanding," Sir Alex said.

If what Sir Alex was saying were true, then they had known that they were going to keep her before she even got here! They knew where she worked and what she did, even where she lived. She stood in the middle of the room, her hands at her side, and she could feel the involuntary shivers start up her spine. She reminded herself to breathe.

"Then I insist on speaking to the American Consulate. You are essentially holding me against my will," Anne said, her voice shaking.

Lord Ashley came up and grabbed her hand. Anne wanted to pull it back but had no strength in her arms. His hands were soft and warm to the touch, and he held hers lightly between his palms.

"Anne, we are not here to harm you. We are here to protect you. If you go out on your own, you could end up dead, like Ginger, and neither of us want that. Besides, you may find that you remember something critical that will help us solve this murder—both of them. Wouldn't that make this ordeal seem worth it?" His voice reminded her of her grandfather again.

"We'll make sure you are well taken care of. The best food and lodging. It'll only be a few days, and then you can go home. We don't think it will take long for us to flush out the murderer. You do want justice for Ginger don't you? We need your cooperation and help to do so. Look, just like when you came here, we'll give you your cell phone and purse. We'll bring a driver – just for you. If you feel unsafe at any time, you can call the police. We'll even give you the number," Lord Ashley said.

Anne knew this was the best offer she was going to get. Once she got her cell phone, and was in the car, she would call Jarred. If she couldn't get him she would take her chance and contact the local police. She just wanted her purse and phone back.

"OK," she said, resigned.

Sir Alex looked at his watch. "In ten minutes your driver will be here. We are going to have you leave by a back entrance; your purse will be waiting for you in the car. I just need your locker key and receipt."

Anne didn't move. Sir Alex had his hand out but Anne didn't want to do it this way. She wanted to get the purse herself.

"Sir Alex, why don't you take her to the security checkpoint and let her get the purse. Then you can escort her to the automobile." Anne liked this much better, and nodded.

"Alright, Anne. Shall we?" Sir Alex opened the door to the office and waited for her to exit. She found the air much better outside the room.

The maze of hallways again made her nervous, until they turned into the main corridor and she willed herself to calm down.

The security guard that took her purse was still there, and Anne walked up to him with Sir Alex beside her, and handed him the key and receipt. The guard went over to the locker and put the key in the lock, but it wouldn't open. He tried it again but with the same result. He then looked at the receipt and went over to another man and showed him the key and receipt. The man pointed to a clipboard and the young guard consulted it, then took another key from the board and went over to the locker. This time it opened and Anne was given her purse.

Anne grabbed her purse like it was a loaf of bread and she hadn't eaten in a week. She looked out the main doors as the young guard pressed a button and indicated they could exit that way. Her heart sank when Sir Alex spoke up.

"John, we're going to take the back exit. Thanks anyway." John shut the door and moved over to someone who had just come through the detector. Anne stood there and realized she had missed the opportunity.

At least she had her purse.

She followed Sir Alex back through the maze of corridors until they exited through an unmarked foyer, out into a small parking lot. There were only a few cars there, and she recognized the blue Rover. The driver sat in the front, and Sir Alex opened the rear door for her, then shut it once she was inside. He went to the front passenger door, opened it, and spoke briefly to the driver, then shut that as well. He waived to Anne as the driver pulled out of the lot into London traffic.

Anne settled back into the seat and opened her purse. Her cell phone sat on the top and she grabbed it, holding onto it as the driver wove in and out of the lanes. At least she had a way to make contact with the outside world.

Anne gazed out the heavily tinted windows and clutched her purse. The sights changed from city to country, and the Estates got larger. Soon, she didn't recognize any more landmarks, and there were no more street signs. She could feel that she was starting to get nervous. Her stomach was in knots and she rubbed it. Anne leaned forward to knock on the glass partition. She noticed that it wasn't glass at all, it was Plexiglas. The driver didn't respond, so she knocked harder. Still, he failed to acknowledge her. Her heart rate started increasing again and she yelled at him. Still – there was no effect.

She tried the door lock and felt comforted when it unlatched. She wanted to open the door and make sure it worked but they were moving at what had to be over sixty mph, so she decided to wait until he slowed down.

In about five minutes the road turned and he had to decelerate for a truck in front of him. Anne poised her hand on the door lock and pulled on it. She expected the familiar feel of the lock mechanism being released and the door to swing open, however the door did not react. She held the lock open and pushed on it with her other hand. Then it occurred to her: they had flipped the child protection lock. She couldn't get out!

Anne tried to calm down and turned toward the opposite side window to give her some protection from the rear view mirror, then looked down at her telephone. For some reason it was off. She didn't remember turning it off, and she was positive that she had charged it the evening before.

With the phone in her left palm, she pressed the on button with her thumb and waited for the reassuring start-up display - but it didn't turn on. She tried it again. Nothing.

She flipped the phone over and opened up the back where the battery was, and slid open the cover.

It was empty.

There was no point in screaming. No point in trying to wave to the other cars that passed periodically. She contemplated trying to break a window, but knew that she would probably only hurt herself. She kicked herself for being so gullible. Then tried to calm down by reminding herself that they said they would protect her. Maybe that is what they were doing. Still, she was beyond uncomfortable. The thought seemed ridiculous, as that is what she had told Jarrred. *'I'm uncomfortable with the friendship.'* That was nothing compared to what she was feeling now.

Anne turned aside and looked out the window. She could no longer see any houses or manors, just pastures of rolling hills broken up by groves of trees. They were well outside of London now. Well outside of her comfort zone.

Chapter 35

May 14, 1939 p.m., Cornwall Estate, Kent

Anne sat at her desk and finished writing the letter on the scratch paper, then took out some of her favorite stationary and dabbed some of her perfume on it. She transcribed the note onto the nice stationary and sealed it in a matching envelope. She put the draft copy in her diary next to John's letter, and addressed the original to him before walking downstairs with it safely in her pocket.

As she walked by the study, she stopped and went in to look at the books. She found her favorite one entitled: *The Woman in White*. It was a new copy, a gift from her mother just last year. After her mother had handed it to her, she had explained that Anne had been named after one of the heroines in the novel, Anne Catherick.

Anne went over to her father's desk, took out a writing implement and, without breaking the binding, wrote an inscription inside the front cover opposite the address label that her mother had affixed.

"Dear John,
I'm sorry. I will never forget you. Love Anne."

She closed her eyes and kissed the writing, then added a faint line under 'never', placed the letter in the book, and wrapped the package in a large sheet of brown paper she found in the kitchen.

She took the package to the only place she could think of that it might reach John, Michael's room, and placed it on the table with a note to her brother pleading with him to deliver it.

Michael did come late that night to collect some things and found the package on his table. He sat down and opened the package and was a little mystified to find the book. He turned it upside down and shook it causing the letter to fall to the table. He was pleased that it had the scent of his sister's favorite perfume and he picked it up and took a slow deep breath of the fragrance, then unceremoniously ripped it open and read the letter. It was, as he would have expected, written from the heart of a teenage girl. He pondered the note for a minute then tore it up and threw the remnants into the trash. He grabbed the book and tossed it in as well, then considered that decision for a moment, removed it, and put it on the top shelf of the bookcase that was built into his bedroom. It blended nicely with the other bindings, and he liked the idea of having a gift from Anne in his room.

:

The next day Anne checked Michael's room and saw that the package was gone. She sat down at the kitchen table and touched the place where she had placed it the day before and said a prayer. With all her heart she wished him safe passage – to wherever he would go.

Chapter 36

2004, Somewhere Outside of London

Anne was taken to a house in the middle of nowhere. In fact, it was the first house she had seen in at least twenty minutes. It was small, and well off the main road. When the car stopped, the driver got out and was greeted by several men whom Anne was terrified to see had guns slung under their arms. The driver and one of the men had a short discussion, then the guard came over to the car door and opened it. Anne stayed inside.

"Miss Compton." The man ducked down and peered inside the compartment at her. "I'm Kevin, and that's my partner Jerry." He pointed to the other man with the gun. "We are here to protect you. Please, I know we are a bit scary looking but we don't bite." He smiled and motioned for her to get out.

Anne ducked out of the car into the sunlight and squinted at the brightness. The first guard stood back at a respectful distance. He was a few inches taller than her, had a stocky torso and a square jaw. The other guard, Jerry, was about the same height, but slender. She looked around at where she was but could see nothing except rolling hills. The house was in the middle of an open field. Anyone approaching from any direction would be seen. Anne doubted that it was a mistake.

"Please, Miss Compton, come on inside." Kevin moved around to her flank and she was left no choice but to walk toward the house to avoid his proximity. The gravel under her feet made her ankles wobble and she almost fell over. Kevin caught her and she quickly pulled her arm back.

"I'm fine," she said, as she pushed him away. She saw Jerry look at Kevin and smile. She stopped, and both men looked at her.

"I want to know why my telephone was tampered with. Sir Alex promised I could make a phone call and I want to do that." She looked at Jerry, who had a friendlier face.

"I'm very sorry, Miss Compton. But we find that often people make phone calls when they are in protective custody and they say something that they shouldn't, then the bad guys find them, or their family, and well... it ends up being very messy. As soon as it's safe, we will make sure you can call whomever you want. For now, please come inside." Jerry stepped aside and Anne passed through the front door. She felt like she was entering a den of lions. It was a bit of a relief to discover that the home was nicely furnished, and didn't smell of mold and dust. She was shown to a room on the second floor, where she found all her clothing from her hotel. It made her feel somewhat comforted but even more concerned.

As soon as she was alone, she dug through everything but did not find the diary or the envelope. She didn't know if that meant they had taken it or had not found it in the safe. She hoped it was the latter.

The room was small but comfortable. It had a full size bed, a dresser and night table, a lamp and an area carpet. There was a single small window and she looked out to see if there was a way to climb down. She had a feeling what the answer was before she checked. It was a straight drop, about twenty feet to the bushes below. Anne walked over to the door and was surprised to find it open. She went down the hallway and, as quietly as possible, tried each door. The door at the end of the hallway opened into an adequate bathroom, and she went in and closed the door but could not secure it. There was no lock.

Anne tried the other three doors on the way back to her room but could not open any of them. The only way down from the second floor was the same stairway that she had come up that exited into the living area of the main floor where she would be in plain sight of the guards. Yes, she wasn't in a locked room, but it might as well have been. There was no way out of the house.

That evening Anne heard a car drive up. She couldn't see the driveway from her window and so she moved to the top of the stairs, and heard some familiar voices from below. She walked down to see them.

"Ahh… Anne, glad to see you are safe and sound. My apologies about the phone but, as was explained to you, it is for your safety. In a few days this will all be over." Sir Alex and Lord Ashley were there.

"I still feel as if I am being held against my will," Anne felt she might as well remind them.

Lord Ashley came over and gave Anne a copy of the London Times.

"Sorry, Anne, but you might want to look at page three."

Anne sat down and turned past the front page. On the bottom left she was horrified to see another picture of Jarred.

"What?" She looked up at Lord Ashley.

"Well, you can read it later but the gist is that Jarred's fingerprints were found at the scene of the murder, *on* the murder weapon." He paused and made sure she heard him. "There is also a witness that has come forward and stated that they saw him leaving the flat around the time of death. I'm afraid it doesn't look good. I know how you must feel."

Anne felt her knees start to give out, and she sat down. She folded up the paper but held it in her hands. "That's impossible..." she stuttered. "He wouldn't do that. I don't believe it! Besides, we were in the apartment the day before. Both our fingerprints would be there." Anne looked up at Lord Ashley.

"Actually, the police do mention that." He pointed to the paper. "An unidentified third person's fresh prints were found at the scene," he said. "So, you are wanted for questioning."

Anne saw the opportunity.

"I'm happy to talk to them. We can go right now." Anne got up and looked at the men, but none of them moved.

"Anne, we didn't want you to be put through any more today so we took the liberty to inform them that you were with us and we would pass on any vital information," Sir Alex said.

"But I don't mind..." Anne said, still standing.

"Thank you, Anne, we will pass on your willingness to Scotland Yard," Sir Alex said, and then turned toward the kitchen and pointed.

"We brought some food for you and wanted to check on your arrival. Glad to see everything is fine. Kevin and Jerry have been informed to let us know of anything you need. We will stop in tomorrow." He and Lord Ashley got up and left the house.

"We are having pheasant and potatoes, Anne. Hope you enjoy good English food. Jerry here is pretty good in the kitchen," Kevin said.

Anne went back up to her room and read the article. It was as they had said, but she could not believe that Jarred did this. She may not have known him a long time, but she felt it in her heart. He was being set up, but she couldn't fathom why. Somehow, all this was connected to the diary and the sixty- year-old murder of Theresa and the stolen gold. But what did Sir Alex and Lord Ashley have to do with it? And why did Lord Ashley have a fifty-year-old picture of the Cornwall estate in his office? Then again, she thought, as Kevin announced dinner from downstairs, she could be wrong, and Jarred could be guilty.

:

Jarred sat in the small London flat with the same newspaper in front of him. The article didn't tell him anything new. He was in Ginger's apartment shortly before her death and, in fact, his prints were likely on the knife that killed her.

He got up and checked his untraceable MI5 cell phone, at least that is what he had been assured. The signal kept coming in and out and he had missed several calls over the last day, including one that he sorely wished he had caught—the one from Anne. By the time he tried her back it must have been too late. His man had reported that she had come downstairs, mailed an envelope, and then had been picked up by a late model Blue Rover with government plates, but that he had been prevented from following. The interrogation of the driver from the white car yielded nothing. He was just a hired pawn.

Now he found himself wanted by Scotland Yard for murder and, worse than that, Anne had been taken somewhere. He had no doubts that, whoever took her, they were definitely not his allies.

Jarred opened a bag of crisps, or, as he reminded himself, Anne would have called them 'potato chips.' His phone rang in the middle of a bite, and he wiped off his hands to pick up the handset.

"I think we found out who took her." It was Logan, the man who had lost Anne at the hotel.

Jarred sat up straight. "And?" he prompted.

"Sir Alex Reinquist's name is mentioned in her letter." Jarred didn't question him about where the letter came from—he already knew.

"Sir Alex Reinquist..." Jarred said. The name was vaguely familiar.

"He is Lord Ashley's aide," Logan said.

Jarred grew very concerned. This was unexpected, and not good news. Lord Ashley was a very powerful man and ran an intelligence taskforce. Worse yet, it was not under MI5 control, and he would have to be very careful about how they were to proceed.

"Is he personally involved?" Jarred asked.

"We don't know. The only person mentioned in her letter is Sir Alex Reinquist. From what I gather though, Sir Reinquist does not do anything without Lord Ashley's knowledge. Of course, this could be an exception," Logan said.

"Alright. We will have to deal with that later. Any idea where she might be?" Jarred asked.

"A couple of ideas: Lord Ashley has several private residences around London. Of course, he also has access to any number of other safe houses if he is using his government cover. Still, if he wanted to make sure that no one knew where she was, it is likely he took her to one of his homes. On the other hand, Sir Reinquist, only has one residence that we can find - and it's in London. I've sent men over to take a look, but I don't think it's likely. If I had to make a wager I'd bet on one of two places: either Huntingdon, out past Cambridge, or an estate out near Bury St. Edmunds way," Logan said.

"And between the two?" Jarred asked.

"Bury St. Edmonds, a place by the Westley Estate. It's not very big, very secluded and surrounded by a very large open field. There is no way to approach the house without being seen; a perfect safe house," Logan said.

"I'll take that one," Jarred said.

Logan paused on the line.

"What?" Jarred asked. He was anxious to get going.

"May I remind of you of the small fact that you are not a field operative?" Logan asked.

"But I've had some training," Jarred said, "I'm authorized to carry a gun."

"Yes. True, but who isn't? A weekend of field ops a year doesn't really prepare you for something like this. Especially if what you suspect is true and Lord Ashley is using professionals. Perhaps even some of our own personnel," Logan said.

The thought had occurred to Jarred.

"Look. It's not like my uncle is going to officially sanction a mission to investigate Lord Ashley. So what other choice do I have? I'll tell you what, I'll just take a look, if it looks promising I'll call you, OK?" Jarred asked.

"Or I could just go with you," Logan said.

"How about you go check out Huntingdon…" Jarred said.

"Fine Jarred, it's your call. I don't like it but she is your friend."

"If you don't hear from me by tomorrow, you know where to look. Can you drop off a map and some night gear?" Jarred asked.

"Yeah. And we are going to spend some time going over exactly what you are going to do in case things go wrong. I really would hate to lose one of my best buds. Besides, you owe me and I plan to collect," Logan hung up and Jarred spent the next several hours thinking about how he was going to do this. He had to assume Anne was being held against her will, and that these men knew that someone might come looking for her. He found himself wishing that he had taken a couple of more weekends of field training.

Chapter 37

May 16, 1939

Michael arrived shortly after 8:00 p.m. and John looked up at him, seeing him shrug. He was tired of trying to be civil.

John had his belongings packed up in his open satchel on the bed. The bag remained unzipped, and there was a small framed picture of Anne looking off into the distance on the top of the pile of clothing. John was dressed in a black turtleneck sweater and black wool pants and boots. Michael sat at the table reading the newspaper.

"When are you going?" John asked.

"I'll leave tomorrow." Michael didn't look up from the paper.

"Where to?" John asked. He wanted to know.

"I've booked passage on a ship going to South America, but I doubt I'll stay there. I'll probably head up to the United States. Seems like it's the only place that's not going to be at war," Michael said. He couldn't think of a port in South America or he would have mentioned it. He quickly flipped the paper to the outgoing ship manifest.

"What's the ship named?" John asked. Michael had just found the page and glanced down the list.

"The Corre," Michael said, and smiled to himself. John was getting better at this game, "it's going to Rio."

John made a mental note of the information.

"Your guy on this boat I'm leaving on: what do I pay him? I don't have much money," John said.

"He said you can work off the passage, and maybe even earn something. It depends on what you are willing to do," Michael said.

"Anything… doesn't matter to me at all." John drifted back to the room and looked one last time at the picture of Anne before zipping it up. He returned to the kitchen and put his canvas satchel on the floor.

"Look, Michael, you've won. I'm leaving. Whatever game you played it's over… I realize you don't like me and you know I don't care for you, but you know I'm in love with your sister…"

"You want something from me Johnny?"

"If Anne ever asks…tell her –" Michael interrupted him.

"Where do you think you'll end up, and what name are you going to use?" he asked.

"Probably New York or Chicago. They're easy to get lost in. I'm planning on going by the name John Harris," John said. Michael smiled at hearing the plan. The information might come in useful some day.

John picked up a glass of water that he had poured earlier and drained the glass. Almost immediately he started to feel funny and he used his arm to brace himself on the table.

"Michael, what did you do..." The last thing he saw was a grin on Michael's face.

"Nighty night, Johnny boy," Michael said, as he sipped his glass of wine.

:

John awoke to the sound of a foghorn. His mind was as muddied as the view he looked out upon. He could smell the salt air, and he slowly got to his feet and looked around. There was nothing but water.

He got up and steadied himself, using the ships railing. He was thankful to see his satchel and he grabbed it and walked down the deck until he found a door. A sailor came out of it and lit a smoke then looked at him.

"Where am I?" John asked. The sailor looked as if he heard the question all the time.

"You're on the Grunion," he took a drag and stared out to sea.

"And where are we going?" John asked.

"Africa," was all that the sailor said as he walked away.

John worked as a steward on the Grunion for over a month. They stopped at Dakar, Abidjan, and then Port Elizabeth in South Africa where he was able to get work on a vessel going to Buenos Aires, Argentina. After a month there he worked his way up the coast to Uruguay, Brazil, Venezuela and finally into Mexico. It was October 1939 by the time he reached Chicago. England had declared war on Germany and the Second World War was raging across Europe.

Even if he was allowed to, there was no way to get back home.

:

Anne and Lizzy's mother passed away a year later in 1940. Lord Cornwall immersed himself in work as World War II engulfed dozens of countries, and Britain found herself the last obstacle to Hitler in Europe. Anne became Lizzy's de facto mother, and raised her at the Canterbury estate until she was eighteen, at which point Lizzy married and moved to London with her new husband.

When the United States finally joined Britain in 1941, Michael was serving on the HMS Exeter, and had fought in the Battle of River Plat. He later spent some time in Uruguay as well as Argentina. He returned to England as a war hero well after the conflict had ceased and the rebuilding had started, his previous life seemingly forgotten.

After the war, the forty million pounds sterling of bullion that was sent to Halifax in May of 1939 was returned to Britain. It was discovered, during the repatriation, that over a half million pounds were missing. The location of the missing bullion was never found however, as the Minister of Finance, Lord Cornwall was, in the end, responsible. The Queen accepted his resignation and she appointed his long time former aid, Sir Percy Harrison to the post of Finance Minister.

Sir Percy knew without a doubt that Michael was involved in the disappearance of his son. Four days after his vanishing he returned to his office and drafted a letter of resignation, which he had hand delivered to Lord Cornwall. He then called one of his best friends, the present acting head of MI5, and took the dangerous and unusual course of opening a file on a royal. Michael Ellias Cornwall II. It was a file that would last Sir Percy's entire lifetime, as well as that of his son. He had no idea how the truth would be found, but he appeased his anger with the thought that, one day, Michael would be held accountable.

At his father's death in 1961, Michael assumed the title of Lord Cornwall and started selling his family holdings in England. The MI5 file on him remained open but despite numerous suspicious events throughout his life, no substantial evidence was ever found. After a particularly disturbing episode in 1963 involving the raping of a fourteen-year-old girl at the family's Yorkshire estate, Michael moved to Hong Kong where he took up collecting Asian and Eastern European antiquities.

John Harrison was never found. Late in life Sir Percy Harrison fathered another boy and a daughter, Jarred & Amelie Harrison. He died in 1977 at sixty-eight years old. As a director of MI5, his last formal wish was that the case on Michael Ellias Cornwall II be left open. He made sure that Jarred Harrison, his youngest son, knew about his older brother John as well as Michael Cornwall. In 1977, the year his father died, Jarred Harrison became an officer in MI5 at the age of twenty-one. That same year Amelie Harrison, then twenty-five, married Theodore Mulberry. A year later she gave birth to Jarred Mulberry, the man wanted in the murder of Ginger Thereaux at her flat in Notting Hill.

Chapter 38

2004

Jarred left the flat a little after eleven p.m. It was cloudy and cold. The drizzle had just started, and he buttoned his leather coat and pulled the wool scarf around him. He had gloves on his hands and he found it difficult to insert the key into his car door. Once inside, he put down his small bag and started the engine. There was no traffic, and Jarred made good time out M11. The road to Bury St. Edmunds was not easy to find, and he turned around several times before finding the correct direction. Logan's map lay open on the passenger seat, and Jarred stopped the car about four kilometers from where Logan had marked, and parked in a grove of trees.

It was lightly raining, and Jarred pulled out a black knit cap and slipped it on his head. He pulled out a nine millimeter gun and put it in his right hand pocket, then strapped a knife and sheath on the inside of each leg. He pulled out a pair of night vision goggles, placed them on his head, and looked through the darkness to where the house should be.

He saw a building, several kilometers in the distance. A single light shone through a window on the bottom floor. He could not see any cars. Jarred checked the laces on his soft soled moccasins and started walking. He first went along the paved road and then exited the pavement for the tall grass. The wet dirt stuck to his feet, and he stopped every ten meters or so to remove the clumps. When he got about three hundred meters from the house, he bent down and swam through grass using his hands as guides, and made his way up to the edge of the parking area. By the time he reached the edge, it was almost 2:00 a.m., and he saw no evidence of anyone awake.

From the grass, it was about fifty meters to the front door. The graveled area extended around the entire perimeter. It would be nearly impossible for him to get to the house undetected if anyone was watching. He used his goggles to look for any surveillance equipment that might be attached to the exterior. He saw none on the front.

Jarred backed into the grass and made his way around to the side to his right and then to the back. There did not appear to be any cameras on the exterior of the house, or wires running along the ground. The final wall of the house had the fewest windows and Jarred thought it would be the best one to make an approach. He was thankful for the rain, and waited for a heavy downpour, then ran with the gun in his hand to the stone wall. He waited in silence, his face pressed against the wet rocks. There was no sound but the water dripping from the gutters above. On the corner of the home the stones had been placed slightly offset from the face of the wall. He looked up and observed a window on the second story that he thought he could see in if he climbed high enough, so he removed his gloves and placed them in his pockets, along with the gun, and pulled himself up like he was climbing a rock face. At about five meters, he craned his neck to see in the window and it looked like there was a bed with someone laying in it. His heart leapt in anticipation, and he strained to see clearer, but the rain was obscuring the lenses of his goggles and he finally gave up. He tried to see if there was a way to climb over to the window but it was impossible, and so he descended back to the ground.

As he stood there with the rain pouring down, Jarred knew he should call Logan, but with the adrenaline pumping through his veins he was confident that he was up to this task. Besides, he reasoned, Anne was really his dilemma, not anyone else's. With Logan's voice chastising him in his head, he determined that he would have to go through one of the main floor windows or doors.

Jarred moved silently around the side of the house and tried each window, but they were all locked. He then tried the rear of the house, but again, nothing was open. He moved over to the door and put his hand on the knob, but thought he saw a movement of something inside and quickly ducked down, pressing his back against the wall. His hand involuntarily moved to his pocket where he grabbed the handle of his weapon. It was slick with rain, and he pulled it out slowly as he waited for several minutes. The rhythm of his heart pulsed in coordination with his breaths. He willed it to slow down and then moved back to the door to look in. The entrance led to a laundry area, and he could see the light of a single dim bulb in what appeared to be the living room. With his goggles on, he could see the outline of several chairs and sofas. The room was furnished, but not lived in, like something you would find in a vacation home or furniture store.

He tried the knob again but it didn't yield, so he pulled on it. The door was firm, with no play. Jarred moved around to the opposite side of the house and then the front. There was only one option left: the main door.

It was a wooden door made of hand-sawn timbers and clad with iron. The lock was at least a hundred years old, and had a thumb release. Jarred carefully pulled the door to him and tried the release. He was not surprised when it didn't unlock. But this one he could open.

He could hear the voice of the field Sargent from his last training session in his head as he pulled out his pack from his inside pocket and removed two small steel utensils, working them into the keyhole, telling him to be efficient and quiet. In a matter of seconds, he heard the click and he winced, holding his breath, but nothing happened so he slowly opened the door. The rain was coming down hard, and he knew if anyone were inside they would be able to hear the change in cadence, but he had no choice. His left hand was on the handle and his right on his weapon. As the door opened he again thought he saw movement and froze in place. The night goggles were helpful for seeing, but peripheral vision was not good and he thought about removing them, then decided against it. Perhaps he was seeing shadows from the clouds, or curtains, which a draft of air was moving.

Jarred stepped inside the door and was delighted that the floors where covered in carpet instead of a hard surface. He took a moment to wipe off his moccasins. If this were the wrong house, he would have a serious cleaning bill.

To his right there was an office that was empty. Straight-ahead was the living room that he had seen from the rear, and about three meters in front of him was a staircase. There were two other rooms to his left that were closed and he made a mental note of their relative locations. If Anne were being held here they would keep her on the second floor. The guards would be on the first floor. Jarred took a step forward and then another. The carpet was soft and yielding, and thankfully silent. He held the gun up with both hands in front of his chest and moved silently to the staircase, where he placed his right foot on the far right side of the second stair, and took a deep breath before putting his weight on it. He was relieved that there was no sound. He moved his left foot up to the fourth step and did the same procedure.

The creak pierced the silence and though he faced upward toward the second floor he knew, for a certainty, he saw movement out of the corner of his eye. With one motion he kicked his feet out from under himself and spun around, the small of his back slamming into the second stair. The flash in front and to his left, was amplified a hundred times by the night vision and he was temporarily blinded. With one motion he fired a shot in its direction then ripped off the goggles and blinked, madly trying to see something. The guard must have been waiting against the far wall. They had been expecting him! The knowledge both exhilarated him, as it meant that Anne was here, and terrified him because he knew it was a trap.

He felt the next shot before he heard the sound. His left shoulder was thrown against the staircase wall like someone had swung a cricket bat at him, and he heard the blow as it resonated up the wall.

Someone on the second floor fell, or threw themselves to the floor, and Jarred let go a barrage of shots into the living room as he stumbled backwards up the stairs. A voice barked out an order below him. That meant there were at least two guards downstairs and he had no idea how many on the second floor.

His eyes were still mostly useless and his ears strained to hear every sound. The pain in his shoulder spread to his upper arm but it kept him alert and he moved along, hunched over, to the first door. Light appeared from downstairs and it cast a shadow down the hallway, which helped him locate the knob. It was locked and he threw his one remaining good shoulder against it and felt the jamb crack. The room was empty. Jarred took a moment to stand still, but he heard no evidence that anyone was moving downstairs so he moved to the next door and tried the knob. It yielded, and he pushed it open while standing with his back against the wall. No sounds. He spun into the dark room with his gun extended in front of him, and saw movement to his right, beside the bed. Someone was huddled beside it and they didn't look like a guard. Jarred held his gun at them and opened his mouth.

"Anne?"

The person looked at him. It was definitely a woman.

"Jarred?" It was Anne's voice.

"Anne. Yes, it's me," Jarred said, as he put up his hand for her to be quiet so that he could hear what the guards were doing. He leaned toward the open door. There were voices resonating up the stairwell. He could hear at least two men.

He looked at Anne, who had gotten to her feet and moved next to him. He felt her grab for his arm and he winced. She released it.

"Are you hurt?" she whispered.

"I took a bullet," he said, surprised at the steadiness in his voice. He turned back toward the open door. There was no way he could get her down the stairwell without risking both their lives. He was trapped, and they knew it. Jarred stepped inside the room and shut the door. His mind was getting cloudy from the pain. He turned on the light and looked at Anne. Her face was awash with concern and fear. She looked at his shoulder and reached out a hand to remove some loose fabric. He looked down to where she touched. There was a dark stain on his left shoulder. The bullet must have missed his vest and hit him.

"Anne, How many guards are there?" he asked. She looked at his face.

"Two," she said. "You need to stop the bleeding. I can't see how bad it is." She looked at him and her face belied her anxiety.

"Are there any men outside?" he asked, ignoring her comment.

"I ... I don't think so. I haven't seen any," she said.

Someone yelled up from downstairs.

"Aye! You up there!" It sounded like Kevin. "I know you can hear me. You've got yourself in a bit of a bind. There's no way out but the stairs. Why don't you just come down and we'll talk about it. No need for anyone to get hurt."

Jarred ignored the voice and turned back towards Anne.

"Did they hurt you?" he asked.

"No. I don't even know what they want," Anne said. "They took my cell phone and insisted I come out here with them. I wasn't given a choice."

"Who took you out here? Who talked to you?" Jarred asked. The dizziness was getting worse, and he reached out to Anne, who helped him sit on the bed. The revolver remained in his right hand. She looked at it, then back at him.

"Lord Ashley and Sir Alex Reinquist." She sat down beside him and held on to his left arm. "Jarred, what is this all about? I haven't the foggiest notion—" She was interrupted by the voice downstairs.

"Hey! You have two choices. Either throw down your gun and come down, or we will come up. Either way, if you don't want the girl hurt, you need to give it up. We'll give you sixty seconds to decide. Then we're coming."

Jarred surveyed the situation. He was in no shape to fight, though if it was just him he would probably try. He took out his cell phone and dialed a number as he opened the door. The phone failed to ring and he looked at it. No signal. He swore and put it back in his pocket.

"We're coming down," he said.

"Remove the clip and throw the weapon down."

Jarred turned to Anne: "Look, stay alert. If I get an opportunity I'm going to go after them. You run. My car is four kilos to the east. Just follow the road," he said.

"No, Jarred. I can't leave you here like this. Maybe they will take us to a hospital. Maybe they really just want to talk," Anne said.

"Anne. You don't understand what this is about. They're not going to let either of us go." The voice interrupted again.

"What's taking so long? Send the girl down first, then you come down. Keep your hands where we can see them."

Jarred looked at Anne and threw his gun and clip down the stairs. Anne followed them.

Anne saw the two men first. Kevin was to the right at the bottom of the stairs and Jerry was to the left. They both had their guns drawn, and Anne gazed down at the floor, awaiting instructions. Her heart was beating so hard that it felt like a herd of bulls in her chest.

"That's it, Anne. You come towards me," Jerry said, as he motioned with his hand.

Jarred followed slowly, his left arm up at his side, but not fully extended. When Kevin saw this he yelled and it made Anne jump, and look back toward Jarred.

"Get yer hands in the air!" he said.

"I can't. I've been shot." Anne was surprised at how steady his voice was.

"Oh, that you have. Must hurt like hell," Kevin chuckled. He signaled for Jarred to join Anne, which he did.

"You realize I'm MI5. They know where I am," Jarred said, as he stared at Jerry, who appeared to be the senior man. Anne didn't give any evidence that she was surprised. She remained with her eyes cast downward, her hands now at her sides.

"Yes. We know who you are. A *desk* operative," Kevin smirked at Jerry's insult, "You're also wanted for murder. If your buds know where you are, it certainly is not officially sanctioned," Jerry said.

"That's just a story that Lord Ashley blew to the press. There's no truth in that, and you know it." Jarred lost his footing. The loss of blood was making him loose equilibrium.

"You have to get him medical attention. He's hurt." Anne spoke up as she looked at Jarred. The two guards seem to contemplate the request, and Anne took that as permission, so she hurried over to Jarred and took his arm to steady him.

"Not going to happen, Miss. I guess you're going to have to be the nurse." Jerry reached over and threw her a towel from off the couch. He had used it as a napkin for dinner.

Anne took the towel and wrapped it around Jarred's arm and cinched it as tight as she could. He winced and she looked at his face. He was obviously in a lot of pain.

"You realize he came to get you for a reason," Jerry said. Anne and Jarred looked at him.

"You put him at the murder scene. You're the last witness," Jerry said. He held his revolver lightly sideways in his hand to make his point with the nozzle.

"What do you mean?" Anne said, and looked at Jerry, then at Jarred. "Are you implying he came here to kill me? That's ludicrous!"

"Think about it. He's wanted for the murder of Ginger. You put him at the scene. He claims he is on a government assignment, but you know as well as we do, this is personal." Anne looked at Jarred, who remained silent. She looked at his forehead, his cheeks, his mouth, then at his eyes, which gazed back at her. In that moment, the connection they had shared explained everything she needed to hear from him. She didn't want to lose him, whatever the cost.

"This is stupid. You kidnap me and hold me here, and then try to tell me that the guy who is trying to rescue me is actually here to kill me?! Do you think I'm an imbecile?" Anne stared at Jerry. *"You're* the idiots." She couldn't resist the jab, but regretted it immediately when Kevin came over and stood with his gun menacingly in front of them both. He obviously meant it to be intimidating, but it also put him in a direct line in front of Jerry and Jarred feigned to be groggier than he really was and fell forward, over his knees. His hand right hand grasped the knife strapped to his shin and he withdrew it from the sheath.

Kevin saw the movement a little too late as Jarred sprung up from his position with the blade in his hand and drove it into Kevin's thigh. The force propelled him back toward Jerry. But Jerry had seen the movement and adroitly dodged the hurtling guard.

"BACK OFF!" He yelled and fired a shot toward the two men, which were now on the floor. Kevin provided a human shield to Jarred. Jarred was about to take the knife and put it to Kevin's throat when Anne screamed.

"NO! Jarred! Please stop!" She was looking at Jerry, who had his hand on the trigger with a clear shot of Jarred's head. Jarred froze and allowed Kevin to roll off him and retreat about a foot away. Kevin held his wounded leg with his left hand and retrieved his gun with his right. His breath was ragged and his face was twisted up in anger.

Jarred laid his head back on the floor, his arms and legs splayed and looked at the ceiling. His shoulder throbbed and he was gasping for air. Anne ran over to him only to be shoved away by Kevin who then kneeled over Jarred, pinning him to the floor with his good knee on Jarred's injured shoulder. A jolt of pain shot through Jarred's neck, and he grimaced.

"You son of a—" It was the last thing Jarred remembered hearing as Kevin's gun crashed down on the left side of his head.

:

Jarred woke up in a barren room. Anne knelt beside him and smiled. She looked exhausted. He tried to sit up, but Anne put a hand on his chest and held him down. He had no strength to resist.

"Where are we?" he asked.

"I don't know. They blindfolded me. I think we're about an hour away from the other house, but I'm not sure. I thought I lost you back there." She looked at him, and her eyes filled with tears. Jarred reached up and touched her cheek. She closed her eyes and nuzzled against it.

"How long?" he asked. She opened her eyes and took his hand with hers.

"About a day," she said.

"A day?" he asked.

"Yes. I can't tell for sure. They took away our watches and the room has no windows... I was really scared." Her face was calm, but showed her exhaustion.

"Are they here?" he asked.

"I think so. Once in awhile I can hear something."

Jarred took stock of how he felt. Other than the splitting headache and his throbbing shoulder, he felt remarkably OK. He turned his head and looked around the room. It was made of cement, with a single light fixture in the middle of the ceiling. There were two mattresses on the floor, a couple of chairs, and some food that sat on a makeshift table.

He was hungry. Anne saw him look at it and got him some bread and water. He allowed her to feed him and then fell back asleep.

When he awoke, Anne was curled up next to him on the bed. The room was cool and he could hear the soft rhythm of her breath, and decided to leave her alone. He sat up and surveyed the room again. The door was the only exit and was made of metal, with the hinges on the opposite side. It wasn't a hopeful sight. He could hear several voices having an animated conversation and walked over to the door, but couldn't make out the words.

Jarred ate some scraps of something that looked like a kind of fowl and drank another glass of water, then sat and watched Anne sleep. It was the most peaceful thing he had every seen. She awoke about an hour later, opened her eyes and smiled when she saw him looking at her, then pushed herself upright. They sat a few feet away from each other.

"How long have I been sleeping?" she asked.

"I really don't know. At least a couple of hours." Jarred looked around the room again. "I wish I knew what time it was. Actually, while we're at it, the day would be nice too." He grinned and she responded.

"I bet you have a lot of questions," he said. Anne nodded.

"Why didn't you tell me about your relationship to Sir Percy?" she asked.

"I honestly didn't know anything until we showed up at Betty's house. Seeing the Cornwall name made me remember the story I had heard from my uncle. You know we are related then?" he asked.

"Yes. I think..." she said.

"Sir Percy Harrison had two other children besides John, Amelia and Jarred, my uncle and namesake. My mom is Amelia Harrison, she married Theodore Mulberry, my father, and here I am." Jarred paused to make sure Anne followed.

"We had been told about John Harrison, the missing son, when we were children. It was an unspoken quest of the family to find out what happened to him. But, until you came along with your inscription and diary, all the information we had ever received amounted to nothing. The diary sheds some light on particulars that we never knew. The family based what happened on the letter that John sent to his father, but that was ambiguous at best. The story of Anne Cornwall explains a lot." Jarred stopped and looked at her again.

"Do you have the diary?" she asked.

"Yes. We managed to remove it before Lord Ashley's men gathered your belongings. For several days I've had a man from MI5, a friend of mine, Logan, unofficially keeping an eye on you. When you disappeared in the blue Rover, another car prevented him from following." Anne remembered the white car behind the Rover.

"Did you read it?" Anne asked.

"Not all of it. There was no time to finish it. I'm sure my uncle Jarred is researching it as we speak. We hope there will be some clues as to the whereabouts of John, as well as evidence against Michael Cornwall. You know he is still alive?" Jarred asked.

"Yes. In Hong Kong, right?"

Jarred nodded.

"So how did you find me?" Anne asked.

"The letter you left. You're a smart girl. We traced Sir Alex Reinquist to Lord Ashley, and that link provided some possible houses. Seems like they were right," Jarred said.

"Do you know what happened to Ginger?" Anne asked.

"Yes and No. The news is correct in that I did go to her flat after our visit I did—late that evening. Ginger called me and was scared about something she had learned. Now we understand why." He gestured to their present quarters. "We had a light supper and I advised her to let me know if something else happened. Lord Ashley's men, or someone connected to him, must have killed her after I left. They used the knife, which I had touched during the meal. It's not a favorable situation for me right now..." Jarred had been so intent on finding Anne that it wasn't until he laid it out for her that the seriousness of his situation dawned on him.

"She must have revealed your name before she died..." The thought made him sick. They must have tortured her.

"Why didn't you just tell me about your uncle?" Anne asked again.

"To be honest, there is no good reason. Perhaps I was hoping that your discovery would end in nothing. John Harrison's story is a bit of a blight on the family... and remember all the other leads we've ever had resulted in dead ends. I had no reason to suspect this one was different. But, of course, it was. By the time I realized you had stumbled on to something real... I'm sorry, Anne. I should have told you," he said.

"Why are you working in a law firm?"

Jarred laughed at her question. "Now, that's a good question! I've asked myself that many times," he said. "MI5 offered to pay for my education if I wanted to go to law school. Unlike the Cornwall's, our family suffered greatly from the war, and my great uncle's search for John, so I accepted. The paralegal job is a way for me to have some spending money while I finish school." The comment reminded Anne that she needed to start studying again if she was going to ever become an attorney. Not that it was a pressing need in the present predicament.

"What does Lord Ashley have to do with all of this? I mean, I understand why Michael Cornwall would want to stop an investigation about a murder that he probably committed, but who is Lord Ashley?" Anne asked.

"I have no idea. MI5 is working on the connection," Jarred said. He hoped it was true.

"You know, he had a picture of the Cornwall estate in his office. It appeared to be taken many years ago, when the estate was still in good repair," Anne said.

"That may be helpful," Jarred said. He made a mental note of it.

They were interrupted by the sounds of the door being unlocked. Before it was opened, a voice, Jerry's, came through.

"Back away from the door! I won't ask you twice."

The door opened slowly and, with his gun drawn, Jerry moved into the room. Anne and Jarred remained seated. Lord Ashley entered behind a second guard that stayed outside of the chamber.

"Good! I see everyone is awake. Glad to see you both are well." Lord Ashley walked over to a chair and sat down facing them.

"I imagine you are having quite the conversation." Lord Ashley paused but neither of them showed any indication that they were going to talk.

"Alright then. To business." He slapped his knees with both hands.

"We have a bit of a situation here, and we require your help." He spoke to Anne.

"Why don't you leave her out of this. She doesn't know anything," Jarred said.

"Well, not so true, but don't worry, you have a part to play as well. You realize that Scotland Yard has released a warrant for your arrest for the murder of Ginger Thereaux?" Lord Ashley said.

"That will never hold up." Jarred dismissed it for Anne's benefit, but he knew that he was in serious trouble. "There is no motive or witness that can place me at the scene."

"True, Jarred. But we are going to fix that," Lord Ashley laughed. "At special request of Lord Cornwall, we need you," he pointed at Anne, "to help us." Jarred and Anne looked at each other upon hearing the name.

Jerry walked up to Anne and grabbed her arm.

"Anne, you come with me. Jarred, sit there like a good little boy or we will kill her," Lord Ashley said. Jerry had his gun behind Anne.

"I won't help you. Why should I? You've lied to me... us, you killed a friend of Jarred's, and you've kidnapped me!" Jerry tugged on her arm. Anne yanked it back and Jerry grabbed her firmly with both hands behind her back, and dragged her out of the room.

"Leave her alone! She has nothing to do with any of this!" They could all hear Jarred yell at them as the door shut. Lord Ashley directed her down a hallway and then into another room. He turned to her and his face softened. Jerry let his grip loosen and Anne wrenched away from him and stood with her back against the wall.

"I won't help you!" Anne repeated.

"Well, that will be your choice. It should make for an interesting one," Lord Ashley laughed again. The cackling really irritated her because there was nothing funny about what he was saying.

"Here's the deal, Anne," Lord Ashley said. His face suddenly was very serious.

"We are going to let you go." He paused for the statement to sink in. "However, you are going to go to Scotland Yard and make a statement to them. You will say that you were the third person in the room, which your fingerprints will bear out, and that you saw Jarred, " he pointed down the hall with his index finger, "kill Ginger in a fit of rage over digging into his Uncle's past. You will explain that Jarred was obsessed with making sure that John Harrison was not revealed as the murderer that he was." Lord Ashley stopped, and tilted his head to look at her. Finally Anne spoke up.

"Why should I do that?" She was afraid of the answer.

"Because if you don't, we will kill Jarred." Lord Ashley said it with no emotion, "We could just do it right now if you want," he signaled to Jerry and he started toward the door.

"No!" she yelled, "But I don't understand why you want me to do this... he will think I betrayed him!" she said.

"Ah yes," Lord Ashley smiled, "that is the conundrum isn't it? But as you have so poignantly mentioned, you will denounce him, or he will die. It's your choice," Lord Ashley said.

"Why kill Jarred?" Anne stammered. "What do you possibly get out of that?"

"A story of remorse for the public. The suicide of a man who bore a terrible secret, closure of the murder of Ginger... a lot actually," Lord Ashley said.

"And if I do this – what happens to him?" she asked.

"Ah. That is a good question! And this makes it so much more interesting." He stopped to see if he had Anne's attention. "If you do as we ask, and go to the police, I will let Jarred go. Of, course he will be on the run, and think that you betrayed him, but he will live."

"How do I know you'll keep your word?"

"I guess you don't. However really, if you do as you're told it will make for a much more entertaining theater than just merely killing him, which isn't our style anyway. We prefer to enjoy watching people... shall we say, alive and miserable rather than peaceful and dead."

"I need to talk to Jarred about it," Anne said. A shiver went up her spine, and she reached across her arms and grabbed them. She stared into the air, and Lord Ashley kept talking.

"Unfortunately, that will not happen. We wanted to present you this… option, but you will not be able to discuss it. Don't you see the satire in this? You must decide whether you betray him publicly, and he lives as a suspected felon, or is killed because you refuse to do so. His life is quite literally in your hands," he laughed again.

"You can't do this! It's not fair!" Anne looked defiantly at the short man.

"Exactly," Lord Ashley said. "That is the point."

Anne kept silent. Anything she could say would be wasted on the ears of the devil who stood before her.

:

A few hours later Jerry delivered some food to Jarred. Lord Ashley was with him. Jarred's mouth had stopped bleeding and he stood as they entered. Jerry had his gun drawn and maintained his distance.

"Why are you doing this?" Jarred pointed to Lord Ashley. "What do you have to do with Michael Cornwall?"

"Ahhh…" Lord Ashley said, "Yes. That is an appropriate question."

"Jerry. Give me the gun, and wait outside." Jerry looked at him questioningly.

"Just give it, and wait outside." Jerry walked over and placed the gun in Lord Ashley's hand, and left. He shut the door behind him. Lord Ashley stood up and put more distance between himself and Jarred.

"You see, we met in Argentina after the war had ended. I was quite a bit younger than Lord Cornwall, but we found that we had… shall I say… similar tastes." Lord Ashley smiled, and Jarred could see the yellow stains of a smoker.

"We became good friends and, in fact, spent much time at the Canterbury Estate and the Yorkshire Estate. My favorite was the Canterbury home, because it had the dubious distinction of being the site of Michael's first… mischief. Yes, I think that is the proper term. Anyway, as you undoubtedly know, there was an unfortunate incident with a young girl out in Yorkshire in the 1960's and, well, let's say my position helped Michael immensely. When Michael left the country I agreed to monitor the Theresa matter, as well as his other indiscretions, in exchange for the Cornwall Estate. As a matter of fact, the last bit of the estate, the home, is being transferred to me for handling this little situation. But really, I must admit, I am doing it more out of pleasure than work. I have no need for more wealth. But Michael is so very good at getting people to sell their souls for a mere pittance, and I enjoy watching him work. "

"You're a sick bastard!" Jarred spit out.

Lord Ashley chuckled. "Well, yes. I guess I am. And I appreciate you asking about Michael and I. I mean, what's the point in doing all this if no one knows?" Lord Ashley walked backwards to the door and knocked on it with the gun.

"By the way," Lord Ashley turned around and faced Jarred as the door opened. "We let Anne go," he said, and paused, but Jarred didn't give him the satisfaction of asking why, so he just continued. "She made a deal to save her own skin in exchange for yours." He said it as Jerry took the revolver from him, then closed and locked the door behind him.

Chapter 39

The men blindfolded and bound up Anne's hands and feet, and put her in the back of a car, making her lie down. She could see that it was light out and, about an hour later, she could feel the car speed up and merge onto a major highway. She could hear the sounds of many cars and trucks around her, and guessed that they were nearing London. The driver pulled off the highway, stopped the car, and got out. Anne's imagination was going wild, and she tensed up her body in case someone tried to attack her. She heard the door by her head open and she tried to flip herself around. A hand on her head pushed her into the seat, and she stopped struggling.

"Listen. We can do this easy or hard. Up to you." It was Jerry's voice. "I'm going to remove the blindfold and you are going to behave yourself, or we are going to have a problem." Anne tensed up when she felt Jerry's hands on her face, then the sunlight flooded her eyes and she blinked rapidly to get accustomed to the brightness. She looked around and saw that they were in some deserted parking lot, and she backed away to the opposite side of the car.

"It's nothing like that. Anne. I'm not going to hurt you," Jerry said. "Look, I can untie you or you can ride into London like that. It's a long drive. What is it going to be?"

Anne contemplated the options and extended her feet toward him first. He was careful to stand back far enough so that she couldn't kick him, and he untied her ankles. Once her feet were free she turned around and offered her hands. He untied them as well and she rubbed her wrists, then acted like she was going to get out of the car.

"You can get out here if you want. Fine with me. It'll save me a drive. But, as you can see, there is nothing around for kilometers. Otherwise, you can sit back and enjoy the ride to your hotel. As you can see, we have your case." He pointed to her bag sitting on the floor of the back seat.

Anne remained silent, but pushed herself back in the car, and Jerry went around to the driver's seat. While she had the chance she tried the door handle, and it opened. Jerry looked at her in the rear view mirror.

"Convinced now?" he asked.

She ignored him and turned her head to look out the window.

An hour later they arrived back at the hotel and Anne got out and grabbed her bag. Jerry made no attempt to help her, but did roll down his window.

"You have forty eight hours to get your story on the news. Your room key is in the side pocket." He gestured toward her bag and drove off.

Anne pulled her bag and walked into the familiar lobby. The sounds and smells comforted her, but she felt a wave of emotion surge in her chest and she ran to the elevators. Thankfully, she rode up to her floor alone. Her key worked the first time she tried it and she pulled her bag into the room, shut the door, flipped the bolt then sat on the floor with her back against it. She thought about the option that Lord Ashley had given her. If she went to the police, Jarred would be convicted of a murder he didn't commit because of her. And she couldn't even explain to him why. He would think she betrayed him to save herself. But the other choice, his death, was unthinkable. She believed they would indeed kill him if she didn't do as Lord Ashley asked. A week ago, when life was less precious than it was now, she may have been able to take what some would consider the honorable choice, but the last several days had changed that. She tried to consider Jarred's wishes, but she knew in her heart there was really only one alternative. She would rather have him alive and feeling betrayed than dead at her own hand.

The thought made her whole body start to shake involuntarily, and she grabbed herself by the arms and tried to stop the shuddering but couldn't. The waves undulated in her chest until they reached her mind, and she broke down and cried uncontrolled on the floor, her feet tucked into a fetal position until she lay spent, the side of her face on the carpet.

She closed her eyes and felt very tired as the fatigue hit her like a drug.

:

When she awoke, her mind ran through all the facts that she knew about both murders and the people involved. Like playing a game of chess, she started to formulate a plan. If she couldn't get a checkmate, she would go for the next best thing. When she had gone through the plan a half dozen times, she opened her eyes and sat up.

She could feel the indents in her face and she rubbed them. It reminded her of Jarred's hand cradling her face just a few hours before. The image was what she needed to motivate her to get up and start to work.

She went over to the television and turned it on. She had been gone for a little over two days. Anne watched the news channel for a half an hour to see if Jarred was making headlines, but saw nothing. At least that was in her favor. Next she checked her luggage and was happy to see her cell phone, which worked, as well as her purse. She would need her credit cards.

Anne pulled out a hotel envelope and placed her passport as well as her company Visa card in it and sealed it. Then she addressed it to her room number, grabbed her ATM card as well as her room key, and ran downstairs. She was relieved to see that she did not recognize the clerk at the front desk, and handed him the envelope, which he accepted. He said he would give it to the room guest when they next checked in. Anne then went to the lobby ATM machine and withdrew three hundred pounds. It was the most that it would give her.

She returned to her room and called the concierge and asked for the number to Scotland Yard. With the number beside her, she opened a bag of nuts from the in room snack bar and ate the almonds while she went over what she was going to say.

She dialed the number and took a deep breath when it rang.

"Hello. Scotland Yard. May I help you?" A man answered the phone.

"Hello. May I speak to the detective in charge of the Ginger Thereaux murder please?" Anne said.

"May I ask what your relationship to the case is?" he asked.

"I'm a witness," Anne said.

"I'll get an inspector. Please hold."

A few seconds later a different voice answered.

"This is Inspector Rowan, who am I speaking to?" he asked.

"Inspector Rowan. My name is Anne Compton. I am an American citizen and I have information regarding the murder of Ginger Thereaux," Anne said.

"Can you tell me where you are calling from Ms. Compton?"

"The Jury's Great Russell St. Hotel," Anne said.

"Ms. Compton, I'll be over in about thirty minutes." Inspector Rowan said. Anne realized he didn't ask for her room number but figured he would just ask the front desk.

She made several more calls on the house phone and then switched to her cell.

"Hello Jen? Sorry, I know it's early." Actually she hadn't calculated the time but it was early.

"Annie? What are you calling at this hour for?" Jen asked.

"Jen. Wake up. I need you to write some things down. It's important," Anne said. She heard some commotion on the other end of the line and waited till Jen came back on.

"OK. Is there something wrong?" Jen asked.

"No. Listen. I sent you an envelope several days ago. Don't open it—yet. I need you to write down a name: Inspector Rowan, Scotland Yard. I'm meeting with him in a few minutes. Are you getting this?" Anne asked.

"Yes. But Annie—are you OK? This is all very weird..." Jen said.

"Everything is fine, Jen. There are just some legal matters that I need to take care of, and I wanted someone to know where I am. Please don't ask any more... write down that Jarred Mulberry is with Lord Ashley and that he is involved with... the situation involving Ginger Thereaux. T-h-e-r-e-a-u-x. Got it?" Anne said.

"Yes. But—" Jen began, but Anne cut her off.

"If you do not hear from me in forty eight hours, notify the American Consulate what I just said, that I called Inspector Rowan today. That's all. Sorry to dump all this on you, but please no questions," Anne said.

"OK. Annie. But this is really screwed up," Jen said.

The next call Anne made was to Harry.

"Hi, Harry. It's Anne. Look, I know I'm doing it again. Sorry, but I need a big favor."

"Anne? Is there something wrong? I've been trying to reach you, but the office said you haven't been there in two days?" Harry said. She was surprised at how awake he sounded.

"I'm fine, Harry. But there have been some legal complications. I'm sorry about the disappearance. I'll explain more when I see you. Harry? I need that favor," Anne said.

"Anything, Anne. I hope this doesn't have to do with that stupid cross..." Harry said.

"Oh. Well, no. Not exactly. Look, Harry. Unless you hear from me, I need you to book and pay for a ticket for window pick up in two days time. Here is the airline and flight number that I need. Please do not book it until an hour before departure. It's a red eye, so I'm sure there will be seats. Can you also do a prepaid reservation under the company name for me at the Newark Marriott. Call them directly and prepay please - tell them I've lost my wallet," Anne said.

"But Anne—" Harry said.

"Oh. And one more thing. Spell my name with an 'e'. C-o-m-p-t-e-n," she said.

"I—I don't understand, Anne…" Harry said

"I'm sorry, Harry. Will you do that for me?" Anne asked.

"Yes. I'll do it. With an 'e'. Air and hotel, please take care of yourself. You'll have to let me know what this is all about," Harry said.

With all of that taken care of, Anne undressed and took a much needed shower. She got out and put on some clean but wrinkled clothes, and waited for the inspector. Her hair was wet, but she didn't bother to try and dry it. She sat on the edge of the bed, finished the bag of almonds, and made several phone calls on her cell phone before the knock came on the door.

Anne got up and checked the bathroom mirror one last time. She was wearing a pair of plain-front slacks, a simple beige short-sleeve blouse and a thin belt. Her eyes were bloodshot, and they had bags under them, but she didn't try and conceal anything.

The knock came again, and Anne unlocked the deadbolt and opened the door.

A man and a woman stood in front of her door. The man was about five foot nine, just a little taller than she was, with a brown herringbone sport coat and solid brown slacks. He looked remarkably like Jarred. The woman was in uniform and was shorter than both of them. She wore a cap.

"Ms. Compton?" he asked.

"Yes. Are you Inspector Rowan?" she asked.

He nodded.

"May we come in?" he asked.

The inspector and his silent female aide entered the room and looked around. They took a seat on the sofa, and Anne sat opposite them in the chair.

"Ms. Compton, perhaps you can explain your relationship to the deceased?" The inspector took out a pad of paper and a pen and looked at Anne.

"Ginger was a friend of a friend. I worked... I mean I work with Jarred Mulberry. He introduced us a couple of days ago," Anne said.

"And do you know where we may find Mr. Mulberry at this time?" Inspector Rowan asked.

"I'm sorry, but no. He hasn't been at work in several days," Anne said.

"Yes. So we have learned... Anne, you are an American?"

"Yes. From Chicago," she said.

"And how long have you been in London?"

Anne stopped and thought a moment. "About five days," she said, though she wasn't sure at this point.

"And what brought you here?" the inspector asked.

"I was sent here by my Chicago office to coordinate the extradition of an Eastern European artifact." Anne thought about this fact for a moment and wondered if she should allow the inspector to think that had something to do with Ginger's murder.

The inspector looked at her and stopped writing.

"That wouldn't be the missing cross from Armenia?" he asked.

"Yes. That's the one," Anne said.

"I've heard about the case. There are some very angry people..." He looked at her again.

"Yes. I'm aware of that inspector. But I don't think the two events are related," Anne said.

"Oh. I see. So would it be fair to say that you and Jarred are just business associates?"

Anne hesitated a little too long then said: "Yes."

"You act as if you are unsure of that answer, Ms. Compton," he said.

"I'm sorry. I guess we are friends as well. It only makes this more difficult," she said.

"I assume you mean about what you witnessed?" he asked.

"Yes." Anne looked at her lap. Her hands were folded together.

"Tell me what you know about the... murder," he said.

Anne took a deep breath and let it out slowly.

"Jarred and I went to visit Ginger... I think, three days ago now. I gathered, by the conversation, that Jarred and Ginger were at one time seeing one another, so it was a bit awkward." Anne paused and looked down. "Jarred needed to pick up some paperwork from her for work."

Anne wanted to see if the inspector knew the real connection between Ginger and the sixty-year-old murder of Theresa. But he seemed to accept Anne's version without question.

"Did something happen during the visit that made Jarred upset?" The inspector asked.

"Nothing in particular. He was having a bad week, so it wasn't the best timing. Ginger said that whatever he needed wasn't ready yet. So Jarred was a bit miffed."

The inspector made some notes and looked up at her to continue.

"We ended up getting caught out on the far side of London and didn't get back until really late. I think it must have been around 2:00 a.m. or so. Ginger was still awake and had been drinking. She wasn't very reasonable. When we got into the apartment it became apparent that she thought that Jarred and I were an item, and she got very abusive. He tried to calm her down, but it just seemed to irritate her more, and she grabbed a knife and attacked him. Somehow, he got it away from her and was holding on to it when she lunged at him again. They struggled. The next thing I knew, she was lying on the floor, bleeding. I freaked out, left the apartment, and caught a cab about three or four blocks from here, then returned to my hotel. I've been just wandering around the last couple of days trying to figure out what to do."

"Have you heard from Jarred?" the inspector asked.

"No. Nothing. I was kind of hoping I would but he hasn't called. I watched the news the next morning and was sick to my stomach, but it was self-defense. Really." Anne looked up at him with tears in her eyes. The policewoman got up, got a Kleenex from the bathroom, and gave it to Anne.

"So why did you wait this long?" the inspector asked.

"I don't know. I guess I was hoping he would come forward, or I could at least talk to him. But perhaps something happened…" Anne said.

"Alright. Well. I will likely have more questions as soon as we are able to do a little checking here. I apologize for this, but I will need to hold onto your passport," he said.

"Oh? Well, I don't know what to tell you about that. I just looked for it this morning and it's gone. I was just going to call the Consulate today. I normally have it with me but, with everything that has happened, I think I misplaced it, or dropped it somewhere." Anne paused and saw that the inspector wasn't buying the story.

"Look. You can look around. Everything I have is in this room," Anne said.

"I'm going to take Anne down to the station for a bit," he said to his aide. "We'll need to get her fingerprints and confirm hers are the third set in Ms. Thereaux's flat. Perhaps you can see if you can discover her lost passport. Anne - let's take a walk," he said. Anne reached for her purse and the inspector looked at it.

"Here, go ahead." Anne handed it to the policewoman and she checked it, then handed it back.

"OK. Thank you, Anne. These things are always a bit awkward… shall we?" He opened the door and offered Anne to go in front. Anne grabbed her coat and walked out the door.

When the elevator doors opened, and they walked out into the lobby, the inspector asked her to wait a moment. Anne stood in the lobby while the inspector walked up to the front desk. Anne could feel her temperature rise and she tried to overhear what he was asking. She managed to pick up something about a 'safe' and then the front desk clerk typed something on his computer and shook his head 'no'. The inspector walked back over to Anne, who was feeling very hot. Her hands were shaking and she stuffed them inside her coat pockets.

"Alright. I was just making sure that someone didn't turn it in to the hotel staff." He again offered for Anne to walk in front of him and she elected to walk beside him. It made her more comfortable than having to feel him behind her.

The ride to the station was in an unmarked car and Anne sat in the back seat.

"Inspector, now that we are alone may I ask you a question?" she asked.

"Sure, Miss Compton."

"Do you know a Sir Reinquist?" she watched him carefully to see if he flinched.

"No. Can't say I do."

"How about a Lord Ashley?" she asked. At the mention of his name the inspector looked in the rear view mirror. Anne braced herself for a response.

"How do you know Lord Ashley?" he asked.

Anne carefully considered her next words. If the inspector was working for Lord Ashley this line of questions could be disastrous.

"Someone just mentioned him. That's all," she said.

"Miss Compton. Some people here in England are not all they purport to be. It is best to be careful when meeting strangers," he said. Anne thought that was the understatement of the year. She took a deep breath and braced herself to take a step into the unknown. Sooner or later she would have to trust someone. It might as well be now.

"Inspector. I need to tell you something…" Anne said.

:

They arrived at the police station and he led her up the stairs and through the double doors. He motioned for Anne to take a seat, and then said something to the officer at the desk before walking back toward Anne.

"It'll only be a few minutes, and after they take the prints you are free to go. I need you to stay in London until you hear otherwise from me. If you do hear from Jarred, I would like to know immediately." He offered his card and she took it. "Thank you for contacting me. It'll be good to get this behind us, and I'm sure you are anxious to return home." He shook her hand and then left.

Anne sat on a long wooden bench, one of several in the waiting area, where all types of people milled around. It smelled of a mixture of smoke and sweat. Anne pulled her coat around her and sat as still as possible until she was called.

Chapter 40

The policeman gave her a towel to wipe the solution off her hands and escorted her to the front door, where he offered her a ride back to her hotel. She declined his offer and caught a taxi back to the hotel, asking the driver to wait. She went inside to the front desk and picked up the envelope with her passport and company Visa in it, then asked the taxi to take her to Avis Car rentals near the city limits.

She confirmed her Avis Express Preferred reservation under her company name, and provided the corresponding credit card. She was given a Vauxhall Vectra and found herself once again in the right hand seat of an automobile. This time, however, it wasn't for the fun of it, and she willed herself to relax and concentrate. She placed the car into gear, and then pulled out into the traffic.

After about ten minutes she started to relax a little. The knots in her shoulders would be bothering her for days, but she found that she could at least look around without running into the cars beside her. She found A2 and headed South without much of a problem, then transferred to M2 and stayed on it until she arrived in Canterbury. The sun broke out as she entered the city. After making several wrong turns she finally found the Cornwall estate, and pulled up the familiar driveway. Before going to see Betty, Anne parked at the front of the house and tried the front door. It was open, just like the last time, and she walked in to the Cornwall house. She could see her own footsteps as well as Jarred's from her last visit. The house had a comfortable, welcome feeling and, with the sunlight pouring in from the windows, Anne felt more at peace than she had for days.

Anne walked around to the stairs and slowly ascended them, like she would walk up the steps of a cathedral. She looked up at the landing and could imagine young Anne Cornwall standing there, looking down. It made her remember what the girl had been through.

Anne gently opened her door and walked into the room. It was undisturbed, except for her footsteps. She could still see the marks on the nightstand where she had bothered the dust with her fingertips. Anne bent down and looked under the bed but saw nothing, except a solid wood base. She walked over to the side nearest the wall and again bent over. There were two drawers, and she held her breath as she gently pulled the first one out, peering inside. It was filled with nothing but books and dolls. Anne moved over to the next drawer and grabbed a hold of the round knob to tug on it, but it failed to move. She tried a better grip, and strained to get it to budge. It finally gave way, and Anne landed on her rear, her back against the wall. The drawer was full of clothing.

She pulled out piece by piece, several shirts, a skirt and two sweaters. The clothing was in perfect condition, preserved by the tight seal of the drawer, and Anne marveled in the preciousness of the moment. It was the very same clothing that young Anne wore so many years ago, neatly folded, and pressed just as Anne would have guessed, with the faint smell of cedar. Anne stacked them neatly on the bed, and then remembered what she was looking for. It wasn't there. She sat on the floor and looked under the bed one last time but there was nothing else. She had counted on finding the scarf to help her with her plan, and now that would require some serious reworking—if it were possible at all.

Anne put the clothing back in the drawer and closed it tightly, then left the room and walked down the stairs. She exited through the front door and pulled the car around to the rear, in front of Betty's cottage. The familiar smoke was emanating from the chimney, and the door was closed as Anne approached it. She knocked on it.

"Come on in," Betty's voice rang out through the wood.

Anne pushed on the lever and the door swung open. Betty sat in front of the fireplace as she knitted what looked like a sweater. It was hot in the room, and Anne was tempted to leave the door open, but she removed her jacket instead.

"Hi, Anne. Good to see you again. I was happy to receive your phone call this morning," she said.

"It's good to see you too, Betty. Is that a sweater?" She sat down across from her, as far from the fire as possible.

"Yes. For the neighbor. I make them one every Christmas. I don't think they wear them, but they act appreciative and it gives me something to do!" Betty smiled.

"It's beautiful, Betty," Anne said. It was harvest gold. Betty had probably kept the yarn since the seventies, but she smiled back and put down her needles.

"You know, I haven't been to London in years. What's it like these days?" Betty asked.

"It's terribly busy. Too much traffic, and there are a lot of strange looking young ones walking around. I don't think you would like it, Betty." Anne smiled and chuckled.

"Well, I don't get around much. Never did drive. Did I mention that my husband passed away? Oh. Probably did. I repeat myself a lot. It's the curse of living alone." Betty picked up her needles and started working again.

"Betty. I had a question about the diary," Anne said. Betty nodded but kept working.

"There is a scarf mentioned in it. Anne said she hid it under her bed." Betty looked up and stopped.

"Did you look for it dear?" Betty asked. Her face was unreadable.

"Yes. There is nothing there," Anne said, and Betty smiled. "Do you know where it is Betty?"

"Hmmm. Why do you want it, dear? It's been a very long time…" Betty looked at her with sad eyes and then averted them to the fireplace.

"I think it is important, Betty. It might help solve a murder that happened here," Anne said.

"Theresa." Betty looked at her.

"Yes, Theresa," Anne said, "do you know where it is, Betty?"

Betty turned away and picked up a picture frame. Anne had seen it before.

"Did you know that you look a lot like my sister did when she was young?" Betty handed her the picture, and Anne reluctantly took it. She looked at the old black and white picture of the two girls next to the horse.

"Chestnut? Right?" Anne tried to recall the name.

"No. That was my horse. This one was Odd fellow." Anne knew she had heard that name before, but couldn't recall where. Betty reached out to take the picture from Anne but it slipped from her grasp and they both held their breath as they watched it hit the carpet and fall apart.

"OH! I'm sorry Betty!" Anne reached over and picked it up. The picture had come out of the frame and there was an inscription on the back. Anne froze as she read it. She reached out with her right hand and picked it up carefully off the carpet, then looked at Betty. Betty held out her hand for it, but Anne turned it over and looked at the photograph and then again at the inscription on the back. It was written in pen with a flowing hand and read 'Anne & Elizabeth '38'.

Anne looked up at her and realized how stupid she had been. Betty & Lizzy—both were abbreviated names for Elizabeth!

"Betty?" Anne asked. She took the old woman's hands as she knelt in front of her. "Anne was your sister?"

Betty nodded as her eyes filled and the tears slowly fell down her wrinkled face.

"You're Lizzy?" Anne asked.

"Yes," Betty said. She took the picture from Anne, and held it in her hand as she looked at it.

"Anne was my best friend. She raised me." She looked down at the young woman in front of her. "She died twelve years ago, in London."

Anne didn't know what to think. This was Lizzy, the child she had read so much about in the diary. She sat there on the floor, the fire crackling, with a person she had only imagined in her thoughts. She might as well have just met the Mad Hatter or Mother Goose. It was like seeing a fairy tale come to life. She had so many questions!

"Betty, why didn't you tell me?" Anne asked.

Betty wiped away the tears. "I was going to, but when you showed up you reminded me so much of my sister that I just couldn't. It was too difficult. Better for you to think that it was all ancient history."

"But the diary?" Anne said.

"Yes. I probably shouldn't have given you that. I just felt like it was time that someone knew what my sister went through. She didn't have much of a life. She never had a husband or children. She always smiled for me, but I knew inside she was not really happy. How could she be? All that doubt…" Betty drifted off and gazed into the flames.

Anne considered telling her everything that had transpired, but decided it would do no good.

"Betty. Do you have the scarf?" Anne asked again.

"Yes. I do. I took it from the drawer a long time ago." Betty got up and went into the bedroom and came back a few minutes later. She had a plastic bag with a blue wool scarf in it. Anne could see the dark stains. She handed it to her.

"Why didn't you turn this into the police?" Anne asked.

"I don't know dear, what would they do with it?" Betty asked innocently.

"Well they could have tested it for DNA and...well, you know, microscopic fibers..."Anne didn't bother to finish because she saw the blank look on Betty's face. She looked around the small living area and didn't even see a TV.

"Never mind, Betty. It's OK," she said.

"Betty?" Anne asked, as Betty picked up her knitting needles.

"Yes dear?"

"Did you ever hear from John?"

Betty looked up again. Her eyes once again filled with tears. "No. If only he had let her know he was safe... but she never heard from him."

Anne saw *The Woman in White* under her chair and picked it up. She opened it up to the inscription and read it again. For the first time she noticed the line under 'never'. She looked at Betty.

"What do you know about this book?" Anne asked.

"It must be the book that Anne hid her letter in that she speaks about in the diary, but I have no idea how it got to America," Betty said. She pointed to the address label. "My mother used to put those on all the books.

"I'm sure Michael never delivered the letter she wrote to John, Betty. He must have thrown it out and kept the book," Anne said.

"That's possible," Betty said. "When I moved back here, many years ago, estate buyers purchased most of the books and furniture, and sold them off. I told them to leave the piano and my sister's room alone. It was her sanctuary, and the piano was the only other love of her life." Betty stopped to dab her eyes. "You know, she always wanted to become a concert pianist, but she gave it up when I was fifteen. I always thought it was me – until I read the diary."

"What do you mean, Betty? Why would she feel that way?" Anne said.

"She didn't feel worthy of being loved, or loving *anything* after what happened to John. She blamed herself." Betty shook her head sadly. "So she gave it up. A kind of penance, I guess."

Anne understood. She was having some of the same feelings herself.

"I don't even know why she died. The doctor said she was in good health. I think she just had no reason to live," Betty said.

"What did she do… before that?" Anne asked.

"She became a secretary for my father's office… She never married, but there were many men that were interested. I don't think she could allow herself to be happy," Betty said. She got up again and took a small plastic box from a shelf and handed it to Anne.

"Here. You should listen to that." It was a cassette tape. Anne hadn't seen one in years.

"What is it, Betty?" Anne asked.

"The last time Anne was here, I begged her to play the piano. She finally gave in and I secretly taped her. I think it is Beethoven, but I'm not sure. Do you play an instrument?" Betty asked.

"The cello," Anne said.

"I like the cello," Betty said. She stood up in front of Anne, and Anne got on her feet. It was time to go.

"Thank you, Betty," Anne said.

"Take the book too, Anne. It belongs with the diary, and my memories are sufficient for me now. I don't want to leave them here for the scavengers to take after I pass. The last we heard, John may have been in America. If you find him, please give them to him." Anne nodded, picked up the volume along with the scarf, and walked to the car. This time Betty followed her.

Anne put the items on the front seat, and then gave Betty a hug. When she was about to pull away, the sun glinted off Betty's gold necklace and something occurred to Anne.

"Betty, do you know anything about a bunch of gold bullion that went missing during the War?" Anne asked. Betty beamed at the question.

"Oh. Yes. I almost forgot about that. There are some gold bars beneath the shed." Betty pointed to the ground. "I found them by accident a decade ago looking for flower seeds."

"Why didn't you report that to the police?" Anne asked. She was almost afraid of the answer.

"I don't know… I was afraid…" Betty paused and looked at her, "Perhaps I just wanted to forget the whole mess. It was an awful long time ago. What Michael did was better forgotten for all of our sakes."

"Betty. I may call you and tell you to contact an inspector at Scotland Yard. That gold may help them catch Michael. But don't do anything until you hear from me."

"I can do that. I guess there's no point in any more secrets. Everyone is nearly gone anyway," Betty said. However, the thought of catching Michael, her good for nothing brother, after all these years made her smile. The only reason why he allowed her to stay at the estate was to keep away the squatters. Betty still remembered the midnight visits to her sister's room. Anne never said anything, but she had known.

"Goodbye Betty," Anne said, as she got in and turned on the Vauxhall. Betty waived at her as she drove down the driveway, and out of sight.

Anne drove slowly back to London. The treasures on the seat beside her could not afford to be lost due to some carelessness on her part. She stopped in Chatham and had a soup and salad for dinner in a local café, watching the news for anything on Ginger. There was nothing reported.

By the time she returned to the car, and took a taxi to the hotel, it was well past dark. She again placed her passport and Visa in an envelope and left it addressed to her room at the front desk. She didn't want to have either of them taken from her.

Chapter 41

Jarred awoke with a terrible headache. His shoulder was swollen and stiff but he saw little evidence of infection, and hoped that the bullet had passed cleanly through the flesh. He sat up on the mattress and listened for sounds, but heard nothing. He wished he knew whether it was day or night. The thought that Anne was released made him happy, but the knowledge of what Lord Ashley said she would do made him sick. He couldn't believe that she would make that kind of exchange. His heart told him there must be more to the story, but he couldn't imagine what. He knew that he would never give in to the demands of these men. Just the thought made him want to vomit. Whatever the outcome of what Anne did, his name would be worthless.

Jarred spent the rest of the time focusing on what he would do if he could escape. It kept his mind active and alive. The options were few but he knew where we wanted to go and whom he wanted to confront.

:

Anne awoke the next morning to the sound of the telephone ringing.

"Hello?" she asked.

"Hello, Ms. Compton?" the voice said. "This is Inspector Rowan of Scotland Yard."

"Yes, inspector, I remember who you are," Anne said, wide-awake.

"I thought we should let you know that I am releasing a statement to the media in about an hour. You may want to make yourself scarce for a while. The press seems to always find out about people." Anne found his comment was not very reassuring. "However, if you do change hotels, please inform me."

"Any idea of how long I have to stay here?" Anne said.

"As far as in the country? I can't really say at this moment. We would like to find Mr. Mulberry first. You realize, once this appears on the wire, he may not be very happy with you?" he asked.

"I am aware of that, inspector," Anne said.

"Look. About our other conversation; I think it is important that the investigation proceeds as normal so, I think I'll send someone over to keep an eye. I'll try and get them to be inconspicuous... or perhaps not, I guess we'll leave it up to the officer. Might be better to send everyone a message." Anne didn't like the idea of a babysitter.

"Inspector, I really don't want that," Anne said.

"I appreciate that. Still, I think it is better. We'll talk soon," he said.

"Dammit!" Anne said, after she hung up the phone. She understood that he was trying to send a message to many parties but this would complicate matters significantly. She was not completely positive she could trust the inspector, let alone any unknown uniformed officer. She thought about packing her bags and leaving immediately but decided that was unwise. She needed to just act normal until the announcement was made. Her plans didn't kick in for another day and a half, and she needed to be patient.

An hour later, she turned off the mute on the television and watched as Inspector Rowan gave a press release about the murder of Ginger Thereaux. He said that a witness had come forward confirming that Jarred Mulberry had indeed been seen at the crime and was considered a suspect. The announcement made her nauseous. She knew, without a doubt, that Lord Ashley would allow Jarred to hear what she had done. The inspector gave a hot line number where information could be given to the police anonymously. Anne waited a few minutes and then used her cell phone to call the House of Lords.

"Lord Ashley, please," Anne said.

"One moment. I'll connect you with his aide," the female receptionist said.

"Hello? May I ask who is calling?" Anne recognized the voice.

"His niece," Anne hoped he had a niece. "Is this Mr. Reinquist?" Anne intentionally withheld the title.

"Yes," Sir Alex hesitated," This is probably not the best idea," he had recognized the voice.

"I realize that. I'm not on a hard line." She hoped the term meant what it did in the movies. "I've kept my end up. I want to know if you are going to keep yours or if I am going to have to—"Sir Alex stopped her.

"Be careful what you say. Hold on one moment," he said.

"You performed very well today. Nice work," Lord Ashley said without identifying himself.

"Look, you pompous aristocrat, I just want to know if you are going to keep your end of the bargain!"

Lord Ashley laughed.

"Of course, my dear. I *always* keep my word. However, I wouldn't make wedding plans anytime soon. Your boyfriend is in a bit of a bind, and, if I might add is quite put out with you. For good reason! It's been nice doing business with you, Anne. It would be better for you if you did not call again." Anne was clear on the threat, and hung up.

She racked her brain trying to think of a way to reach Jarred but came up empty. She was sure he wouldn't trust her enough at this point to contact her, but still, her heart hoped that he would.

:

Jarred had no idea what time it was when Jerry opened the door and tossed him a loaf of bread.

"Well? Is it done?" Jarred asked, before the door closed.

Jerry turned around to face him.

"I don't see it matters if you know or not." He reached behind the door and threw in a London Times. Jarred picked it up to check the date, then looked at Jerry. Almost two days had passed.

"So, if it's done, let me go. I'm as good as dead anyway," he said.

"Page four. You're slipping, Jarred. Last week you made page two." Jerry shut the door and Jarred opened the paper to the article. It showed a picture of an Inspector Rowan, as well as a photo of himself. He recognized it from his MI5 file. Anne had done it, just like Lord Ashley said she would. He wondered what exactly she had told them, but it didn't really matter. There was no going back now. Jarred tore off a piece of the rye bread and ate it. He tried to comprehend why Anne would betray him, but nothing made sense.

About an hour later the door opened and several men stood behind Jerry.

"It's your lucky day, Jarred. These men are going to blindfold and bind you. Then we are going to let you go. You can make this easy, or hard. Up to you." Jerry said, his hand signaling the men behind him to wait.

Jarred turned around and laid on the mattress with his hands behind his back. He really didn't care either way. The two men put on the blindfold and put plastic ties around his wrists and ankles, then carried him out. Jarred could feel the warmth of the sun touch his body, as well as a cool breeze. He was taken outside and tossed in the back of a van. The corrugated metal was uncomfortable and chilly. He refused to let them hear his pain or discomfort and lay quietly while they drove. He estimated he was in the van several hours before it stopped. With the amount of turns the driver took, Jarred knew that they were intentionally backtracking.

The truck stopped on gravel and the men opened up the rear doors, and pulled him out. They stood him on his feet and removed the blindfold, then let go of him and Jarred almost fell over. One of them caught him by the arm and Jarred blinked until he could see clearly. There were two of them. One stood about three meters away in front of him and he could feel the other, behind him, cutting off the tie on his hands. He rubbed his wrists when they were free.

"Get on your knees." The one in front of him said.

Jarred got on his knees and was shoved hard in his back. He rolled over as he fell and landed on his bad shoulder and groaned.

"Have fun, Jarred. We'll be watching the news to see if you make it." He heard the two men hop in the van and take off. The acceleration sprayed gravel over him like hail.

Jarred pushed himself up to a sitting position and used a sharp stone to chip away at the tie on his ankles until it gave way. He stood up and looked around. He had no idea where he was, but it was broad daylight and he could see a busy highway a hundred meters in front of him.

He walked to the highway and stood by the off ramp hoping someone would stop before a patrol came by. At least with two days of growth, and as bad as he must look, he doubted anyone would recognize him. In a few minutes a dark brown Ford rolled up and a man stuck his head out the window.

"Are you all right?" he asked.

Jarred almost found the question humorous, but he was in too much pain to laugh.

"No. Actually, I'm not. I was carjacked yesterday and got the tar beat out of me. I just woke up over there." Jarred pointed to where he had walked from.

"My God, man. Get in and I'll take you to the hospital." The man got out of his car and walked over to Jarred.

"Could I possibly use your phone. My wife must be worried sick," Jarred said.

"Oh. Sure. Here." The man pulled out a little Nokia from his jacket, and handed it to Jarred.

He dialed a number and it was picked up on the first ring.

"London, Distributing." A female voice said.

"Hello, this is Othello. Is my wife there?" Jarred used the name that meant an agent in need of assistance.

"One moment please," the woman said. A few seconds later another woman answered.

"Othello?" she asked, "where are you?"

"Where am I?" Jarred asked the driver.

"Two exits West of Colchester," the man said.

"Did you get that?" Jarred asked.

"Yes. Give us twenty minutes. You will be met by a gray unmarked van with London plates. Do you need medical attention?" she asked.

"Yes." He hung up the phone and turned toward the good Samaritan.

"Thank you. She wasn't there but they said they would find her and send her right away. I'll be fine. Thank you so much for stopping." Jarred said.

The man looked at him, concerned. "Are you sure? You look pretty bad."

"Yes. I've been through worse. Served in Iraq for a term. *That* was bad," Jarred lied, but he didn't want to have the man wait around.

"Well, as you say… are you hungry? I have a bag of chocolate malts." The man was truly kind.

"No. That's OK… you know what? That does sound good. Thank you," Jarred said. The man walked back to his car and gave him the bag. He still looked concerned.

"Really. I appreciate it. Good to know there are some decent people still around," Jarred said.

"Goodbye, sir." The man drove off, and Jarred popped a malt ball into his mouth and bit down on it before he realized that his jaw was still very sore. He decided to let it melt instead.

The van arrived a short time later and Jarred was put in the back again. At least this one was carpeted, and he fell asleep on the drive back to London.

Back at the safe house that he had left two days ago, a doctor checked his wounds and cleaned them. He was told that he was extremely fortunate that the bullet had not hit a bone or major artery. Jarred was instructed to keep the dressing clean and get some rest. More than anything, he was thankful for the bottle of painkillers and swallowed two of them as Logan walked in.

"You look like something the dog wouldn't even bother to drag home," he grinned.

"Thanks. I feel like it too," Jarred said.

"You realize that your uncle is none too pleased with your actions? He said something about your lack of training and 'botching' it up, threatened to just leave you out in the cold," Logan said, and smiled.

"I guess I wouldn't have been surprised if he had. Please give him my apologies and thanks. Maybe when this thing blows over he'll be willing to see me," Jarred said. He made a mental note to buy him a bottle of his favorite Scotch if he was ever able show his face in England again.

"Did you see the paper yet?" Logan asked. He put a London Times on the table.

"About Anne?" Jarred asked.

"Yes. What in the world was that all about today? She knows you didn't kill Ginger," Logan said.

"I don't know. We were captured together. The next thing I know she was dragged off to another room, and then this." Jarred pointed to the paper. "Lord Ashley said she did it to save herself... a deal with Satan," Jarred said.

"Do you believe him?" Logan asked.

"I don't know what to believe. She definitely did this?" He pointed again to the paper.

"Yes. We confirmed it," Logan said.

He sat on the bed with a glass of water and sipped from it.

"I was wondering how she got away. You know we checked on the house the next morning when you didn't show. It was vacant," Logan said.

"It was a trap. They knew someone would come for her. Seems they know everything before we do. We were taken somewhere—I have no idea where. Underground, I think."

"So why let you go?" Logan asked.

"Sick game of his. With Anne's statement to the police he knows I can't surface publicly. He's probably counting on me leaving the country. This whole thing seems to be about the murder of that servant girl sixty years ago. They're obviously afraid of something," Jarred said.

"So now what? Your uncle can't be officially involved but you know he will help," Logan said.

"I need a new passport and a ticket to Hong Kong," Jarred said.

"Hong Kong? I don't think he'll go for that. It's too obvious. You can't take on Lord Cornwall by yourself. Remember the last time you tried to become a field operative," Logan waited for the point to sink in, "If *he* catches you, you'll be dead, or extradited to England to stand trial for murder." Jarred thought about it.

"I don't really have a choice. If I don't clear my name, I can't come back, no matter what," Jarred said.

"And how do you plan on doing that? Get Lord Cornwall to confess to the murder of Theresa and Ginger and exonerate you?" Hearing Logan explain it made it sound implausible.

"I don't know…what about the diary? Is there anything in there that could implicate him?" Jarred asked.

"According to our boys there are a couple of things: the missing scarf for one. We have sent someone out to look for it but after this much time who knows…The other is that the diary alludes to another murder. We looked up the date and there was a shooting at a Port that killed two army guards. There was also the murder of the original inspector, but the incidents were never officially linked. No one was ever arrested for any of the crimes. Keep in mind this was during the outbreak of World War II. Almost everything took a back seat to that in 1939. The last thing, possibly, is some missing gold," Logan said.

"Gold? How?" Jarred started, and Logan put up his hand.

"Remember your history lessons? The Crown moved forty million pounds sterling to Canada right before the War. When it was returned, a half million pounds were missing. It's rumored that is why Lord Cornwall lost his Ministry—and your great uncle received it a few years later. Imagine if Michael was involved with all that. Talk about motive!" Logan finished.

"And no trace of the stuff, right?" Jarred said.

"Lots of suspicions but nothing concrete, everything from a band of gypsies to robbery on the high seas. There is even a mention of our dear Lord Cornwall. A very delicate mention," Logan said.

Jarred thought for a moment. That was the key then. Michael must have stolen the gold. If he could find a trail…

"Alright. Do you think you can get me a ticket to America? I'll take it from there." It would take a little longer, but Jarred was still determined to get to Hong Kong.

"May I again remind you –" Logan started.

"That I am not field trained. Yeah. So I've heard," Jarred said.

"I need some cash. Do you have any?" he asked. It made Logan laugh.

"Me? I already spent next week's check!" He looked at Jarred and got serious. "Let me see what I can do."

Logan left the room and Jarred lay back on the bed, staring at the wood paneling on the ceiling. The painkillers were starting to work and it made him very tired.

:

Logan knocked on the door and it woke Jarred up. He looked at the clock. It had been almost three hours. He came in and sat down next to the bed with a bag.

"First of all, here's some bangers and mash from your favorite pub. I know how you like that. Second, here is your passport. You are now 'Jarred Harris'. Thought you would find that easy to remember. Nice photo 'eh? I took it from your last physical exam." Jarred opened it up and looked at it. "I strongly suggest you do something to change your appearance a little. Your face has been on the news a lot lately. Third, the money: I could only come up with five hundred pounds, but I did come up with a company cash card. Untraceable." Jarred took the card and grinned.

"Your Uncle doesn't know about that. Well, he probably does but doesn't. You know what I mean. He said to tell you that you need to sit tight for a couple of days and check in. They're working through the channels to see if they can do something," Logan said.

"Thanks Logan. I appreciate it," Jarred said.

"So what about the girl?" Logan asked.

"Is she safe?" Jarred asked.

"Appears so. The police have her under surveillance. I think she'll be fine. Though I don't know if she should be. I still can't believe what she did," Logan said, and then reached into his breast pocket. "Oh, and a one-way ticket to New York. It's a very nice city, by the way. Lastly, a GSM cell phone. Prepaid with one thousand minutes, also untraceable. No chats to anyone that the police might be monitoring looking for you," he grinned.

"What can I say Logan, I owe you," Jarred said.

"Yes. And I do plan to collect on that," Logan said, and smiled. He shut the door behind him. As soon as he left, Jarred eagerly opened the food. It smelled heavenly.

Chapter 42

Anne stayed in her room most of the next day, only taking a break to exercise and get some food in the restaurant. The supposed inconspicuous policeman was very conspicuous. She hoped he was the only one. She wondered if she dared try Jarred's cell phone but realized the dangers in doing so. If they did let him go as they promised, she hoped he would make himself scarce until she could attempt to finish her plan. If all went well, perhaps he would forgive her. If not… she decided not to think about that eventuality.

At around 10:00 p.m. she called down to the front desk and asked if anyone had left anything for her. The night desk clerked checked and said yes. She asked for it to be delivered, and a few minutes later a bellboy knocked on her door and handed her the envelope with her passport and credit card in it. After he left, she gathered the diary, book and scarf, together with a few other things, and put them in a paper bag that she had picked up. Then she grabbed her purse and her favorite coat and walked out the door. She put out the DO NOT DISTURB sign, and took the elevator to the second floor where she got out.

The stairs to the main lobby opened near the elevator into a small foyer. There was a sofa table and two chairs as well as a house phone. Anne peeked around the corner and observed the policeman in plain view of the path out the front door. There was no other way to exit the hotel. Anne picked up the phone and dialed a number.

"Could I have the restaurant bar please," Anne asked when the voice answered.

"Hello?"

"I'd like to order a drink to be delivered to someone. Is that OK?" she asked

"Sure. Do it all the time," the man said.

"Gin and tonic to the nice policeman in the lobby," she said, as innocently as she could.

"Sure ma'am but I don't think they're allowed to drink on duty…"

"I know, but I think he is just about to finish his shift," Anne said.

"Should I bill it to your room?" he asked.

"Yes," Anne gave her room number and hung up.

She waited a few minutes until she saw a waitress walk out of the bar and deliver the drink. When she heard an animated, but muted, conversation she took a deep breath and walked out of the lobby onto the streets of London.

Anne continued for several blocks, then hailed a taxi to Heathrow and paid with cash. She arrived at a little before midnight and walked up to the counter of United Airlines.

"Hello. I have a prepaid reservation to New York. Anne Compton," she said.

The woman typed for awhile.

"Is that C-o-m-p-t-e-n?" she asked.

"Well, it's a common mistake but its with an 'o' not an 'e'." Anne handed the woman her passport. Anne hoped the intentional misspelling would obfuscate any cursory monitoring attempt by anyone that might be interested in her whereabouts although she figured Lord Ashley would actually be happy.

"Oh. Let me correct that," the woman typed some more and then handed Anne a boarding pass. "The ticket has been paid for. Here is your boarding pass. Do you have any luggage to check?"

"No. They lost it on the way over," Anne said.

"Oh. I'm sorry. I hope it wasn't us," the woman said.

"No. It was a competitor," Anne said, and the woman smiled.

"Terminal three. Gate twelve C," the woman said. "They should begin boarding in about ten minutes."

Anne left and started the long walk. So far, so good, she thought.

The security checkpoint was being very zealous, and Anne tried to pick the fastest line. She handed the inspector her passport and felt her stomach flip as he consulted a checklist that he held. After a moment he waved her through, and she wondered if he noticed the sweat on her brow. She removed her coat and waited in line for the metal detector. The guards were being very thorough, and she removed her watch, rings, shoes, and placed all of them, along with the unopened bag, her purse and coat, in the plastic bin. She held her breath as she walked through the gate and hoped to god they didn't open the bag.

Once on the other side, she quickly gathered her items and walked to Twelve C, just as they announced the final boarding call.

She walked up to the gate agent and handed her the boarding pass and her passport.

The woman scanned it, then tried it again.

"One minute please," she said, and walked over to the counter.

Anne looked around at the terminal. There were very few people left in it and she wondered how far she could run before getting caught. It was a ludicrous idea, and she knew it. She looked back at the agent who was animatedly pointing at the screen. Anne was stuck. If they caught her now, not only could she be in trouble but also Jarred would almost certainly be lost.

Anne tensed up and watched the agent approach.

"Sorry, Miss. There is a bit of a problem." Anne's heart sank, and the agent noticed the angst on her face.

"Don't worry. It's not a big problem. It's just that your seat was double booked. Here, I've just changed yours and, since we are full tonight, you get to go Business Class." Anne laughed, and thanked the agent profusely. They both walked away delighted.

The flight was uneventful. Anne was very thankful for the recliner seat and the safety of the airplane. She slept peacefully and was finally awakened by breakfast, which was really odd because she arrived at almost the same time she had departed. It was very early in the morning. Still the omelet, sausage and fresh fruit were just what she wanted.

They arrived at Newark, Terminal B3 and cleared customs and immigration without incident. The airport was eerily quiet in the wee hours of the morning, and she walked down the exit corridor with the other passengers from her flight.

Anne exchanged her remaining British Pounds into US currency at the only foreign exchange booth that was open, and followed the signs to ground transportation. She took the Marriott shuttle to the hotel and, after a brief hassle about her lack of identification she checked in, then went to the self service business center and logged on to the Internet.

She had only a few priority emails but nothing looked important, so she skipped them and emailed Jen to let her know that she was fine and that she would be in contact with her in a few days to explain everything. She then checked the Hong Kong Auction houses until she found what she had been waiting for. In a few days the XiXi Auction house on De Voeux Road was holding several auctions for everything from eastern antiquities to European religious artifacts. The European listing showed a first century cross, claiming to have provenance back to the time of St. Jude. It was just the reason she needed.

The next email was to Harry.

Harry,
Thank you so much for your help. You were perfect. I am back in the good old USA. I need to find a Starbucks…! I apologize for not keeping you in the loop on the goings-on, but it has been rather hectic. I have managed to locate the cross. It is coming up for auction in a few days… Get this! In Hong Kong! I've gone so far with this thing, I figured I would just finish it. Besides, I have all the necessary paperwork with me so… How about getting someone to make me an airline reservation to leave tomorrow from NY, as well some nice (I deserve it, right?) accommodations in the Kowloon district? (It's centrally located) Also, have the insurance company wire a buyer's deposit to the XiXi auction house on De Voeux Rd; estimated price is $400,000 to $700,000 USD. If they squawk, remind them that it is just to hold the cross and, once the extradition papers are done, they should get it back?! (no guarantees, eh?)

OK. I'll check my email later in the day. If all goes well, I should be back in Chicago in less than a week. I never thought I'd miss my little apartment so much.
Anne

Anne next looked up the address of the Chinese consulate in Manhattan. It was on Twelfth Avenue. Before she logged off, she contemplated writing a short note to Jarred, but all she remembered was his work address, and she figured it was probably being monitored. She really wished that she could somehow get a message to him. The thought that all he knew was what looked like her blatant betrayal weighed heavily on her heart, but there was nothing she could do about it tonight. She looked at her watch and decided to try and catch up on some sleep. It was going to be a really long day.

:

That morning Anne was thankful the hotel had a full assortment of complimentary bath items, as she had nothing but her toothbrush with her. It felt good to have the hot water on her face and body. It was like she was washing away the past, if only temporarily. Feeling rejuvenated, and with her plan well in mind, Anne checked out of the hotel with her paper bag and purse to take a taxi to Manhattan. The first stop was the Chinese Consulate General. She was surprised at the lack of people in the consulate. Then she remembered the SARS issues. Anne asked for directions to apply for a Visa to Hong Kong, and was directed to a nearby window.

The application was painless, and much easier than she thought. She gave the reason for visiting as 'business', and it seemed like her employment with a law firm was all they needed to hear. They probably had a lot of attorneys visiting these days to support the increasing number for foreign corporations doing business in China. By what the woman said, she wasn't even sure a visa was required, but the woman gave one to her anyway and, with her approved visa in hand, Anne left the building and took a taxi to go shopping. She needed a small suitcase and some clothes. As she went in and out the shops in Manhattan, she thought to herself that Jen would have really enjoyed this. But she knew it was bad timing.

For lunch, Anne stopped into a New York pizzeria and sat in the window to eat her slice. She wondered about all the people walking by. What kind of lives did they lead? Were they having problems at work? In their relationships? They all looked 'normal' but, given the turmoil inside her and the facade she carried, she realized that there were a lot of people in pain, and no one else realized it.

Around late afternoon, Anne found a Kinko's and paid for twenty minutes of Internet time. She was happy to see that Harry had written back. He was surprised that she didn't want to come home and he offered, albeit not persuasively, to go himself. Anne smiled at his transparent proposition. He had made reservations on the Cathay Pacific non-stop flight for that afternoon, and hotel reservations at some place that she couldn't pronounce. She printed out the email and put it in her purse.

Before she left Manhattan, she visited a bookstore and picked up a pocket guide to Hong Kong, complete with maps and phrases. During the long taxi ride to JFK she tried to memorize some of the

Cantonese and Mandarin phonetic greetings, but they sounded all wrong, and the East Indian taxi driver kept looking at her funny, so she finally gave up and watched the traffic jams like everyone else.

She boarded the plane and was relieved to see that it wasn't full. They gave her an entire row of economy seats to herself, and she took a pillow and several blankets on the way down the aisle in order to make a bed. She placed her new carry-on and her bag below the seats in front of her and took out her guidebook for some reading material. According to her ticket, the flight was going to take nearly a full day.

The flight was smooth, but went by terribly slow and Anne was more than ready when the familiar squeal of the tires hit the pavement. She was surprised to see that the airport was on an island, and she could see beyond it to what appeared to be the densest gathering of skyscrapers she had ever seen.

Thankfully at least some of the signs were in English and she followed the other passengers to immigration. She had nothing to declare and was passed through without incident. Finding her way into the city was going to be much more difficult. She took out her paper, approached what looked like a taxi line, and showed the attendant the address of the hotel, before she realized that she didn't have any Hong Kong Dollars. She was relieved to notice on the windows of at least some of the cabs the familiar Visa logo, and was hurried into a cab as the line pushed behind her.

"Ni hao ma?" Anne waved at the driver in the rear view mirror as she attempted the traditional Mandarin greeting. She couldn't tell if he understood or not, because he just waved back at her. It was either a wave 'hi' or a dismissal.

She had never experienced traffic like this before. It was almost as if there were no traffic rules or laws. Periodically, she would see a policewoman standing in the middle of an intersection, but it was like she had given up, the traffic in gridlock around her. The weather felt around seventy, and it was overcast but not raining, enabling Anne to look around and observed an incredible amount of people going in every direction. From her seat inside the taxi it was like looking out a picture window to another world, which it was to her.

The amount of stares and finger pointing she received was also disconcerting. There were other Caucasians periodically, however they were mostly men, and when the cab stopped for a light or traffic hundreds of people would look in at her. She couldn't tell whether they were curious or disturbed by her presence, and she learned to cower to the back of the cab when it wasn't moving.

After what seemed an hour or longer, the cab arrived at a clean and Western looking hotel. She paid the driver with her company credit card. He either complained or talked to himself about something, but it was soon over and she departed the taxi and entered the revolving doors to the lobby.

There was a short line at reception and she waited behind a woman who looked like she was from the US. It made Anne a little more comfortable knowing that she wasn't the only white female in Hong Kong.

"How long are you staying, Miss?" the Chinese man's English was perfect. In fact, he had a British accent. She found it a little strange, but pleasant to listen to.

"I'm not sure, several days at least," Anne replied.

"May I have your passport please?" The man checked her name and authorized a key, then handed both of them back to her.

"Please sign here." He indicated a space on the room receipt.

"Do you have a business center with Internet access?" she asked.

"Yes, we do, Miss. It is around the corner." He indicated around the hotel gift shop. "However, all our rooms have Internet access through the entertainment center." She was delighted with the information.

"Oh. And I have a friend who lives somewhere in Hong Kong that I've lost track of. How would you suggest I locate him?" she asked.

"Certainly, the concierge could help you locate a detective if necessary, however, you may just want to look in the telephone book. You will find one in your room," he said.

"Thank you," Anne said. Perhaps a detective would be a very good idea to locate Michael Cornwall.

Anne got her self settled in, and took a shower. She put the scarf and diary in the room safe and placed a call to the Concierge. She was given the name of a local investigator, whom she was assured spoke English fluently. She dialed his number.

"Wei?" the voice said.

"Hello?" Anne asked.

"Hello? This is Bradley Johnson. How can I help you?" She was relieved to hear him revert to English.

"My name is Anne. I work for a law firm in Chicago in the United States. I was looking to find a particular person I believe is here in Hong Kong," Anne said.

The man laughed. "I know where Chicago is, Anne. Not a problem! Where are you staying?" Anne told him.

"Good. That's only a couple of blocks away. Shall I come over and we can talk about it?" he asked. "Say, in about thirty minutes, in the lobby?"

"Uhh. Sure. That would be great," she said. She didn't know why she was surprised at his offer.

Anne changed and went downstairs to greet Bradley Johnson. The name humored her and she had a mental picture of a forty-year-old, balding and slightly overweight man with bifocal glasses.

When he arrived she discovered she was quite incorrect. He was about her height, with brown curly hair, well dressed in a tailored two-piece suit, and a gold tie. He was about forty, but in good shape with a nice smile.

She was the only white woman presently in the lobby and he walked up to her.

"You must be Anne?" he asked, and proffered his hand.

"Yes. Thank you for coming," she said, as he sat down kitty corner to her.

"Shall we talk about rates or how can I help you first?" She liked that he was cordial but very business like.

"Well, I suppose I should hear about your rates," she said.

"I charge four thousand dollars a day." He smiled at the shocked look on her face, then added, "Hong Kong dollars, which is a little over five hundred U.S."

Anne looked relieved. "That's fine," she said. "I don't think it will take very long for the information I want." He just smiled.

"So, who can I find for you?" he asked.

"A man named Michael Cornwall. He's English," she said.

Bradley looked at her with concern. "You don't mean Lord Ellias Cornwall, do you?"

"Yes, I— " he cut her off.

"You said this man is a friend of yours?" His look of concern didn't dissipate.

"No. Not exactly." Anne watched him to see if he relaxed at the news, and he did. "Actually, I've never even met him. Let's just say he has something I need, but I don't want him to know I'm here," Anne said.

"Lord Cornwall is quite well known in certain circles. He is not a man to be trifled with and takes his privacy very seriously. Prior to the return of Hong Kong to China in 1997, Lord Cornwall was very friendly with several of the Governors. Even now he is a personal friend of the Chief Executive." Anne was not too happy to hear this news. The last person she had asked to help find out information was now dead.

"Look. Perhaps you already have the information I need. I just want to know who his daily associates are, does he have family and, specifically, is he going to be at the XiXi Auction starting… tomorrow?" Anne asked. She was uncertain what day it was.

Bradley looked at her. She knew he was deciding what to do. "I believe the auction starts tomorrow, Sunday. And I can tell you that he does not have any family that is publicly known, at least. As to who his associates are, and whether he will be at the auction, that should be relatively easy to find out. I'll make a few phone calls and get back to you… I don't suppose you would care to enlighten me with what you plan to do with this information?" Bradley asked, as he stood up.

"If you are wondering if have I been sent here to kill him, the answer is no. Other than that, I can't really say, but it won't be lethal." At least not for him, Anne thought.

"Alright. You can pay me on receipt of the information." Bradley shook her hand and then took his leave.

Anne stayed in her room and made some phone calls to the auction house to make sure they were expecting her. They confirmed that she was registered, along with the insurance company, and that a reserve account had been set up. She reviewed the extradition and artifact registration paperwork that she had brought with her. Everything looked in order. If all went well she would retrieve the cross tomorrow and deal with Michael by Monday. Of course, she doubted that all would go according to her plan.

Anne went downstairs and exchanged her US dollars into Hong Kong, then walked down the street looking for a café in which to have a late lunch. She picked a small café that was packed, and she was a little shocked that they seated her at a table with another family, but everyone acted as if it were the normal thing to do. She took the seat, and observed that people were ordering various dumplings from trays that were being wheeled around the room by Chinese women who seemed to talk non-stop. All the smells were as exotic to her nose as the sights were to her eyes. She finally got up enough courage to select a couple of dishes that had items that at least looked vaguely familiar. The only utensils given her were chopsticks, and the children at the table made fun of her bumbling efforts to get the food in her mouth. One of them finally took pity on her and was kind enough to demonstrate their use, and she was able to eat enough to at least satisfy her hunger.

She arrived back at the hotel and was greeted by Mr. Bradley. "Hello Anne. I believe I have what you requested." He handed her an envelope.

"It appears that Lord Cornwall is usually accompanied by at least one guard, sometimes two. He must be in his mid-eighties and perhaps one of them is his nurse. He appears to be quite active, and has a full schedule, including attending auctions on a regular basis. He collects Asian and other antiquities. My contact at XiXi seemed to confirm that he is registered for the Asian auction tomorrow morning. I believe it starts around ten a.m."

"How much do I owe you?" Anne asked.

"I think this shall be complimentary," Bradley said, and smiled. "It would be better for me if I can truthfully say that I was not hired to investigate Lord Cornwall. Please be careful. His reputation is, shall we say, not one of a mild tempered man."

"Thank you very much," Anne said, as she shook his hand. Even sixty years later this man was still terrorizing people.

Between the lunch and the time change, Anne suddenly felt very tired, so she went up to her room and set the alarm for 8:00 a.m.

Chapter 43

Jarred arrived in New York shortly after Anne. Instead of going to a hotel Jarred caught a cab to the Chinese Consulate, and also obtained a visa, as Jarred Harris, an import-export businessman. He booked his flight for later that day and spent the afternoon at the airport waiting for his flight. He carried only a single duffel bag that had a couple of changes of clothing, his cell phone, and some toiletries. As he waited for his flight, he checked his email at a kiosk and wrote down some information that Logan had sent him, including Michael Cornwall's address and favorite clubs. Jarred noted on the list that, despite his age, he still enjoyed the company of women. His flight left New York that evening, and he arrived in Hong Kong Saturday night. He paid cash for his taxi to the Central District where he obtained a room at a hostel, which he also paid for with cash.

Early Sunday morning, after a bowl of noodle soup for breakfast purchased from a street vendor, Jarred took a taxi to The Peak, Hong Kong's most prestigious district, where the Tai-Pan's used to live. Jarred had allowed his beard to grow, and wore dark sunglasses with a Marlin's baseball cap that he had purchased at an airport gift shop in New York. He had on a pair of khaki pants and a blue knit polo shirt. He hoped he looked like a lost tourist.

Lord Cornwall's residence was a three story colonial house on a gated compound. There were cameras on the home, and walls, as well as several German Shepherds roving the grounds. Jarred walked by the home twice and could see no easy way to enter it undetected. He stood a half block away to see if anyone stirred, and was slightly surprised to watch the gates open at a little past 9:00 a.m. and an older grey, but very well maintained, Bentley exit the premises and pass by him. The rear windows were heavily tinted, but he could see the profile of at least one older man in the back seat. The driver was a large British looking fellow, with a black cap and matching driving suit. He looked like a thousand other bodyguard/chauffeurs that adorned the streets of London on any given day, and didn't give Jarred a second look.

Jarred considered trying to enter the house now that it appeared Michael had left, but he decided against it. He really had little interest in the home. What he wanted was Michael or his gold.

As the car drove by Jarred, he wished that he could follow it but had no way to do so. He turned toward the Central district and started walking back down the hill. At least he knew that Lord Cornwall was in town.

:

Anne arrived at the XiXi Auction house a little after 9:30 a.m. She had spent over an hour getting ready, and she hoped that she looked like the part she was about to play. Her auburn hair was severely straight and unadorned. She had on dark eyeliner and bronze lipstick, as well as a pair of square, purple tinted sunglasses with bronze rims. She wore a simple silk black dress, with a portrait neckline, three-inch black leather pumps, and a simple gold necklace. A jade bracelet was on her right wrist. Her purse was, she hoped, this season's periwinkle Prada, which she had bought from a New York street vendor for twenty bucks. The entire ensemble made her feel both uncomfortable and exhilarated. It was a bizarre combination of feelings. By the looks that she was getting from the men and women, she hoped she looked more avant-garde than ridiculous, which is how she felt.

The auction room was a vast open space, about seventy feet long and forty feet wide, with ceilings at least ten feet high. There was a podium in the front, as well as a lectern, and various employees were hurriedly making preparations for the opening in less than half an hour. The room had over a hundred seats in it for the general bidding public, as well as three private glass fronted rooms on the right, and a bank of phones with seats on the left.

Anne registered with a beautiful young Chinese woman, dressed in a red traditional Cheongsam dress. Her hair was pulled up in a bun and held with a pair of ornamental chopsticks. Anne was again surprised by her British accent. It was going to take a while to get used to hearing Asian people with English inflections.

She was assigned number four fifty five and given a small placard with which to bid, as well as a catalog and information sheet.

Anne took a seat in the back where she could observe the crowd that was beginning to gather.

A few minutes before 10:00 a.m. she was horrified to see Peter, the priest's son, enter the room with his entire black frock. At least, she thought, he definitely looks more out of place than she did.

Distracted by Peter, she didn't notice the people who entered the private rooms until right before the auction opened. In the middle room, there was an older but still very distinguished, and very obviously British, man along with two guards or assistants. The older man looked to be about five foot ten, with a full head of silver-white hair and a weathered face. He stood straight, and walked without the assistance of a cane. He was dressed in a traditional gray three-piece pinstriped suit with a red bow tie. There was no doubt in her mind that it was Lord Cornwall. Several people acknowledged him as they took their seats, and he nodded to their gestures. She watched him walk up to the glass window and survey the room. Her heart skipped a bit when he looked directly at her and held her gaze for a moment before moving on. She wondered whether he saw the panic in her eyes through the purple lenses.

The auctioneer opened the bidding on a Qian porcelain vase. The guide showed it as a late example, in fair condition, and it drew some relatively active bidding. Next was a beautiful, rare Hunan bronze mirror, which drew considerably more activity. After that there were a series of Ming, Qian and Jin dynasty artifacts in bone, stone and bronze. The bidding fluctuated like a series of waves, and most of the estimated prices were easily exceeded. Anne was almost tempted to bid on some hairpins inlaid with different stones from the Qing Dynasty. But the thought quickly disappeared when the bidding reached ten thousand Hong Kong dollars. Through the entire auction, Lord Cornwall merely observed. After nearly two hours, the auctioneer finally paused and the entire room became silent. An assistant brought out a gold scepter that looked like an inverted door handle. It had a head on it that appeared like a mangled fist. The description was read to the patrons from the auction brochure:

"A rare Ruyi, or scepter of solid gold. The shape of the scepter was supposedly formed from a mythological fungus (phallic) called the Linzhi that was said to imbue eternal life. The Ruyi was typically made of jade or wood, and was used by princes and the Emperor as their symbol of power. This gold specimen is in exceptional condition and is said to date from the period of the so-called mythical Emperor Yu."

The reading prompted a murmur throughout the room. And the bidding was started at fifty thousand Hong Kong dollars. At two hundred and fifty thousand dollars, Lord Cornwall joined in. At Four hundred thousand dollars most of the bidders dropped out, and there was a stilled hush as the remaining three bidders successively raised the price. It was like watching a high stakes game of poker, where no one would call the hand. At one million dollars one of the bidders dropped out shaking his head. That left a woman in a gold suit and Lord Cornwall.

"One million, one hundred thousand."

"I have one million, two hundred thousand."

"I have one million, three hundred thousand."

Lord Cornwall exited his private room and entered the main auditorium. All eyes followed him. He looked at the woman in the gold suit and announced.

"One million, five hundred thousand."

The woman ignored him. The auctioneer continued.

"One million, six hundred thousand. To the lady."

At this point an assistant ran to the lectern and handed the auctioneer a piece of paper. He looked concerned as he announced: "We have a bid of two million dollars to bidder eight, eight, eight." Another murmur, louder this time, ran through the audience. Anne couldn't tell if it was because of the bid or the bidder's number.

The auctioneer waited for the chatter to die down.

"To you." He signaled to the lady in gold.

She shook her head.

He then looked at Lord Cornwall, but he made no movement.

"Sold for two million dollars to bidder eight, eight, eight."

Applause broke out and Anne looked at Lord Cornwall to revel in his disappointment, and was confused when she saw him smiling. The man next to her saw her face and explained.

"The bidder on the phone was working for Lord Cornwall. That's his number – eight, eight, eight. Everyone that regularly comes here knows that, except for her." He nodded to the lady in gold in the front. "Triple eight is a Chinese lucky number," he added.

The Ruyi concluded the auction and the auctioneer took a break. The assistants changed out the displays and signs and put up ones that indicated the next sale, Eastern European religious artifacts. The audience was abuzz after the last frenzied sale, and Anne watched many people congratulate Lord Cornwall on his purchase. Anne couldn't resist the opportunity and walked up to him.

"Congratulations on your purchase. It is quite beautiful," Anne said.

"Thank you. I'm sorry but you have me at a disadvantage. What is your name?"

Anne hadn't anticipated the question and felt suddenly flushed.

"Umm... Anne," she said. At hearing the name Michael looked puzzled. His face lost his smile.

"That was my sister's name... Have we met?" he asked.

"Oh. No. This is my first visit to Hong Kong. That is a coincidence, about your sister, though." Anne felt the panic rising in her stomach and wanted to turn around and leave. What a stupid stunt!

"Well, good to meet you," Anne said, and turned around and left.

She waited in the woman's restroom until the announcement was made for the next auction. She stopped in the hallway to get a drink of water, and was relieved to see Michael was gone when she returned. Anne proceeded into the auditorium and glanced at the private rooms, but they were empty. She couldn't believe she had been so foolish, and made a promise not to do that again until she was properly prepared.

She was happy that the cross was scheduled early in the auction, and when it came up, she readied her paddle. Peter sat in the front and, when he saw the cross brought to the stage, he stood up and started screaming at the auctioneer.

"You thieves! That is stolen property. It belongs to me!" He looked around to make sure everyone was looking at him. "We told them it was stolen; that it was a national treasure, but they refused to do the honorable thing."

The auctioneer looked bewildered and so did his assistants. Two guards walked up to Peter, but he dwarfed them, and they stood a few feet away, obviously hesitant to try anything. Peter continued his ranting until two more men arrived. They were armed with guns and were much larger.

"Sir! You must leave. If you do not, we will have you arrested," one of the new guards said.

"You could try and force me to…" Peter leaned into the man's face, but while he was distracted the other one took out his club and hammered him behind the knees. Peter yelled something in Armenian and lashed out as he fell, but the man in front of him dodged his blow and hit him on the side of the head with his stick. Peter went silent. The crowd nervously chattered, and the auctioneer finally spoke.

"Ladies and gentlemen. We apologize for the disturbance." Several other guards showed up as he was speaking, and dragged Peter out of the room. The auctioneer continued.

"We believe that the icon in question is of clear legal title and will proceed with the auction." Anne thought to herself that he was in for a bit of a surprise.

The bidding started at ten thousand dollars US, at the request of the owners and experienced a flurry of activity. Anne stayed silent until the bid hit two hundred thousand dollars, then she left her placard in the air until the rest of the bidders gave up. She felt like she was in grade school and she was waiting for the teacher to call on her.

The cross sold for under the estimated price at three hundred thousand dollars. Bidder four fifty five was announced as the winner, and the audience broke out into applause. Anne didn't know whether to stand and take a bow or just smile. For that moment she felt like a celebrity.

She waited until the auction was finished and most of the people had left before entering the winner's room. There was a well-dressed couple seated with the agent. She recognized them as the ones who had purchased a Greek Icon of the Madonna. She looked down at her purse and removed the extradition paperwork. When she looked back up, she was surprised to see Stephen and Natasha, Peter's sister. She hadn't seen them since the fiasco in New York. She saw that they were holding hands, looking around nervously, and hoped that her disguise would fool them. They seemed to disregard her, but Stephen went back to the main door and looked out while Natasha stood by wringing her hands. Perhaps they knew that Peter had been there.

Anne moved to the back of the room and allowed them to approach the agent. They had an animated conversation and were given some paperwork to sign. As they left, Stephen grabbed Natasha's left hand and kissed it. Anne noticed the ring immediately.

After they had departed Anne approached the agent, paperwork in hand, and sat down.

"Ms. Compton. Congratulations on your successful bid. It is a remarkable piece." He smiled at her and extended his hand.

"Thank you," Anne said. She accepted his hand and sat down.

"How would you like to take possession of it? We can have it shipped to anywhere in the world or you may take it with you," he said.

Anne pulled the paperwork out from under the desk and put it on the table. The agent looked at it puzzled, then looked at her.

"Actually I—" Anne stopped herself and thought about all the misery that the cross had caused.

"I would like it held here for now. I will personally advise XiXi Auctions what is to be done with it in the next forty eight hours," Anne said.

The agent wrote down her instructions and she signed them.

"Where would you like the remaining funds sent," he asked.

"Actually I am requesting that you hold all the funds until a matter concerning the legal ownership is established," she handed the agent her paperwork and he looked at it concerned.

"Look. This is just a legal matter that will be cleared up shortly. I'm sure your attorney's will be able to clarify it. Have them contact the person listed on the paperwork," Anne said.

The agent made a phone call then wrote for a minute or so and returned his attention to her

"Well I believe that concludes our business Ms. Compton. Have a good day," the agent stood up and Anne took that as a dismissal. He handed her two slips of paper.

"That is the receipt for the payment on the auction. You will need to present it *in person* when you pick up the cross. The other is an acknowledgement for the paperwork," Anne thought he was quite efficient.

Anne got up and left. Stephen and Natasha were nowhere to be seen. In fact, the hallway was vacant, and she walked down to the elevators and stood there waiting. The voice behind her made her spin around.

"Anne Compton." Lord Michael Cornwall appeared. He must have been waiting in one of the rooms by the elevators. There was a single guard with him. Anne stood there, her mind vacant, her feet nailed to the marble floor.

"Yes. I know you. That was a foolish stunt," he said.

She didn't feel a reply was necessary. The same thought had been pounding in her mind since she had done it.

"Why are you here, Ms. Compton? You really wouldn't be foolish enough to—" Lord Cornwall was interrupted by another voice, and heavy footsteps from the stairwell behind Anne. She saw the surprised look on Lord Cornwall's face and turned to her right to confirm the voice.

"I want my cross!" Peter said, the side of his face swollen from the blow he had taken just a few hours before.

Anne looked at him, dumbfounded, then in a flash of inspiration she pointed to Lord Cornwall.

"I just gave it to him," she said. Peter reacted immediately, and so did Lord Cornwall's guard. Anne took the opportunity, as the two men struggled, to leave quickly. She turned around and fled down the stairs where Peter had come from.

Only a floor down, she heard the door above her open, and Peter's voice rained down from above her.

"You lie to me! I will have the cross!" Anne tried to figure out what he thought she was doing there. His father definitely knew that she was attempting to return the cross to him. What was the matter with Peter? Didn't he understand that he was going to get it back? Then she thought that perhaps the priest and his son had not communicated. The enlightenment presented an opportunity, and she stopped on the next landing to wait for Peter.

"Wait, Peter!" She yelled at him with her hands fully extended and he came to a halt five feet away.

"I can get you the cross, but that man," she pointed upstairs, "wants to harm me."

He looked down at her and took a step forward.

"I swear! I will give you the cross, but you must help me, otherwise, if that man gets me first, you will never have it."

Peter considered this and stood fixed where he was.

"Why does he want you?" he asked.

"Look, that doesn't really matter. What does matter is that you understand the instructions I am about to give you. If you do not do this just right, I will likely die and you will not have your inheritance."

For the first time she saw a look of concern on his face. "I will do this. But if this is a trick…" Anne could see his face become red again and stopped him.

"This is not a trick. I promise. You know whom I work for. I have no reason to lie to you. We need to return your cross so that you will drop your lawsuit against our client, but this man, Lord Cornwall, is very dangerous and if he kills me you may never see the cross again."

She could see that Peter was considering what she was saying.

"But you just bought my cross upstairs!"

"That is true but, as you can see, I do not have it on me," she pulled out the receipt and showed it to him. He looked at it, puzzled, like he couldn't read it. "That receipt shows that it can only be released to me, however, if something happens to me, you may never get the cross," the statement was at least partially true. If something happened to her it could take a long time to unwind the legal mess.

"OK. But you must give me something so that I know you will keep your promise."

"Like what?" Anne asked.

"Give me your passport," Anne wasn't about to do that.

"No. You can keep the receipt," she could see that he liked that idea. It was going to be a mess if he lost it, she thought.

Peter took the receipt, looked at it, then put it in his shirt pocket.

"OK, but if I don't hear from you within a day I'm going to come looking!" Peter said.

"Fine," she said. She believed him.

He then gave her a telephone number and allowed Anne to leave. She walked down the remaining floors where she caught a taxi to her hotel. She stopped to speak to the concierge and the front desk then went up to her room.

Later that afternoon Anne called Lord Cornwall's residence. To her surprise, he answered.

"Lord Cornwall?" She decided to use his title in order to avoid aggravating him.

"Yes," he said. His voice was stern.

"This is Anne Compton. I have a proposition for you," Anne said.

"Why would I need anything from you?" he asked.

"Remember a scarf—a blue scarf, with several dark stains?" Her question was met with silence.

"That would not be of any use to anyone after all this time," he finally replied.

"Normally that would be the case, however, by a series of small miracles, it does exist, and in perfect condition. I have sent a picture of it to your home that you will receive shortly."

"Ms. Compton, this is a waste of time. So what?" he asked.

"Lord Cornwall, forensics have come a long way in sixty years. Are you sure that you can afford to have this item in the wrong hands?" Again she was met with silence.

"Assuming that you have what you claim, what do you want for it, money?" he asked.

"No. It is much simpler than that. You just have to make a phone call," she said.

"To whom, and what for?" he asked.

"I don't care to whom. What I want is to clear Jarred Mulberry's name in England. You forced me to make a false statement to the police…"

She was interrupted by Lord Michael Cornwall's laughter.

"Yes. That was quite a good show! But it is done. How can I change *your* statement to Scotland Yard?" He asked.

"I don't know and I don't care. Give them the real murderer, make up a story, apologize, whatever it takes."

"And if I do this you will give me the scarf?" he asked.

"Yes."

"It is not enough. I want this mysterious diary too," he said.

The request shouldn't have surprised her, but it did. It made her heart sad to agree to this.

"Fine. The scarf and the diary for the clearing up of Jarred's name," she said.

"And you," he said.

"Wh-at?" she asked. She must have heard him incorrectly.

"You. Do you think I would fulfill your request without assurance that you have what you say? The deal is simple. You come to my house and surrender yourself in exchange for Jarred's name.

After I have completed my end of the deal we will escort you to the items. If you do not have them, well, it will be very uncomfortable for you," he said.

Anne considered his request and she thought it could be workable if it was done just right. She was aware of the very real danger however it was a risk she was willing to take for Jarred. It was the only way that she could make up for her seeming betrayal.

"Fine. You send your driver to the XiXi Auction house. I will be there in one hour."

Anne hung up the phone and wrote letters to Jen, Harry and her mom and dad. She wanted to make sure in case something happened that someone who cared knew what had transpired. She didn't want to end up like John Harrison. Anne logged on to the Internet in her room and wrote one final letter. The similarity to Anne Cornwall and John Harrison's tragic end did not escape her.

> *Dear Jarred,*
> *I do not know whether you will ever receive this. I know you must think I have betrayed you to save myself. I promise you that I would never do that. It was a choice that I was forced to make, an impossible decision, and I did what in my heart I had to. I promise I am going to try and remedy what I have done. Whatever happens, please believe me. I did not mean to hurt you.*
> *I'm sorry…*
> *Love Anne.*

Anne clicked the send button before she could change her mind and went downstairs to the lobby where she gave the desk clerk an envelope with her room key in it, and addressed it to Peter.

The Bentley arrived at the XiXi Auction house on time, and Anne got in it and was taken to The Peak. Lord Cornwall met her at the door and she was escorted to a room, and locked in. She had no intention of leaving anyway.

Chapter 44

Jarred was immediately concerned when he read the email that evening. It sounded like she was going to try and do something, but he had no idea what. There was only one person in Hong Kong that he could think of that might know the answer.

He put on his coat and walked to the Wanchai District where he intended to purchase any kind of weapons that he could find. He managed to obtain a decent knife and a heavy wooden bat. It looked like something a fisherman would use. He then took a taxi to Lord Cornwall's estate. He had no idea what he was going to do but, at this point, he only had his own skin to lose, and the value on that had gone down dramatically in the last few days.

:

At around 10:00 p.m. Anne heard a loud commotion outside the house with several voices yelling at each other. In a few minutes, things had seemed to dissipate and Lord Cornwall unlocked her door and came into her room.

"You had a visitor tonight." Anne looked at him.

"It seems Jarred Mulberry is here and is under the impression that I've done something to you. You wouldn't know anything about that, would you?" he asked.

"No. I have no idea." She really hadn't. "What did you do to him?" she asked, apprehensively and sat down on the bed to steady herself.

"Nothing. Well, not much at least. He'll live. However, we need to make him go away. His presence here..." Lord Cornwall indicated his home, "or in Hong Kong, is not the kind of attention that I need."

"I don't understand," Anne said.

"Very simple. You and I are going to walk out of this room and go talk to him. You are going to say that you are my guest and that he should leave Hong Kong immediately. You are going to convince him that you do not want him here."

Anne's heart fell. She couldn't do that to him again. The whole point of what she was doing was to repair the last time she abandoned him.

Lord Cornwall saw her hesitation and said: "Or I'll have to kill him. I really won't have a choice. He just draws too much attention. It is your choice."

Anne bowed her head and nodded.

"Get your pretty face together. Let's go." He opened the door and she slowly followed him.

Jarred was kneeling on the floor, his hands tied behind his back. His face was bloodied and bowed toward the floor. It was obvious that he was in a lot of pain. Anne looked at his shoulder where he had been shot and it was bleeding again. The fight had probably reopened it.

"Jarred?" Anne said.

Jarred raised his head slowly. The surprise on his face hurt Anne's heart.

"Anne? What are you doing…" he said, then stopped and pursed his lips to look at Lord Cornwall.

"Jarred, what are you doing here?" Anne asked.

"I… I was looking for information about you." He kept looking back and forth between Lord Cornwall and Anne.

"You shouldn't be here. I have business with Lord Cornwall and your presence is causing us problems." Anne couldn't feel her hands or feet anymore. She was numb. He looked at her and she could see he was trying to understand.

"Look. Lord Cornwall has agreed to let you go, but you must leave Hong Kong immediately—tonight. His driver will escort you to the airport. It is better for all of us if you leave." Lord Cornwall stood by, smiling, and nodded at the last part.

"Please go!" Anne said, then turned around and ran back to her room.

"Well, what is it going to be Jarred? You heard her. We have an arrangement, and you aren't part of it. Shall we take you to the airport?" Lord Cornwall laughed.

"Get me out of here." Jarred glared at him and stood up. The guard grabbed him and escorted Jarred out of the house.

Anne sat on the bed and tried to fight back the tears. If she could only hold on for a few more days, Jarred would understand—at least she hoped he would. Otherwise he would hate her for the rest of his life. The thought made her depressed heart even heavier. She lay down on the silk comforter and willed herself to sleep.

The next day, Anne remained in her room all day. She was allowed out only to use the bathroom when she requested to do so on the intercom. The same guard that she had seen the day before always attended to her, and she wasn't sure if Lord Cornwall was even in the house. The day went by so slow. She felt as if she was six years old, waiting for the next day in order to go to the neighbor's pool. It was excruciating.

On Tuesday, Lord Cornwall awakened her. He entered the room without knocking and walked over to the bed. Anne was glad that she had slept in her clothes.

"It's done. Now *your* turn," he said.

"Where… How?" Anne roused herself out of sleep and sat up.

"Follow me." Lord Cornwall exited her room and she followed him, rubbing her eyes. She was taken to an office where there was a computer. He pointed to it.

"Take a look at either London Times or CNN International edition. We made both agencies," he said. He sounded proud of his accomplishment.

Anne sat down at the desk and typed in The Times web address.

"Go to 'Britian' and type in Ginger Thereaux," Lord Cornwall said.

Anne followed his instructions and a single article came up from that morning.

> **London Times:** *In a bizarre twist to this week old murder, another suspect has been arrested. Scotland Yard has just announced that they received a tip from a domestic intelligence agency with information concerning the Notting Hill crime. Also provided were clothes with Ms. Thereaux's blood on it as well as DNA from the now in custody suspect. A picture of the suspect leaving Ms. Thereaux's flat was also provided to Scotland Yard. Inspector Rowan reported that the arrest warrant for Jarred Mulberry, a previous suspect, has been rescinded; though he is still wanted for questioning.*

Anne checked CNN and found the same information. That's for you, Ginger, she thought.

"I want to make a phone call. I need my cell phone," Anne said.

"Thought you might want to do that." Lord Cornwall called for her purse and, a few moments later, the guard brought it in to her.

She dialed a number.

"Scotland Yard."

"Inspector Rowan, please. This is Anne Compton."

"One moment, please," the connection took a few minutes. It occurred to Anne that she had no idea what time it was in England.

"Ms. Compton," Inspector Rowan sounded awake, "I've been wondering when I would hear from you. "

"I'm sorry about that, inspector, things have been rather… difficult to explain," she said. She hoped that he would take the hint that she may not be alone.

"So, I've gathered," he said.

"Should I ask where you are?"

"I can't really say," Anne said, "Inspector, I was calling about the report on the news this morning. Is it accurate?" she asked.

"Yes. This is the most peculiar case I have ever seen. We received the suspect and the evidence hand delivered to us this morning. Looks like *he* is the real killer. Of course, the suspect is saying he was framed..."

"Thank you, inspector. I have to go," Anne started to hang up the phone but he kept talking.

"Ms. Compton, I appreciate that you were forthright with me about your predicament however there is still some unfinished business that will have to be attended to. I'll be in contact," the inspector hung up. Anne was not surprised that there would be consequences for her actions. They would have to be dealt with later.

"If you are satisfied, let's go finish this," Lord Cornwall said.

"Actually, I don't have the items. I gave them to an associate." He stared at her with a look that sent chills up her spine. She quickly added: "But he has instructions on how to deliver them to you once I give the OK," she said.

"Let's get on with it," he said.

Anne dialed Peter's phone. He answered in one ring.

"Peter?" she asked. There was no doubt that it was him.

"Yes."

"Everything is ready. Please proceed as planned. Let's meet at noon," she said, and hung up.

"We are going to the Central District," Anne said, and grabbed her purse.

Lord Cornwall got into the back of the Bentley with her and Anne directed the driver to go to the Nanyang Plaza.

The morning traffic was intense and they arrived a few minutes late. Anne saw Peter by the Fed Ex depository box. It was a chute that went directly into the building. He held a package in his hand.

"Let us out on the other side of the street from the Plaza," she said. The driver did as she requested. He stopped in traffic and Anne and Lord Cornwall got out to a chorus of blaring horns. Lord Cornwall stared at the closest driver and he stopped leaning on his horn.

"Now what?" Lord Cornwall asked. The enormous amount of people flowing on the sidewalk made it difficult to stand in one place. They were constantly being jostled, and Anne moved toward the curb as Lord Cornwall held her forearm in a vise-like grip.

"Look over there." She pointed toward Peter, who had seen her and held the package in his hand. It was half way in the drop box. All he had to do was let it go.

"You release me. Once I get to the corner and cross the street you can go get the box from him," Anne said.

Lord Cornwall looked at her then at Peter.

"If this is a trick, you *will* regret it. You are not a difficult person to locate," he said. He let her arm go and Anne stepped a foot away, then stopped.

"One more thing. What name did John use when he left England?" she asked.

Lord Cornwall had not taken his eyes off of Peter. "Harris. John Harris. I'm sure he's long dead," he said.

Anne quickly blended into the flow of pedestrians. When she had crossed the intersection, she looked back and observed Lord Cornwall making his way to the Plaza. She waited until Peter handed him the box and then disappeared into the crowd.

:

Anne caught a taxi back to the hotel and packed up her luggage. At the front desk, she faxed to the auction house the instructions that they had requested in order to allow Peter to pick up the cross. She walked out the door where she took a cab back to the airport. As she lay back in the seat and watched the Hong Kong skyline rescind into the distance, she thought; it was finally over. She prayed that Jarred would somehow hear the news.

Before getting on the plane Anne made one final call.

"Hello, Betty?"

"Yes. This is Lizzy." Anne was tickled to hear her use her childhood name.

"Lizzy, this is Anne."

"Hello, Anne. How are you?" Lizzy said.

"I'm fine. Do you remember our conversation about the gold?" Anne asked.

"Yes, of course, Anne. Is it time?" she asked.

"Yes. It's time, Lizzy," Anne said.

"I'll do it right away. Please come by and see me, Anne." She paused and then said.

"If my sister were here she would thank you. She deserved better," Lizzy said.

"Yes, she did. Goodbye Lizzy." Anne hung up the phone.

Chapter 45

It was a small one-bedroom apartment on the West side of Lincoln Park. The old man rose every morning at 5:00 a.m. He always started the water boiling for his old fashioned oatmeal, and then poured himself a cup of coffee as he waited for his breakfast. When the oats had set, he scooped out a bowl and sprinkled some brown sugar on it and walked to the living room where he sat down in his favorite maroon Lazy-Boy chair and turned on the TV with his remote.

He tried to never miss the CNN International edition. It was the only news he got from the home he had left sixty-five years ago. The first thing that caught his attention was a picture. It was of a house that he remembered. He could still see the window above the driveway that he used to look at so longingly. He remembered the sitting room where he touched Anne's face for the first time and the study where his life fell apart.

John Harris turned up the volume.

"MI5 agents, investigating a tip that was called in sometime yesterday, have discovered a stash of gold bullion that is said to be remnants of a shipment stolen from the Crown during World War II. The estate is owned by Michael Ellias Cornwall II, who currently resides in Hong Kong. Her majesty's government has formally requested that Lord Cornwall be held by Hong Kong police until he can be remanded to British agents who have been sent to escort him back to England."

John put down his cup of coffee and pushed himself to the back of his chair and smiled. It had taken over sixty years but now, when he died, he would at least know that Michael had not gotten away with everything. To him, it was the best possible news that he could have heard.

He looked to his right, picked up a photograph and held it in his hands. The frame was tarnished and the photo showed signs of yellowing, but to him it was the most beautiful picture in the world. He had been there that day with the photographer. A horse had passed behind Anne, and she had turned to look at it. The photographer captured that perfect moment.

He was no longer hungry, so he got up and walked back to the kitchen and put his untouched bowl in the sink. The knock at the door was almost imperceptible, but he went over and opened it, just in case.

On the carpet, leaning against his door jam, was a small package. He bent over and picked it up, carrying it back into the apartment.

The package had his name on it, and so he sat down in his chair and opened it. Inside he found a red, hardbound book. He turned it over. The spine read *The Woman in White* - Collins. He reached over, put on his glasses, unwrapped it and opened the cover. At the sight of the handwriting his arms shook and his eyes filled with tears. With wrinkled, old fingers he removed his glasses and wiped the wetness away with the back of his hand. He could feel every beat of his heart as he put them back on and then read the inscription.

"Dear John. I'm sorry. I will never forget you.
Love Anne."

John Harris sat there with the book open on his lap, his fingers touching the words she had written. The swell inside his chest came from the deepest part of his soul and it poured out like a torrent. He sat there and looked straight ahead as the tears ran down his face his frail old body convulsed by the waves of the silent sobs. He had spent a lifetime holding on, waiting to hear from her.

Somehow, she had finally found him.

Chicago, 2004

Anne returned from John's apartment and could only imagine what he was going through. She felt joy and sadness; relief and pain. The story had come to an end, but she couldn't help but feel a loss.

She went to her purse and took out the tape that Lizzy had given her, dug out her portable cassette player from the closet, and brought it into the living room. Her cello sat in the corner and she removed it from her case and leaned it against her chair. She lit a single vanilla candle on the coffee table and turned off the lights, then took a seat in her chair and started the tape. Anne gently held her cello in her arm, and laid her head against it - waiting.

The music started and she could see the fingers of a beautiful young woman dancing across a keyboard. Soon the sounds of a piano and cello blended into one as the two Anne's crossed time and death, and together, played a lullaby by Brahms.

The End

Epilogue

"So *where* are you?" Jen asked.

"I'm in Seattle, knucklehead! I'm standing at a place called Pike Place Market, looking at a green and white ferry on Elliott Bay. It's beautiful," Anne said. Jen could hear the breeze whistle through the cell phone.

"Seattle? You didn't get enough rain in London?" Jen said.

"Actually—it's sunny and beautiful today. I'm standing here in just a shirt," Anne said.

"So why are you there?" Jen asked.

"Well, Jarred wanted to come here, and he has some distant relative that lives in Issaquah or something. And besides, I've always thought about visiting the Space Needle," Anne said.

"Well, enjoy yourself, Sis. You deserve it. Have you decided what you're going to do with your life after all the adventures?" Jen asked.

"Um. Not really. Mom and dad have always…" Jen interrupted her.

"My question was. Have *you* decided what you want to do?" Jen asked.

Anne stopped for a moment and gazed at the sunlight reflecting off the bay.

"I… I'm not sure. Maybe become a cellist?"

"I think that would be a great." Anne could hear Jen's husband say something to her sister. "Hold on, Anne." Anne couldn't make out the conversation and turned around to look at the Seattle skyline.

"Can I call you back, Anne?" Jen said.

"Sure. Bye." Anne hung up the phone just as Jarred walked up. They started heading back into the market.

"So, what do you want to do?" Jarred asked.

Anne shook her head. Another person, same question.

"I don't know. I was thinking of taking up cello lessons again or becoming a writer or something," she said. Jarred stopped walking and Anne looked at him, puzzled. The Space Needle was protruding from behind his head like he was sprouting an antenna.

"That's fantastic, Annie. But I meant: what do you want to do for lunch? I saw a Filipino place a floor down," Jarred said, and smiled at her.

"Oh..." Anne said. "Whatever you ..." She stopped herself, grabbed his left arm and spun him around in the opposite direction—toward the Needle.

"Actually," Anne said, as she towed him along, "I know exactly what I want to do."

Moments

A journey filled with laments
Both heard and unuttered.
A road with a defined end,
All too clearly in view.

A trail upon which we struggle along,
In an incessant quest for happiness
Found in a few precious moments
Between episodes,
Weighted by a preponderance of uncertainty
And mediocrity,
Which weigh us down
While we yearn …
For love.
Even if just a modicum,
Found in the exhale of a single breath upon the nape,
Or
The light caress of a finger,
Slowly drawn across our brow.
As long as it is for us to possess.

As long as it is an
Acknowledgement that we are needed,
If only as a mentor,
Or a muse.
Even a friend.
To be held,
If only in a thought,
By a person who cares
About us.

To be wanted,
If only within the heart
By someone we cherish,

Though unobtained.

Minutes of life,
Tokens and fragments of promises
Broken by endless advertisements for existences
Not of our making
Or choice.

We are pushed along a road not of our will
By a world which has found no satisfaction.
To achieve a goal in which we loath,
The only reward we are given.

What have we done with our years?
When it is only in looking back
That we discover what we truly ached for
Were moments of time.

When we were at peace.

When we were safe.

When we were loved.

Caveat

Although this story is based on certain historical figures and facts, it is fiction. Any resemblance to any actual person or event probably took place only in the mind of the author.

Andrea Peters